UNTIL THE STARS FALL

UNTIL THE STARS FALL

AN IMMORTAL REVERIES NOVEL

VANESSA RASANEN

Crab Apple Books
P.O. Box 4220
Cheyenne, WY 82003
www.crabapplebooks.com

Visit the author's website at www.vanessarasanen.com

Cover design by Franziska Stern
Map by Gerralt Landman
Chapter illustration by Kateryna Vitkovska
Character artwork by Natalie Bernard, Anastasia Vasilevich, Kiley Freshwater, Mary Begletsova, and Panna Mara

ISBN: 978-1-7327652-9-0
Also available in hardcover, ebook, and audiobook

To the hopelessly romantic, stupid-in-love, heart-on-the-sleeve individuals who love with all of their being:

Never change.

AUTHOR NOTE:

This book contains some strong language, physical and verbal abuse (secondary character), and sexual intimacy on page with tame language.

A "spice rack" is provided in the back for readers who prefer to know when to expect intimate content.

HOERDA

CASTLE
ARENYSEN

ARENYSEN

DOLOBARE

RENWICK

PRONUNCIATION GUIDE

Characters

Lieke: LEE-kuh
Connor: CON-er
Durand: der-AND
Brennan: BREH-nen
Matthias: muh-THY-uhs
Orelian: uh-REH-lee-uhn
Calla: CA-luh
Vael: VAYL
Nevan: NEH-vuhn
Cian: KEE-uhn
Ellae: EH-lay

Places

Emeryn: EH-mer-in
Arenysen: uh-REH-nuh-sehn
Dolobare: do-lo-BAR
Engle: EHN-guhl
Linley: LIN-lee
Shoerda: SHOR-duh
Fairden: FAYR-duhn

PROLOGUE

Lieke

I was still holding the bloody knife when they found me.

I didn't know what they were yelling, because his words echoed in my ears.

I didn't fight them when they grabbed me, because I couldn't look away from the male at my feet.

I was no stranger to death, but facing my own was a different story altogether.

I still had hope, though, because I had a friend in the royal family.

He could save me. He could protect me.

But he didn't.

His father flicked his fingers in the air and ordered the guards to take me to the dungeons where I'd wait for the gallows. My friend didn't speak. He didn't move except to look away from my desperate eyes, pretending not to hear my pleas for help.

He was a coward, and I told him that, screaming it across the crowded room.

This couldn't be happening.

This couldn't be how it ends.

A voice cut through the air, yelling, "Stop!", but it wasn't the voice I expected or wanted.

I might have been saved from the gallows, but how would I survive what came next?

CHAPTER ONE

Lieke

ove killed my mother. I wouldn't let it hurt me.

My mother died shortly after my father when I was barely old enough to understand. The healers said her heart had broken, weakened by the loss of her husband, and my young heart scrambled to protect me from the same fate. I promised myself I would never be one of those lovesick fools. I would never give my heart over to another or let my entire life revolve around someone else's affections.

I held fast to that vow as I focused on learning my mother's craft, taking her place in the palace kitchen, until the day the fae prince waltzed by. My heart never stood a chance with him, not when his smile rivaled the sunrise and his green eyes outshone the damned stars. We might have only been friends, but when he looked at me, I forgot my promise, and I nearly forgot I was a lowly human and a servant. I almost believed he would one day love me in return.

Then the queen died, and everything changed.

The nation lost their queen.

He lost his mother.

I lost my best friend to his own grief.

I tried to forget him and let him go. I might have succeeded too, if I hadn't been stuck working as a cook in the palace. Unfortunately, it was one of the only safe places for humans in Emeryn, and it was the only home I'd ever known. So I stayed and tortured myself in the process.

"Where is your mind off to now?"

The question cut into my daydream, and I quickly looked up from the dough I was kneading—or was supposed to be kneading—to find Mrs. Bishop peering at me from under her long lashes. The tips of her pointed ears poked through her graying hair that was trying to escape the pins she'd attempted to tame it with.

"What?" I asked, trying to buy myself some time to find an excuse by pretending not to have heard her question. The head of the kitchen staff was kind enough, but I wasn't particularly in the mood for her teasing today.

"You're neglecting that dough as much as Prince Brennan neglects his duties, Lieke," she said, pointing her finger at the pale lump under my hands.

"Oh, right," I stammered. Why did she have to mention him? I shook my head—as if I could shake his name from my thoughts—and threw myself back into my task, slamming the heels of my hands into the dough before turning and folding it and repeating the movement.

"So?" the fae pushed. "What's got you distracted today, Sunshine?"

My brow tightened as I concentrated on working the dough. "Just thinking about Mother," I said. It wasn't a complete lie at least. Mrs. Bishop could taste lies in the air as easily as she could taste the food she prepared.

She hummed but thankfully said nothing more.

The door to the kitchen flew open, pulling our attention to Marin, one of the only other humans still employed by the Durand family. Her bright red hair fell over both shoulders in two tidy plaits, and a bright smile lit up her freckled face, her brown eyes dancing with excitement.

"You should see the ballroom!" she gushed, running into the kitchen and leaning against the worktable in the center. "And the terrace! His Majesty has really gone all out this time."

Mrs. Bishop snapped her chin up and jabbed a finger in the air at Marin and then at me. "Don't even think about it. Either of you. You know the rules."

Marin rolled her eyes and dismissed the old cook with a wave of her hand. "Oh, Mrs. B. You worry too much. I'm not insisting we crash the actual party, but nothing in the king's command says we can't be out and about before the guests arrive. How else would we be able to prepare everything?"

"Still. It bears repeating. You know the reason for his rules. You know the—"

"Yes, yes," Marin said around a sigh. She wiggled her fingers in the air. "We know the danger."

Mrs. Bishop shrugged and resumed her chopping. "Just as long as you know."

Marin scooted around the table and sidled up to me, giving my ribs a good elbowing. "So, want to come look?"

I didn't stop my kneading and didn't look at the woman. Though we weren't friends exactly, I liked her well enough. She wasn't as catty as most of the fae staff, but I didn't have time to go gallivanting around the palace with her. I shook my head before tossing my chin toward the balls of dough stacked in a pile on the table.

"I can't. I have all of those left to prepare still."

Marin's shoulders slumped, and she sighed again. "What good is having a mostly fae staff if they can't use some magic to make the work go faster?"

"Tell me about it," Mrs. Bishop said with a quiet laugh. "If only all fae were gifted with such talents."

The image of Brennan's scowling face popped into my mind—a memory of one of the many times he had lamented to me about how unfair it was that his older brother, Connor, had a gift when he didn't. What that gift was, I didn't know. The humans in the palace weren't allowed to know, and if the fae staff knew, they didn't tell us—which was surprising, given their propensity for gossip.

The memory shifted into Brennan flashing one of his cocky grins. With a growl, I slammed my hands into the dough.

Why did Marin have to talk about magic?

And why did every stars-damned topic have to remind me of him?

"Whoa there, Lieke," Marin said teasingly. "What did that bit of dough ever do to you?"

My face warmed from embarrassment, and I swiped the back of my hand across my brow in a shit attempt at hiding it.

"I just want to get my work done so I can get back to my room for the night," I said, hoping the fae across from me couldn't detect the lie on my tongue.

Marin lifted her hands in surrender. "Fine. I'm going."

As she spun on her heel and made for the door, I caught Mrs. Bishop staring at me again. I didn't need magic to recognize the knowing gleam in her eye. When the door closed, I dropped the dough onto the table and met her stare.

"What?" I asked, though I could already guess her response.

She pointed her knife at me, but her brow crinkled with more of a worried expression than anger. "Don't do anything stupid, Lieke. This is a bigger party than usual, with a much longer guest list."

I selected my words carefully, sure to keep them all within the realm of truth. "I know. After I finish up here, I'm going straight back to my room."

After scrutinizing me for a moment longer, she finally returned to her work, saying, "Don't say I didn't warn you, Sunshine. The king has his rules for a reason."

"So you've reminded us, Mrs. Bishop," I said. "I'll be careful."

It was no lie either—though my definition of careful likely differed from hers.

I had grown up in this palace and on its grounds, exploring and observing. I knew my way around as well as anyone else, and I had places I liked to go, places no one else ventured. Every season the Durands held a party like this for all the fae nobles, and I had attended every single one of them. Even if only in secret.

Prince Brennan may have walked away from our friendship, but on these evenings, from among the trees, I could pretend that maybe—just maybe—I still had a future with him.

Tonight, though, I refused to simply watch and dream.

Tonight, I would take a chance.

Tonight, I would talk to him.

＊

Once all the bread loaves were prepared and left to rise, I waved to Mrs. Bishop and headed straight for my room. No, I didn't plan to stay there all night as required, but there was no way I was going to wear my flour-dusted, butter-smeared clothing tonight. While I knew the unlikelihood of Brennan showing up at our old hiding spot, I refused to look like a simple servant.

Even if that was all I was.

Back in the servants' hallway, I nodded and gave a tight smile to two fae maids as they hurried past me to take on the duties of the humans who would be confined to their quarters for the evening. If they were upset about this arrangement, it didn't show on their faces. Inside my room, I closed the door and leaned back against it, letting my body crumple under the exhaustion. My arms ached from the morning's work in the kitchen, and part of me wanted to fall into my bed and rest. Stars knew the extra sleep would do me good after the week-long preparation these parties demanded of the kitchen staff.

But no.

As tempting as that was, I couldn't.

I pulled open the doors of my mother's old wardrobe and couldn't help but smile at the sight of the colorful array of clothing hanging inside. Soft velvets. Wisps of silks. The remnants of my parents' life before the war when humans and fae had lived in harmony and prospered alike. I had once asked Mother why she'd hoarded them since she'd been forced to wear the drab staff uniform. She had offered a one-word answer: *Hope.*

Marin had once insisted I seek some sort of closure by tossing out all of Mother's belongings, but Marin didn't understand grief. She didn't understand me. I didn't keep her clothes because I couldn't let Mother go; I kept them out of the same hope my mother had held onto. A hope that life in Emeryn and beyond might go back to how it once was, that one day fae and humans would live together as equals, partners, true neighbors.

What would it take to make that happen?

What could possibly convince the fae to stop blaming the humans for the war?

What might encourage the humans to forgive the fae for the oppression that came with the treaty?

My gaze landed on the simple white dress tucked along the left wall of the wardrobe. Mother's wedding gown.

Marriage.

Love.

"Love can conquer all evils, sweet girl."

My mother had said that so many times, and I'd believed her.

Until love hadn't protected her from death.

While I'd never believed the healers' claims regarding the cause of her death, I couldn't deny how the light in her spirit had dimmed when my father was killed on that distant battlefield.

With a shake of my head, I pushed the past out of my mind and pulled out the dress I had selected for tonight. It was a simple gown of navy-colored satin overlaid with delicate lace. I slid out of my work clothes, leaving the dirty garments piled on the floor as I quickly moved to the small basin of water in the corner. Dipping the washcloth into the too-cold water, I washed away the day's sweat and grime with the amber soap Marin had given me for my birthday last year.

I didn't have time to wash my hair, but I was able to brush out the tangles at least. Using the mirror above my desk, I carefully pinned up my blonde waves, leaving a few tendrils to fall here and there. A pinch of my cheeks to give them color and a swipe of rose pigment across my lips, and I was ready for the dress. Carefully I stepped into it, lifting it over my hips and bust before sliding my arms into the cap sleeves. Thankfully the dress had a low backline, which allowed me to secure the buttons without assistance.

When I dropped the hem of the dress back to the floor, the reality of what I was about to do settled into my stomach. I clasped my hands over my gut in a futile attempt to quell my nerves. Slowly I drew in a breath and counted backward from ten before exhaling.

I could do this. I had to give my heart a chance, and tonight was as good as any other.

Yes, I might walk away with a bruised heart, but I would wake up tomorrow knowing I had at least tried.

CHAPTER TWO

Connor

I wished my father had put an end to these royal parties when my mother died. But at the same time, I understood why he continued to host them. Planning the festivities, having the castle decorated with her favorite flowers, bringing in the musicians, requesting that all her favorite foods be prepared—this was his way of holding onto her.

He held his grief closely guarded, tucked away like a withering flower in his pocket, but I still saw it as if he bore it plainly. It lingered at the edges of his weary eyes, giving the appearance that his tears—long since dried out—might burst forth at any moment. It coursed through him, pulling his muscles tight and setting his jaw in a constant state of tension. And when he couldn't contain it any longer, it propelled from his heart in bitter rage, flung at whoever was unlucky enough to have sparked the fuse.

King Nevan had always had a temper. It was rare to find a fae who didn't. But the loss of his queen—my mother—had increased that inner anger beyond anything we'd seen from him when we were younger. My brother, Brennan, and I had learned to identify the signs of our father's coming rage and had become adept at skirting away from him before it landed squarely on our necks.

It was that rage—and my desire to avoid being its target—that had me storming through the palace before dawn had broken. The thumping of my boots against the stone echoed through the cold hallway like a heartbeat thundering away with purpose and drive.

Forcing my breathing to settle into a steady rhythm to match my footsteps, I tried to clear my head and focus only on what needed to be done. But fuck I hated having to do this. Every single season.

I turned a corner, and my stomach tightened as I recognized the unmistakable sounds of Brennan's favorite pastime. As I reached his door, I rolled my eyes at the rhythmic pulsing of bodies meeting, the uninhibited moans and deep growls, and my brother's name on whoever's lips they were this time.

I had no time for this. I had men to train and security measures to review with the general.

Yet here I was, needing to pull my brother off some female he'd picked up at the pub in town, all so I could spare him—and myself—from our father's next tirade if we weren't both there to meet him this morning.

I banged the door open, slamming it against the stone wall, and strode into my brother's chambers, then moved through the foyer to the doorway of his bedroom. My breath fell to the floor in a sigh, but it was not loud enough to interrupt the scene before me—a scene I'd had the misfortune of witnessing far too many times. A few times I'd tried knocking before entering or shouting around the corner, but nothing could break up the festivities except physically pulling him away.

With calm and deliberate steps, I approached the bed, where Brennan was thrusting himself deep into a redheaded wench I didn't recognize. Her hair was spread out on the bed around her head like a flaming halo, though there was nothing holy about the moans she let out. I cursed inwardly at my body's reaction to the scene, ignoring how disgusting it was to be aroused by watching my brother screw someone.

Bending over, I forced my mind to focus and picked up a pair of Brennan's pants. I flung them in his face. Though his movements slowed and his hand pulled away from the female's neck, he didn't stop. Instead, he turned his attention to me and gave me that stupid grin I hated.

"Hello, brother," he said in a ragged breath. "I never knew you to be the voyeuristic type. Or were you hoping to cut in and take Maeve here for a ride yourself?" He wagged his brow and tossed his head toward the female on the bed. At the sound of her name, she turned to me and shot me a wink. "She's good for a release, and I don't mind sharing."

Clearing my throat, I forced myself not to look away, not to let either of them see how uncomfortable this shit made me. Commander of the king's army, firstborn to the throne of Emeryn, and here I was having to constantly break up my baby brother's trysts and pull him back to his princely duties.

"Maybe next time," I said, trying my best to sound apathetic rather than annoyed. "The king needs us. Now."

"Let me—" Brennan started to protest.

I tossed my head toward the door, saying, "Maeve. It's time to go."

Neither were happy with me—understandably—as they pulled away from each other and proceeded to get dressed. Maeve pressed a passionate kiss against Brennan's lips and gave his backside a slap before turning to leave, slamming her shoulder into me as she passed by.

I ignored it.

I was used to it.

Same thing happened every stars-damned time.

Pulling a shirt over his head, Brennan sat on the edge of his bed to step into his boots.

"Is it already time for another of Mother's parties?" he asked, his tone soaked in boredom.

"Indeed. Thought you liked the parties though. Or have you finally fucked your way through every female in our kingdom?"

Brennan's mouth fell into a frown, and he rolled his eyes to the ceiling, as if he was actually recounting all of his escapades. "I'm sure there's someone I haven't bedded yet. There are always the humans."

"Don't even joke about that, Brennan." The warning came out as a growl. "You know the rules."

"And I'm nothing if not respectful of all our rules." He took on an air of mock chivalry.

"Right. Let's go then. The king is waiting."

With that, I turned away from him and left his room, hoping he would follow as I needed him to. Last thing I wanted to do was drag his sorry ass all the way to Father's office.

✳

I found my father bent over a massive pile of papers atop his desk, one finger working at his temple. His office used to be one of my favorite places when I was a young, ambitious prince, eager to take my father's place as ruler of Emeryn. I would run my fingers past the long row of leather tomes that contained the histories of our family and our lands. He never allowed me to actually read them, so I quickly learned to stop asking. They would be mine one day. I could be patient and wait for my time to come.

My father looked as old as those books now, and he was—for all intents and purposes—equally off-limits. Any fatherly affection he'd shown before had disappeared with Mother's death, and now he only spoke to us out of necessity.

Today was no different.

Without looking up from his work, he harrumphed.

"Where's Brennan?"

I cleared my throat, preparing to offer up one of the numerous excuses I kept tucked in my back pocket for whenever my brother let me down. But Brennan's voice, as casual as ever, wafted over my shoulder.

"I'm here."

The king's dark eyes shifted and pinned us both with the sharp glare we'd grown up with. When his attention settled on me, my chest involuntarily constricted, as if bolstering my defenses against whatever was coming.

"Who was he busy screwing this time?"

Why doesn't he ask Brennan? Who am I, the keeper of my brother's sexual conquests?

Unable to voice any of those questions, I replied with a lazy lift of one shoulder. "A redhead from the pub, I assume."

A growl rumbled in our father's throat, but he seemed eerily calm when he sat back in his chair and looked Brennan up and down.

"I used to bed any fae wench back in my youth too, so don't think I don't understand the appeal."

Brennan's cocky grin appeared in my periphery, but it was shot away with the king's next words.

"But it all ends eventually. It has to end." He stretched the last sentence out to hammer home his point, and for a long moment he stared Brennan down, as if willing him—with a mere glare—to understand.

"And it will, Father," Brennan said.

Stop now, I silently urged him.

But, of course, he didn't.

"When I'm ready, it will—"

Our father's fists slammed down on his desk as he rose to his feet, sending his chair crashing to the floor. The entire desk shifted forward from the force of the blow. Brennan was lucky there was such a heavy piece of furniture standing between them to keep our father from strangling him.

"IT ENDS NOW!" the king bellowed so loudly that the oil lamp on the corner of his desk shook.

Without turning my head, I peered at my brother to find him fighting that familiar battle between retreating and holding his ground against the beast he'd foolishly poked. But something new flashed across his features. The muscles along his jaw and around his eyes tightened. His eyes briefly met mine, and I shifted my head just enough for him to get my message to stand down.

Brennan understandably wanted to live his own life, but he was a prince. The sooner he accepted this, the easier life would be for him. Maybe he wouldn't be happier, but he'd at least stop having to take the brunt of our father's outbursts. Harsh words were the king's typical disciplinary tool of choice, inflicting a different kind of damage than his fists ever could. With only words, he could leave hidden wounds that ran deep, cutting our souls down with each tongue-lashing and pushing us down into the muck of our own self-loathing.

I'd learned to tread carefully around our father, but Brennan hadn't yet. He needed to soon. Thankfully, though, he was heeding my advice today and backing down from the challenge he'd wanted to raise.

"Yes, Father," he finally said.

A heavy exhale pulled King Nevan's shoulders low, and after righting his chair, he sat back down. For several breaths he remained silent, glancing from one of us to the other and back again. I tried to relax under his intense scrutiny, but I couldn't draw in enough slow breaths to ease the discomfort.

When his gaze landed squarely on Brennan, I nearly gave an audible sigh of relief.

"As you've been otherwise preoccupied, Brennan," he started, a smirk threatening to pull at his lips, "you may not be aware of the turmoil brewing among the four kingdoms."

Brennan shook his head, and I couldn't help but envy my younger brother for not having to deal with the constant political tension.

Our father continued. "As second-born, the likelihood of your taking the Emeryn crown is slim, and with your brother's expertise in combat and political maneuvers, it is slimmer still. I expect him to have a long and prosperous rule."

While I worked to keep my chest from puffing up from his praise, Brennan seemed to be struggling to not deflate. He might not want to rule, but that didn't mean he wanted his lesser station thrown in his face.

"But you may be exactly who we need to stave off ruin."

"Excuse me?"

Brennan and I asked the question in unison. How could my promiscuous and unreliable brother be the answer?

"The King of Arenysen is as anxious about another war as I am," said my father, "and he's concerned about the future of their crown. He only has a daughter, and as much as she would like to rule by herself, her need to continue the family line necessitates her search for a husband. The ruling families from the other kingdoms will no doubt be vying for her hand, and we cannot let them succeed. We cannot afford for anyone else to form such an alliance. We need you, Brennan, to do what you do best. Woo the princess. Enchant her. Secure her hand—and her heart if you wish—and secure Emeryn's future while claiming a throne and crown for yourself."

I had to admit the logic was flawless, perfect. Surely Brennan would agree.

Then I remembered who my brother was.

Straightening, Brennan rose to his full height and kept his voice calm and professional—more so than I had possibly ever heard from him—as he said, "Marriage has no appeal for me, Father. And an arranged marriage? I cannot—"

"You can, and you will. Because you must," our father said calmly. Laying his forearms atop his desk, he leaned forward and regarded Brennan with an expression of understanding rather than anger.

"Think of it as a challenge. Your greatest challenge yet."

"And I must start—"

"Tonight."

Brennan's eyes widened, and it was a marvel his jaw didn't drop to his chest at that single word.

The silence stretched on as they stared each other down, and I was just about to step in and argue in Brennan's defense, to request he have one final night of freedom before he was tasked with such a mission. But our father turned his attention to me, staying my tongue.

"Connor, you will ensure your brother does not falter or fuck this up. Do you understand?"

How in the stars did he expect me to do that?

As if he could hear my unspoken inquiry, the king added, "Yours might be the harder of these two tasks, I know. But our family's legacy and the very future of this kingdom require this of him. I cannot trust him to do this alone. Do whatever you must to keep him focused."

Lead an army. Devise military strategy. Navigate political drama. Those things I could do. I was confident in my ability to succeed in those areas.

But constraining my brother? Keeping him in line?

That seemed altogether impossible.

And Brennan's infernal smile and wagging brows didn't have me feeling any better about this task.

CHAPTER THREE

Conner

It was still early in the night when I lost Brennan. Silently cursing both my brother and our father, I carefully maneuvered through the crowd of guests with as much of a smile as I could muster. I should have just let Brennan take the king's punishments all these years instead of protecting him. Maybe then he wouldn't have become such a cocky prick.

Instead, all I'd done was convince our father that I was, in fact, Brennan's keeper.

And I was doing a shit job of it at the moment.

Where in the fuck was that bastard?

I winced at the thought, as an image of our mother flashed in my mind. Brennan wasn't a bastard by definition, and it was unfair to her to give him such a label.

As I neared the far corner of the terrace, Matthias Orelian, my second in command, approached with two glasses of faerie wine. He offered me one without a word, but I waved it away as I continued to scan the crowd for any sign of my brother. If I was to do the impossible, the last thing I needed was to have my head swimming in drink.

"Did he scurry off again?" Matthias asked. I nodded. He took a sip from his glass, passing the other to one of the staff walking by. "I still say we—"

"We can't lock him in the dungeons," I said, though the idea was sounding more and more appealing with each passing second. "He has to woo Princess Calla, remember? Hard to do if he's imprisoned."

"Was only a suggestion, Connor. And the princess isn't even here tonight." He shrugged and started to step away but then turned to look over his shoulder, saying, "If he's not here, you know where he'll run off to."

He offered me a sympathetic grin before disappearing into the mass of fae dancing and chatting. He wasn't wrong. Brennan was as predictable with his escapades as the moon was with its path across the sky. Taking a final glance at our guests to make sure he truly wasn't among them, I stepped backwards onto the lawn as casually as I could. Spinning on my heel, I shoved my hands into my pockets with a growl. The clamor of the party faded behind me as I made my way toward the trees. I might have welcomed the silence if I wasn't forced to come here.

How long had it been since I'd stepped foot in this forest?

Too long.

Even all these years later, though, the scent of orange blossoms and pine lingered in the air. It swept over me like a comforting hand across my forehead, my mother's kiss in my hair, her sweet words bidding me goodnight. Grief pricked my heart, threatening to pull me back into the pit I had barely managed to claw my way out of after her death. I couldn't afford to fall into it again.

Gritting my teeth, I huffed out a breath.

I didn't want to be here, but searching every inch of our property would take all night.

Unless I shifted.

While my abilities weren't a secret, at least among the fae, there was something about leaving my skin and giving up my voice that held little appeal.

That was an understatement.

I hated it.

The animal might be just as much a part of me as my fae form, but it felt wrong, leaving me with an intense need to peel it away and return to myself.

Still, as uncomfortable as it was, it had its benefits.

Sniffing out my brother, first and foremost.

And then maybe biting him if he gave me any trouble.

Any *more* trouble.

I took another look around. When I was sure no one was nearby, I reached into my mind and pulled at that neglected thread of power. Before I could reconsider my plan, it was done. I shook myself out from snout to tail, already itching to get out of this wiry black and gray fur as soon as I could.

I froze as I caught a scent.

It couldn't be. They knew the fucking rules.

Maybe it was from earlier in the day. Maybe they weren't really here.

I sniffed the air again. No. Too strong.

A human.

And here I had thought this day couldn't get any worse.

CHAPTER FOUR

Lieke

The servants' hallway was always quiet during these parties, with all the fae staff upstairs serving the guests. Mrs. Bishop, despite all her warnings and worry, never kept watch over us humans. She always retired early after spending the entire day working to prepare so much food. Still, I held my breath as I slipped slowly past her door, praying to the stars above that this wouldn't be the first night she caught me breaking curfew—and in a fancy gown, no less.

Creeping down the back hallway, I took the side door out to the gardens that lay between the north side of the palace and the surrounding forest. The moon hung high in the sky, full and bright, bathing the palace grounds in its soft light.

My heart thumped away in my chest, picking up speed until it was beating in time with the music wafting from the ballroom. With each step forward through the soft grass, my pulse pounded in my ears. The terrace finally came into view, but I pressed on until I could make out the expressions on the guests' faces and the points of their ears. Looking to my left and right, I tried to remember the exact spot where I had seen Brennan leave the parties time and time again, but everything seemed so similar from up close.

I would just have to guess.

And watch for any females heading this—

A noise, like the rush of air through thick leaves, snapped my attention around to my left, but I saw nothing except dark grass and looming trees.

It was probably just the wind, but the branches overhead lay still, their leaves motionless. I had just started to chide myself for letting my imagination run amok when I heard it again. It was nearly impossible to pinpoint over the music, but it was most definitely not my imagination. Once more, I spun around, knowing I must look ridiculous, but if it kept me from being attacked, I didn't care.

There, behind a tree, something shifted, coming into view briefly before disappearing again.

What was that?

It wasn't big enough to be a fae, or even a human for that matter.

"Who's there?" I asked with barely any sound to my voice.

No one responded, but—was that a growl?

Fear traipsed up my arms and across my shoulders. Why had I spoken?

It probably knew you were here already, I reminded myself.

Though that didn't make me feel much better.

I should leave. Return home. Crawl back into bed and wait until next season's event.

Spinning on my heel, I started to retreat toward home, regret and frustration mixing with the fear in my gut. But then movement pulled my gaze back toward the tree, where an animal now stepped into view.

It was nearly the size of a small horse, with coarse, scraggly fur of black and gray. Even in the darkness, its eyes shone as clear as gems, sparkling with curiosity and humor. The hound padded toward me, its gaze locked on mine as if searching my face for answers to questions it couldn't voice. My fear should have remained high, but there was something about this animal that put me at ease. It stopped an arm's length away from me, but it didn't sit, didn't seem to relax at all. It simply stared.

Then it cocked its head to the side, and I could have sworn its brow tightened with that same look Mrs. Bishop always gave me when she became suspicious. I mirrored its movements if only because I had no idea what else to do. Running seemed foolish. Even if it meant me harm—which I somehow doubted—I certainly wouldn't be able to outrun this animal.

"What do you want?" I asked, still keeping my voice barely over a whisper. At this, the animal sat, and there was no question now that its brow pushed up at an angle, as if to remind me it was an animal and therefore couldn't speak.

I rolled my eyes to the darkness above and pulled the night air deep into my lungs before looking back at the dancers and the lights of the party. No one was coming this way, so I still had some time. Leaning back against a tree trunk, I ignored the bite of the bark against my bare shoulders and returned my attention to the dog's piercing eyes.

"I am probably wasting my time," I admitted. "What could a prince—a fae—see in me? What could I offer him that he couldn't find in one of those females? Why did I have to fall for Brennan?"

I reached my foot out from under my dress to poke my toe into the dirt. It felt good to give my worries a voice, even if this was only a dog. I couldn't talk to anyone about this, but here were two ears to listen to me.

When I looked up, though, the hound was gone.

Even a dog doesn't want to hear your petty problems, I told myself.

Searching the lawn, I saw no sign of the animal anywhere, as if it had vanished. Then a giggle tickled the air, and I quickly hid behind a tree. A female with short, dark hair curling around her pointed ears glided across the lawn, heading for the trees.

My heart raced as she passed by and disappeared into the forest. Brennan would be here soon, and if I didn't act now, I might never find the courage to try again.

The clearing of a throat had me turning back toward the palace.

Brennan Durand.

My nerves sparked, forcing my pulse to go even faster until I was sure he would know I was here by its thundering alone. With a hard swallow, I pushed my feet to move around the tree until I stood right where the female had bounded by.

And then he was there, stopping and staring at me quizzically.

My cheeks heated with the realization that he could probably sense all the emotions that swarmed me, but somehow I managed to open my mouth to speak.

"Your Highness," I said, dipping my chin and dropping my eyes to the ground between us.

A seductive chuckle answered my greeting, and I looked up to see him offer me a lopsided grin. His hazel eyes seemed to laugh—not in an unkind way, but like he was sharing an inside joke with me alone.

"Lieke?" My name on his voice pierced me squarely in the chest, and my lips began to curve up into a smile…until he spoke again. "You can't be here."

Pulling my bottom lip between my teeth, I shifted my gaze away from his, as if looking for an escape.

"King's orders, you know," he reminded me. When he stepped closer, my breath hitched, and I couldn't bear to look up and see the dismissal in his eyes.

"I know," I said with a meekness that sent fresh warmth over my skin. This was not going well, but stars above, I wasn't going to give up now. "You're worth breaking the rules for though."

Silence.

Look at him! Don't be a coward!

My thoughts shouted at me, but my body wouldn't listen, remaining frozen in this awkward standoff.

He stepped toward me and stood so close the air warmed around me, making it difficult not to melt into him.

"Go home, Lieke," Brennan whispered, placing his hand on my shoulder as he stepped past.

CHAPTER FIVE

Connor

I had been so distracted by Lieke's confession that I nearly missed the approaching female. Brennan would surely be following soon after. It wasn't until I had darted off that I realized I had left Lieke behind, unprotected, vulnerable, and stupidly smitten over my idiot brother.

I should have nudged her back home, but who would listen to a wolfhound?

I could have shifted in front of her, but I didn't want to frighten her more.

So you abandoned her, I mocked myself. *Good job, Connor.*

No matter. This would be quick enough.

In no time, I locked on to the scent of the female. I soon found her in a small clearing in the forest. She stood leaning her back against a tree at the far end. With a roll of my body, I reined my magic in, pulling the wolfhound back until I was once again in my fae body. I didn't have time to appreciate the feeling of being back in my own skin, though, and with a single breath, I shoved my hands in my pockets and stepped out from the trees.

The female didn't bother looking up from where she pretended to pick at her well-manicured nails.

"Hello, shifter prince," she said, her voice a sultry velvet, slow and smooth. "Come to steal away your brother's plaything?"

At this, her gaze flicked up, and she peered at me from under her long lashes. A devilish half-smile pulled at her red lips, which highlighted the shades of red in her hair.

I shot her a bored look. "In a manner of speaking, Marletta."

Lithely she pushed away from the tree and stepped toward me.

Watching her, I kept my senses fixed behind me, waiting for any hint that Brennan was approaching. When she was within arm's reach, I lifted my hand to her shoulder and forced her to stop.

"That's close enough," I said, ignoring how her dark eyes shifted down to my lips and then back up.

She wrinkled her nose. "Agreed. You smell like dog."

"Brennan isn't available," I said, though I knew this wasn't going to be that easy.

A laugh rumbled low in her throat as she shook her head. "Seemed otherwise when he invited me here."

"Seems he still lacks any sense of self-preservation."

Footsteps. To my right. He was here.

"Hello, brother," I said, never pulling my eyes away from the female sneering at me.

Brennan stepped into my periphery and lifted his arms out to his sides, stopping just inside the clearing. "Connor, interrupting my fun twice in one day? What am I to think?"

I snapped my glare to him. "Maybe you should think about what the king will do to you if you fail to obey his orders."

"You mean what he'll do to *you* if *you* fail," he countered. I really should have stopped covering for him years ago. Should have let our father unleash his anger where it was warranted instead of across my back.

I turned to Marletta. "Leave. Now," I commanded. The fae's eyes twitched before she swung her attention to Brennan, sending him her silent question.

"You heard your prince." Brennan merely pointed behind him, no disappointment on his face.

Marletta growled and pulled her shoulder violently from my grasp. I lifted my hands in surrender, and she stalked away, snarling at Brennan as she passed him. "You'll never have another chance with me."

Brennan laughed—he actually *laughed*—and I almost felt sorry for the female. Almost.

"I hope that's not how you treat all the females you entertain," I said, mentally cringing at his callousness.

Brennan sauntered over, giving me a casual shrug. "They all get over it. Eventually."

"You won't treat Princess Calla like that." My tone came out more commanding than I'd intended, but he didn't seem to notice or care as he rubbed a hand over his chin.

"You never know. Maybe she's attracted to assholes." He turned his palms face up as if asking me to seriously consider this possibility.

"Yes, I'm sure the sole heir to Arenysen, who could have any number of suitors in our lands and beyond, will swoon over your prickishness."

He shrugged again, an upside-down smile appearing on his face. "It could happen."

Before I could think of any response for him, a snarl—faint but undeniable—yanked at my attention, pulling my gaze back behind me. It came again, but this time, it was wrapped around a word—*now*.

A male.

Had Marletta run into someone when she'd left?

My heart picked up its pace with each second that passed.

No. This had come from behind me, not from where Marletta had retreated.

Lieke.

"Shit."

I was already turning when Brennan said, "What's the big deal? Our guests can take care of themselves."

Over my shoulder I said, "She isn't a guest. Get back to the party before the king realizes both his sons are missing."

I didn't wait to see if he complied before I was bounding back into the trees, shifting into my wolfhound form as I ran. The male had gone quiet, but I picked up his scent—and Lieke's—soon enough. When her muffled cries finally reached me, I pushed myself faster.

As the trees thinned, I could see them. Could see how her feet dangled above the ground, kicking and struggling. Could see how his hand wrapped around her throat, holding her up and threatening to end her.

I didn't think about who this fae was or why he was attacking her.

I didn't care.

I only needed to stop him, to save her.

With a growl, I lunged.

CHAPTER SIX

Lieke

The moment my world was fading away, the edges of my vision darkening with each squeeze of the fae's strong grasp around my throat, and the next moment, I was falling.

I blinked rapidly, sure I was imagining the scene before me, but it remained the same.

The wolfhound from earlier had returned and latched its jaws onto the fae's forearm. Its teeth clamped down tightly, biting into his flesh. The fae growled with more ferocity than he'd shown me, but no matter how he moved, stumbled, fought, or screamed, the wolfhound held fast.

I scrambled backwards as best I could, my feet slipping in the grass until my back pressed against a tree. I should move, skirt around the trunk and hide, or run all the way home. But I couldn't leave, not without knowing if the hound would be okay. Ignoring how my backside ached from my fall and how my throat throbbed from the attack, I pushed myself to stand, but I didn't retreat.

I watched as the hound finally released the fae and stared him down with a terrifying snarl, as if he were daring the fae—who was now holding his wounded arm to his chest—to attack. Surely he would. A fae was far stronger than any hound, far quicker too.

But the fae only backed up a couple of steps, hatred blazing in his dark eyes.

Would he run? Was he feigning his surrender?

My eyes flicked back and forth between the two until the fae spoke.

"Seems rather unfair to come at me in hound form, Prince."

Wait. *Prince?*

I snapped my attention back to the hound in time to see him instantly shift into a fae male. Tall. Handsome. Familiar.

Prince Connor.

My heart stopped.

My breath caught.

My mind spun into chaos.

I'd almost been killed, of course, but somehow—as ridiculous as it sounded—that would have been better than this.

I had spoken to this hound.

I had spilled my heart to him.

About his *brother!*

The prince didn't look at me as he straightened and casually slid his hands into his pockets. Nothing in his expression indicated he'd been on the offense moments earlier, attacking this male. No fury blazed in his eyes. No tension laced his jaw. His anger, instead, seemed to be quietly simmering behind his calm exterior.

Connor tipped his chin up slightly. "Griffin." The fae didn't return the greeting, so the prince spoke again. "You know the rules. Humans are not to be harmed, on our property or anywhere in this kingdom."

The fae—Griffin, apparently—curled his lip. "You mean like the rule that humans are not to attend these events?"

I swallowed hard.

I had broken the rules. Brennan had warned me.

The prince shrugged. "This is one of our staff. She was not a guest. She was not in attendance."

At this, Griffin faced me with a look of disgust so potent I wanted to sink into the earth and disappear. I was nothing. I was no one.

"Odd attire for a staff member," he said.

Connor sighed. When he slid his gaze to mine, I looked down at my mother's dress.

My face might have flushed with embarrassment if I wasn't facing the king's punishment. Instead, the blood rushed from my cheeks and my stomach sank as I berated myself silently.

Love made us stupid.

Of that I was becoming more and more certain. With each passing second, I waited to be grabbed and dragged back to the palace.

"She will be dealt with," Connor said simply, with no hint of emotion, as if he were commenting on the migratory pattern of birds rather than my fate.

I jerked my chin up when Griffin growled and rushed at the prince. He didn't attack Connor or even touch him. Rather, he flashed him a wicked grin.

"Why don't we take her to your father now then?" Griffin challenged.

Connor didn't back away but narrowed his eyes. "You dare tell me how to run my household? You overstep, Griffin. You answer to us, not the other way around."

Griffin inched back, his smile never wavering. "Things can always change, Your Highness. The war proved that. The humans—"

"Are not your concern right now," Connor said. His calm expression faltered for the first time, as if there was something he didn't want to speak of. Whether he was being generally reticent or simply wanted to avoid revealing something in front of me, I couldn't be sure, but I had little doubt he was hiding something.

With a nod of his head, Connor said, "Go back to the party. Now. Before I have to drag you before my father and explain why you got bitten."

The fae's smile dissolved into a grimace. Before he left, he gave me one more glance. "Next time, Goldie, you might not be so lucky."

CHAPTER SEVEN

Connor

It could have been worse. Lieke was alive. Griffin too.

Yet, watching Griffin stalk off, I couldn't shake the chill that settled under my skin. This wasn't over. He wouldn't let this go. I'd have to watch my back.

While watching Brennan too, I reminded myself. *And the humans.*

I dropped my chin to my chest.

"So you're the hound," a sweet voice said from behind me, and my eyes fell closed so I could prepare myself for an inevitably awkward moment. Awkward or not, at least she was safe. I shifted my head to glance over my shoulder at Lieke before slowly turning on my heel to face her fully.

"I am," I said. I didn't have the energy to try to lie to her. Despite her stupid actions tonight, she was anything but stupid. I'd known her—and her family—long enough to recognize that.

But stars above, love made you stupid, didn't it?

Lieke chewed on the inside of her lip for a moment, searching my eyes as if she hoped to find the answer to the question she was too embarrassed to ask aloud. I could save her from that bit of embarrassment at least.

But I still wouldn't lie to her.

"Yes, I heard all you said." Her face immediately flushed pink, and her eyes darted away from mine to look up at the leaves overhead. "I won't tell him though. I promise."

Slowly she turned her dark eyes on me again. Though the color was slowly fading from her cheeks, her heartbeat—faint but clear in my ears—refused to settle.

"You swear?" Her voice trembled with uncertainty.

Offering her a tight-lipped smile, I nodded, and grief lodged itself in my throat as I said, "Upon my mother's grave."

Lieke's shoulders slumped with relief, and she huffed out a heavy breath. "I'm so stupid."

"Even the smartest of us do stupid things sometimes. Let's get you to your room though. I need to get back to the party." I nearly mentioned my having to babysit Brennan but decided against it. "Now, I assume you didn't exit through the main door?"

She shook her head and pointed at the door on the other side of the garden. As I stepped past her, Lieke turned to walk beside me. We continued in uncomfortable silence, but when we reached the door, she grabbed my arm, her feet skidding to a stop.

"You can't tell Mrs. Bishop," she whispered as her eyes pleaded with me to keep this secret.

Stars, this woman.

I was glad she was safe, of course, but I'd already been charged with handling my brother's shit. I couldn't shoulder her problems too.

Dropping my head to the side, I looked at her squarely. "Pick one."

The spot between her eyes crinkled. "What?"

"I'll keep one of your secrets. But not both."

Yes, this was a good compromise. She couldn't argue with this.

I was wrong.

"No, I can't. You must—"

"I must do nothing of the sort, Blondie." My patience was wearing thin. What part of my needing to get back to my guests didn't register with her? "Did you not hear me back there with that fae? I don't answer to you. Quite the opposite. Now, I'm willing to offer my help with one of your problems, but not both. I have enough on my plate as it is without taking on a human's drama."

She didn't cower at all as I expected, but rather seemed to do the opposite. Pushing her lips into a tight line, she stared confidently into my eyes as she ground out the word "Fine" through her teeth. I waited another breath, but she didn't say anything more. Neither did she make any move to keep walking.

"If you don't pick one, I will. I'm sure my brother would be most amused to learn of your infatuation." Perhaps it was a low blow, but I was quickly running out of grace for her. For all I knew, Brennan had found another fae to go frolic with while I was occupied with Lieke.

"No," she said, cutting off my thoughts with her sharp retort. "We'll tell Mrs. Bishop."

With a silent nod, I resumed leading her inside and through the servants' wing. The confidence she'd exuded moments ago withered away, and she refused to walk beside me any longer. Behind me, she released a shaky breath, whispering, "She's going to kill me."

CHAPTER EIGHT

Lieke

I stood behind the prince like a child, clutching the skirt of my dress, as if I might be able to hide myself from the old cook's view. Without hesitation, Prince Connor rapped on the door with three knocks that matched the pace of my runaway heartbeat. After several painstaking moments, the door finally opened, revealing the cook. Mrs. Bishop hastily wrapped her robe tighter around herself as she greeted her prince.

Connor's head dipped in a sharp nod, and he stepped to the side to reveal me. "Can I assume you didn't know she was out?"

I winced, even though there was no denying I was in the wrong.

"Is she all right?" Mrs. Bishop asked. At least she was inquiring about my well-being. That had to be good news for my fate, even if her tone indicated otherwise.

"I believe so."

"Did anyone see her?" Normally I would have been annoyed that they would speak about me as if I weren't here, but tonight I was more than willing to delay my consequences as long as possible.

"Unfortunately, yes. A male—"

"Which one?"

My chin snapped up at her casual interruption of the prince, and I held my breath as I waited for him to rebuke her.

But he didn't.

"Griffin."

She cursed under her breath. I couldn't recall the last time I'd heard her use such language.

"Exactly my thoughts," the prince said. "He won't be calming down about my attacking him anytime soon."

"You attacked him?" she asked with a mix of concern and humor.

"Of course. I couldn't let him strangle one of our staff, even if she made a mistake. He will be expecting for us to take some course of action in response to her transgression though."

My stomach clenched. I'd only been worried about disappointing Mrs. Bishop, maybe getting a long lecture about safety and being saddled with additional kitchen duties as punishment. I hadn't considered that I might still be taken before the king.

"I will handle that, if you'll allow it," Mrs. Bishop said.

"I will," the prince said, giving her another nod. Then he cocked his head. "But this is a one-time agreement. If she breaks the rules again, I cannot protect her from the king's judgment."

"Understood, Your Highness."

Without another word, Prince Connor turned to give me space to pass him by. Our eyes met briefly, but I couldn't read any emotion there, as if he'd already wiped his hands clean of this situation and of me.

"Thank you again." Mrs. Bishop took my arm and pulled me inside her room. As she closed the door, I braced myself for the coming reprimand. But she didn't speak, let alone yell. Instead she released me and turned to go back to her bed. She sat, resting her elbows on her lap and rubbing at her temples. I stood there in this ridiculous dress, watching her, unsure what to do.

"Mrs. Bishop," I started, even though I still hadn't found the right words to offer.

She didn't look at me as she responded, "Go back to your room, Lieke, and go to bed. We will talk in the morning."

"But—" I took a step toward her, but she held up a hand, still not lifting her eyes.

"Now."

My lip quivered slightly as I continued to watch her. She wouldn't change her mind, but I couldn't force my feet to move. When she repeated the word, though, with a whisper coated in anger and disappointment, I pushed my muscles to listen and did as I was told.

*

The next morning, I rose before the sun—and before Mrs. Bishop—eager to get the inevitable over with. I paced my room, wringing my hands as I pondered what she might have decided to do with me.

Scrubbing the dishes for the rest of my life would be too lenient.

Locking me in my room for all eternity seemed too harsh, not to mention impossible.

What punishment existed between the two?

A knock at the door startled me, and I bounded for it, pulling it open to find Mrs. Bishop holding two cups of tea. I invited her inside as she proffered one of the drinks to me. Taking it in both hands, I blew across the top of it and moved to sit on my bed. She dragged my desk chair to the center of the room and sat in front of me, studying me silently for a moment.

At least she was finally looking at me.

Sadness swirled in her soft blue eyes. Sadness and loss and dread.

"You can't stay here," she said in a steady but quiet voice.

My heart thudded to a stop.

My vision blurred.

My breath quickened.

What? I had to leave?

But this was all I had. This was my home.

I couldn't fathom this.

Couldn't think.

Couldn't protest.

"Not forever, Lieke," the fae said around a strained smile.

I squeezed my eyes tightly closed, unable to look at her as I asked, "How long?"

"That depends on you, Sunshine."

What in the stars did that mean? When she didn't elaborate, I dared to open my eyes to find her staring at me with what now looked unnervingly like hope.

"Where am I to go?" I asked.

She reached a hand into the pocket of her skirt and pulled out an envelope that was brown with age, its edges worn smooth. "Your mother left this with me long before she passed. Told me to give it to you if you ever got into trouble."

"Glad to see she had such confidence in me," I muttered as my head swirled with questions.

Mrs. Bishop's gaze settled on the bruises on my neck for a moment before dropping down to the envelope. She let out a slow exhale. "As hopeful as she was, she worried what life in Emeryn would look like for the humans after Queen Durand died. The war taught us all the fragility of peace. You can't fault her for taking precautions."

I bit the inside of my lip nervously. "What does it say?"

"I've never read it myself, but I do know she arranged for you to be trained."

"Trained in what exactly?"

"Defense." She said the word as if it should have been obvious. "Your mother wanted to trust the fae, and she hoped you would be safe here with us. Unfortunately, the fae you encountered last night is not one to be trifled with. There won't always be a prince nearby to save you. As much as the Durands and I strive to protect you and the other humans on this staff, the fact of the matter is our world is dangerous and hostile to your kind. Humans who stayed in Emeryn after the war have had to learn to protect themselves. Your mother's family helps train anyone who needs it."

Trained to protect myself? I had never considered this as an option before, but the more my mind tossed around the prospect, the more excited and intrigued I became. But there was one thing I didn't understand about this plan my mother had hashed out.

"But I'm human. I have no chance of protecting myself against a fae. Trained or not, I could never gain the strength and speed necessary to defeat them."

"Defeating them is not the goal. You only need to be able to survive and get away. Your mother had—stars, all of us have had—enough death and fighting for a million lifetimes, so no, defeating them is not the aim. Your mother truly thought you'd be safe here on the palace grounds, but I think she forgot whose child you are. You got your father's curiosity and her stubbornness."

I offered her a wry smile but said nothing. I didn't want to leave. The palace held the only memories I had of my family. But if my mother had thought this was best for me, if she had gone to such great lengths to plan this out ahead of time, then I had to trust her.

Mrs. Bishop held the envelope out to me, and I took it cautiously. "No need to read it with my staring at you, but when you're ready, let me know. I'll have Mr. Pruitt get the carriage ready for you."

I shot her a perplexed look. "I'm to take the carriage?"

The cook rose from her seat and placed the chair back at my desk before heading for the door. "Yes. Prince Connor thought it best to have you escorted to wherever you needed to go, especially with that fae bastard possibly lurking about waiting for you." My face warmed at the mention of the prince's name, as if he were here staring at me, but Mrs. Bishop continued. "I wouldn't delay too long, though, Sunshine. Best to travel during the daylight if possible."

CHAPTER NINE

Connor

Two glasses of faerie wine had done little to erase the taste of that fae's arm in my mouth, but they had at least dulled my senses enough to allow me some rest after the evening's excitement—and give me a twinge of a headache this morning.

Downing the last sip of coffee in my mug, I reread the message Mrs. Bishop had included with my breakfast. Lieke was leaving today to stay with her distant family who would train her to protect herself. While this prospect raised some suspicions in the back of my mind, I trusted Mrs. Bishop's judgment. She hadn't specified how long Lieke would be gone, but with any luck, she wouldn't return until after my brother was successfully married off.

I wandered over to the small dining table in my front room and grabbed a roll from the breakfast tray. If Mrs. Bishop returned to find I hadn't consumed anything but coffee, she would repay me with a quick swat upside the head, no doubt. I started to head for the door, but the thought of angering our cook—and former governess—sent me back to the table for a few slices of fried meat as well.

There, now she'd only scold me for not touching the fruit.

I had nearly made it to Matthias's office on the first floor of the palace when he came storming around the corner from the front entrance. His hardened expression—made more concerning by the cold anger in his eyes—sent my stomach straight to my feet.

"What happened?" I asked around the last bite of my breakfast, obliging him when he spun and waved for me to follow him out into the courtyard toward the stables. He was already leading my horse, Rosie—saddled and ready—out of her stall when he finally answered.

"There's been another. To the south. Not too far from here."

Another.

Taking the reins from him, I bit back a curse. Another attack so soon? The last had taken place only a couple of months ago. They were becoming more frequent, and apparently more serious. Normally we would have sent one of our junior officers or a squad leader to investigate and report back, but if Matthias was insisting I see it for myself, it was likely worse than the previous strikes. With great effort, I shoved back the horrors that sprang to life in my mind, the ghastly memories from my brief time fighting at the end of the war.

With a click of my tongue, I had Rosie following Matthias and his mount down the long drive and out the front gates. For hours we traveled through the forest in silence, with nothing but our horses' hoofbeats and steady breathing to tick away the passing time.

We were nearly to Linley when our horses slowed of their own accord and laid their ears back against their heads. The forest had grown notably quiet, and despite the late-morning sunshine streaming brightly down on us, the air itself seemed wary. Up ahead, the road curved to the east, keeping whatever had happened here out of our line of sight. I listened for any sign of a potential ambush or lingering danger. Finding none, I nodded to Matthias to proceed. Whispering words of comfort to the horses, we urged them forward.

In the middle of the road a carriage stood like a deadly omen. The horses were gone. The doors were flung open. Unlike previous attacks, the scene was devoid of any blood, and no bodies littered the ground. I was about to allow myself to breathe easier when I saw a foot peeking out from behind the carriage.

My stomach lurched.

It was far too small to be an adult, but they had never—not since the attacks started several years ago—attacked a child.

I dismounted and handed my reins up to Matthias. While I didn't expect Rosie to run away, I didn't want to take the chance of anything spooking her. Surveying the ground, I carefully stepped up to the carriage. No one remained inside.

Behind me, Rosie stomped her foot. Apparently she was as eager to be away from this scene as I was. I pushed on, swallowing hard as six victims came into view. Two females. One male. Three young ones: a boy and two girls. All fae. All dead.

But this was no scene from a battlefield.

This was new. Different. Puzzling.

These fae—a family, most likely—were not scattered about the ground as if they had been struck down while fighting off their attackers. They were lined up; their bodies lay prone, side by side, with their arms touching. Their eyes didn't look to the sky but remained closed as if they were merely sleeping in the middle of the road.

While this wasn't the gruesome sight I had anticipated, it left me with an uneasy feeling all the same.

Leaning back, I peered around the carriage and beckoned Matthias to dismount and come over. He stopped short next to me, and his head tilted as soon as he saw them.

"The messenger said it was different," he said, "but this isn't—"

"Agreed. Notice anything?"

"You mean other than the fact that they've been arranged so neatly?"

I nodded and watched as he examined them again. His eyes narrowed, and he clicked his tongue slowly like he always did when he was concentrating. Then his forehead twitched, and he snapped his head around to look at me.

"No blood."

"Exactly." I shook my head. "We haven't seen a human among the dead in, what, years? But even then we always found traces of their blood, a sign they were injured, that they had to fight to escape. Here? Nothing."

Matthias glanced back at the dead fae and asked, "What if the humans aren't to blame for this one? There's no trace of their scent."

"Their scent hasn't lingered around any of the attacks for the last several months. They must be masking it somehow. We only knew it was them because of their spilled blood at the scenes."

"What if the night stalkers—"

I shook my head and gestured to the dead with my hand. "There are no marks on the bodies to indicate that. Plus, they've isolated themselves on Dolobare since before the war. Why would they return now?"

"Could it be fae?" Matthias offered.

"It's possible, but I don't think so. The humans have been doing this for years. It has to be them."

"But how?" Matthias walked away, circling the bodies. His hands fell open in front of him. "How would a human do this? Against fae? Without losing any blood?"

"And without leaving any noticeable wounds on them," I added.

Matthias frowned. "So not ash or rowan wood—"

"All destroyed anyway," I said. "And not likely lyrite."

"Agreed. The last fragment of that went missing how many years ago?"

I didn't bother to answer his question but continued to stare at the dead. "Whatever it is, it's new. We'll need to get feelers out to see if we can find out anything about what they're using now. And send some of the guard to bring this family to our healers. Maybe they can determine what new weapon is being used against us."

Matthias offered a sharp nod as he passed me and remounted his mare. I afforded the fallen fae one last look over my shoulder, hoping I'd be able to make this right, to find the rebels and put an end to their violence.

All while babysitting Brennan.

CHAPTER TEN

Lieke

Mother had arranged for her cousins to take me in whenever needed. With fae-human relations being what they were after the war, they had gone into hiding in the northern forests when I was still young. Thankfully, my mother had included instructions in her letter explaining how to contact them.

This was all a bit too much to take in.

I'd never even known she had living relatives remaining in Emeryn, and now I was to go live with them? One stupid mistake and I found myself banished from my home and forced to live with strangers. Mrs. Bishop had reassured me she would keep my mother's belongings safe for me while I was away and instructed me to pack as little as possible. So with a small bag of clothes, a book, and my mother's necklace around my neck, I stepped out of the palace and walked toward the waiting carriage.

Mr. Pruitt had been hired as the carriage driver and horse master after my father died. He appeared to be around the same age as Mrs. Bishop and was just as pleasant to be around. As I approached, he touched the brim of his cap and pulled open the door. While he offered me his hand to help me inside, he asked, "So where are we headed, Miss Berg?"

"The Garrison Tavern at Engle," I said, noticing how his eyes tightened briefly.

"It's none of my business, of course, but you aren't planning to stay in Engle, are you?"

"Why do you ask?"

He shifted nervously. "The towns are growing less and less safe for humans, is all."

I swallowed around my growing nerves and smiled as best I could, placing my hand on his arm. "No need to worry. I'll be meeting friends of my mother's there." A slight pang of guilt twisted in my chest at having to lie to this kind fae, but to be fair, I wasn't entirely sure what to expect when I arrived. I was to go the tavern and ask for a Mr. Marstens, who would somehow put me in touch with my family.

"Very well then," Mr. Pruitt said, nodding. "We should arrive in a couple hours. Not too far from here at least."

The journey might as well have been twice as long with how exhausted I was by the time we arrived that evening. While I had planned to take the time to rest and prepare myself for whatever awaited me, I instead spent the entirety of the ride with my worries festering in my uneasy gut. When Mr. Pruitt finally opened the door, I took as deep a breath as I could, grabbed his hand, and stepped out.

My mouth fell open.

"First time away from the palace?" Mr. Pruitt whispered as he handed me my bag.

I managed to snap my mouth closed before nodding quickly. Even if Mother hadn't forbidden me from leaving the palace grounds, I would never have considered venturing outside the gates anyway, as I'd had no need to. I had seen illustrations of towns before, of course, but seeing one with my own eyes was another story entirely.

The buildings—homes and businesses alike—lined the wide street on either side. They might not have been as grand or regal as the palace, but they fascinated me all the same, with their steep-pitched roofs, colorful doors, and round windows. The tavern sat between an inn and a bakery. Even at this late hour, the aroma of freshly baked bread floated on the air along with the faint sounds of conversation and laughter.

Mr. Pruitt gestured to the tavern with a toss of his hand. "Would you like me to accompany you inside?"

"If you would? At least until I get in touch with this Marstens character. I don't want to keep you too long."

"It's no trouble, miss," he said, then led the way down the neatly paved walkway to the bright green door of the tavern. A torrent of sound rushed at me when he pulled the door open, but it quieted as soon as I stepped inside. All eyes turned toward me, and my breath snagged on the fear rising in my throat.

Mr. Pruitt tucked my hand under his arm and guided me to the bar. The room filled with murmurs and whispers, which I tried my best to ignore. There were several empty stools at the bar, and we settled ourselves onto two at the end. The bartender strode over to us, fixing a suspicious eye on me.

"Don't get many humans around here these days," he said, his voice carrying easily across the quiet room. "What brings you to our humble village?"

This fae seemed to be close to the king's age, with faint traces of gray in his dark hair. The rough stubble gracing his jaw gave him a rugged appeal.

I lifted my chin slightly. "Just passing through actually. But I am supposed to meet someone here."

The male dropped his large hands, rough and calloused, to the bar and scoffed. "Oh? And who might that be?"

Mr. Pruitt stiffened beside me but remained silent. The whispers stopped. Somewhere behind me a chair scraped against the floor.

"Mr. Marstens," I said. The bartender's eyes narrowed as he studied me for a long moment, and then he barked out a laugh so loud I flinched. I cast a sidelong glance at the carriage driver beside me, but he only shrugged. The patrons behind us resumed their muttering. I turned back to the bartender, who now wore a crooked smile.

"What's so funny?" I asked.

"I should have known," he said. His dark eyes seemed to gleam with recognition. "You look so much like Alora."

"You knew my mother?"

He nodded, and then the light in his eyes dimmed and his smile faded. "I was sorry to hear of her passing. She was one of the good ones. As was your father."

My throat tightened as grief swept in, but I managed to swallow around it. "Are you Mr. Marstens then?"

The fae dipped his stubbled chin and waved a hand in front of him. "Hugh Marstens, at your service." Turning to Mr. Pruitt, he raised a brow. "And I assume you're the..."

"Driver," Pruitt offered.

"Ah, the royal coachman," Mr. Marstens said, pursing his lips. A cloud passed over his eyes briefly. "Is Mrs. Bishop still at the palace?"

"Yes," I said, and for some reason I decided to add, "not sure anything could get her to leave the Durands—"

Mr. Marstens was already speaking again. "Do tell her that the young Miss Berg is in good hands."

Pruitt shifted in his seat. "And how do I know your hands are good?"

The bartender showed no sign of offense at the question but lifted a shoulder, saying, "Because her mother sent her here for a reason, and I do not think she would have sent her into harm's way."

For several breaths, the two fae stared at each other across the bar, as if engaged in a silent argument I wasn't invited to. This was getting ridiculous. Yes, there was a risk here. This bartender could be pretending to be my contact, pretending to know my mother. But life would always have risks, and I refused to live in fear.

Clearing my throat, I broke the silence. "Mr. Marstens, excuse us for not taking you at your word. We mean no disrespect, but these are odd times. Is there any proof you might be able to offer that would put us more at ease?"

The bartender seemed unperturbed by my request and promptly

smiled. "Of course, of course. Alora—smart woman that she was—planned for your skepticism. Told me to mention her necklace, the blue stone on a silver chain. Given to her by the late queen herself to celebrate the birth of her daughter—you."

My heart swelled as I listened, and my hand itched to reach for the pendant hidden beneath my shirt. I refrained. While any doubts surrounding Mr. Marstens were quickly fading, it seemed unwise to assume the others in this room could also be trusted.

"Is he right?" Mr. Pruitt asked, leaning into my line of sight.

I blinked rapidly at him before nodding. "Yes. About all of it."

"And you're sure you are all right being left here alone?"

"Yes, Mr. Pruitt. I'm sure. Please let Mrs. Bishop know I arrived safely, and I will send word to her as soon as I'm able to."

"Very well," the driver said, rising from his seat. "I will be off then. Please do take care, miss. Mrs. Bishop will have my head if anything happens to you."

As I watched the fae exit the tavern, I hoped I was making the right decision to stay.

*

I woke the next morning to the unfamiliar scent of stale beer and dust, panicking for a moment before remembering where I was and why I had come here. My back ached from the lumpy mattress I'd slept on, but I reminded myself it could have been worse.

Exactly, you could have been killed.

Yawning, I reached my arms overhead, wincing when I slammed my knuckles into the hard wall at the head of the bed.

"Sleep well?" a male asked, and I shot up to find Mr. Marstens sitting in a wooden chair near the window. Why was he in here? How long had he been watching me sleep?

As if he could read my thoughts—and I wasn't completely convinced that he couldn't—he smiled warmly. "As you said last night, miss, these are odd times, and there is only one reason you would be showing up in my tavern as you did. I would be remiss if I let anything happen to you before I could get you to your family's camp."

"So you sat there all night?" I asked, dropping my eyes to verify I was still dressed in the riding clothes I'd worn yesterday.

His eyes widened slightly, but he shook his head. "No." I exhaled with relief. "I stood most of the night. Over there, by the door."

My mouth fell open like a dying fish.

"Don't worry, Miss Berg. I promise I was perfectly proper." I scrounged for words but found none. "You can close your mouth now. And if you'd like to freshen up before we leave, there is a privy down the hall with a soaking tub. I can have hot water brought up for you."

"Thank you," I managed to say. "That would be wonderful. But can I ask you a question?"

"Of course," he said, smiling.

"How did you know my mother? How do you know where to find my family?"

His eyes turned wistful for a moment, but his good humor returned quickly. "Ah, your parents used to visit Engle quite often. It's where her cousins—who you'll be staying with—had their home before the war. I never had the pleasure of fighting beside your father, but I was sad to hear of his falling. I only saw your mother once more after that, when she came here to arrange for your training."

"But that doesn't explain why you've remained in touch with them. Not with how fae and humans now hate each other."

Mr. Marstens nodded slowly. "Ah, well. Technically, I'm a demi-fae, so I have ties to both of our kinds. Truth be told, I'd love to see an end to this unrest and division."

Pulling in a breath, I squared my shoulders and rose to my feet. "So when do we leave?"

He offered me another warm smile. "As soon as you're ready. I have a pair of horses waiting in the stables out back. You're lucky you came when you did. Any earlier and your family would have still been in the mountains."

I swung my legs over the edge of the bed and cringed when my bare feet hit the cold floor. I didn't bother mentioning that it was, in fact, poor luck that had brought me here in the first place.

※

I stood at the edge of the campsite watching Mr. Marstens ride away until he vanished from sight. A throat cleared behind me. I turned to find a man and woman watching me. My mother's cousins, Anna and Owen. Despite their kind expressions, something about them unnerved me.

You're being ridiculous, I told myself.

They were family. Mother had trusted them. I could too. What other choice did I have? I couldn't go back home, and I couldn't stay in Engle or any other village.

Anna, an older woman with dark hair that was graying at her temples, moved a half-step forward and dipped her chin. "Our daughter, Raven, has prepared your tent for you. If you'll allow me to show you the way?"

My mouth went completely dry. I tightened my hands into fists to try to keep their shaking from being too noticeable. All I could manage was a quick nod. I bent down to pick up my bag, but her husband reached it first.

"Allow me," Owen said, and before I could even think to protest, he had my belongings in his arms and was walking off with them.

"Come," Anna said with a wave of her hand, and I stepped alongside her without another look back.

For the first time since I'd arrived, I allowed myself a look at what would be my home for the foreseeable future. The clearing was as large as the grounds around the palace, but there were no buildings here. Instead, rows of large tents had been erected. These weren't the flimsy type meant for temporary shelter; rather, they seemed to be sturdy structures.

"Over there are the training grounds." Anna pointed to the right, and I swung my head to see several circles where the grass had been worn away, leaving only dark soil. In one of them, two women sparred, and I instinctively flinched each time their wooden swords met with a loud crack. My steps slowed as I watched. They moved quickly, expertly, as if they were performing a dance.

I stopped short when one of the women spun around and slammed her elbow into the nose of her opponent, causing her to drop her weapon into the dirt. With blood streaming from her nose and over her lips, the injured woman managed to hook her ankle behind the other's leg and knock her onto her backside.

A hand nudged my jaw up from where it had fallen open, and I caught Anna's eye.

"Don't worry, Lieke," she said. "Your training won't start until tomorrow. Come, let's get you settled."

I shifted my gaze back to the women in the training ring, who had resumed their practice. How long would it take for me to learn how to do that? And how much would it hurt in the process?

As we walked through the large camp, Anna pointed out the area where they prepared meals, a larger fire where everyone gathered together, the privy and the baths, and the row of sleeping tents. There seemed to be enough room for at least thirty people, but the clearing was nearly empty.

"How many people live here?" I asked as we continued past the tents.

"Oh, you *do* talk," she said, giving me a kind smile that I returned easily. "At the moment, we have barely a dozen. Some others come and go when traveling through, but for the most part it is just the eleven of us. Twelve, I suppose, now that you're here."

"And where is everyone? Did I scare them away or something?"

Anna offered me a sympathetic laugh and stopped in front of one of the tents. "Of course not, Lieke. Those on night watch are sleeping. We may seem secluded here, but we have to be vigilant."

"And the others?"

"Out hunting, I believe. We try not to visit the town markets unless we absolutely have to. Better to know how to survive on our own. Never know when the fae may become even more hostile toward our kind, when we may not be welcome to visit or trade."

Was our world truly that broken?

My hand lifted to my neck as I pondered that question, and I remembered how that fae had gripped my throat. What would have happened to me had Connor not appeared?

I knew the answer, yet I still hoped things could be better, that anger could be quelled and wounds healed, that whatever was broken in our world could be fixed. But standing here in this camp, with the clacking of the wooden swords behind me, I began to wonder if that was nothing more than a foolish dream.

CHAPTER ELEVEN

Lieke

Anna had left me to get acquainted with my new home, and aside from her husband, who brought me a plate of food for supper, no one interrupted my settling in. The bed and furnishings were comfortable enough, but they weren't home.

You'll need to get over that.

Between the unfamiliar surroundings and the excitement of what I was to learn, my sleep that evening was fitful at best. Thankfully, the smell of food the following morning was enough to help me overcome my exhaustion, pull me out of bed, and get me out of my tent.

"Lieke!" a voice I didn't recognize called from the fires, and a young woman stepped out from a group of people and trotted over, her long dark hair bouncing against her shoulders. I held my hand out in greeting, but she brushed it aside before wrapping her lean arms around my shoulders and pulling me into a hug. I stiffened, unsure what to do with my arms.

"You must be Raven?" I choked out the question, and she finally released me with a giggle that would have probably been infectious had I not been so caught off guard.

"That's me," she said, beaming. "How'd you sleep?"

I lifted my shoulders to my ears. "Could have been better."

Raven pursed her lips and nodded. "You get used to it, so I'm told."

"You don't know yourself?" I asked.

"Been here since I was a baby. This is all I know."

"I know what you mean," I mumbled.

Raven's brown eyes widened as she donned a crooked smile. "Mama said you've lived your whole life in the palace. What was that like? Were there lots of parties? I bet the food was amazing. Speaking of which, you should eat."

Grabbing me by the elbow, she half-led, half-dragged me toward the cooking fires, not seeming to notice when I tripped several times on tufts of grass and my own toes. She loosened her grip and pointed to a thick log lying on its side.

"Sit here. I'll grab you a bowl."

Silently, I obeyed, clasping my hands together as I leaned over and placed my forearms atop my knees. A moment later, she returned with two bowls of what appeared to be a thick, rich porridge. She offered me one, and I eagerly accepted it, my stomach growling away. I blew a cooling breath over my breakfast, marveling at how Raven gobbled up a steaming spoonful without hesitation.

Swallowing loudly, she swiped the back of her hand across her lips. "So the palace. What's it like?"

I lifted my spoon and glanced past it to meet her gaze. "It's big, I guess."

She bumped her shoulder into mine. "I asked you about the palace, not the prince."

My face warmed, and I braced myself for some teasing remark about my blushing. She said nothing but simply raised a brow at me, urging me to expound.

"I wouldn't know about the prince, honestly," I said, immediately wishing I hadn't.

"Really? Not even rumors? I mean, even I've heard he's rather…
impressive."

"Well, rumors are hardly reliable," I said, scooping up another bite.

"Why are you trying to ruin my fantasies here?"

I raised my empty spoon toward her. "You know, he could have
started those rumors to compensate." My skin warmed again.

Raven flashed me an incredulous look. "Oh please. Even the smaller fae outshine any human, and you know it."

"I know nothing of the sort," I said, shooting her an innocent look.

She studied me for a moment, squinting her eyes. "Liar," she finally
said.

I couldn't help but laugh. "Swear to the stars," I said, raising my
hand as if this were some solemn vow I was making.

"You lived your whole life around fae, and not once?" she asked,
her shock written plainly on her features. She jabbed a finger into her
own chest. "You mean, I—a lowly human who's been hiding out in the
forests my entire life—have been with a fae before you, someone who
grew up with them?"

I shrugged. "Obviously you weren't hiding your *entire* life if that's
the case."

Smacking my shoulder with the back of her hand, she scoffed.
"You know what I mean."

Dropping my spoon into the now empty bowl, I faced her. "Sorry
to disappoint you, but no, I haven't."

She stared at me blankly before her lips slowly dropped into a
frown. "If anyone's disappointed by this, it should be you, not me. You
don't know what you're missing, Lieke."

How could I tell this woman—who looked genuinely concerned for
me—that I wasn't interested in sex just for the fun of it? Despite balking
at romance for most of my life, I now craved love more than anything
else. And not just any love, but his. Brennan's. The very prince whose
body Raven had just been gossiping about.

Pressing my lips together, I bobbed a shoulder as I stared down at
my empty bowl. "Trust me, I know what I'm missing. But I need to get

over him."

"Get over who now?" she asked, and I mentally kicked myself for letting those words slip out.

Shaking my head, I stood and asked, "Where do we take care of our dishes?"

I expected her to ignore me and keep pushing for an answer, but instead she offered me a warm smile as she rose from her seat and pointed to a washbasin on the other side of the fires. She looked up at the morning sun and sighed.

"Training starts soon, so I guess we'll have to resume our chat later."

"Who is training me anyway?" I asked, hoping it wouldn't be one of the brutal women I'd witnessed fighting yesterday.

Raven donned an easy grin and lifted her brows high as she answered, "Me."

✳

My breath came out in painful wheezes, and no matter how much air I sucked in, I couldn't find any relief. Bent over at the waist, I stared at my feet. My lungs burned almost as much as the sun beating down on the back of my neck, and my legs angrily protested this abuse I'd inflicted upon them.

Not me, actually.

But Raven, at the direction of her parents.

Her toes came into view as she bounced her heels off the ground in front of me.

"You weren't lying when you said you weren't athletic. We haven't been running that long."

"Why—" I took another unsatisfying gulp of air as I tilted my face up to look at her. "Why would I lie about that?"

She beamed a smile that begged to be smacked off her perfect face. "Oh, you know. Some people play up the humility to make their performance more impressive. You though..." Her words trailed off into a string of giggles.

Pushing my hands off my knees, I forced myself to stand upright. "At least I'm good for a laugh," I said, thankful that my voice was finally coming out a bit more evenly now.

Raven stepped forward and gripped my shoulders with both hands. "We'll make sure you're good for much more than that before we send you back to the palace. But it won't be easy. You ready to head back?"

A groan rumbled in my chest as my head fell forward.

"I'll take that as a yes. We're already late, and I really don't want to miss lunch," Raven said, spinning away from me and bounding off through the trees before throwing a final command over her shoulder. "Hurry up, Lieke!"

✳

The wooden sword smacked into my hip, pulling a hiss from between my teeth as my shaky, weary legs did their best to spin me away from Raven. Every muscle in my body, from my calves up to my neck, screamed. Between the run this morning and the last hour of weapons drills, they'd been pushed beyond their limit.

"Lift your weapon," Raven commanded patiently, gesturing toward the sky with her palms.

My shoulders slumped, and I rolled my neck in a fruitless effort to stretch out some of the pain. "I can't," I said, defeated.

Tucking the tip of her practice blade behind my elbow, she nudged my arm up. "You must learn to, Lieke. Up." I winced as I forced my muscles to obey, and gritting my teeth, I reset my feet as she'd demonstrated earlier. "Good," she said.

I didn't wait for her to give the word before I lunged forward, putting any energy I could muster into thrusting the blade toward her. She easily pivoted back and to the right, avoiding my strike. Still, she smiled and offered another word of praise.

"Now what do you do?" she asked.

Instead of answering verbally, I growled as I pulled the blade in a wide arc toward her, stepping my left foot forward so my body could turn to face her.

"Yes, exactly," she said, lifting her weapon to meet mine with a *thwack* that reverberated up my arm. I fought through the fatigue as best I could, trying to ignore how my entire limb shook uncontrollably from the exertion.

"Now, shift your weight more to your back foot," she instructed. "More on the balls of your feet. Yes, like that. See how that makes it easier to back away from me as I pursue?"

Lightly I stepped back several paces, and she moved with me, circling her blade away from mine. My arm dropped heavily to my side.

"I can't do this," I said, shaking my head slowly.

Raven sighed and offered one of her warm smiles as she relaxed. "Not yet, but you will."

"I'm glad one of us is optimistic."

Nodding toward the edge of the circle, she said, "Come on, let's get you some water."

"When does this get easier?" I asked as I trudged along beside her to where two canteens of water waited for us in the grass. I stood there, letting her kneel to pick them up, knowing if I did it, I might never stand back up.

She shrugged and handed me my water. "Here, drink it slowly." She took a small sip of her own before finally answering my question. "Everyone is different, obviously, but you'd be surprised how quickly the body can learn. The mind, however, can take a little longer."

"What do you mean?" I asked, wiping a stray drop of water from my chin.

"A muscle is created to become stronger, right? We train it, build it up. We're not trying to force it to do anything it wasn't designed to do. But the mind? It's set in its ways, averse to change, stubborn beyond measure. Training it to see past what you know and pushing it beyond its own limits? That takes time. But don't worry. You're not the first person I've trained—and not the first my parents have helped either. We know how to get you where you need to be. Trust me."

"But what am I training for anyway?"

When she didn't respond but merely dropped her canteen onto the grass, my heart plummeted into my stomach and my muscles locked up. Was our break already over? My mind scrambled to find some excuse to get out of continuing our training for the day. She flashed me a quizzical look and cocked her head.

"You don't need to look so scared, Lieke."

"I can't," I said, hating how pathetic I sounded. I wanted to be stronger, wanted to be able to push through all the pain to keep going, but I didn't know how.

"Can't what? Go relax?" I blinked slowly at her, which earned me a laugh. I was too tired and sore to be offended. "We're done for the day, friend."

CHAPTER TWELVE

Conner

This was a disaster.

I stared down at the map stretched across my desk. I'd been here in my study poring over it all morning, but my vision had long since blurred. My body ached. My head pounded. My stomach growled. All in protest to my insistence on sitting here until I had devised a plan.

But all these hours later, I still had nothing.

A slow *creak* filled the room. Matthias had poked his head around the door.

"So you are alive," he said, stepping inside and shutting the door behind him.

I rubbed a finger into my temple, trying to ease the pain there. "Am I?"

My best friend huffed out a single laugh. "I've never seen one of the undead before, but I imagine they would be more…rotted."

I shook my head and gestured for him to sit.

"How are the soldiers?" I asked, knowing there wouldn't have been much improvement since I'd looked them over yesterday. Sloppy. Slow. Slovenly. The war had ended over twenty years ago, but our troops had still not fully recovered.

"They're…" Matthias started to answer but then looked up to the ceiling, tapping his finger against his lips. "Well, they're alive?"

I drew in a breath to steady myself. For the past year we had received regular reports of growing discontent across the kingdom, all while our neighbors continued to fortify their own fighting forces.

The threat of rebellion and war loomed over my head daily, and my armies were simply *alive*.

Matthias settled back in his chair and elaborated. "As you know, a good portion of our experienced troops are still recovering, plagued with nightmares and unpredictable fits of madness. We've had to relieve many of them of their duties. That leaves us with a relatively new and untested force."

"Are they at least showing promise?" I asked, foolishly allowing a little bit of hope to leak into my voice.

My second offered a shrug. "Perhaps. Anyone can be taught and trained, but only if they're willing. A good leader would help a lot, to be honest."

"Are you saying you're a poor one, Matthias?"

"Last I checked, Your Highness, I'm not the leader of the Emeryn armies. You are."

Running a hand behind my neck, I dropped my eyes back to the map, but I could see nothing except a blur of papers and ink. For all intents and purposes, I was their commander, but lately it seemed to be in title alone.

I had a new assignment.

Brennan.

The ass had been a pain in mine since our father charged me with controlling him. I had assigned guards to track him and keep an eye on him for me, but all that had done so far was confirm my suspicions that he hadn't changed his ways at all. Princess Calla had visited a few times during the past year, and he had done a good job charming her as commanded. But after each visit, I still found him tangled up with a brunette. Or a blonde. Every single time.

Fact of the matter was, Brennan had little to fear if he failed. When he screwed up, I was the one our father railed against. As unfair as that was, I didn't fight it. Not after the promise I'd made to our mother.

A promise I wished she had never asked me to make.

A promise I never could have denied her.

Protect your brother, she had said. *Promise me you will be there for him when I cannot.*

And I had protected him, at least from the king.

But I had failed to save Brennan from himself. That needed to be remedied.

Something moved in front of my face, and I glanced up to find Matthias now standing, waving his hand over the desk.

"Where did I lose you just now, Connor?" he asked with genuine concern. "It's your brother, isn't it?"

I nodded once before shaking my head slowly. "I don't know what more to do. What can I possibly try that I haven't already?"

Matthias returned to his seat with that mischievous look of his. "You never did take my suggestion of locking him up."

I envisioned shoving Brennan into one of the cold cells with nothing but urine-soaked straw for bedding. Bread. Water. Darkness. Solitude. As cruel as that sounded—and as guilty as it made me feel to consider it—I was starting to think it might be the only way to turn the little shit around.

"Maybe," I muttered, ready to be finished with this topic altogether.

"It really is unfair for you to have to manage marrying off your brother," Matthias said. Before I could agree, he continued. "When does the king expect you to focus on your own marriage prospects? After all, our kingdom will need an heir just as much as we need this alliance with Arenysen."

I suddenly wanted to go back to discussing Brennan.

"Maybe he thinks we have time," I said with a shrug, trying not to let him see how this new topic grated on me. Not that I could hide much from him, though.

"And what do you think?" Matthias asked, all humor gone from his tone. He honestly thought I had time to think about finding a wife? As if he could read my thoughts, he jabbed his finger toward me. "And don't tell me you don't have time to think about it."

I settled back in my chair and laid my head back, lifting my eyes to the ceiling. What *did* I think about it? I wasn't averse to the idea like Brennan was, but I wasn't exactly gearing up to bind myself to anyone just yet.

"I have time—to find her, that is," I said, still looking at the ceiling instead of at my friend. "If it's meant to happen, it will happen."

Matthias started laughing before I'd even finished speaking, and I raised a brow in question.

"Don't tell me you still believe in that mate nonsense!" His forehead crinkled as he ridiculed me. "You know that's just a fanciful bedtime story. It's not real!"

"And how do you know? When exactly did you become an expert on romance?" I tried to keep my tone flat, uninterested, even as something tightened defensively in my chest. If I dared try to explain to him how my parents had actually been mates, bound to each other by fate, he would have scoffed and denied it. Funny how a war—a war fought for love, at that—could turn everyone's hearts away from the truth.

"Sure it's not just your way of putting off marriage for as long as possible? *Oh, she's not my mate. Can't marry her.*" He wagged his head as he proceeded to mock me, and I would have thrown something at him had there been anything handy.

"Why are you so eager to marry me off exactly?" I asked. My love life—or lack thereof—had never come up before this, and it seemed an odd time to mention it.

Matthias's smile faded slightly, but he didn't let it disappear completely. "Watching you working so hard to pair your brother off had me thinking, I guess. Arenysen needs a future king. And we need a future queen. That concerns everyone in our nation, does it not?"

He wasn't wrong. It would need to be addressed sooner or later.

Later was all I could handle right now though.

"Someday, Matthias. But not yet. There will be time for that."

The door slid open behind him, and Brennan entered, looking as disheveled and haggard as I felt.

"You wanted to see me," he said, as if I might have forgotten sending the page off to fetch him.

I peered over Matthias's head.

"Yes, hours ago actually," I said before meeting Matthias's gaze and giving him a silent command to leave us.

"Remember, Your Highness," he said as he rose to leave, "time's ticking."

He laughed once when I rolled my eyes but quickly left without another word, only giving Brennan a polite nod as he passed him.

Brennan rocked back on his heels and shoved his hands into his pockets.

"What was that about time ticking?" he asked.

I scowled at him and ignored his question. "Have you any idea what you're doing?"

"Besides standing here awaiting another lecture from my brother?"

"If you don't want to hear it from me, I'm happy to take this to the king," I offered.

His eyes twitched with humor before he let a single laugh escape and dropped himself into the chair. "No you're not. Because then you'd have to admit to him that you've failed."

He wasn't wrong, but at this point I was nearly considering taking the beating from our father if it meant getting Brennan in line.

Nearly.

Rubbing my fingers against my temples, I stared down at my desk. "We all have things to do, Brennan. What happens if you fail? Have you thought about that at all?"

Why I bothered asking him, I didn't know. He'd never cared about anyone or anything beyond his own whims and fancies. He'd never had a care for the future or for anyone else.

"That's your business, Connor, not mine," Brennan said with more emotion than I would have expected from him. I opened my mouth to argue, but he pinned me with a bitter glower. "We all know everyone hates me."

"No one hates you," I argued. "Frustrated with you, perhaps, but we don't hate you."

He leaned closer, his glare darkening. "Regardless, it's been made perfectly clear that I'm the lesser son who can be tossed aside and forgotten. This is no different. I'm nothing more than bait needed to lure some politically beneficial pussy."

"You really see it that way?"

"How could I see it any differently? Mother doted on you. Father confides in you. And I'm just here, like some accessory the family parades around when needed."

My throat tightened, and I couldn't find the words to convince him otherwise. If he didn't see how much the family cared for him, how could I say anything to help at this point? My heart ached as I stared at him, but then something in me snapped.

Brennan. The princess. The armies. The rebels. Everything. Rested on me.

The least this fucker could do was marry a princess for the good of the kingdom.

"Which is it, Brennan?" I asked, all my pity for him slipping away.

"What do you mean?"

Leaning forward, I laid my forearms on the desk and glared at him for a long breath.

"Do you hate being inconsequential? Or do you want to be needed?"

His eyes darted around the room as his lips tried to form words his mind hadn't yet selected. Then he focused back on me. "To be needed, but—"

I raised a finger between us. "No. No *but*, Brennan. We don't get to choose how we are needed. We either help or we don't. We either do what needs to be done or we walk away and accept the consequences of our cowardice. You can absolutely choose to tell the king and me and the entire kingdom to fuck right off, but you don't get to sit here and bitch to me about feeling insignificant when the whole of our future sits on your self-centered, prickish shoulders."

Brennan stared back at me, but I couldn't read him, couldn't tell if any of my words had gotten through to him. How many times had I reminded him of the stakes, of the consequences of his failure, only to have him brush them aside. But I didn't have time to sit here in silence while he wrapped his head around something that should have been an easy decision. I had shit to do. Maybe time in the dungeon would help him make up his mind.

Slamming my palms down onto the desk, I pushed myself up to stand, ready to tell him just that, when he lifted his face to look at me.

His lips crept up into one of his lopsided smiles. "I guess I'll be the bait the kingdom needs."

CHAPTER THIRTEEN

Lieke

I woke before dawn and stepped out of my tent, breathing in the crisp morning air. Clasping my hands together, I reached my arms high above me and stretched away the stiffness in my joints. At least the ache of my muscles was now a pleasant reminder of my improving strength rather than the agonizing torment it had been when I'd first arrived.

"You ready?" Raven's question pulled my attention over my shoulder.

"Of course," I said, giving my shoulders one more roll before I took off running across the camp toward a barely-there trail.

Raven caught up to me easily, and within moments we had instinctively matched each other's gaits so our feet hit the ground in unison. We continued along the path without speaking, accompanied only by the noise of our steady breathing and footfalls. As I looked around at the trees, I recalled how difficult this run had been just over a year ago.

Had it truly been a year since I'd left home?

This entire time, I'd received only a handful of letters from Mrs. Bishop. She claimed her infrequent communication was for my safety—and the safety of my hosts, who couldn't risk being discovered by the fae, but I still wasn't completely convinced of the threat. Not even the attack at the Durand party last year could convince me that the entire race was a danger to humans.

After an hour, Raven and I closed in on the camp and slowed to a walk.

"Feels good to be back here. I missed these trees," she said quietly. We had finally returned to the forests near Engle after spending the last year migrating about the country, settling in different regions each season to avoid detection. We hadn't returned to the same campsite as before, but we were near enough that these woods felt familiar.

"Certainly beats running in the mountains. Reminds me a lot of home," I said with more than a hint of sadness.

"You'll get back there soon," Raven said encouragingly.

I frowned. "But not yet."

"Not yet," she said. The smile she offered me, though, seemed more apologetic than comforting, and I bristled.

"What aren't you telling me, Rave?" I asked. When she bit her lower lip and dropped her gaze to the ground, my gut tightened. "Is it that bad?"

She shifted her attention toward camp, where the others were preparing the morning meal. "It's not going to be easy," she finally said.

"As if any of this has been easy," I said, trying to laugh, but it came out hollow.

When Raven finally turned back to me, gone was the lightheartedness that had been present before. As I waited for her to speak, her dark eyes burned into mine with such intensity that my breath caught. Quietly, as if she were apologizing, she said, "I'd say this will hurt me more than it will hurt you, but I hate to lie to a friend."

✳

A rough circle of stones had been placed in the grass at the edge of camp, designating the new training area. Eventually, once the grass got worn down with all the sparring, they would be removed.

I stepped over them and into the ring. Raven's words had conjured such fear in me that I had barely been able to choke down my breakfast.

"You should have eaten more," she said from behind me, and I pivoted to see her entering the ring carrying two knives. We had long ago stopped sparring with wooden blades, so the sight of the weapons wasn't what sent my stomach lurching into my throat. It was the remorseful gleam in my friend's eyes.

"I would have if you hadn't scared the shit out of me earlier," I said, trying to smile. She said nothing but opened her left hand, offering me the knife in her palm. As I took it, I eyed her suspiciously. "Why do you look like you're about to do something you don't want to do?"

Raven swallowed hard. "Because I am," she said.

She moved in a flash, sweeping her blade toward me and catching me off guard. I shuffled backwards in retreat, but I wasn't fast enough. The edge of her knife slashed across my left bicep, biting into my flesh. Instinct forced my knife-hand up to cover the wound, but Raven smacked it back down with a sharp reprimand.

"No! Fight through the pain, Lieke," she commanded, her eyes stern and focused, then lunged toward me again. This time I was ready for her, and I leaped out of her reach. "Good," she said, but I barely heard her as I tried to ignore the stinging heat in my arm and the blood dripping down from beneath my sleeve.

I backed away from her, keeping my weapon up, but I faltered when my heel struck one of the training ring's stones. Raven took advantage of my misstep. Sweeping her left arm up and out, she slammed her forearm into my wrist, forcing my knife to fall to the grass.

She didn't stop.

In one fluid movement, she sliced her knife down my collarbone before quickly changing directions and slashing my ribs, cutting through my shirt with ease. Growling, I shoved her hard with both hands and crouched to retrieve my weapon. My fingers frantically searched the grass for the handle as I watched her regain her balance. When her foot came flying toward my face, I had to give up on the knife. At the last moment, I managed to get my hands up, but I failed to grab hold of her. Pain shot up my arm as she landed a kick against my hands. The blow forced me onto my backside, and I rolled onto my back, barely stopping my head from hitting the stones behind me.

I couldn't think, couldn't focus, couldn't understand.

But then her earlier words screamed through my foggy mind.

Fight through the pain!

This was part of the training.

This was necessary.

This was what I told myself anyway in the mere seconds I had before Raven attacked again. Flipping her grip on her weapon, she flung herself toward me, aiming the blade down at my right shoulder. I managed to roll away from her onto my stomach just as her knife stabbed the ground inches from my face.

"Good, Lieke," Raven said, her tone surprisingly encouraging.

I scrambled back onto my hands and knees, desperate to get off the ground and grab my knife, but she was already there, standing over me, poised to strike yet again.

I peered up at her and noted the silent apology on her face as she buried her knife in my back.

✳

My breath hissed through my teeth as the needle pierced my skin and pulled the thread through, pulling the edges of my knife wound closed. Raven whispered yet another apology, but I still wasn't sure I believed her. When a blast of pain shot through my back, I clenched my jaw tightly and willed myself to stay silent.

"You did good," she said. I only huffed in response. "I know you don't think so—"

"Don't tell me what I think," I snapped over my shoulder.

"You're angry," she said quietly.

Rolling my eyes, I stood so quickly that the stool I was sitting on toppled over. I spun around to face her. "Don't tell me what I'm feeling either."

Raven blinked evenly at me, no sign of apology or regret in her expression, and pointed to my left shoulder. "I need to put some salve on it so it doesn't get infected."

I gritted my teeth and glowered at her, my nostrils flaring. "You stabbed me."

She looked almost bored as she said, "I'm well aware of that."

"You didn't have—"

"Yes, I did." I raised my brow in question, and she retrieved a jar from the ground and stood before she responded. "Remember what I told you at our first training session?"

"Obviously not," I sneered.

"We're not just training your muscles here."

I scowled as I grumbled, "You're stabbing them too."

She ignored me. "This is part of teaching your mind to learn new limits in strength, courage, pain. Now turn around."

Without another word, I obliged, relaxing as Raven applied the cooling salve over my injury. Through the tent's open flaps, I watched as others in the camp strolled past. Some offered knowing smiles, while others conspicuously averted their eyes. One woman, though, approached us directly, a bandage peeking out of the collar of her shirt.

"Who got you this time, Caroline?" Raven asked casually.

The woman laughed and said, "Philip, this morning. Healing nicely though."

Raven stilled behind me. "So the new tonic is working?"

Tonic? I steeled my features, hoping Caroline wouldn't notice my confusion.

"Seems to be. It's why I'm here actually. Have you seen your mother?"

"Saw her over at the healer's tent when I stocked up on stitching supplies not long ago."

Caroline nodded her thanks and pivoted to leave without another word.

Once she was gone, Raven tapped my arm lightly. "All done, Lieke."

I winced as I moved my left arm, testing its mobility. "So what's this miracle tonic?" I asked, aiming for a benignly curious tone.

"Oh, just some new healing medicine my mother discovered years ago."

"Healing medicine? Yet I'm sitting here getting sewn up with no numbing ointment."

Raven's lips slowly lifted into an almost remorseful smile. "Part of the training, I'm afraid."

CHAPTER FOURTEEN

Connor

Drawing in a calming breath, I pushed open the door to my father's office and found him standing at the large window near his desk, looking down at the palace grounds with his hands clasped behind his back. He didn't turn around as I approached.

"Do you think he'll propose as he claims he will?" the king asked in a calm voice that did little to put me at ease. Not that I had much reason to be on edge, with everything finally falling into place with Brennan. It had taken us two years to get to this point, but I knew all too well how quickly things could go to shit.

As I pondered my answer, I joined him at the window. Three stories below us, the staff was preparing for yet another party. The gardeners pruned the hedges and straightened up the flower beds while the kitchen staff bustled around, moving tables into place and throwing cloths over them.

"I do," I said, knowing full well how unconvincing my answer sounded.

"You've done well, Connor."

I froze, unable to breathe or move or even blink. When was the last time he'd given me a compliment? When was the last time he'd said anything that wasn't a command or a reprimand? I swallowed hard.

"Might want to save those words for after the nuptials," I said.

My father laughed—not the boisterous laugh that had marked much of my youth, but as much of a laugh as I had heard since Mother passed.

"Fair enough, son," he said. "Remind me to commend you later."

"And what if he backs out?" I didn't know what compelled me to ask that, and I immediately wished I could shove the words back into my mouth.

The king stiffened.

His jaw pulsed.

I opened my mouth to backtrack, as if that were possible, but before I could, he said with his signature fierceness, "Make sure he doesn't."

Failure was not an option. It never was for me.

Finally turning to me, the king gave a single nod before gesturing for me to follow him to the sitting area in front of the fireplace. I waited for him to sit first and then perched myself on the edge of the chair opposite him.

"Relax, Connor," he said, but that was almost as difficult as everything else he demanded of me. Still, I did my best to fake it and scooted back in the chair. Once I'd settled, he gave me a tight smile. "That's better. Now tell me, what has the general reported? How are our armies faring?"

At least Matthias had given me good news to deliver on this front; his tireless efforts this past year had paid off.

"They're improving every day. We estimate they will be up to previous standards in another three months or so."

"Just in time. Good."

I eyed him, genuinely confused. "Sir?"

"If Brennan can't secure this alliance with Arenysen, we will need every single soldier ready to defend our borders. As you know, our scouts are reporting increased traffic from both Wrenwick and Kinham to

Arenysen. No doubt they are doing everything they can to undermine the pairing of your brother and the princess. King Vael is leaving this decision completely in the hands of his daughter, so we can't secure this alliance without your brother."

"So if he fails—"

"War."

The word fell from his lips like an ax. I'd known of this possibility for the past two years, but the way my father said the word now sent the reality of it slamming into my sternum. The blood. The screams. The chaos. The horrors.

"But why?" The question was out before I could constrain it, but I didn't care how desperate I sounded. My father had been there on the battlefields with me, and he was as determined to avoid it as I was.

Roughing a hand over his stubbled chin, my father gazed into the cold, dark fireplace for a moment. I wondered where his mind wandered. Was he tormented by the same images I was? Or did he think of his brother and the love that had plunged our nations into that bloody mess? Did he wonder if it could have been prevented? Did he doubt his brother's claims that the woman had been his mate?

Because I did. I had pondered all of this for the past two decades.

His sigh filled the room as he turned his weary eyes back to me. "The heart is a fickle thing, Connor. Easily swayed. Easily stolen. Easily corrupted. And the mind is of little consequence once the heart has been overtaken—whether by love or greed or power. The heart can convince even the smartest among us to do foolish things—dangerously foolish things, especially when it is the desire for vengeance that has blackened its fibers. I fear this is exactly what has happened to Wrenwick's king."

If anyone had reasonable cause for wanting revenge, it was indeed Nils Olander. His brother, Leif, had been betrothed to the woman my uncle claimed as his mate. That claim had started the war.

"You think Wrenwick would break the treaty?"

"I think their king has had a good deal of time to stew over the perceived wrongs against him and his family. Humans are just as stubborn and single-minded as we can be."

"And where does Kinham's allegiance lie? Any idea? Think they will side with the Olanders?"

My father was shaking his head before I even finished speaking. "Even if they weren't both human kingdoms, Kinham would be unlikely to give up what they gained all those years ago. No doubt they'll seek to keep their kingdom's sovereignty at all costs."

"Including war."

He nodded.

"And we are sure a marriage will be enough to stop the threat?"

"Can we be sure of anything? No. But it's the best plan we have so far. Especially with the increasing attacks on our roads. Where do we stand on getting that under control?"

My stomach tightened, and I nervously roughed my hand over my mouth and chin as I searched for the right words.

"The attacks have become less frequent, but they have continued with the same pattern. No blood. No human casualties. Clean kills."

The king's expression tightened. "Have the healers determined how they're dying? Humans don't have magic, after all."

"They're currently looking into the possibility of..." I swallowed my next word, unsure how my father might react to it. Thus far, our conversation had been fairly pleasant, and I hated to ruin it with this information.

"Possibility of what?" He eyed me suspiciously, but something in his hardened stare told me he'd already guessed.

"Poison."

"Is it the *same* poison?" he asked with more timidity than I'd expected.

"We don't know yet. That's what they're working to determine. It's similar, but different. Works faster, unlike what—"

"Killed your mother," he whispered as he lowered his eyes to the table between us.

"Whatever it is—whether it's what took her from us or something else entirely—we are nearly certain it is not native to our lands. Either someone is creating it here or it's being brought in. Since Arenysen is the primary importer from Dolobare and the lands beyond—"

My father's head snapped up, his blue eyes burning into mine.

"Then we have even more need to ensure Brennan doesn't fuck this up."

CHAPTER FIFTEEN

Lieke

Gritting my teeth, I focused on the corner post of my tent as Raven removed the bandage from my side. Studying the wound, she blew out a slow breath.

"You're getting better with your stitches," she said. "Nice and even, and it's healing nicely."

"Better than the ones on my back that I couldn't reach," I said flatly, shifting in my seat. Raven's reasoning for not helping me close my wounds seemed logical enough, but it was difficult to appreciate the lessons she taught when I was nursing painful gashes and tears with nothing more than an herbal salve and bandages.

Raven didn't seem to notice my jaded tone. "True. Those scars will last years longer, but scars aren't bad as long as you're willing to learn from them."

I swung my chin around to face her, not bothering to hide my frustration. "Sometimes it seems like the only thing I'm learning is not to turn my back on a friend."

The corners of her mouth turned down as she raised her brows high. "That may be one of the more important lessons to take away from this, but certainly not the only one. I get that you're bitter. I was too when I was in your position, but trust me. You'll appreciate this when—if—you ever find yourself in that situation again."

That situation.

Thankfully the nightmares had become less and less frequent, but the memory of Griffin's fingers lifting me up off the ground, choking the life out of me, refused to leave me alone completely. Three years later, and it still tormented me. Raven was right. I never wanted that to happen again. I never wanted to be helpless and weak.

"Look on the bright side, though, Lieke," Raven said, securing a new bandage over my stitches and stepping in front of me. "You're improving in your defenses. You're sustaining fewer and fewer injuries."

She wasn't wrong. This cut in my side had been the first I'd sustained in over a month. The first non-superficial one anyway. I had come so far in my skills, and I owed all of it to Raven. Yet all I did was sulk and let my bitterness fester.

For all the times I'd wondered why my mother would send me here to endure this, I'd rarely allowed myself a moment to be grateful for it. But I had to admit I was stronger. I was faster. I was more resilient. I was more confident.

Because of Raven.

"I'm sorry," I whispered, dropping my chin to my chest.

"For what?"

"For being so unappreciative."

Raven laughed softly. "It's okay, Lieke. I expected it. It's part of the job. But I'd take your scowling at me every day for the rest of my life over what is about to happen."

My eyes widened. What more could she possibly do to me? I'd already been isolated for days on end, left to fend for myself in the forest for weeks, forced to stitch my own wounds without numbing herbs. All so I could learn how to survive, to push myself mentally through pain and hunger and fear.

A sad smile spread across Raven's face. "This time it really will hurt me more than you," she whispered. "You're going home, Lieke."

My heart leaped into my throat, cutting off my breath. Home? Three long years, and I was finally going home. It was all I'd wanted since I arrived, but an ache lodged itself in my chest. What waited for me back there besides loneliness and rejection?

"I wish you could come with me," I said, pressing my lips together to keep them from trembling.

"Me too. I'd love to catch a glimpse of that prince of yours," she said, mischief sparking in her eyes.

"He's far from mine," I corrected, ignoring the sharp sting of that truth.

"Yet," Raven said. "Wait until he sees how you've grown. He won't be able to ignore you any longer."

I couldn't keep myself from snorting. "I think you underestimate my fae competition, Rave. New skills or not, I'm still just a human."

She rolled her eyes at me. "*Just* a human. You say it as if it's a weakness, like we truly are the lesser creatures they believe us to be. And I know you don't believe that, Lieke. Even if you don't share most humans' hatred for the fae."

Leaning back in my chair, I lifted my eyes to the ceiling of the tent. "It would just be easier if I could get over him."

I didn't bother to mention how difficult this had proved to be. Every time I'd contemplated the reasons he couldn't be with me, every time I'd been close to convincing myself we were an impossibility, something seemed to tighten around my heart and pull me right back to my *need* for him. Three years away from him hadn't cured my affliction, and I was beginning to think there was no cure, that I would simply have to learn to live with this pain forever.

"Would it help if I told you he's spoken for?" she asked quietly.

I straightened in my seat. Her eyes danced with a false innocence I'd come to know all too well.

"What do you mean?"

"My parents received a message from Mrs. Bishop yesterday evening after you'd turned in."

Hardening my glare, I scooted forward in my chair. "Stop stalling. What's the news?"

She shrugged and looked casually around my tent. "Oh, you know, just that he's courting Princess Calla of Arenysen. Seems there does exist a female who can tame him. They're expecting a proposal within the month, so she says."

My heart tumbled into my gut.

For years I had watched Brennan sneak off with one female after another, and it had hurt, but I'd always known his trysts weren't serious. Nothing more than distractions.

But a proposal?

Marriage?

I was out of time.

Maybe that's best for you.

This could be the very thing I needed to help me finally move on.

As if in answer, my chest tightened at the mere thought of being parted from him. This was preposterous. I didn't belong at the palace. I didn't belong with the fae royals. I was nothing but a mortal human, the daughter of a cook. A nobody.

And yet I did belong there.

I couldn't explain it.

I couldn't ignore it either.

Like something was calling me back home with more intensity than ever before.

I needed to get home.

And soon.

Raven caught my gaze. "There's the fire I wanted to see in you."

✳

We walked through camp in silence until we came to Raven's parents' tent. She announced our arrival, and Anna bid us enter, where we found her sitting with Owen at the table. I dipped my chin to them in greeting, and with a toss of her hand, Anna dismissed her daughter.

"Meet me after?" Raven asked, and I nodded as confusion set in. In all my time here, I'd never known them to exclude Raven from one of our talks.

Anna beckoned me forward, proffering the chair opposite her. "Come, sit, sit."

With a tight-lipped smile, I obliged, my curiosity and apprehension growing.

Owen laughed once, and the kindness in his eyes helped put me at ease. "No need to look so frightened."

"Then why—" I started, but Anna raised a hand and shook her head slightly. I expected her to offer an explanation. She didn't.

"You are not the first we have trained, Lieke. And with fae-human relations deteriorating as they are, you won't be the last, I am sure. But you are the only one we expect to ever send off to the palace."

My forehead twitched and my shoulders tightened as questions swirled around my mind.

Why had I really been sent here?

What was expected of me?

Was I to be some pawn in a political game?

Again Owen laughed, as if I had uttered every question aloud. "What has you so worried?"

I searched his eyes for a sign that there was any validity to my suspicions, but I detected nothing more than his usual quiet humor.

"Oh, nothing. Just nervous to go home after all these years away, I suppose," I said with a smile, waiting for him to look away first. He was still staring at me when his wife spoke again.

"That is understandable, especially after the attack that brought you to us. I hope you will trust the training we have provided if that fae—or any other—seeks to do you harm."

"It's not that actually," I said, regretting the words as soon as they were out.

"Oh? What else could have you so nervous?" Anna asked.

My cheeks warmed, but I ignored them and searched for anything to say—anything that wasn't the embarrassing truth. But before I could, she asked dreamily, "Is it by chance the prince?"

There seemed to be no sign of mockery in her voice, and the smile she offered appeared genuine enough.

I only nodded in response, though my blushing face was likely all the answer she needed.

Anna reached across the table and took my hand in hers, stroking the back of it with her thumb.

"The heart doesn't always know what's best for us, unfortunately. But sometimes we must let it lead for a while before we truly know our path."

"I shouldn't love him," I admitted. "I've tried to get over it."

"Are you certain about how he feels?" she asked.

I nodded. "Fairly certain. He only sees me as an old friend he doesn't have time for anymore."

"Ah," Owen said, "but he hasn't seen who you have become."

I wanted to find encouragement in their words, believe there was truly some hope that Brennan might ever see me the way I saw him. But I couldn't. I couldn't even picture it. Especially with his pending proposal—assuming he hadn't already proposed.

"That may be so," I said, "but he's to be married soon. To the fae princess of Arenysen. That's who he belongs with. Not me."

Owen waved away my excuses. "He's not married yet though. And the last thing we need in our lands is more fae. Especially with how they've treated those of us who survived and remained."

Anna released my hand to reach for her husband's forearm. "Hush up, Owen. We have no right to say who our prince can and cannot marry. And there may still be hope for our kinds to live together in peace. Someday."

Shrugging, Owen looked over at his wife. "I'm just saying, it would be beneficial to all of us—fae and human alike—if both races ruled the kingdom as equals."

As hopeful as I was to see that change made—and as much as I wished I could be the one to help make that happen—it seemed so far out of reach that I might as well try to touch the stars.

Anna cleared her throat, drawing my attention back to her. "Regardless of what happens with the prince, I know your friend, Mrs. Bishop, is eager for your return."

I smiled at the thought of being home again—and of spending my time kneading dough instead of my sore muscles.

"Before we send you off though, we have a gift for you," Anna said and nodded to her husband, who reached down to the floor between them. He lifted a small bundle of dark cloth and placed it on the table before unrolling it with care. Inside were two small knives in simple leather sheaths. Their handles were also simple, made of smooth, dark wood. Owen selected one and cradled it in both hands as he passed it to me.

"These may not look like much," Anna said, "but there is no need to ornately decorate weapons that are to remain hidden."

I slid the sheath away to reveal the steel blade, but as I moved to touch the tip to feel its sharpness, Anna reached forward and pulled my hand back. My eyes went wide with an unspoken question.

"These blades are special. They will protect you from the fae, but you must only use them as a last resort."

I glanced down at the blade in my hand. It looked like plain steel to me, like most other knives I'd seen.

"Special how, exactly?" I asked.

Owen answered this time. "Magic."

Quirking a brow, I lifted my eyes to peer up at him.

Anna sighed heavily. "Magic is one way to look at it. But really, they're made with rare materials that are fatal to immortals."

"Just immortals?"

"Well, the knives can kill anyone as well as any other blade if used properly, but yes, the materials aren't fatal to humans."

"So why stop me from touching it then?"

"Because the more they're handled and touched by humans, the less effective the—"

"The magic," Owen said, ignoring how his wife glared at him for finishing her sentence for her.

I eyed the pair sitting across from me, unsure what to make of this tale. Magic existed, of course; I knew that. The prince's ability to shift was evidence enough, but something felt off here. Something I couldn't quite figure out. What weren't they telling me?

You're being paranoid, Lieke.

They've trained you.

They've cared for you.

They're family.

Yes, my unease was surely unwarranted. I was just nervous about returning home. Sliding the blade into its sheath, I placed it back with its mate on the table and watched as Owen wrapped them both up again. When he extended the bundle to me, I accepted it with a forced smile.

"You said they were to remain hidden?" I asked as I pushed myself away from the table to stand.

Anna stood as well, lifting another parcel from beneath the table and handing it to me. "Here is a new riding skirt for you, along with a knife garter for your thigh and a wrist sheath for under your sleeve." She waved a hand toward the screen in the back corner of the tent. "Would like to make sure everything fits before we send you on your way."

Once I had changed out of my leggings and into the riding skirt and secured both knives to my thigh, I stepped out and nodded my thanks to the older couple.

Anna smiled. "Perfection, Lieke. Do you have any questions?"

I frowned slightly, looking from Anna to her husband and back. "Just one. Why do I need a riding skirt exactly? Am I not taking the palace carriage back?"

Anna said nothing as she waved for me to follow her out of the tent and into the morning sunshine. Raven was already approaching, leading a beautiful chestnut horse toward us. I reached a hand toward the mare, and she nuzzled my palm, her warm, breathy snort tickling my skin and pulling a giggle from me.

Raven handed me the reins and scratched the mare behind her ear. "This is Honey. Trained her myself since she was just a filly."

"I can't take your horse!"

"Of course you can, and you will. I want you to. I'd trust her to no one else."

"This is all too much," I said as tears began to surface.

Shaking her head, Raven offered me a tight smile. "Not too much for you, friend."

Anna reached an arm around my shoulders. "Mr. Marstens has arrived to escort you back to Engle before you make your way home."

I swung my gaze toward the edge of the camp. The demi-fae waved from where he sat atop his horse, waiting patiently. Before I could say anything more, Anna placed a kiss on my temple.

"We will miss you, Lieke. Truly," she said. I started to protest that the goodbyes could wait until I had retrieved my belongings from my tent, but then Owen came walking up with my bag in his arms and proceeded to tie it behind the saddle.

Raven pulled me into a tight hug and stepped back quickly. She seemed to hate goodbyes as much as I did, so I lifted myself into the saddle, adjusting the skirt to cover my legs on either side. Thankfully, it was only the three of them—and not the entire camp—here to see me on my way. With a small wave, I clicked my tongue quietly to Honey and gave a light squeeze of my legs to nudge her into an easy walk toward the edge of camp. Tears pooled in the corners of my eyes as I rode further into the trees.

CHAPTER SIXTEEN

Lieke

The sun lingered high in the sky—albeit barely visible through the dense forest canopy overhead—when Honey and I made the final turn onto the road to the palace. The tall stone wall that protected the palace came into view. A pair of guards stood on either side of the road, leaning against the wall and watching me as I approached. Though they didn't move, I could sense their keen eyes on me. The immense wooden gate lay open, but I knew better than to try to simply ride on through.

With a slight tug on the reins, I urged Honey to a halt before the entrance and the guards. Lazily, the one to my right pushed off the wall and sauntered over to me, using the long spear in his hand like a walking stick. His sword bounced in its sheath against his leg as he advanced. Neither guard wore armor, only a tunic emblazoned with the royal seal—a dark blue shield lined in gold and adorned with a gilded silhouette of a hound beneath two crossed daggers.

The guard stopped a good distance away and scrutinized me, his dark eyes roaming over my body. When he spoke, it wasn't to me.

"Evan! Are the Durands expecting any human visitors today?" he asked over his shoulder.

His companion didn't budge as he answered, "Not that I was told."

The guard in front of me lifted a single brow and asked, "What business do you have with the royal family?"

"Are you new here? I work for them," I said, lifting my chin into the air. "In the kitchens under Mrs. Bishop. I've been away visiting family."

At this, the other guard stepped away from the wall. I looked from one guard to the other, willing my face to remain calm and not reveal the fear that was beginning to take root in my stomach. The guards moved closer. Honey huffed out a snort as if to tell them to back off. They didn't listen. Either that or they didn't understand horses.

"Have any proof?" the guard on my left, Evan, asked, and I slowly turned to face him.

"And what kind of proof might you need? Shall I recount all the meals I have helped prepare for the Durand family throughout my relatively short lifetime? Or shall we drag poor old Mrs. Bishop out here and have her vouch for me?" I forced a sweet smile and addressed the other guard now. "Both would seem a waste of time for two busy males such as yourselves."

The fae shared a look, and for a moment I wondered if my words—and attitude—hadn't sealed my fate. Would they turn me away? Arrest me? Or worse?

Evan locked eyes with me before tossing his chin to the side. "Come on down, miss. We'll need to search you and your belongings before we can let you pass."

Stars.

Why hadn't I planned for this? Why had I thought I would simply be allowed to ride onto the property with ease?

Clearing my throat, I leaned forward and swung my leg back behind me and dismounted. I gave Honey a pat on her neck before slipping the reins over her head and holding them out to Evan. Mentally I moved through the possible maneuvers I might need if the situation soured, but I hoped I wouldn't have to use any of them. I simply wanted to go home, not cause a scene or get into trouble.

Evan nodded to the other guard, who began to untie my belongings from the back of the saddle. Honey stepped away from him, but I calmed her with a quiet breath, and she steadied herself. I turned my attention back to Evan.

"I can't say this is altogether proper for you to search…" I gestured to my body with both hands.

His face wrinkled with disgust. "You're not exactly high on my list of things I want to touch today either, but it has to be done. Especially with the party tonight. Now raise your arms."

Heaving a heavy sigh, I lifted my arms and watched him as he held the reins in one hand and used the other to feel along my waist, over my torso, and behind my back. My body tensed when his fingers briefly grazed the space between my breasts, which earned me a short laugh from him. As he continued to feel along my arms, I shook my head at him.

"Since when are humans seen as such a threat to the Durands, warranting such thorough scrutiny?"

It was the other guard who answered. "Since they started picking off helpless fae along the road, that's what."

Evan growled. "Shut your mouth, Willem. For all we know, she's one of them."

My eyebrows shot up. "Humans are behind the attacks? How do you know?"

Evan glowered at me. "Yes, and I don't owe you any further explanation, girl. And you can lower your arms. I need to check your legs now."

My heart thumped faster, and I tried not to think of what they might do if they discovered the knives I had concealed there. I needed to stop them, but how? I racked my brain for ideas, but it had inconveniently blanked.

"Is that truly necessary?" I asked, trying to control the quavering in my voice. Not that it mattered. I knew they could hear my quickening pulse.

"Her pack is clear," the other guard announced before I could get an answer.

"Quite necessary, miss," Evan said. "I'll be quick about it though. Willem, come take these reins for me, would you?"

After handing them off, he knelt before me and began to lift my skirt. What could I do? I couldn't be found with the knives. I couldn't risk these guards touching the blades either. How would I be able to explain a dead fae if that happened? My mind raced, seeking out every possibility and thinking about every action I could take in response. My heartbeat pounded in my ears like a galloping horse.

Wait. That wasn't my heartbeat. It was an actual horse. Someone was approaching. Surely the guards heard it, but they didn't let it distract them from their search.

Evan had my skirt lifted to my knees when the thumping of hooves stopped. Someone called from behind me, "What's this? My guards having fun without me? Why wasn't I invited?"

Brennan.

That voice. I'd know it anywhere, no matter how much time had passed since I'd heard it last.

The guard paused, dropped my skirt back into place, and rose. I dared not move.

"Just a human trying to break into the palace, Your Highness," Willem said.

Brennan laughed. "Seriously? Even a human would know not to use the front gate if they were trying to break in."

The guards mumbled something I couldn't hear, but by the way they bowed their heads and stepped back, I assumed it was an apology.

Brennan came into view as he stepped around me, handing his mount's reins to Willem. I forgot how to breathe. He looked even better than I remembered, with his face freshly shaved and an unruly lock of his brown hair falling into his green eyes. I chided myself for being so ridiculous, like some young girl with her first crush.

He is your first crush though, I reminded myself. My cheeks dared to warm at the thought.

"And who exactly is this supposed infiltrator?" he asked. Humor graced every syllable. His eyes roved over my face and body, and I waited for him to recognize me.

With curiosity flashing through his features, he leaned toward me slightly. "Well? Are you going to answer my question, or are you expecting me to guess?"

"You don't recognize me?" I sounded like an idiot, but he smiled.

He smiled at everyone though.

"Am I supposed to?"

My heart sank. I hadn't changed that much, regardless of what Raven and her parents said.

Evan cleared his throat, and Brennan turned to look at him sideways. "We haven't finished searching her yet, Your Majesty."

Brennan swung his attention back to me, his eyes dancing with mischief. "I'll take over the searching from here," he said. He stepped to the side and gestured for the guard to bring his horse. "Shall we, Lieke?"

My eyes widened.

"Oh, don't look so shocked," he said around an intoxicating smile. He leaned in again and whispered, "You didn't really think I could forget you, do you?"

CHAPTER SEVENTEEN

Connor

I pulled the pocket watch from my waistcoat, checked the time, and frowned.

He should have been back by now.

Maybe he'd gotten hung up somewhere.

Maybe he had become distracted.

Maybe he had been attacked.

The rhythmic pounding of horses' hooves pulled my thoughts out of their downward spiral and had me spinning on my heel and heading for the courtyard. At first, relief swept over me that Brennan had made it home before the royals had arrived, but I heard two horses. Not one.

If it was my brother, he wasn't alone, and that was undoubtedly bad news.

I didn't want to think about what my father would say—or do—if Brennan mucked everything up after all.

Maybe it's just a friend.

My mind whirring, I tried to find some silver lining in this moment.

But Brennan had no friends.

Their voices hit my ears before they came into view. My brother's flirtatious charm answered by a female voice that sounded vaguely familiar and not at all like Princess Calla.

I turned the corner of the house to find one of the staff walking a pair of horses—Brennan's and another I'd never seen before—toward the stables. My brother's back was to me, blocking my view of the female. They didn't notice me when I stepped into the courtyard, nor did they react when the gravel crunched loudly beneath my boots as I approached them. My mind turned the female's voice over and over, trying to place it, until a breeze swept past them, carrying their scents my way.

I froze mid-step.

No. It couldn't be her.

I shook my head, hoping I was wrong. She'd been sent away. Mrs. Bishop hadn't mentioned any word of her return. Why was she back?

Squaring my shoulders, I drew in a deep breath and pushed myself forward. As I stepped alongside Brennan, I cleared my throat. They both turned to look at me, but it was her face that held my attention.

"Well hello, brother," Brennan said, giving me a single slap on the back. "Look who I found being frisked by our guards at the gate! You remember, Lieke, don't you?"

All I could manage was a dip of my chin as I fumbled around for the right words to say.

"Hello, Your Highness," she said with her own graceful nod. Her dark blue eyes sparkled with delight, though her voice held a hint of apprehension.

"You're back," I said flatly.

My brother frowned at me. "That's no way to greet an old friend, is it, Connor? You could at least smile at the woman."

Slowly I turned to face him, but I couldn't manage a smile, not when we were so close to sealing the alliance with the Arenysens and my brother was here flirting with one of our cooks.

"It's okay, Brennan," Lieke said. "He doesn't need to smile for me."

"Can I have a word, brother?" I asked, trying to keep my tone serious but not rude. Not waiting for an answer, I turned to Lieke. "Please excuse us, Miss Berg."

"Of course," she said, lifting her chin toward me before turning back to Brennan. A small smile pulled at one corner of her lips. He watched her walk away toward the palace.

"Can you believe it, Connor?" he asked, giving her a wave when she looked back from the open doorway.

"Brennan," I said with icy venom coating my tongue. He didn't seem to notice as he continued to watch the now closed door. I repeated his name, and he finally turned to me with that stupid grin still on his face.

"If I'd known she would one day look like that—"

"Like what?"

"Are you blind, brother?"

"She looks the same to me," I lied. Her time away and the training she'd received had, in fact, honed her muscles, tightened her curves, and given new life to those sapphire eyes. Confidence suited her. Not that I needed to admit any of that to my brother. Especially when it would be the death of me—and our kingdom—if I didn't fix the trouble she was already causing.

"Liar," he said, calling me out.

"Is this going to be a problem?" I asked him, waving a hand between him and the palace door where she'd disappeared. "You have a princess to propose to, you know."

Brennan offered me a casual shrug. "As if I could possibly forget. My plans haven't changed."

My breath escaped me in a rush of relief. "Good, but just promise me you'll leave the human alone."

He held up his hand with his palm toward me—a sign of honor and promise—as he continued to retreat, but my insides twisted with dread all the same. Now that Lieke was back, I wouldn't get to relax or celebrate tonight after all.

CHAPTER EIGHTEEN

Lieke

Apparently, three years of training had done little to save me from the aches and pains of working on my feet all day. At least my shoulders and arms seemed to be handling the return to work better. They barely felt fatigued, even after being in the kitchen since sunup.

Swiping my hand across my brow, I surveyed the empty kitchen and made one final check to ensure everything was clean and in its proper place. The morning would be here soon enough, and the last thing I wanted was to have Mrs. Bishop scolding me before I'd even had my coffee.

Satisfied with the work I'd done, I wearily turned and headed down the hallway to my room—or rather, the room I now shared with Millie, the head maid. When I'd left, Mrs. Bishop had shifted the staff around to give everyone more space, but unfortunately, no such changes were made upon my return. I missed the old room that had been Mother's and mine. If I'd still had that private room, I wouldn't be forced to wear my knives at all times and worry constantly about a roommate catching me with them.

When I got to my door, I drew in a deep, steadying breath and sent my wish up to the stars that Millie would already be asleep. Although she'd never come right out and told me she hated me, the disdain in her eyes when she looked at me was hard to miss. Even though I knew she wouldn't talk to me if she was still awake—as she never spoke more than a few words and only said those out of necessity—I didn't particularly want to deal with her silent scrutiny either.

But today held no luck for me. As soon as I opened the door, a low grumble hit my ears as her chair scraped against the floor. Entering the room and closing the door, I kept my eyes down and forced a tight-lipped smile onto my face. I hadn't made it even halfway to my bed in the far corner when Millie stepped in front of me. Slowly I lifted my eyes.

Ah, there it was. The annoyance and bitterness.

I raised a brow in question.

In a flat tone, she said, "A message for you."

She held up a folded piece of paper.

Who would send a message to me?

The only person outside of this palace who even knew I existed was Raven. My heart perked up and then immediately ached at the memory of my friend.

When I still hadn't taken the paper from her, Millie pushed it toward me. "Just read it, Lieke."

"How did it arrive?" I asked, gingerly fingering the smooth paper. Why was I stalling? Why was I so nervous to read it?

"The page brought it. Said it was urgent. From the prince."

My heart thudded to a stop.

The prince?

"Brennan?" His name was on my breath before I could think better of it.

Millie rolled her eyes and shook her head as she turned back toward her desk. She mumbled something under her breath, and although I couldn't hear it, I was sure she was questioning my sanity.

I didn't open the message until I was on my bed, where I sat with my legs pulled up like I used to do as a child. My veins thrummed with anticipation and wonder.

Every day since I'd returned home last week, I'd gone about my tasks, hoping to catch a glimpse of him, wishing our paths would cross so I'd have a chance to speak to him again. It hadn't worked out at all, though I had seen his brother a few times. And Connor might as well have believed I didn't exist with how little attention he paid me. Like he truly didn't remember how close Brennan and I used to be.

Maybe he didn't.

Stars, even Brennan had forgotten our old friendship for years.

Until I returned. Until now. Until this message.

You don't even know if it's from him.

It could be from Connor.

Unlikely. Just open it already.

Holding my breath, I unfolded the paper. My heart stopped. In his casual scrawl was a single line:

Lieke, meet me. Tonight, in our spot. - B

Our spot.

I reread the note several more times. Millie still sat at her desk, showing no sign of turning in anytime soon. If I left now, she'd be suspicious. Unless…

Standing up, I stretched my arms high overhead and yawned. She didn't seem to notice until I walked across the room and opened the door.

Without turning around, she said, "I wouldn't do that if I were you."

"I'm just heading to the privy, Millie," I lied. "Or would you rather I need to go in the middle of the night and bother you while you're asleep?"

At that, she groaned and waved a hand over her shoulder, shooing me away.

Before she could change her mind and question me further, I left, shutting the door quietly behind me. I rushed down the servants' hallway on light feet.

My heartbeat was an erratic mess as I quickly made my way through the dimly lit hallways of the palace and up the stairs. As soon as I stepped into the queen's personal wing, the air turned cold. Our spot wasn't too far from me now, but it was impossible to be in this hallway without thinking of the queen.

Keeva Durand had been a kind ruler and a loving mother, a friend to everyone, including my mother. She had been the one to ensure the humans on the staff were protected and cared for. When she died, some of the humans had worried about their future and expected to be sent away, but my mother had always believed the surviving Durands would uphold the queen's wishes, even after she was gone. While my mother had been right, and King Nevan had continued to protect his mortal staff, that didn't mean that nothing had changed.

The palace—once a happy home full of love and warmth—seemed to have died along with the queen.

As I neared the door to the parlor, I slowed my pace, and all the grief my thoughts had conjured stuck in my throat. For the first time since Millie had handed me the note, I wondered what Brennan could possibly want from me. My heart hammered in my chest as my nerves flared.

It's just Brennan. Your friend.

Yeah, the friend I dreamed of marrying one day.

Your friend who is to marry someone else soon.

He's still your friend. Just talk to him.

My fingertips had barely touched the doorknob when it turned and the door opened, revealing the face I'd dreamed of for most of my life.

"Brennan." His name fell from my lips on a whisper. I didn't realize I'd said it until the corner of his mouth pulled back in a cocky smirk.

"I got tired of waiting for you to find the courage to come in," he said, his green eyes teasing me like they had so often when we were younger. Before I could respond, he grabbed my hand and guided me inside.

A shiver ran up my arm at his touch, and I winced, knowing he could hear the change in my pulse and my breathing. Thankfully, he didn't comment on it as he led me past the furniture draped in white cloths. By the moonlight shining in from the far window, I recognized the shapes of the chaise and the grand piano. Sorrow threatened to resurface, but I drew in a deep breath and forced myself to focus on the prince holding my hand.

He led me to the bay window—which was tucked between two large bookcases—where a wide, cushioned bench awaited us. Brennan sat first and tugged lightly on my hand until I sat facing him, releasing my hand when I did. I tried not to frown at his retreat, instinctively pulling my legs up and crossing them in front of me.

For a couple of breaths, he stared at me in silence, searching my face as if he were trying to commit it to memory.

Was he waiting for me to say something? He was the one who had summoned me.

I opened my mouth, but he lifted a finger between us and closed his eyes.

"I owe you an apology, Lieke," he said.

"What? Why?" I asked, genuinely confused. This was the last thing I'd expected him to say. Well, that wasn't entirely true. The last thing was a heartfelt declaration of love, but an apology was a close second.

When he finally looked at me, all his earlier teasing had vanished.

"I left you," he said. "You were my closest friend, and I abandoned you."

I leaned forward and took his hand in both of mine. "Your mother died, Bren. I never blamed you for needing space."

He didn't pull away, though he did turn to look out the window at the moonlit grounds below. "Is it too late?"

I knew he didn't mean it the way I wanted him to. I knew I shouldn't get my hopes up. But something Raven had said the day they sent me back home came to mind.

Don't give up on him, Lieke.

"Too late for what?" I asked quietly, hoping he didn't hear the sliver of hope I still clung to.

Slowly he faced me, and I could have lost myself in his stare.

"For us," he whispered. When he lifted his hand and trailed his fingertips along my jaw, I froze, as if any movement might break the spell he was obviously under. His eyes drifted down to my lips, and my heartbeat thundered.

He started to lean toward me but stopped when the door opened. "Brennan?"

He pulled away and stood, leaving me sitting on the window seat alone.

"Yes, brother?" Brennan asked.

Connor stepped into the moonlight, both hands shoved into his pockets. He glanced at me quickly, no recognition on his face.

"Father wants to see you." His voice was regal, cold.

"At this hour?"

Connor stepped closer. This time he regarded me more carefully before addressing his brother again. "Yes. If you can meet *her* at this hour, surely you can see the king as requested."

Brennan nodded and turned back to me. "I'll find you tomorrow?"

All I could manage was a timid "Sure."

Connor turned to the side to let his brother pass, but he didn't move to accompany him. Ignoring the growing tension in the room, I rose to leave as well. Connor pivoted to block my exit, so fast that I nearly ran into him.

Clenching my jaw, I raised my gaze to his and waited. My skin prickled under his glare, but I forced myself not to break the stare.

"I know what you're doing, Lieke," he finally said.

I narrowed my eyes slightly. "I'm just trying to get back to my room, Your Highness."

He gave me a withering look as his tongue slipped out to wet his lips, drawing my attention to his mouth against my will. I snapped my attention back to his eyes quickly, and I could have sworn I noticed him fighting a smirk.

"My brother," he finally said, "is to be married soon."

"I know."

Connor's jaw pulsed with obvious irritation. "I cannot let anything—or anyone—stop that from happening. Do you understand?"

"I understand," I said, nodding. "But I do not control Brennan. Neither do you."

When he didn't respond, I moved to step around him, but he grabbed my wrist and challenged me with a hard glare.

"Nothing good will come from this, Lieke. He's using you, like he does everyone else. You'll only get hurt."

Yanking my arm out of his grasp, I inched closer to him. "Why do you care?"

He swallowed as he searched my eyes. Then, with a deep breath, he turned on his heel and strode for the door, calling over his shoulder, "Don't come here again, Lieke. This room is not yours."

Stopping at the doorway, he waved for me to exit, and part of me wanted to refuse to leave just to spite him and his pompous ass. But then I remembered who I was—a mere human servant. Disobeying the crown prince would lead to nothing good, and I'd already had the audacity to challenge him just now.

With my chin lifted, I marched past him and out into the hallway. If he followed, I didn't know.

And I didn't care.

CHAPTER NINETEEN

Connor

Once Lieke disappeared down the stairs, I hurried toward the king's study and opened the door without bothering to knock. Darkness greeted me.

Along with a firm punch to my jaw.

I grunted, stumbling into the room and kicking the door closed behind me, only to have two strong hands shove me back against it.

"What the fuck was that?" Brennan growled.

Rubbing my jaw, I pushed past him and headed for the desk. "You know what," I answered before striking a match to light the lamp. I turned to find him scowling at me. Slowly, his lips shifted into an amused smirk.

"I didn't think you had it in you," he said with a huffed laugh.

I narrowed my eyes at him in question.

Brennan slowly walked forward, shaking his head. "Lying. The great Prince Connor, commander of the royal armies, protector of all"—he waved a hand in the air with mock reverence—"told a lie." He gasped and placed his hand over his heart. "What would Mother think?"

My teeth slammed together. He knew exactly how to push me, and I hated it. I drew in a long breath to ease my temper, refusing to take the bait as I had too many times in the past.

Dropping my head to one side, I considered him for a moment and asked, "What *would* she think, Brennan, about you consorting with a damned servant in that room?"

My words missed the mark, though, and he shrugged, leaning forward a bit.

"We're just friends—"

"Do you attempt to kiss all your *friends*?"

He ignored my question. "And I think Mother would be fine with it. I mean, she was fine with every other time Lieke and I were together in there."

Exasperated, I stepped toward him. "But you weren't about to propose to another back then. You weren't commanded to marry someone else back then! If she were here, she'd be—"

"She'd be convincing our father to find another way, Connor!" His arms flew up at his sides.

He couldn't be serious. He couldn't be this stupid.

I shook my head in disbelief, laughing quietly as I stared at him.

"You really believe that?" I asked.

He didn't respond, but his eye twitched slightly. His jaw tightened.

I softened my voice as best I could. "She would have ensured you did as you were told, because she understood the meaning of sacrifice."

Brennan lifted his chin and peered down his nose at me. "When did you become such a momma's boy?"

Stars, I wanted to hit him. My hand had already balled itself into a fist, but I took another calming breath, refusing to let him goad me.

"If it wasn't for her, I would have stopped caring about you a long time ago."

"She's gone. You don't have to give two shits about me anymore. Why bother?" he asked, his eyes wild with frustration.

"Because I promised her I would. It was the last thing she asked of me, and I couldn't refuse," I said quietly.

Brennan's eyes fell closed, and he exhaled sharply. For a long moment, he was silent. Finally, he dropped his chin to his chest and asked, "That's why you always stepped in? Why you took all my punishments for me?"

"Yes."

Slowly he met my gaze, fresh determination filling his eyes. "Well, you can stop now, brother. I'm old enough to face my own consequences. Consider yourself free of that responsibility."

"I didn't make that promise to you, dumbass, and I'll honor it as long as I'm drawing breath or until our mother comes out of her grave to free me from it herself."

"Always the fucking hero, aren't you?" Brennan spat at me.

This time I did hit him, burying my fist in his gut.

He doubled over with a pained groan and staggered backwards slightly, his hands clutching his belly.

When he straightened, though, he was laughing. He lifted his hands out to the sides, palms toward the ceiling. "Well, brother, if you want to keep standing between me and our father's fists, so be it."

Grinding my teeth, I shook my head. "I wouldn't have to if you'd stop being a selfish prick and just do what you're supposed to for once."

His forehead creased as his eyes danced with comical confusion. "That's not exactly incentive for me to behave now, is it?"

I rubbed my forehead, silently cursing my brother and this whole damned situation. Blowing out a breath, I lifted my shoulders in a shrug and turned back to the desk to extinguish the lamp. I shoved past him, not bothering to say anything more until I had the door open.

"Look, I'm riding out early in the morning," I said, but he kept his back to me. "I'll return at the end of the week, in time for the princess's arrival. Don't forget what you have to do, and don't fuck this up, Brennan."

When he said nothing and made no move to follow me out, I turned on my heel and left.

Stars, let him not fuck this up.

CHAPTER TWENTY

Lieke

Two days passed, and life basically went back to normal. I filled my time with whatever I could, taking on extra duties for Mrs. Bishop, foraging for mushrooms and berries in the royal forests, testing out new recipes—basically anything to try to forget that Brennan had been about to kiss me before his brother had so rudely interrupted.

Unfortunately, today was my day off, and not even my morning run could help keep my mind from wandering back to the memory of the prince caressing my cheek and leaning in.

Damn Connor!

Why had he barged in at that exact moment?

Why couldn't he have waited just ten more seconds?

I stopped short and pulled my ponytail up off my neck before lacing my fingers behind my head. Pacing around in a circle, I greedily sucked in the crisp morning air and lifted my eyes to the leaves overhead. They were just starting to change colors, signaling the fast-approaching autumn.

And the upcoming banquet.

The princess would be in attendance, and the staff was abuzz with rumors that Brennan would propose.

What would I do if he actually went through with it though?

"You'll let him," I said aloud.

The thought of having to watch him recite the sacred vows to someone else, having to prepare the food for their wedding feast… What if Mrs. Bishop tasked me with making their damned cake?

A growl escaped my throat as I threw my hands back down to my sides. Shaking out my arms, I tried to relax, but there was no getting rid of the prickly unease that settled under my skin. I needed to move, to run, to take all this angst and pound it into the ground under the soles of my feet. After quickly rolling my shoulders and stretching out my neck, I spun around and ran straight into a broad chest.

"Woah there, Lieke," Brennan said, gently gripping my arms and nudging me back a pace.

I smacked him on the shoulder with the back of my hand and glared at him. "You scared me!"

"I guess your hearing hasn't improved with age. I wasn't even trying to be sneaky." He flashed me a smirk.

I couldn't help but roll my eyes at him. "Not really something that happens for humans, you know. What are you doing here?"

"Scaring you."

I continued to glare, though it was anything but annoyance coursing through my veins. Stars, he looked good. He smelled good. Everything about him—

"I wanted to see you," he said, as if it was the most natural, obvious thing in the world.

"And what about your brother?"

Brennan's lips twisted into a devilish grin. "What about him?"

I shrugged, trying to mimic his earlier nonchalance. "Oh, you know, his command that I stay away from you."

"He doesn't need to know," he said, stepping forward slowly.

"We shouldn't—"

My breath caught at his invading warmth. I shifted my eyes down to his chest, reminding myself he wasn't mine and could never be. His finger slipped under my chin, and I let him lift my face.

"Is that what you want?" he asked in a near-whisper, trapping me in the deep green pools of his eyes.

Swallowing hard, I scrounged for words.

What *did* I want?

I wanted him. I always had.

"Your thundering heartbeat is answer enough," he said.

He traced his fingertip along my jaw, then slid his hand beneath my ear to cup my neck.

"Maybe it's thundering out of fear," I said shakily.

He smirked again, wetting his lips with his tongue. "I might believe that if you weren't looking at me with such desire."

When his gaze lowered to my mouth, I reflexively pulled my bottom lip between my teeth. My mind went utterly blank as he leaned forward until his lips whispered over my own, so close I could almost feel him. All I had to do was shift forward slightly, and I'd get the kiss I'd yearned for.

He finally saw me as more than just his human friend.

He finally saw me the way I saw him.

Wait. Why now?

After all this time—after he stopped speaking to me or even seeing me—why?

I pulled back just enough to escape his breath on my skin.

My heart raged against my thoughts, cursing me for not simply seizing this moment.

Connor's warning rang out in my head at the same time. *You'll only get hurt.*

Damn him!

Nothing good can come from this, Lieke.

Cursing silently, I retreated further to look Brennan in the eye.

He gave me a shaky and uneven laugh. "I don't know that I've ever been rejected before."

"There's a first time for everything," I whispered.

Slowly, his hand slipped off my neck, gliding over my shoulder and down my arm. Lacing his fingers with mine, he turned back toward the palace, tugging on my hand to urge me to follow.

I resisted, planting my feet in the grass. If I wasn't going to kiss him in a secluded forest, I surely wasn't going to traipse back to the palace hand-in-hand with him.

Rolling his eyes, he laughed again. "Come on, Lieke. I'm allowed to spend time with friends, aren't I?"

Friends?

Friends.

My chest tightened around the word, as if it were a weight pressing into me.

I gritted my teeth and slipped my hand slowly out of his.

"Do you try to kiss all your friends?" I asked. He opened his mouth but said nothing. "Is that what I am to you? Just a *friend?*"

Try as I might, I couldn't keep the hurt from my voice, and I had to press my lips together to keep my chin from trembling like a child. He reached his hand up to my cheek again, but I turned away from his touch, eyeing him skeptically as I waited for him to give me a bloody answer.

When he still hadn't responded, I raised my face in challenge. "It shouldn't be that hard to answer. What do you want from me? Do you want a friend? Fine. We can be friends, but I will not stand here and let you toy with my emotions like I'm one of those fae tarts you bring home from the tavern."

Sheepishly, he rubbed the back of his neck, clearing his throat as he averted his eyes. Did he really not have an answer for me?

"It's complicated," he finally said quietly.

"You don't say!" I slammed my eyes shut and fisted my hands, trying to calm down. Of course it was complicated. Still, he didn't deserve my anger.

"I'm sorry," Brennan said, pulling my attention back to him. A confused sadness played in his eyes.

I shook my head. "I shouldn't have yelled."

"But you're right. I'm being unfair."

For a long moment, we both remained quiet, but my mind was in chaos with questions I didn't want to ask him. I didn't know if I could stomach hearing his answers. Yet I also couldn't move forward without knowing.

I stared down at my toe as I dug it into the grass, but then I looked up to regard him curiously from beneath my lashes. "What am I? To you, I mean."

He drew in a deep breath and took a tentative step forward, not looking away. "Would you hate me if I say I don't know?"

Lifting my chin, I angled my head and searched his eyes, as if maybe the true answer was hidden in their depths. "I could never hate you, Brennan. Be mad at you, yes, but hate you? Never."

His whole body relaxed, and a hint of a smile played at the corners of his lips.

Lips you could be kissing right now.

No. I didn't want to be kissed like that.

"Can we just be together, Lieke? Like old times?"

Old times. I repeated the words to myself, mulling them over.

Was that really what I wanted?

No. I wanted to live in a world where he loved me, where he chose me, where he *could* choose me and didn't have to marry someone else.

But we didn't live in that world. If this was my only way to have him in my life, I'd take it.

"Sure, Bren," I said finally and shrugged. "So what do you want to do?"

His smile grew, lighting up his face as he raised a single brow. "Cards?"

CHAPTER TWENTY-ONE

Connor

Another evening. Another tavern.

I settled myself into a chair at a back table while Matthias retrieved two pints of ale for us. It was the sixth such tavern in as many days, and the patrons here greeted me in the same way as those at the previous five had: with wary stares and grim half-smiles.

I couldn't blame them.

Their fallen spirits were the reason for this week's trip around the country. Traveling to meet my people face to face was one of my favorite parts of being the crown prince, even if it meant enduring lumpy mattresses and bland food. It got me out of the palace and away from my brother and his drama.

Of course, these visits weren't nearly as relaxing as they had once been. Everyone had been on edge since the attacks had begun. Still, the journey was a much-needed respite from dealing with Brennan and his supposed *friendship* with Lieke.

Matthias slumped into the chair beside me with a weary sigh. He handed me a pint glass filled to the brim with ale, foam tumbling over the edge and dripping onto the table. I took a long draught, savoring the rich drink with my eyes closed. This was much better than being home.

Matthias laughed lightly, and I opened my eyes to find him watching me with a comical grin. "Either the ale here is really good or you're particularly worried about this town's concerns."

"A little of both actually," I said. "We really need to get a brewer on staff at the palace."

Leaning closer, Matthias whispered, "Maybe we can entice the one here to move?"

"Let's see how tonight goes first. If they're as angry as the people we've met elsewhere, I'd hate to stoke that ire by cutting off their access to good ale."

Matthias nodded and lifted his own tankard to his lips. As he was drinking, a pair of fae, a male and a female, slowly approached our table. Their stern glares bored into me, and the pub grew quiet.

"Your Highness," the female said with a quick nod.

I dipped my chin in return and smiled warmly at her. "Please sit," I said, gesturing to the empty chairs at my table.

"No need," the male said gruffly. His eyes narrowed. "This won't take long."

Placing my folded hands on the table, I leaned forward and raised my brow in an invitation for them to proceed.

The male cleared his throat and pulled his shoulders back. "Our son, sir." His lip quivered once before he stilled it with a deep inhale. "He and his wife were killed two weeks ago."

Matthias set his glass down and pulled the ledger from inside his jacket, asking, "Where?"

"They were traveling back from Fairden," the female said quietly.

Thumbing through the pages, Matthias searched his records. When he stopped, he glanced at me and nodded.

"It was them, wasn't it?" the male asked. "The humans?"

I drew in a breath and fought the urge to survey the room and the citizens who waited to hear my response. These parents deserved my full attention. This was why I made these trips—to connect with my people, to listen to their concerns, to reassure them that their rulers were here for them.

But I knew what would happen once I confirmed their fears.

Their anger was inevitable. And justified.

"We believe so, yes," I answered. "We are—"

The male stepped closer, shrugging off his wife when she reached for his arm. "What are you doing about it?"

"Your High—" Matthias started to rise from his seat as he spoke, but I quieted him with a raised hand, never once breaking eye contact with the distraught male.

"What's your name?" I asked gently.

The male flinched in surprise at my question. "What does that matter?"

"Humor me," I said, opening my palms to the ceiling.

"The Jamesons, Your Highness," the female said, stepping up alongside her husband. "Opal and Lars Jameson."

I nodded my thanks to her before addressing her husband again. "Mr. Jameson, rest assured we are investigating. My second here, Mr. Orelian, has his best-trained men hunting for those responsible. Unfortunately, it is a complicated situation."

"How exactly is this complicated?" Mr. Jameson asked. "Seems rather simple to me. Fae are being murdered on the roads, and as far as I can tell, the crown has done nothing to protect us or to punish those responsible."

"I understand your frustration," I said, ignoring how he scoffed at my response. "But you must remember the humans are citizens of Emeryn as well."

"And what if they're not?" Mrs. Jameson asked quietly. "What if they're from Wrenwick?"

I dropped my head to one side as I met her gaze. "Then there is an even greater need for us to protect everyone in Emeryn—fae and humans alike. The humans in our land are already living in hiding; they have been fearing for their lives ever since the war ended."

"As they should!" a male's voice barked from somewhere in the middle of the crowded pub, and a chair scraped loudly against the floor.

The Jamesons stepped to the side to allow for this new speaker to come forward, and my stomach tightened uncomfortably at the sight of Griffin Ford, the fae who had attacked Lieke a few years ago. He glowered menacingly at me, as if he might try, right here in this pub, to get his revenge for me thwarting him that night. But instead of approaching me, he began to turn slowly, addressing those gathered.

"The humans don't belong here! Humans started the War of Hearts! Humans bring nothing but trouble! This prince and his father do nothing to stop them from picking off fae while we are told, what? To not hurt them? To not defend ourselves?"

The crowd murmured their agreement, and this time I didn't stop Matthias when he stood. I ground my teeth together as I waited and watched my second move around the table and stalk toward Griffin.

Griffin pivoted on his heel to face me again, only to find Matthias standing between us with a hand on the hilt of his sword. The fae looked over my friend's head to stare at me. His smile gave way to a sneer.

"Can't fight your own battles, Prince?"

Calmly, I leaned back in my chair and crossed my arms over my chest. "I'm happy to give everyone here a demonstration of what happened the last time we met. Just say the word."

I didn't particularly want to shift here, but I would if he decided to push me. The asshole needed to be knocked down a bit before he got anyone hurt. He didn't accept my challenge though. Instead, he chuckled quietly and stepped back from Matthias, keeping his attention on me.

"You mean the last time you attacked me in an effort to protect a human?"

Shit.

It didn't matter that the law forbade fae from hurting humans, and it didn't matter that I had every right to stop him from doing so. With humans attacking the fae and killing them throughout the kingdom, the fae in this room—and in every taproom I had visited this week—had little sympathy for the mortals.

Gasps and whispers filled the pub. Every eye turned to me with suspicion, as though I was some kind of traitor. Matthias was in Griffin's face in an instant, though, giving the same explanation I had been about to offer.

"You broke the law and attacked a human." Matthias jabbed a finger into Griffin's chest. "And a human under the direct protection of the king, no less. You attacked one of his staff, and you're lucky your prince let you off with nothing more than a scratch. Next time you might not receive such leniency."

Griffin stared silently at Matthias in disgust for several tense moments until he finally lifted his hands in surrender and retreated a step. He backed toward the door, saying loudly, "Don't expect the crown to protect you from these attacks! Their loyalty lies with the mortals, not with you! It's up to us to stop these humans—"

"ENOUGH!" I shouted, slamming my hands on the table. I stood, sending my chair toppling over behind me. Then, tamping down my anger as much as I could, I made my way to stand beside Matthias in the center of the room as I continued speaking.

"Anyone who goes against our laws is an enemy of the crown, and we will not hesitate to dole out punishment as needed. We will find the human rebels. We will stop these killings. But you need to trust me."

Silence hung over the room. No one moved. Everyone stared.

And then Griffin barked out a single laugh.

"You're all fools if you trust this prince!"

He stormed out, slamming the door shut behind him. Matthias shook his head angrily, muttering something under his breath. I studied my people and noted the fear and concern worn plainly on their faces.

"I know you're afraid," I said to them. "I know you're angry. I am too. But I am here. For you. Now, if anyone has anything further to discuss, concerns to be relayed back to your king, I will be at my table for the rest of the evening."

With a nod, I turned on my heel and returned to the corner, righting the chair and settling back down. Picking up my pint, I downed the last of my ale and tried to enjoy it.

CHAPTER
TWENTY-TWO

Lieke

"You're such a damned cheater!" I shouted, tossing my cards in Brennan's face as he laughed.

"It's not my fault you're still so easy to read." He shrugged but made no move to pick up the cards scattered across our laps and the window seat in between us. "Does this mean you don't want to play anymore?"

Shaking my head, I scoffed and looked about the music room. "What else is there to do in this palace?"

Brennan tapped a finger to his lips and glanced up at the ceiling before eyeing me mischievously.

"Not that."

"What?" he straightened, his face falling into an expression of pure innocence.

"I know you."

"You *think* you know me."

I barked out a laugh. "All those years you pretended I didn't exist? I was still here, having to watch you drown your cares in all the females of the kingdom. And other kingdoms, I'm sure."

Brennan's eyes narrowed briefly, and a twinge of regret pricked my chest. But he was smirking at me again before I could try to remedy my callousness.

"That's only one part of me. I'm not as shallow as everyone seems to think."

"No one thinks—"

He raised a finger. "No need to lie to me, Lieke. I know what everyone says. It's fine."

I leaned back against the bookcase and turned to stare out the window at the grounds below. For four days we had been meeting here to play cards and talk. Always at different times to avoid raising suspicions. Today we had agreed to meet in the late afternoon, and the sun was now easing its way toward the treetops, signaling the approaching end of our time together.

I hated these moments.

Hated having to walk away from him, having to pretend like I was content with just being friends, having to act like he wasn't preparing to propose to the princess in a matter of days.

We never talked about that though.

"I don't want to do this, Lieke," Brennan whispered.

"Do what?"

He kept his eyes lowered as he gathered up the playing cards. "Marry her."

My stomach twisted. "Then don't," I blurted out, immediately regretting it. It wasn't that simple.

"I don't have a choice," he said, sliding the cards back into their pouch and setting them on the bookcase behind him.

"Don't you?" I asked, though it was such a ridiculous question. He was a prince. Of course he didn't have a choice.

Still, he seemed to ponder the question as he stared at me with sad eyes. "We need the alliance with Arenysen. If we don't secure it, we could be dragged into another war with Wrenwick."

"Why can't Connor marry her?" I asked.

Brennan's laugh fell flat, humorless, as if the notion was absurd. "My father would never give his throne over to me unless he had to. Connor is the true ruler. I'm just the pretty face they needed to woo a princess into marrying me and aligning our countries."

I wished I had some solution for him, but no matter how I looked at his situation, I came to the same conclusion. Brennan had to do as he was told. He had to marry someone else.

"Is she nice at least?" I attempted a smile, but it was as fake as my interest in his answer.

He raised a questioning brow. "You don't really want to know, do you?"

"No, but if you're going to have to marry her, I'd like to know she's not a shrew."

Shrugging, he frowned and looked away from me. "She's nice enough, I guess. But she's not you."

My heart stilled, and I chided it for being so easily persuaded by him and his careless words. Still, that little bit of hope glimmered in my mind and twisted my gut into nervous knots.

Don't read into it, Lieke, I told myself.

But when he lifted his eyes to look into mine, there was something new in them. No, it was probably just what I wanted to see, what I had hoped to see since I was fifteen.

It wasn't real.

It was my imagination.

"What do you mean?" I asked, internally wincing at how awkward I sounded.

Brennan scooted himself closer to me until our legs touched. Taking my hand in his, he held my gaze and said, "I can't say I love you, because stars know it's too soon for that to be true. But I *want* to love you."

My heart ceased to beat.

My lungs failed to pull in air.

I had died.

I was sure of it.

Somehow, though, I managed to whisper, "What?"

"Lieke. I don't want to be friends." He groaned in frustration. "That came out wrong. I mean, these last few days with you have been better than any I've lived in years."

Part of me wanted to push back and ask him if that included the years he'd been allowed to live with such abandon. But there was something so genuine and heartbreaking in his voice that I couldn't bear to question him.

He leaned closer still, and I swallowed hard, unsure how he expected me to react. "I want to be with you, Lieke. To get to know you again and to see—"

"But you can't," I whispered, shaking my head. "I've waited so long for you, Bren, but it's too late. Like you said, you don't have a choice. You have to marry her."

It hurt to even say it aloud.

The hope on his face sparked my own once again as he said, "No. I can figure something out. When Connor gets back today, I'll talk to him. Our father trusts him. If anyone can help me—help us—it's him."

But Connor's warning reverberated in my mind.

I cannot let anyone stop that from happening.

"He won't. He told me—" I started, but then Brennan's hands were cupping my face, his thumbs brushing over my cheeks as he stared at me.

"I'll find a way, Lieke. I promise." I wanted so much to believe him, to believe there was some way this could work out and we could be together.

This time when he brought his lips to mine, I didn't pull away. His lips were a whisper, soft and sweet, a silent request for more. Then, with a trembling sigh, I closed my eyes and melted into him, letting his tongue coax my lips to part.

For that one brief moment, nothing else mattered. Not the proposal or the princess or the king or the war. Nothing existed but us.

The door to the music room burst open, and Brennan recoiled. Before I could see who had come in, Brennan was standing with his back to me, blocking my view. Whether he was trying to protect me or hide me, I wasn't sure, and I didn't have time to ponder it before a male's voice boomed, "Do you think I'm a damned fool?"

Not Connor. Older.

The king.

I froze. Staring at Brennan's back, I waited for him to be shoved aside so the king could snatch me up and throw me out of the palace—or worse.

But instead, a hand grabbed hold of Brennan's neck, yanking him forward, dragging him toward the door as his feet scrambled to stay beneath him.

I couldn't scream.

I couldn't protest.

I couldn't fight.

Not against the king himself.

So I remained there, sitting on the window seat, watching helplessly.

Just as they reached the door, Brennan managed to slip out of his father's grasp and shout over his shoulder, "Get Connor!"

CHAPTER TWENTY-THREE

Connor

The ride home from Linley had been long and tense, and I was ready for a good meal and a night in my own bed. The sun had just fallen below the treetops when we turned our horses onto the road leading up to the palace.

I side-eyed Matthias. "I hate feeling like I'm lying to everyone," I admitted, shaking my head.

His lips tightened into a line as he scanned our surroundings for any signs of danger. "How are you lying?"

"I know I'm not actually lying, but my words sound empty even to my own ears. How is it that we haven't been able to find the humans? They're mortals. Weak. Slow. Clumsy."

"And clever," Matthias added. "The worst thing we can do right now is start underestimating them, Connor. You know that. And it's not like we haven't tried. They have to be using something to mask their scent and remain hidden. Maybe it's time we ask Minerva."

Slowly I turned to face him, the familiar ache of grief stabbing me in the chest. "No."

"I know there's bad blood between your family and—"

"She let my mother die, Matthias!" I bellowed, and a pair of birds flew out of the trees above our heads.

"And your father has forgiven her," he said calmly.

"No," I repeated. "We can do this without her."

Matthias replied with a sharp nod. "Yes, Your Highness. We'll start with the locations of the most recent attacks and work our way from there."

Drawing in a deep breath, thankful to be off the topic of the old mage, I faced forward again. "Maybe see if the healers have any thoughts on herbs or stones or some magical something that could be hindering our search. Maybe if we can find—"

"What about the girl?"

"Girl?"

"You know, the blonde human who's currently distracting a certain brother of yours?"

"What about her?"

"Where did she go after you saved her? I'm assuming she didn't go live with some benevolent fae somewhere, right? If she was in hiding with humans, maybe she could help us find who is responsible."

I was already shaking my head. "I don't know. Obviously I've considered it, but her parents served my family for years."

"Maybe her other family isn't as loyal as her parents were."

"And maybe her family has nothing to do with these attacks."

Matthias shrugged lazily and muttered, "And maybe they do. You could at least talk to her?"

"I'll think about it," I said. He wasn't wrong. I did need to consider the possibility, especially given how much time Lieke had been spending with Brennan. Maybe there was more than just her idiotic love for my brother at play here.

We continued on in silence for a bit, but my mind was in chaos. Someone, or something, was helping the humans elude us, keeping us from tracking them down despite our natural advantages.

But what if the rebels weren't humans?

What if we were chasing the wrong adversary?

I was about to pose these questions to Matthias when we entered the courtyard and someone shouted my name. Lieke sprinted out of the palace's front entrance toward us, her dark blue eyes lit with panic. I dismounted quickly and threw my reins to Matthias before I rushed to meet her.

"What is it?" I asked. My hands gripped her arms as I searched her wild expression for any answers. Had Griffin come here? Had he tried to attack her again?

"It's Brennan," she said breathlessly. "The king…"

Shit.

My heart plummeted into my stomach, and I pushed her aside as I ran.

No, no, no. I should have been here.

My mind repeated the words with each step I took up the stairs and down the hallway.

And then I stopped.

A pair of guards stood outside my father's study.

He never placed guards here.

Never.

Then I heard it.

The sounds that haunted my memories, echoed in my mind, tormented me.

The steady voice counting.

The fists hitting flesh between each word.

The groans and whimpers and hisses of pain.

It should have been me.

I should have been here.

I had promised our mother I'd be here.

I ran for the door.

The guards tried to stop me, but I elbowed one in the face and slammed a fist into the stomach of the other. And then I was inside.

Whether my shouts were only in my head or managed to escape

my mouth, I didn't know, but my teeth slammed together at the sight of my brother slumped in a chair, his face battered and beaten. Our father stood in front of him, rubbing his bloodied knuckles.

The king turned to look at me, but I couldn't move.

All I could do was stare.

My heart thundered in my ears.

My lungs gulped for air.

My mind whirred around nothing and everything all at once.

"Connor," my father said, his tone so casual I wanted to retch. What had happened to him? Where had our loving father gone?

But I knew. I knew what had blackened his heart and why his temper raged.

He had lost his mate.

That's no excuse for this!

"What happened?" I asked, my voice shaky.

But the king didn't respond. Instead, he leaned down and grabbed Brennan hard by the chin. His fingers slipped in the blood that covered my brother's face, but he still managed to yank his head up.

"I don't care if that human is your fucking mate, Brennan," our father hissed. "You will propose to Calla. You will marry Calla. You will forget the human. Do you understand?"

Brennan choked and swallowed hard before nodding.

My father growled, "Good" and then flung my brother's face away from him, sending him backwards in the chair, which toppled over and slammed into the floor with a crack so loud I winced.

The guards rushed in behind me.

"We're sorry, Your Majesty."

"He just—"

With a wave of his hand, the king quieted them. "It's okay. He needed to see this. Take Brennan to the healer." He tossed his head toward my brother, and then his hostile eyes met mine. "You can't always protect him, Connor. You can't always take his punishments for him. And I should never have allowed it all these years. I did you and him both a disservice by doing so. But this had to be done. You know what is at stake. You know what he needs to do. You know what we stand to lose if he fails. And now hopefully he does too."

I had no words. I had no thoughts. I had nothing.

I was nothing.

I was good for no one.

CHAPTER TWENTY-FOUR

Lieke

y feet wouldn't move. As I watched Connor race into the palace, I didn't know if I'd done the right thing. Connor didn't particularly like me, and he certainly didn't like my relationship with Brennan.

Any hope that my fear for Brennan's safety was unfounded had been dashed away by the horror in Connor's eyes when I'd told him. No, Brennan wasn't okay. Rumors of the king's temper had circulated the palace hallways since the queen's death, but few of the staff had ever witnessed it firsthand.

Those who had seen it refused to talk about it.

"What happened?"

I spun around to find the other fae, Connor's friend, walking toward me while a page led the horses off to the stables. I couldn't speak. All I could manage to do was stare dumbly at him as he approached. He assessed me, his brows lowering over his dark eyes as if I were some wild animal who didn't speak his language.

He stopped a respectable distance away but leaned forward slightly as he said, "I'm Matthias. You're Lieke, right?"

I nodded, still incapable of speech.

"What happened to the prince?" he asked gently, concern softening his features.

"The king dragged him away," I said.

Matthias's eyes widened slightly. "Why?"

Something in this fae's eyes gave me the impression he was well aware of my relationship with Brennan.

"You seem to know already," I said, pursing my lips.

"I have my suspicions, but I'd like to hear it from you all the same."

My face warmed, and I dropped my gaze to the ground between us.

"Well?" he pushed, though not unkindly.

"He was spending time with me."

"Doing what exactly?"

My chin snapped up. "Oh, nothing like that. We were just playing a game of cards and talking, I swear."

Angling his head, he studied me for a bit. "*Just* playing cards?"

I tossed my hands in the air with a huff. "Fine, there might have been a kiss, but only one."

Matthias's eyes flitted over my shoulder, but when I turned, the doors were still closed.

"Is Brennan going to be okay? What's the king going to do?" I asked quietly.

Taking a deep breath, he shrugged and started to walk past me toward the palace, but when our shoulders touched, he stopped and said, "You seem to know already."

❋

I didn't know how long I stood in the courtyard watching the palace doors, but it must have been a while, because the sunlight was fading fast by the time I coaxed my feet to finally move. My guilt and fear over Brennan—and whatever punishment he was receiving because of me—

were painfully twisting my insides. And now I was late getting back to the kitchen.

Mrs. Bishop would not be happy.

When I reached the door to the kitchen, I took a deep breath and braced myself for the oncoming tirade. It didn't help. My nerves were still pulled taut, and my hands were shaking.

Being even later isn't going to help you any.

I held my breath as I pushed open the door.

The kitchen was quiet but not empty. In addition to Mrs. Bishop and Marin, two fae—Britta and Lola, sisters from the dining room wait-staff—silently flitted about the space, carrying dishes and fetching utensils. Part of me longed to back out quietly before they all noticed me standing here, since Mrs. Bishop appeared to have enough help preparing dinner. But the idea of going back to my room, being alone with all my what-ifs—or worse, having Millie present while my thoughts plagued me—was unbearable.

"Nice of you to join us, Sunshine," Mrs. Bishop said in a flat tone. "Their Highnesses are all taking their meals in their rooms this evening."

No one looked up from their work, though I could have sworn I saw Marin bristle. Trying to keep my tone casual, I asked, "Does anyone know why?"

Four faces lifted in unison, gawking at me as if I'd sprouted a second head.

"You haven't heard then?" Marin asked skeptically.

"Of course she did," Lola said. "She's been sneaking off to see the prince every day this week."

My stomach shot straight up into my throat.

They knew? How?

We'd been so careful.

But have you? My thoughts poked at me.

There were no secrets in this place, were there?

As Britta passed by me, she leaned in close and whispered, "It's okay. We all would do the same if Prince Brennan fancied us."

"And some of you have," Marin muttered in a somewhat jealous tone.

Lola snickered, and Mrs. Bishop clapped her hands loudly.

"That's enough of that talk, girls," she said, a look of genuine concern in her eyes. "We don't deal in gossip in my kitchen. You hear? The king requested a change in the dinner arrangements. We do as we're told. End of story."

"I—" Lola started, but Mrs. Bishop's sharp glare forced her mouth shut.

The old fae looked pointedly at each one of us, jabbing a finger in the air as she repeated her instructions. "No gossiping about the royals. No guessing about what happened. No assuming you know the truth. Now, get back to work!"

Hurriedly I rounded the table to join Marin, who was ladling a hearty lamb stew into three gold-rimmed bowls. Without a word, I took each bowl and placed it on its respective tray. Soon we had the trays filled with steaming hot rolls, butter, and a cup of strawberries I'd picked from the garden this morning.

As Marin placed the silver lids over the trays, I cleared my throat and asked, "Shall I help deliver—"

"No," Mrs. Bishop said without looking up from where she was cleaning the table. "Britta, Lola, and Marin will be doing that."

Although I'd known it was a long shot, especially after Lola's earlier accusation, my heart sank a bit. I needed to check on him, to know he was okay.

While they removed their work aprons, dusted off their hands, and picked up the trays to leave, I busied myself with wiping up spilled stew from the table before tossing the towels and linens into the laundry basket in the corner. Thankfully the dinner was a simple one, and most of the preparation had been done earlier in the day, so there was little left to clean.

As Marin and the two fae waitstaff stepped out of the room, I bit the inside of my cheek and counted to ten. I could still catch up to them before they reached Brennan's room, but I couldn't risk raising Mrs. Bishop's suspicion. When I was sure I'd given them a reasonable head start, I pushed out a sigh and forced a yawn.

"I'm pretty tired. Mind if I leave a little early tonight?" I kept my tone as casual as possible, repeating the words in my head to ensure I hadn't slipped up. No, there was no lie in what I'd said. I was indeed tired, and I certainly wanted to leave early.

She slowly surveyed the kitchen, and stars, I had to force myself to breathe slowly, to calm my heartbeat and prevent it from galloping away with my impatience. She might not detect a lie, but there was no way to hide a panicked heartbeat from her.

Finally she shrugged. "Go on then."

I dipped my chin, careful to keep my movements slow, and offered her a quiet "Thank you" before slipping out of the kitchen.

With a glance down either side of the hallway, I took off for Brennan's room. I hoped whoever was delivering his meal would hand over the tray without a fuss—assuming I made it there in time. I ran as fast as I could, skipping the servants' stairways and heading for the main stairs that led up to the royal wing. It was a risk, but hopefully the king and Connor had already retired to their rooms and were awaiting their own meals.

Thankfully, I met no one on the stairs or in the upstairs corridors until I rounded the corner and spotted Lola about to knock on Brennan's door.

"Lola!" I whispered as loudly as I dared, still running toward her. She slid a sideways glance my way and pulled her lip back into a devious smirk.

When I finally stopped beside her, my labored breathing made it impossible to say anything beyond a pathetic "Wait!"

She turned her head fully toward me. "Forget something, Lieke?"

I sucked in another long breath and shook my head. "Can I deliver his meal to him?"

Lola pursed her lips, and I clenched my teeth, fighting the urge to smack that smug look off her face. "How do you know he'll want to see you? From what I hear, you're the one who got him into this mess. If I were him, you'd be the last one I'd want walking through my door."

I stifled a sigh. I didn't have time to worry about how she'd heard or who had found out. The longer I stood in this hallway, the greater my risk of being caught by another servant—or worse, Connor.

"Please," I said, the desperation in my voice earning me another wicked smirk.

"What's to stop me from going straight to the king about this? I bet he'd be most interested to know the servant distracting his son weaseled her way into his bedroom."

"I'll take your dining room duties for a week," I offered.

She scoffed at me and rolled her eyes. "And earn yourself even more opportunity to be in the same room as the prince? I don't think so."

"What do you want then?" I asked. What could she possibly expect me to have that held any value? What could I offer her that didn't involve taking on her duties?

"Your necklace," she said quickly, dropping her eyes to where Mother's pendant hid beneath my dress. My hand flew up protectively to where it sat near my heart as I shook my head. I couldn't. She raised a single brow and shrugged. "No necklace for me? Then no prince for you."

My mind spun in circles, going so fast I thought I was going to be physically ill.

I can always see him another time. It doesn't have to be right now.

But I need to make sure he's okay. I won't be able to sleep unless I check.

Then why not ask someone to check on him for you? It's not worth handing over Mother's necklace to this wench.

He's fae. He'll probably be healed in no time.

"Well? Do we have a deal? The prince's food is getting cold," Lola said, her expression turning bored.

Footsteps echoed from somewhere behind me, their steady thumping slower than my thundering heartbeat but growing louder, closer.

"Fine," I growled, pulling the pendant out from my collar and slipping the chain over my head, wincing as it caught on the hairs at my neck.

Lola shoved the tray of food into my arms before swiping the necklace dangling from my fingers. Without looking at the door, she reached out and rapped on it three times before whispering, "Better hurry, Lieke.

Someone's coming."

She spun on her heel and scurried off toward the servants' stairs. Dropping my chin to my chest, I let my hair fall over my shoulder, hoping it might hide my face from whoever was approaching. The footsteps were louder now. I held my breath, waiting to be spotted, but then the door opened. Without looking up, I hurried inside and kicked it shut behind me.

"Lieke?" Brennan's voice was weak, sad, and distant. "What are you doing here?"

The room was so dark I couldn't make out his features or how bad his injuries were, but I could hear his pain in each syllable.

"I brought you a puppy," I said, holding up the tray and trying to smile.

He didn't laugh at my attempted joke but simply rubbed his hand on the back of his neck. Averting his eyes, he pivoted and started to walk away, saying, "You shouldn't be here."

"Yes, I know. If I get caught—"

He continued to walk away from me as he said over his shoulder, "That's not what I mean."

Grinding my teeth together, I breathed deeply before following after him. "Do you want to eat in your bedroom then?" I asked, not actually knowing where he was going since I'd never been in his rooms before.

He pointed to his right. "No, there's a table. You can set it there for now."

But he didn't move in that direction. Instead, he turned to his left and disappeared from sight. Gingerly I stepped through the dark room, not wanting to trip or bump into anything. Before I turned to move in the direction he'd instructed, I stole a peek to the left. The door was open, but I couldn't see anything except the edge of what appeared to be his bed. My arms ached under the weight of the dinner tray, so I rushed over to the table and set it down, leaving the lid in place.

And then I waited.

Should I look for him?

Should I leave?

He doesn't want me here.

I'd come here to ensure he was okay, and while I'd verified he was at least alive, I needed to know what had happened. If he'd been hurt because of me, I needed to—to what? What could I possibly do for him?

"Brennan?" I called. When there was no answer, I tiptoed slowly toward the bedroom door.

Then he was there, standing in the doorway, blocking my way. Startled, I flinched and skidded to a stop. He didn't say anything, so I took another step forward until I was close enough to touch him. I dared not look up at him. Slowly, I reached a hand up between us, letting my fingers lightly graze his chest. He didn't move, didn't even seem to breathe. So I took a chance and pressed my hand against him fully.

His hand shot up, grabbing my wrist and pulling my hand away from him.

I was surprised when he allowed me to rip my hand from his grip, but when I finally looked up into his eyes, I didn't find the prince I'd been playing cards with just hours before, the prince who had been so willing to beg for his brother's help in order to be with me.

This prince was cold, distant...

And pained.

While his body had started to heal itself, his left eye remained swollen. His bruised nose was now crooked. Fresh scars sliced across his upper lip and through his right eyebrow.

"What happened?" I asked, swallowing hard when his eyes narrowed slightly. "What did he do to you?"

Pressing his lips together, he set his jaw but said nothing.

"I'm sorry," I said, though it wasn't enough. Such insufficient words for how my heart ached for him. "I wish—"

"You can't be here," he whispered firmly.

"But I am here, and before I leave, I need to know you're okay."

"For you own peace of mind?" he asked, his stare freezing over. "So you can sleep all right tonight?"

"Because I care about you, you jackass! Don't make me out to be selfish! I've been so worried about you! So worried he was going to kill you! Is it so bad for me to want you to be safe and alive?"

His eyes searched mine as if hunting for a lie somewhere.

"I got Connor like you told me to," I said, as if that made up for any of this.

"I know," he said. "But he was too late."

"I'm so sorry, Brennan." My hands yearned to reach out to him, but I couldn't, so I clasped them together tightly in front of me. "I never meant for—"

"For me to be beaten mercilessly by my father?" he asked, his expression eerily calm compared to his words.

I could only nod. We stood there in silence for a while. Not touching. Just staring. There was nothing I could say or do to make this better.

Finally he dropped his gaze and cleared his throat. "You were right, Lieke. I have no choice. I can't be with you no matter how much I want to. I have to marry Calla."

Even though I'd known this—even though I'd been the one to insist on it before—hearing him say it now tore open old wounds in my heart. I had to let him go. I couldn't push for this—for us—not when it earned him such treatment from the king.

My voice faltered when I tried to answer him. Drawing in a steadying breath, I started again. "I understand, Bren. I know I said before that it was too late. But I've changed my mind. Until you walk down that aisle and say those vows, I'll wait for you."

Slowly he lifted his face, and his eyes found mine. Whether the hope in them was real or something I only imagined, I didn't know, but I grasped onto it all the same.

Without saying another word, I turned on my heel and left.

CHAPTER TWENTY-FIVE

Connor

It had been two days since Brennan's punishment, and he was still holed up in his room. The healers claimed he should be fully recovered by now, aside from a few scars. Apparently, injured pride took longer to heal though, and he refused to see anyone.

Even me.

Not that I could blame him. No doubt he expected some sort of lecture from me, since I'd been on his ass constantly over the past few years. He'd been careless, yes, and a complete fool to think he could sneak around with a servant in a palace swarming with staff and scouts. I could only hope Father's reprimand—as painfully brutal as it was—had been enough to knock some sense into him.

Stars knew I didn't want to spend one more minute rebuking Brennan, but I would have no choice if he insisted on staying locked away today.

Since early this morning, the staff had been buzzing about the palace preparing for the arrival of Princess Calla and her parents this evening. Flowers were brought in by the cartload to adorn every room—except those in the queen's wing, of course. Fresh meat and fish arrived from the various merchants in Linley and Engle, and baskets of produce were shuffled inside to supplement the fruits and vegetables our gardeners grew on the grounds.

With all this commotion, I would have preferred to stay in my rooms—like my brother—but I needed to ensure he was ready to greet our guests. Even if I'd had a page available to send word to him, I knew he would just turn them away or ignore them completely, as he'd done with the last two I had sent.

So now I stood outside his door, almost wishing for the old days when I had to drag his sorry ass away from conquest after conquest. At least then he always had a smile for me—an irritated one at times, but still a smile.

I didn't bother knocking but opened the door cautiously, as if I were checking on a sleeping infant instead of a sulking grown-ass prince. The curtains had at least been pulled back, and Brennan stood in front of the window that overlooked the courtyard. He didn't turn as I approached, but his shoulders tensed.

"What do you want, brother?" he asked, his tone weary rather than annoyed.

I stepped up beside him, keeping my gaze forward, and slid my hands into my pockets. "Just checking in on you."

"Isn't that what you have the healers for? I assume they've reported back to you already."

"'Trust but verify,' as our father always says." I winced. Not the best time to mention the king.

Brennan huffed out a sigh and spun away from me, stomping toward the front room, where he dropped himself onto the sofa. Giving myself time to organize my thoughts and words, I followed slowly behind him. I couldn't risk another slip of the tongue. I needed him to cooperate.

After getting settled into one of the armchairs, I studied him as he stretched his legs out and leaned against a large pillow. His head fell back and his eyes closed as he said, "Well, you've verified. I'm fine."

He raised his hand lazily, giving me a thumbs-up to emphasize his point, and I nearly laughed. We used to use the gesture often as kids when we didn't want our parents to know we were about to indulge in a bit of mischief. The last time we'd used it was before the war actually, when we'd devised a devilish plan to put a frog in Mrs. Bishop's shoe.

We had earned ourselves two weeks of fetching water for her after that.

What I wouldn't give to have an angry cook as the worst of our worries.

Shaking my head, I urged the memories to fade away.

"You finally ready to come out of your rooms then?" I asked. "Our guests arrive later today."

He didn't look at me, didn't move, except to reply, "If I must, I must."

"And you're prepared to do what needs done?"

At this, he reached into his pants pocket, his face contorting into a wince as he twisted his body so he could retrieve something. With a grunt, he relaxed again and held up his hand, a delicate silver ring pinched between his forefinger and thumb.

"Is that how you're planning to propose?" I asked, unable to hide my smirk.

He sat up, swinging his legs around and planting his feet on the floor. Leaning over, he rested his forearms on his lap and stared at the ring as he turned it around in his fingers. Then his eyes snapped to mine, and he asked, "Maybe. Think it would work?"

"You know Calla better than I do," I said, shrugging.

"Barely," he muttered, and I didn't bring up the fact that he'd spent far more time with her than I ever had. His point was clear enough.

"For what it's worth, I am sorry," I said. He didn't respond, didn't even nod in acknowledgement, but at least I'd said it. I cleared my throat before I asked, "Do you love her?"

Maybe there was no point in asking, because ultimately it didn't matter. He'd have to marry Calla regardless. But part of me wanted some reassurance that I wasn't forcing my brother to abandon someone he truly loved.

"No," he answered quickly.

"I mean the woman. Lieke."

"I know who you meant," Brennan said quietly. "And no, I don't. Not yet anyway."

"What does that mean?"

He shrugged, his eyes once again focused on the ring he held. "I wanted the chance to fall in love with her, I guess. As stupid as that sounds."

I shook my head. "Doesn't sound stupid to me."

"She's not my mate though. Part of me hoped she was, that the bond might form when I kissed her. I thought maybe if she was my mate, the king would have been willing to call the alliance off. Doesn't matter either way now, I suppose."

"I'm sorry," I said again, hoping he could detect my genuine regret.

"You're just doing as you're told," he said. Taking a deep breath, he turned to face me. "Now I guess it's time for me to do the same."

For a long moment, I studied him, searching for any sign he was merely telling me what I wanted to hear. Last thing I needed was for him to sabotage the years of work we'd put into securing this match.

"What?" he asked, eyes widening.

"You're sure?"

"If I was planning some daring escape to elope with Lieke, do you really think I'd tell you about it?"

Shrugging, I smirked at him. "Never know. You were never good at keeping secrets as a youth."

He scoffed. "Not my fault! It's that damned cook of ours with her taste for lies."

I laughed at the memories of all the times he'd gotten caught fibbing to Mrs. Bishop, remembering in particular how our mother had struggled to hide her amusement when she'd needed to dole out his punishment.

"Well, brother," Brennan said as he stood, placing the ring back in his pocket, "if you don't mind, I'd like to rest a bit longer before I must *do what needs to be done*." He waved his fingers in the air with those last words.

Heaving a sigh of relief, I stood and made my way to the door. Before I left, I turned and said, "I'll be back to get you before they arrive."

✳

I was about to head downstairs when a page rushed toward me, his face flushed.

"Your Highness," he said, and I raised a brow in acknowledgment. "Master Orelian needs to see you. He's waiting for you in your chambers, sir. Told me to fetch you as quickly as possible."

"Thank you." I nodded as I stepped around him.

The corridors leading to my rooms were relatively quiet compared to the rest of the palace. Only a few servants here and there passed me as I walked, until one stopped directly in front of me. It took a moment for me to recognize the intense blue eyes that burned into mine.

Of course things were going too smoothly, weren't they?

Of course this girl was going to interfere. Again.

"Miss Berg," I said casually, focusing all my irritation into squeezing my clasped hands together behind my back. "What can I do for you?"

"How can you do this to him?" she hissed more loudly than I had expected.

Although the hallway was currently empty, it might not be for much longer. I couldn't risk having anyone witness a servant—especially *this* servant—speaking to me in such a manner.

Opening the nearest door, I grabbed her elbow and forced her into an empty guest room. I nudged the door shut with my foot, then ushered her further into the dark, cold space. Lieke glared at me, tearing her arm from my grasp.

"Don't touch me!" she said.

Rocking back on my heels, I studied her for a long, silent moment. My frustration with her threatened to erupt in a growl, but I managed to tamp it back down.

"I warned you, did I not?" I asked, crossing my arms over my chest. Confusion flashed in her eyes for a second, and then she sneered.

"And I warned *you* that Brennan wouldn't be controlled by either of us."

"You could have denied him," I said plainly. "You could have turned down his invitations. Or am I mistaken? Were those little trysts your idea?"

She didn't answer my questions but asked one of her own. "Is he not allowed to spend time with a friend?"

I barked out a laugh and stalked toward her. She stumbled back a step, fear briefly sweeping over her features as if she thought I was going to strike her.

"A friend, perhaps. But you're far more than that, aren't you? Can I assume your affections for my brother haven't waned at all?" She didn't move, didn't answer. "A *friend* would understand his situation, Lieke. A *friend* would have protected him from the repercussions if he refused to do as ordered. A *friend*—"

"Would help him find a way out of this!" She dared to step closer to me, the fire reigniting in her eyes.

I leaned my face down toward hers, ignoring how her sweet scent wrapped around me. "You're naive, Blondie. This is our life as royals. This is his life—his duty—as a prince. There are more important things than a childhood infatuation."

Lieke stood her ground, not flinching once. She pressed her finger into my chest. "And you are pathetic, Your Highness, leading a sad excuse for a life."

I gritted my teeth and retreated a couple of paces, not surprised when she continued her pursuit. Narrowing my eyes, I challenged her to keep talking.

She raised her chin to look at me with all the haughtiness of a princess instead of a servant. "You have nothing good in your life, do you? So you can't let anyone else have anything good either. Especially your brother!"

My resolve vanished.

Before I could think better of it, my hand was at her throat. Pivoting, I drove her back against the wall. Then I released her neck, slamming my hands against the wall on either side of her head. I was in her face in an instant, so close that her shaky breath warmed my skin.

"You know nothing. Nothing!" I hit the wall again, and she flinched. I lowered my voice to a deadly whisper. "Everything I do is to make life better for everyone else. Everything I do—everything I sacrifice—is for the peace and security of our country! Do not presume to know anything about my life. Or about me."

Lieke only stared at me in silence. She swallowed hard once, wetting her lips as if she were readying to speak, but she didn't.

"Next time you interfere, Blondie, I'll drag you before the king myself. You want to remain here? Stay out of the damned way."

CHAPTER TWENTY-SIX

Lieke

What had I been thinking, confronting the prince? Why had I pushed him like that? Who did I think I was?

I remained in the guest room long after he left, replaying the entire encounter in my head. I'd never witnessed that side of Connor—except once, that night when he'd shifted into his wolfhound form. As I lifted my hand to my neck, to the spot where he'd grabbed me, I wondered why I hadn't been scared of him just now. Shouldn't I have been?

Something in his eyes—despite the anger I'd obviously stoked—had put me at ease. Well, as much at ease as I could be with a powerful fae prince intimidating me in a dark room. Even when he'd grabbed me and pushed me against the wall, he hadn't hurt me.

Stars, why could I not stop thinking about his hand on my throat? What was wrong with me?

I shook my head and squeezed my eyes shut, desperate for the memory to leave me alone before my core traitorously warmed again. I drew in a deep breath, but the scent of Connor's cologne had transferred to my shirt, making it impossible to be rid of him. As a distraction, I focused instead on what he'd said. I was naive. I didn't know anything. I needed to stay out of the way.

Or I'd be dismissed.

Stars, what had I done?

My gut lurched as I thought of how close I'd come to being thrown out of the palace. Sure, I missed Raven and her family, and they would no doubt welcome me back. But this was my home.

Logically I understood all Connor had said—about their duty and the sacrifice required of him and his brother—but I couldn't let go of this idea that it didn't have to be that way. Surely a prince should be able to choose who he married?

Even if it's a mortal servant?

You're reaching for the damned stars, I told myself, sighing.

I was yearning for something that couldn't be mine, no matter what Brennan wanted.

I needed to let him go for good this time.

I couldn't see him again.

My chest ached at the notion, and my shoulders curled in as if to protect my heart from the pain. How in the stars did I expect to stay here in this palace without seeing him? Or his damned brother?

No. I would find a way. I had to find a way.

But why did I want to stay in a home tainted with memories of Brennan?

Sure, I'd done so for years after his mother died, but there had always been some hope that one day our separation would end, he'd remember we were friends, and he'd stop pretending I didn't exist. But now it was different. Now there was no hope. He was to marry another. He'd never be mine.

Growling in frustration, I lifted my face toward the ceiling and rolled my shoulders.

"Smile," I said aloud, as I had every day since my mother's passing. Life could be over at any time, and I didn't want to waste too much of it fretting over things I couldn't change. Closing my eyes, I thought of her and the way she used to brush my tears away and say, *"It's good to feel things, sweet girl. It's how we know we're alive. As long as we have breath in our lungs, we have reason to be thankful, for it means we still have time to make a difference and have a chance to be someone else's joy."*

I could do this, because the alternative—leaving and never coming back—was unacceptable.

Taking one more deep breath, I opened the door and stepped out into the hallway, making my way down the servants' stairs toward the staff quarters. Assuming I hadn't lost all track of time while contemplating my predicament, I would find Mrs. Bishop on her break in her room rather than in the kitchen. Whether she would grant my request was another concern entirely, but I had to at least ask.

Her door was at the end of the hallway, furthest from the kitchen. I had once thought it ridiculous for her to have to walk all that way each day, but then she'd explained how keeping work and rest separated—even by such a minimal distance—kept her sanity intact. Then she'd rambled on about boundaries. It had never made sense to me until now.

I needed boundaries.

I needed to find a way to work in this place without my feelings distracting me.

I rapped my knuckles on her door a few times and waited. Silence. Maybe she was asleep. Or maybe I had sulked longer than I'd thought.

"Sunshine?" Turning, I spotted Mrs. Bishop walking toward me. Flour was splotched on one of her cheeks. "What is it, Lieke?"

My mind went utterly blank, as empty as the shell of a heart that remained in my chest. I must have looked pathetically distraught, because her eyes swelled with concern and she cupped my face in her hands.

"What happened?" she asked, but I could only shake my head, my vision going out of focus as I searched for some way to explain this to her. "Come on in and we can talk."

She quickly unlocked her room and ushered me gently inside. Pulling a chair out from the small dining table that sat off to one side, she gestured for me to sit. She poured a glass of water and set it in front of me.

"Drink up, Sunshine, and then tell me what is going on before I have to fetch a healer."

I obeyed, gulping down the water greedily. Setting the empty glass back down, I finally lifted my eyes to find her staring at me.

"You were right," I said quietly.

She flashed me a tight smile and shrugged. "I usually am, but you'll have to be more specific."

"About Brennan."

Her face immediately fell. She didn't say anything but reached out and took my hand in hers, giving my fingers a gentle squeeze.

"I knew better," I continued. "I did, but I didn't listen to you."

"You may not believe me, Sunshine, but I wish I had been wrong. After your mother passed, your grief consumed you. Understandably so, of course, but I didn't know how to help you except to wait and try to keep you busy. When you found Brennan though—when the two of you grew to be such close friends—I thought it was the best thing that could have happened to you."

My chin fell to my chest as I closed my eyes. "Until I fell in love with him, that is."

She slowly inhaled. I prepared myself for her admonishment, but she simply said, "You can't help who your heart falls for, Lieke. Unfortunately, it isn't always meant to be, and we have to live with that heartache."

"I don't know if I can."

Sliding her finger under my chin, she lifted my face. "You can, Lieke, because you must. The alternative is to wither away, to become a living ghost until eventually your life leaves you. Your mother wouldn't want that for you."

"I know, but—"

"But nothing." Her tone was firm but not unkind. "I won't tell you to ignore this hurt, because that is no way to live either. But you cannot let it consume you."

"How do I stay here though?"

For a long moment, she studied me. The longer she waited to speak, the more nervous I became. Would she send me away again? Would she insist I couldn't stay here?

Finally, she nodded slowly. "Focus on your work—and I'm not just saying that as your boss. Throw yourself into something outside of your thoughts. If your hands are busy, your mind will be too. I know it's tempting to want to lock yourself away in your room and hide from the world, and I'll let you have today and tomorrow to wallow a bit. But after that, it's back to work. Okay?"

I could do this. I could. I had to.

I managed a small nod and a half-smile. She patted my hand.

"And who knows, Sunshine. Perhaps the stars have someone in store for you yet."

I had to work to stop myself from rolling my eyes at that. She was from an older generation, so it shouldn't be surprising that she held onto long-gone traditions and beliefs. I hadn't heard anyone speak of stars-guided matches in years, except to ridicule the idea. Mrs. Bishop, though, appeared as serious as ever.

"Do you really believe in all of that?" I asked.

"You mean do I believe in mates?"

I raised a brow in silent question.

She looked up at the ceiling for a breath or two before returning her focus to me. "I do actually, though I'm one of the few, it seems."

"How does it work exactly?" I tried to hide the skepticism in my voice, but I was certain I failed miserably. Mrs. Bishop pursed her lips, but instead of answering me, she glanced over her shoulder at the small clock beside her bed. Humming a sigh, she stood from her seat and faced me again.

"I'm afraid I need to get back to work. We can chat about that more another time." She reached out a hand. Taking it, I rose from my seat. "I'll walk you to your room before I head to the kitchen, but remember: two days to wallow. Then I expect you to get back to work."

CHAPTER TWENTY-SEVEN

Connor

The clashing steel filled my ears as the force of Matthias's strike sent a jolt up my arm, producing a new ache in my shoulder. I shoved him back and stepped away, trying to put some distance between us as we continued to circle each other in the training ring. He was going easy on me, slowing his movements to match my own sluggishness. I might have been offended if I wasn't grateful for his understanding.

That didn't save me from his taunting though.

"You're sloppy today, friend," he said with a smug grin. "Perhaps I should speak to the king about replacing his esteemed general. Temporarily, of course."

"Don't tempt me," I said, lunging forward with my sword only to have him easily parry the strike, twisting his blade around mine so that I nearly lost my grip. "I could use the break."

At that, Matthias attacked a bit more aggressively, and I barely managed to bring my sword back up in time to meet each blow.

"You're distracted," he said.

He wasn't wrong, and I hated it. My mind simply wouldn't clear, wouldn't focus.

Matthias straightened, lowering his sword as he studied me. "She's left quite the impression on you."

Rolling my eyes, I growled and attempted an overhead strike that he effortlessly avoided by pivoting out of the way.

He offered a single laugh. "Is that your way of denying it? It's not very convincing."

Defeated, I relaxed my shoulders and faced my friend. I had hoped some training time would help, but it hadn't. Every failed strike, sloppy deflection, and slow movement of my feet merely reminded me of how much the incident with Lieke had affected me.

"I think I'm losing my mind," I admitted.

Shrugging, Matthias slid his sword into the scabbard at his waist. "Females tend to do that to us, don't they?"

"Not to me," I said, sheathing my own sword.

"Until now. What is it about this one?" Matthias gestured to the pitcher of water waiting at the edge of the ring and moved to pour two glasses.

As he handed me one, I shook my head. It wasn't that I didn't know the reason. I simply didn't like it and didn't want to admit it. But if I could trust anyone, it was Matthias.

"She's infuriating!" I explained. He grinned at me from behind his glass as he took a long draught. "And she brings out the worst in me. I hate who I am around her."

"Are you sure it's really the *worst* in you?" he asked, quirking a brow.

Raising my hand out to the side, I balked at him. "Of course. I grabbed her by the throat, Matthias."

His mouth curved into a knowing smile. "I don't know. Sounds kind of hot."

At that, I rolled my eyes. I was not about to admit to him how inappropriately my body had reacted when I'd had her neck in my hand as I forced her against that wall. My core heated just at the memory, and I silently cursed my body and its carnal needs.

"Hot or not, I shouldn't have done it. I let my temper get the better of me. I don't want to be like that."

"You mean you don't want to be like your father," Matthias said, all humor now replaced by calm understanding.

"Exactly."

Matthias set his glass on the table and roughed a hand over his jaw. "I know you don't want to hear it, but you need to harness that part of yourself and learn how to use it. If you keep running from it and pretending like it's not there, you'll find yourself in this spiral of shame every time it awakens. This is part of who you are, like it or not. It's only a weakness if you allow it to be."

Could my temper really be a strength?

I wasn't convinced.

Anger only led to bruises and scars and regrets, but maybe he was right. Maybe it could be honed like any other skill. Perhaps I could control it rather than being controlled by it.

"How?" I asked quietly, not expecting him to have an actual answer.

"To be honest? I don't know. Practice?"

"So I should seek out opportunities to be angry?" I asked, shaking my head at how absurd that sounded.

Matthias shrugged. "Shouldn't be too hard. I hear there's a girl down in the kitchen who could help."

Lieke's glowering face immediately came to mind, and I groaned loudly enough that I earned a laugh from my friend.

"Or not. Is Brennan no longer a reliable option?"

The change in my brother over the last several days had been remarkable. Upon Princess Calla's arrival, he'd smoothly slid into his role of doting suitor, taking her on a tour of the grounds and escorting her on visits to the village.

"No, actually," I said. "He seems to have finally accepted his circumstances. I expect a proposal any day now."

"Should happen today if my scout's information is reliable," Matthias said, gesturing for me to follow him back to the palace.

"Good. The sooner we get him married off, the sooner I can focus on other things."

"And the proposal should help with your anger management," he said.

"How so?"

"A proposal means a big announcement dinner." He raised a brow as we reached the front steps. Groaning, I dropped my chin to my chest, and Matthias slapped me on the back. "If that prick at the pub the other day shows up, you can practice controlling your anger with him instead of needing to seek out the girl."

Without fail, Lieke appeared in my mind, her contentious smile mocking me for my desire to avoid her.

CHAPTER TWENTY-EIGHT

Lieke

Mrs. Bishop held me to my promise not to sulk too long, and when I returned to work, she seemed more than willing to give me additional duties to help me avoid thinking about Brennan. No amount of fatigue, though, could protect me from my dreams. Every night, I fell into bed with my muscles screaming from the day's work, and every day, I woke with my heart aching even more than my body.

The pain would dull eventually. Losing Mother had taught me that. According to Mrs. Bishop, I'd suffered a loss—the loss of a dream, a future—and that deserved to be mourned.

For the last week, I had been following a rigorous schedule to keep my mind busy— waking early to run, then trudging to the kitchen and grabbing a bite to eat before diving into the day's chores. I baked bread for the Durands' breakfast, picked vegetables in the garden, harvested fruit from the orchard, and helped Mrs. Bishop plan the menu for the next day.

Today, however, upon stepping outside, I was greeted with a torrential downpour, which prevented me from going on my usual run around the property, so I made my way to the kitchen earlier than usual.

I immediately wished I hadn't.

"It's not like he loved her," a voice said from inside. It sounded like Marin. I paused. Glancing around to ensure the hallway was empty, I pressed my ear to the door.

"Doesn't matter though, does it?" There was no mistaking Mrs. Bishop's lilt. Despite her kind tone, overhearing her gossiping about me twisted my stomach.

You don't know they're talking about you though, I reminded myself.

"I suppose not, but what exactly did she expect?" Marin asked. "She had to know she couldn't have him. He's a prince. She's a human."

"But she loves him," the old fae noted. "And you know she's the optimistic sort. She was holding onto hope, and there's nothing wrong with that. We could all use a little more hope these days."

Marin scoffed. "Nothing wrong with that? Her broken heart would say otherwise. Look where it got her."

Broken heart? Marin could tell? I'd spent all this time trying to hide it, attempting to do my best to move on, but apparently I'd failed.

"And what would you have her do exactly, Marin?"

I shifted uneasily at my perch by the door, suddenly feeling bad for eavesdropping—even if they were discussing me and my broken heart.

Marin sighed loudly, and I could picture her shoulders slumping dramatically. "I don't know. It's not like I want her to leave. I just want her to be happy."

My heart swelled, and I pressed my hand against my sternum. She actually cared? All these years, I'd felt so alone. Brennan had been my only friend, and then I'd lost him. Again. I made a mental note to be kind to Marin.

"If that's true," Mrs. Bishop said, "then you will not breathe a word about the engagement. Let me tell her. She doesn't need to hear it blurted out insensitively."

Engagement.

He'd proposed to her.

My heart plummeted into my stomach, landing with a frozen, dull thud.

No, I told myself. *You knew this was going to happen. You expected this. This will not break you.*

Smile, Lieke.

Drawing in a steadying breath, I pushed open the door with as much confidence as I could muster. Marin and Mrs. Bishop both whirled around to face me, their eyes growing wide.

"Good morning," I said, forcing my lips to curl into a half-smile. After grabbing my apron off the hook beside the door, I tied it around my waist and joined them at the worktable. They stared at me in silence as I began to collect the ingredients to make the croissants the king had requested this morning.

"Oh, come now, both of you," I said. "I've already heard. There's no need to pussyfoot around me. I'm fine."

Marin leaned forward and whispered, "What have you heard?"

I waved a hand casually in the air. "The proposal? Brennan and Calla?" I swallowed past the discomfort of having their names together on my tongue. "It's not as if it's any big secret. We've been expecting it all week."

Mrs. Bishop inched closer to me until her hip nearly touched mine. "And you're fine."

Nodding, I returned my attention to the butter and flour as I answered, "Yes. I'm fine. It's fine."

"Say it one more time and we'll know you're lying," Marin said, pointing a finger at me.

"If I was lying, she'd already know." I nodded to Mrs. Bishop, whose eyes narrowed briefly.

She didn't break her stare as she said to Marin, "Leave her be, girl. She's fine."

Marin straightened and smiled widely. Mischief sparked in her eyes as she studied me. "Great! Then you'll come with me?"

Confusion pulled my brow low over my eyes. When a quick glance at Mrs. Bishop yielded no answers, I asked, "Come with you where?"

"The engagement announcement dinner tomorrow night, of course." She said it as if it should have been obvious.

"We aren't allowed, Marin," I said, not mentioning how it was the last place I wanted to be.

She scoffed and looked up to the ceiling. "Not the actual dinner, dummy. I just want to check out the decorations once they're ready. I hear this is to be the most elaborate banquet King Durand has ever held. Even grander than the queen's were!"

"I don't know," I muttered, glancing down at the rolling pin in my hands.

Mrs. Bishop huffed out a breath and dropped her own hands hard on the table. "Marin, don't push her. She doesn't have—"

"What?" Marin asked innocently. "If she's truly fine, as you both claim, a quick jaunt around the palace is no big deal."

The old fae began to protest, but I held up my hand. "And we'll be back in our rooms before the guests arrive?"

Marin's smile grew, and she nodded once. "Promise."

Slowly, I drew in a breath and shrugged. "Fine."

✳

I shouldn't have come.

I shouldn't have been so intent on proving I was okay with Brennan's engagement, because I was far from it. I didn't want to be here, pretending to be excited about the obnoxiously fragrant flowers gracing every table with their perfect velvety petals. I didn't want to touch the thick gold curtains that adorned each window, taking the place of the more than adequate navy drapes that usually hung there.

And I *didn't* want to be walking into the ballroom, having to fake a smile as I stared at Brennan's and Calla's names irritatingly written in impeccable script on a single place card in the middle of the main table, as if they were already married and not simply engaged.

Engaged. I hated the word almost as much as I hated this room and those curtains and the flowers and the ridiculous predicament I'd allowed my heart to fall into.

"Incredible, isn't it?" Marin whispered to me, poking my ribs with her elbow.

Grinding my teeth, I hummed in response.

"You okay?"

Angry tears threatened to surface, creeping toward the edges of my eyes, but I blinked them away. Still, I could only nod; I didn't trust my voice not to betray the stars-damned bitterness burrowing under my skin. Whether she believed me or not, I didn't know, and I didn't rightly care at this point. I simply wanted to get out of this room.

As if Marin could sense my discomfort, she wove her hand under the crook of my arm and led me out into the hallway without a word. We should have left sooner. No, we should never have come here, because then I wouldn't have ended up standing here at this moment, staring down the long corridor straight into the eyes of the fae prince I'd sworn my heart to.

Brennan.

His name was vinegar and honey, leaving a trail of sweet acidity as it ran through my mind. On his arm, a gorgeous fae wearing a purple gown clung to his elbow. A delicate crown was nestled in the dark waves of her hair. Princess Calla. She seemed pleasant enough, but she held onto Brennan's arm with an air of indifferent possessiveness, as if she couldn't be bothered to care that she held a claim to him but wasn't about to let anyone else strip her of that claim either.

His eyes locked onto mine, and I was lost, tumbling down into those starry pools of green. He didn't smile, didn't even acknowledge my presence except to stare into my soul.

But then something in his gaze shifted.

Sadness. Regret. Apprehension. Yearning.

No. You're only seeing what you want to see.

Was I though?

He was my best friend, and nothing—not years apart, nor death, nor marriage—could break the connection we had. I knew him as well as he knew me. Without thinking, I inched my foot forward, but the princess shifted too, pivoting on her toe and pulling Brennan away from the hallway and from me. Brennan's eyes glazed over, finally dropping from mine as he followed his fiancée. Just before they disappeared around the corner, he glanced at me one last time over his shoulder.

My breath rushed from my lungs once they were gone, but I couldn't move.

"I'm so sorry," Marin whispered. "I didn't think they'd be here. I swear."

For a long moment, she and I stood there in silence.

"Are you okay?" she repeated. "And don't say you're fine, because I can tell you're not."

Slowly, I turned toward her, scrunching my brow. "Then why ask?"

She shrugged. "To be nice? But really, are you going to be okay?"

I nodded, slowly redirecting my attention to where they'd retreated.

"He's backing out of the wedding," I whispered.

Marin started, and her eyes widened dramatically as she leaned in closer. "What do you mean? How do you know?"

"He told me," I said. "He said, 'I don't want to marry Calla. Please, Lieke, help me.'"

"What? When did he say that? I didn't think you'd seen him since the proposal."

"Just now. Brennan told me with his eyes," I said calmly.

Marin slumped away from me, her head falling backwards as she released an exasperated sigh. "Oh, I thought you were talking about something real."

Of course she didn't believe me. Stars, I wouldn't believe me either if I were her, but I didn't need her to. I needed to talk to Brennan. Alone.

Pursing my lips, I shifted my weight and sighed. "I suppose that does sound crazy, doesn't it?"

Marin nodded slowly. "Eye conversations? Really, Lieke?" She paused to glance up and down the hallway. "We should probably leave before anyone else spots us in here though. The guests are going to be arriving soon."

Silently we made our way back downstairs, but when we arrived at my door, I couldn't go in.

"I think I need some fresh air actually," I said.

Marin's eyes narrowed with suspicion. "You're not going to go chase down the prince are you? Have more *eye conversations?*"

I laughed half-heartedly. "No. Just need to be alone to think for a bit. Millie may not be much of a conversationalist, but she's not the best of company either."

"Well, I'll be in my room for the night, if you need anything," she said, and I pushed her playfully down the hallway. When she was halfway to her door, she glanced over her shoulder. "Careful out there, Lieke."

Once she was inside her room, I spun around and headed back up the stairs to find Brennan before the fae nobles started to arrive. Hopefully the princess wouldn't be with him.

CHAPTER TWENTY-NINE

Connor

"What do you mean, you saw Lieke?" I hissed at Brennan as I paced in his living room. He lounged casually on the sofa, watching me with a bored expression.

"What else could I mean? Calla and I were strolling around the palace, we turned a corner, and she was there with one of the other staff."

I stopped to shoot a pointed glare his way. "Did she say anything?"

He shook his head.

I resumed pacing.

"And what did Calla say?" I asked.

"To Lieke?"

"*About* her," I clarified.

"Nothing. And why should she? For all she knew, we had simply stumbled upon some servants in the hallway. Not like I was about to offer an unsolicited explanation. How exactly would that have gone?" He waved his hand dramatically in the air before him. "*Ah, yes, dearest, here is the human on our staff who was my friend until she developed a hopeless attraction to me. But don't worry; she means nothing."*

I rubbed my hand over my mouth as my mind raced. Brennan was right. Calla had no reason to be wary or suspicious, and he had no reason to explain the situation. Exhaling heavily, I dropped onto the sofa beside my brother and leaned my head back, closing my eyes. Pinching the bridge of my nose, I asked the question I'd been dreading since he'd told me about the encounter.

"Do you think Lieke's going to be a problem?"

Silence answered me. It lasted so long that I lifted my head to ensure Brennan hadn't drifted off to sleep or slipped away from me without my knowing. But he was still there, staring into the dark fireplace. A muscle in his jaw twitched.

"Honestly, I don't know," he said quietly. "You should have seen the look in her eye when she saw us. I'd never wished I was invisible until that moment."

"It's understandable that she'd be sad."

Brennan swung his head around to peer at me. "Not sad, brother. She looked...hopeful."

I groaned. Why couldn't she just listen? Why couldn't she let him go?

I'd warned her repeatedly, even threatened to kick her out of the palace.

Why had she been upstairs near the banquet hall in the first place? Had she been looking for him? So many questions, and no good answers.

I shot Brennan a sidelong glance. "You didn't happen to give her reason to be hopeful, did you?"

He blinked at me slowly as his brow lowered, as if I had just suggested something totally preposterous. "How could I have? I was standing at the end of the hallway with Calla on my arm. We saw them, turned, and left. That's it."

Rubbing my fingers on my temples, I forced my breathing to slow. I needed to think, but there wasn't time. Guests would start to arrive within the hour, and if Lieke didn't adhere to the rules and stay hidden, I couldn't guarantee her safety. She might be a thorn in my side, but she was still a thorn under our protection.

Until you have to banish her from the palace.

If she tried to interfere and I didn't hold to my word to take her to the king, there would be no hope of her ever listening in the future. She'd never take me seriously if I gave her too many chances.

And I'd already given her plenty.

"What do you—" Brennan started to ask, but a knock at the door cut him off. He checked the clock above his fireplace. "It's not time yet, is it?"

"We still have a half hour or so, but if it's a message from the king, you'd best not leave the page waiting."

Brennan nodded, muttering, "Right, right," and dashed over to the door.

My nerves frayed when he opened it and stiffened. His heartbeat took off. His jaw tightened.

"You shouldn't be here, Lieke," he said.

I dropped my face into my hands, shaking my head as I growled in frustration.

CHAPTER THIRTY

Lieke

Brennan answered the door with his cravat hanging loose and untied over his unbuttoned and untucked shirt. He seemed relaxed, calm, and possibly even happy—until he recognized me and uttered those damned words.

You shouldn't be here.

How many times had he said those words to me? And yet I never listened. This was quite possibly one of the worst ideas I'd had in a long time, perhaps even worse than confronting Connor last week. For all I knew, Brennan wasn't alone in his room. What if the princess was here? Or the king?

"I know I shouldn't be," I said, "but I needed to see you. Can I come in?"

Shoving his hands into his pockets, he rocked back on his heels, but he didn't move to allow me to enter. "Why?"

"I'd rather not get caught standing outside your door, Brennan."

He shook his head. "Should have thought about that before you came."

Narrowing my eyes, I searched his face for any hint of the hope-lessness I had noticed downstairs. He had seemed so desperate to escape his circumstances, but now he was treating me as an annoyance. Had I imagined his dread before? Or was someone here, keeping him from speaking to me plainly?

"Who's with you, Brennan?" I asked.

His brow lowered slightly. "What does that matter?"

"Because this isn't you. You wouldn't treat me like this."

"Exactly how am I treating you?"

I scoffed. "Like I mean nothing to you."

His right eye twitched, but he kept his apathetic expression other-wise in place. "Maybe I..." He paused to look over his shoulder, behind the door, and I took the opportunity to slip past him into the room. "Shit," he muttered, turning around to catch me by the wrist, keeping me from getting too far inside.

"Let me go, Brennan," I hissed, trying to free my arm, but instead he tightened his grip.

"Shut the door," another voice said. I jerked my head up, and my stomach lurched into my throat at the sight of Connor leaning against the back of the sofa, his arms crossed in front of him.

I stumbled a little as Brennan, still holding my wrist, moved to do as his brother instructed.

"You can let her go, brother," Connor said. "She's not going to do anything."

Brennan's hand slipped away, and I stepped back tentatively. My heartbeat thundered in my ears.

Connor's lips lifted into an easy smile that didn't reach his eyes. "No need to be so scared, Lieke."

"Oh? So you're not going to try to choke me this time?" I asked with more attitude than was wise, but I couldn't stay my damned tongue. Brennan swung around to throw an accusing glare at Connor, who didn't seem at all perturbed by my question.

"I didn't try to choke you."

I pursed my lips and nodded slowly. "Oh yes. My apologies. Choking is merely an unfortunate byproduct of throwing someone against a wall by their throat."

"You did what?" Brennan's eyes went wide, and he took several quick steps toward his brother, but Connor lifted a hand to stop him, never diverting his focus from me.

"I apologize for my rash behavior the other day, Miss Berg." He seemed anything but sorry as he addressed me though. "I see my actions didn't deliver the message as intended. Or are you that desperate to be thrown out of this palace and out of our care?"

Not for the first time—and probably not for the last—I cursed my heart and this love that made me so stupid. I kept making the wrong decisions, kept stumbling about, kept hoping for something that wasn't mine to want.

Tears rose against my will, and I tried to push them back with a deep, steadying inhale as I turned to Brennan.

"Tell me one thing, Bren, and I'll leave you alone. I'll never bother you again."

"Tell you what?"

"Do you want to marry the princess?"

Brennan swallowed hard. Wetting his lips, he let his eyes flick down to my mouth briefly before raising them again to mine. "I do," he said.

"Well then, I apologize for my intrusion, Your Highness. Congratulations on your engagement." Nodding to him and his brother, I started for the door. But when my shoulder brushed his, I stopped and said, "I wish you both the best."

Neither prince said another word as I stepped out into the hallway and closed the door behind me. The tears pushed their way to the surface, lining my eyes and blurring my vision, but I refused to break down here. Not when they would be able to hear me no matter how quiet I tried to be.

I couldn't go back to my room and explain my tears to Millie though, so I let my feet carry me to the only place I had ever felt at ease in this palace.

＊

For hours I sat in the window seat where Brennan and I had played cards just a week ago. The whole time, I replayed the scene in my head—Brennan kissing me, the king storming in and dragging him away, me running to find Connor. That moment had changed everything, and it had tainted this room for me, stealing my safe haven in the process.

Yet I remained seated on the cushion, hugging my legs to my chest. I rested my chin on my knees as I watched—through quiet tears—the sun make its way toward the treetops. The faint clatter of hooves on the gravel driveway below pulled my attention toward the front of the house. From this window I didn't have a view of the palace entrance; I could only see the gardens and the patio of the grand ballroom.

The ballroom where Brennan's engagement would soon be announced before all the fae nobles—where Connor and the king would celebrate their success.

The knot in my stomach tightened, and I wiped away my tears with the back of my hand.

He didn't deserve my tears.

He didn't deserve my love.

He didn't deserve me.

Yet here I was, my heart still pining for the damned prince like an imbecile.

What if mates are real and Calla is his? Would I stand in the way of such a bond?

No, I wouldn't. The mating bond might be a mystery to me, but I didn't need to know how it worked to understand its significance. Mother had always called my father her soulmate. I'd thought it was a mere term of endearment, but I wasn't so sure anymore. What if someone else had loved my mother? What if he had tried to come between my parents, to steal her away from him?

Dejected, I dropped my forehead onto my knees. Brennan had said he wanted to marry Calla. No matter how sure I was he had lied, I owed it to him—and to myself—to take him at his word.

A growl rose from somewhere deep in my soul, filling the music room with my bitter frustration. Why did love have to make us so stupid?

My knees whined in protest from being in this position for so long. Sitting up, I moved to stretch out my legs but then stopped. The sun had fully set now, leaving the sky to the west illuminated with soft lilac and lavender hues.

I had stayed too long. Getting back to my room now would be even riskier with so many fae in the palace, but I couldn't stay here any longer either. Millie would happily report me to the king's guard for breaking the rules.

My hand reached under my skirts until I found the knife at my thigh. Gripping the smooth handle, I began to pull it free from its sheath but then hesitated. Being caught after curfew would be bad enough. If I were caught outside of my room with a weapon in hand…

Reluctantly I slid the knife back in place and smoothed my skirt, standing up. I could pull it out easily if needed. I only hoped I could do it fast enough.

Quietly, I tiptoed toward the door. Holding my breath, I inched it open and checked the hallway. Empty. I stepped out and shut the door silently behind me. The fastest way back to my room was down the main staircase, but that was obviously not an option right now. Instead, I turned left and moved further into the queen's wing toward the servants' stairs.

I'd only made it halfway down the hallway when panic sliced through my heart. Footsteps approached me from behind, slow and steady. I willed my feet to keep moving, pushing them faster.

"Where are you going, Goldie?" a male taunted me. *Griffin.* His voice—the voice that had haunted my dreams for years—shot a chill up my spine, and I froze. My instincts told me to keep moving, but I'd never be fast enough to outrun him unless I injured him first.

With my back to him, I slowly lifted my skirt, inching my hand toward the knife. My heart continued its thundering even as I wrapped my fingers around the handle and slid it free.

Within seconds, he was upon me, standing so close behind me that the heat of his body warmed my back. His breath snaked over my ear as he whispered, "Remember me?"

I didn't nod, didn't move, didn't breathe. My eyes closed as I envisioned my move, imagined my knife cutting across his chest. I didn't need to kill him—if that were even possible—I merely needed to wound him badly enough to give me a chance to get away.

"Your mutt isn't here to save you this time," he said.

"I don't need saving," I hissed. Spinning myself around, I aimed my blade at his ribs.

If I had surprised him at all, it didn't give me enough of an advantage over his innate speed. He glided to the side, and my knife met nothing but air. Raven had used that tactic enough in our sparring, though, that I was able to react to it instinctively, planting my right foot on the floor quickly and lunging for him again almost immediately.

This time, he flung himself backwards, out of my reach. A smirk pulled at his lips. Venom filled his eyes.

"Learned some new tricks, I see," he said, backing away from me and the knife I held up between us.

"Just a few," I said.

"Won't be enough against me, though, Goldie." He winked, and then he rushed me, moving so fast I had no hope of reacting in time. His arm slammed into mine, knocking the knife from my grasp. It hadn't even hit the floor when his fingers closed around my throat, crushing my airway. He lifted me off the ground and slammed me down hard on my back, never releasing my neck.

I kicked wildly and grabbed his wrist with both hands, trying desperately to get free, but it was hopeless. Panic spread through me, infecting my thoughts with doom and dismay, as he knelt on top of me, straddling my torso.

"If I'd known it was so easy to get you on your back..." he said, flashing me a wicked grin.

Raven's voice echoed from some faint memory.

Never give up, Lieke. Never stop trying.

Relaxing my arms, I let them fall to my sides. I squeezed my eyes shut and tried to focus on what I could do here.

Nothing.

I was too small, too weak, too…tired.

Never give up! I screamed at myself.

"Giving up already, Goldie?" Griffin asked, loosening his fingers slightly.

My eyes snapped open, and I shot him a deadly glare. "I never give up," I choked out, then slid my right arm up in a slow arc until my fingers found the wooden handle of my knife. It was just out of reach.

My other hand slammed into his wrist, and I pushed with all my strength to get him to release my throat. He laughed cruelly as I pressed into him, not realizing that with every push my other hand drew closer to my weapon.

He squeezed tighter, and the edges of my vision darkened.

With one last burst of energy, I thrust my left hand at his wrist once more, and he—in all his foolish confidence—swayed just enough for my right hand to snatch the knife and swing it up toward his ribs.

It was a shallow cut, but even still, his fingers released my throat to clutch his wound. His eyes widened, and his mouth fell open as he began to lean to his left. I took the opportunity to wriggle my way out from under him, scooting away until my back hit the far wall.

"What did you…" he started to ask, his breathing labored.

"I told you I never give up," I said, sneering at him.

"But how?" The fae swayed, trying to keep his balance. His dark eyes pierced mine, full of confusion and fear. "It's not possible."

The knife's magic.

Did it truly work this fast?

As if in answer to my question, blood spilled from Griffin's lips. His eyes glazed over before he fell backwards, hitting the floor hard. His chest rose with a slow breath and then stilled.

Pinned against the wall, I stared at the fallen fae in disbelief, not daring to move even as footsteps approached. I didn't see them turn the corner. I didn't hear them yelling at me. I didn't look away from the dead male until someone grabbed my arms and began dragging me away.

CHAPTER THIRTY-ONE

Connor

This night should have been a happy occasion. While I still needed to get my brother to the actual altar and ensure he made it through the vows, we had at least reached this pivotal point. The engagement was set. Instead of celebrating though, I spent the entire meal on edge, watching the doorways, scanning the faces of the servers, searching for any sign that Lieke hadn't truly given up and was going to do something stupid. Again.

I barely heard our father announce Brennan's impending nuptials, but I managed to lift my glass and smile when appropriate during the toasts. Brennan, seated to my left, didn't seem to notice my lack of focus, but Matthias leaned over from my right and whispered, "Are you going to tell me what's wrong, or do I need to guess?"

Waving a hand casually between us, I shook my head. "It's nothing."

"Nothing?" Matthias breathed a laugh. "So are you worried about your weight?"

I swung around to look at him. "What?"

He shrugged and pulled the corners of his mouth down as he pointed at the table. "You're not touching your dessert. Last I knew, Mrs. B's chocolate torte was your favorite. So either you're distracted by something serious, or you're trying to protect your girlish figure. Which is it?"

Exhaling slowly, I surveyed the ballroom and our guests once more before turning back to my friend.

"It's her," I whispered, and Matthias's eyes darted around the room. I smacked his arm with the back of my hand. "Not here, jackass. Not yet anyway."

"You really think she'd waltz into a crowd of fae? And with the king here?"

I roughed a hand over my mouth, shaking my head. "I don't know. Maybe. She came to Brennan's room earlier."

Matthias almost appeared impressed. "The girl's got balls; I'll give her that."

"Balls over brains, you could say."

Matthias laughed heartily. "Maybe she and Brennan are a better match than we thought."

I glared at him. "Quiet. That's not funny."

He shrugged again. "It kind of is. Admit it. You wanted to laugh. Just a little."

Rolling my eyes, I turned away from him and noticed the staff had begun clearing away the dessert plates.

"Seriously though," Matthias said, elbowing me in the arm, "if you're not going to eat that…"

With a sigh, I shoved the plate in his direction. He wasn't wrong about it being my favorite, but this sense of foreboding was twisting my stomach into a knotted mess.

"Better eat it fast though," I said. "Looks like the king is about to dismiss everyone to the terrace."

"Nothing like dancing and wine to help with digestion," Matthias said before greedily shoving a large bite into his mouth.

He hummed with satisfaction, and I rose from my seat, planting my hand on his shoulder. "I'm going to get some fresh air. Let me know if you spot her."

Matthias nodded as he forced another forkful into his mouth.

At least the torte wouldn't go to waste.

＊

Out on the terrace I meandered around the crowd, nodding and greeting our guests as my station required. All the while, I searched for any sign of Lieke's blonde hair or dark blue eyes. This proved quite the challenge, with everyone swarming around like bees in a hive.

I settled myself against one of the columns lining the space, bemoaning this irritating sense of duty that had me standing on the outskirts of the party watching for threats instead of enjoying myself. Was this what it meant to rule?

Always sacrificing.

Always watching.

Always serving.

Glancing over to where I'd last seen my father, I found him chatting with an older female—a widow, if I remembered correctly. He seemed genuinely happy, more so than he had in years. Perhaps ruling didn't have to be nothing but work. Then again, the king had his sons to help keep the peace and protect the people. He could afford to relax and enjoy himself now and then when he had me to deal with the nation's problems.

Movement to my right caught my attention, and I turned to find Matthias walking briskly toward me, his mouth set in a hard line.

"Is she here?" I asked once he got closer, but he was already shaking his head.

"No. Worse."

I pushed myself away from the column. "What could be worse—"

"Griffin."

A curse echoed through my mind. "What about him?"

Matthias's brows shot up. "He's gone. He wasn't too far from me when we came out here. I lost track of him for a second, only to catch sight of him going back inside. By the time I pushed my way through to follow, he was gone."

Griffin. In the palace.

Lieke.

"Shit."

"My thought exactly," Matthias said. "Think he's looking for some way to sabotage—"

"He's looking for her." I started to walk away, but my friend caught my arm and pulled me back.

"Her as in *her?*" he asked, his eyes widening. I nodded. "But why?"

Pulling my arm out of his grip, I nodded toward the doors. "I'll explain later. But we need to find him, before he finds her."

When I made to step toward the palace, Matthias stopped me again. I followed his line of sight until I spotted them. Two of my father's personal guards stalked through the crowd, heading for the king.

"I think he already found her," Matthias whispered.

"I hope you're wrong."

CHAPTER THIRTY-TWO

Lieke

My feet slipped on the stone floor as I scrambled to get them under me. The guards carried me through the hallways, their hands like vises on my upper arms. My shoulders screamed under the weight of my stumbling body.

"Slow down!" I pleaded as tears spilled down my cheeks. "Please, stop! Where are you taking me? I didn't mean to. It was an accident."

The guards didn't respond, didn't shout any orders to be quiet, didn't scoff at my claims. Their blank faces stared straight ahead as they marched down the stairs, dragging me and my useless feet with them. The steady tempo of their boots hitting the floor and my soft sobs echoed in the empty hallways.

I could have struggled more. Perhaps I should have.

But doing so would have been pointless.

Even if I had the strength to fight them off me—even if I still had my knives—injuring or killing the king's guards wouldn't help my case. I swallowed hard as we turned the corner. Two more guards stood in front of a pair of large, ornately carved doors that led to the great hall, where the king met with his subjects…and where he sentenced criminals.

The guards exchanged silent nods, and the doors opened.

The room was deathly silent despite the assembly of guests standing to my left. I quickly forgot about them when I noticed the three males waiting for me. King Durand, seated in a large chair atop a slightly raised dais, glared at me with disdain. On either side of him the princes stood. I couldn't meet their eyes, couldn't bear their scorn. Being brought before the king with a room full of fae nobles and merchants was already bad enough, but having to be humiliated in front of Brennan? And Connor?

My stomach lurched.

My head pounded.

My heart thundered.

My breathing quickened.

And then my knees struck the floor.

The guards threw me down roughly, and I fell forward, my hands smacking against the hard stone. A sharp wave of pain shot up my arms, drawing a hiss from between my teeth. I stared at the floor, surprised that my tears—which had flowed so freely earlier—had completely ceased, as if they were intimidated by the king as well.

"What happened?" the king said, his eerily calm voice ringing out.

I waited. No one answered.

Calloused hands gripped my arms again as someone pulled me up to face my king. I refused to lift my head, keeping my chin tucked into my chest and my eyes locked on the gray stones that dug into my knees.

"Look at me," the king commanded.

Shame held me captive, and I was unable to raise my face.

A guard fisted my hair and yanked my head back so hard I couldn't suppress my yelp. The tears still didn't come, even as I locked eyes with the king.

I refused to glance at Connor.

I couldn't look at Brennan.

"What did you do?" the king asked.

My arms shook as I searched for the words.

Just tell the truth. The truth will save you.

But would it?

"I…" My voice was weak and quiet compared to the king's booming tenor. I tried to swallow, but my mouth had gone completely dry, and my lips stuck together when I tried to continue. Panic seized my chest as I watched the anger simmering in the king's eyes.

"A fae noble is dead," he said. The crowd behind me became a sea of mutters and gasps. The king raised a hand high, and they quieted instantly. His gaze narrowed. "How did you kill him?"

"I…didn't mean to."

"That was not my question." He drew in a deep breath. "How?"

"I don't know. The knife…"

"Yes? What did you do to it to make it so lethal?"

"Nothing."

"TELL ME!" he screamed, and for a second I expected him to lunge out of his seat and strike me, but Connor dropped a hand onto his father's shoulder and whispered something into his ear.

The king looked up at his son and nodded once before settling back in the chair. He remained silent for a long time, steepling his fingers in front of his mouth as he studied me. What had Connor said to him? What was he contemplating? Did they even want to hear *why* I had killed him?

Finally, King Durand lowered his hands and tilted his head to the side, scrutinizing me like a falcon tracking its prey.

"You have broken the law and killed a fae. And a noble at that. Under other circumstances, I might have been able to show some leniency. But the fact is, none of this would have happened if you had any respect for this crown and its rules! Rules intended to keep you safe!"

"Please," I whispered before I could think better of it. He didn't seem to notice.

"What you did not only resulted in a preventable death, but also threatened the very peace and security the other humans here in the palace enjoy. I cannot have the other mortals viewing the rules as arbitrary, so I see no other option but to punish you to the full extent of the law."

Brennan's eyes flicked to his father briefly, but Connor only straightened.

"Miss Berg, you are hereby sentenced to death."

"No!" I screamed, but a guard kicked me in the back, cutting off my breath. I barely got my hands up fast enough to keep my face from smashing into the floor. As I lay there trembling, I sucked in air but found no relief for my aching lungs.

This was wrong. This was not okay. Human or not, noble or not, if I hadn't killed him, he would have killed me. Balling my hands into fists, I forced myself to sit back on my heels and face the king.

"It was self-defense, Your Majesty," I said as calmly and politely as I could. I needed him to understand. I needed him to fucking care. "He was going to kill me!"

The king flicked a finger in the air, and his guards pulled me up by my arms. "Take her to the dungeon until her execution at dawn."

This couldn't be happening. In desperation, I finally turned my attention to Brennan, my supposed friend, this prince my stupid heart had chosen to fall for. "Brennan! Please! Do something!"

He didn't move except to drop his eyes to the floor. The fucking coward. I didn't need him to love me. I wasn't asking him to marry me. But stars, I expected him to at least act like my friend.

"You coward!" I screamed at him as the guards began to drag me backwards toward the door. The least they could have done was turn me around so I didn't have to watch Brennan betray me like this. I closed my eyes tight, shaking my head, not wanting to witness how little he cared for me. Soon we'd be through the doors, and he'd be free of me. They all would.

"Stop!" a male voice said, piercing the heavy silence.

My eyes flashed open.

There the prince stood, his arm raised in front of him, his golden-brown eyes staring straight into my heart.

Connor.

CHAPTER THIRTY-THREE

Connor

Stars, I was going to regret this.

My father pushed himself out of his chair and rounded on me. "What do you mean *stop*?"

"You can't kill her," I insisted.

He jutted his chin out, his eyes blazing with indignation. "And why not?"

Over the king's shoulder, a pair of dark blue eyes watched me with awed suspicion, but I forced myself to meet my father's stare. I set my jaw.

And my mind went blank.

I should have probably thought of a reason before shouting, but all I was sure of was that she couldn't die. Not like this anyway. Not over the death of a fae who fucking deserved it. But that reasoning wouldn't work. I needed something else.

I scrambled for words. Giving any response at this point would be better than just standing here. I looked to my brother, who was shaking his head at me, as if he knew what I planned to say. I couldn't use him though. He'd just proven to everyone in this room that he didn't care about her—at least not enough to save her life.

But what would change my father's mind?

The king's brow shot up in a silent question.

If I was going to persuade him to alter her sentence, I'd need to better understand his reasoning. While he'd claimed it was because of the precedent this could set for our other human staff, there had to be more to it.

The crowd at the far end of the great hall began to murmur and whisper again as I remained silent.

The crowd. Of course.

My mind raced through the memories of every public gathering I'd witnessed over the last few months. The people were all angry and afraid. Each attack stoked their ire against the humans a bit more. My father couldn't be lenient with a human in front of them.

Not without a good reason.

I froze as a thought struck me. He couldn't argue with this, not when it could mean fixing everything—stopping the attacks, calming the unrest, and protecting the alliance with Arenysen.

I wanted to sink into the floor or maybe request a private council with the king, but there was no whispering these words. For this to work, I needed everyone in the room to hear.

My gaze shifted to the woman being held by the door. She wasn't going to like this. Stars, no one was going to like it, but at least she'd be alive.

Drawing in a deep breath, I looked at my father and said, "She's my fiancée."

CHAPTER THIRTY-FOUR

Lieke

I opened my eyes to a darkness so deep I couldn't see anything.

Everything hurt, so I couldn't be dead. My head throbbed. My knees and hands ached.

The more I tried to recall what had happened, the stronger the thumping against my temples became. Everything remained fuzzy and confusing.

Well, not everything.

Griffin was dead.

I had been found.

They had taken me before the king.

He had sentenced me to death.

But then…

I jolted up but clamped my hands around my head when the movement delivered a burst of pain.

What had happened?

It couldn't have…

He wouldn't have…

Slowly I lowered one hand until it rested beside my leg. I was not sitting on the cold, hard floor of the dungeon as I'd expected, but on something soft, plush, luxurious.

No. No. No.

Where was I?

What had he done?

As my mind whirred, I blinked rapidly but still couldn't see anything. How was it so damn dark in here? Turning my head, I searched for any light—from under a door or between some curtains or something—but there was only blackness. I scrambled backwards, then winced as my knees protested. When my back hit a wall of pillows, I released a less than attractive whimper.

Then the scratch of a match being lit pulled my attention to my right, where someone sat lighting a lantern. I didn't see his face until the light was adjusted and the entire room was illuminated.

Connor.

Slowly, he turned to me, and the flame reflected in his eyes—eyes that roved over me. Fumbling, I clutched the blankets at my waist and dragged them up to my neck to cover myself.

"How's your head?" he asked as he rose and walked across the room. He proceeded to start a fire in the large grate opposite my bed, and confusion swept over me. The fire caught quickly and was soon blazing, granting me my first view of my surroundings.

The room was larger than the one I shared with Millie. Stars, the bed itself was nearly the size of that room. No decorations adorned the walls except for a gilded mirror above the mantel. The lantern Connor had lit sat on a low table beside a chaise lounge, and to my left, beside curtained windows, sat an elegant desk and chair.

"You can still speak, yes?"

Connor's question startled me. He was sitting once again on the end of the chaise, his elbows resting on his knees. I blinked at him, still not quite convinced this was real. But even if it was a dream, Connor wasn't likely to accept silence. Talking was the best way to get him out of my hair as quickly as possible.

"It hurts," I said curtly, pursing my lips.

"Understandably," he said with a faint tilt to his lips. "You hit your head pretty hard."

That drew a frown from me. Yes, I must have hit my head. Maybe I'd imagined the whole thing. Maybe all of it was just a dream—the encounter with Griffin, the sentencing, the...announcement.

Yes, it must have been the result of a head injury.

But some small part of me still wondered, pushing me to ask, "What happened exactly?"

"Well," he said, lifting his eyes to the ceiling, "you collapsed and smacked your head on the floor."

I reached a hand up to the back of my head and pressed lightly against the tender spot. At least there didn't seem to be any blood. That would have been embarrassing.

"But why did I faint?" I asked, and his expression turned into one I'd never seen on him before, like a mix of amusement and concern, as if he wasn't sure whether to laugh at me or worry about me.

"You don't remember?" he asked.

Was that hurt in his eyes? Had my poor memory offended him in some way?

"No," I lied, not wanting to share my ridiculous dream with him.

Tapping a finger against his lips, he watched me with such intensity I had to look away.

He let out a loud exhale. "Well, Lieke, I announced our engagement, and in the excitement of it all, you lost consciousness. Not a particularly flattering reaction, by the way."

I forgot how to breathe.

It was true?

It hadn't been a dream?

"But why?"

I didn't realize I'd asked the question aloud until he was answering me.

"It was the only way to save you," he said, dropping his chin toward his chest and hiding his eyes from me.

To save me?

Why did he even *want* to save me?

I had done nothing but irritate him and cause him problems, and now he wanted to *marry* me?

Shaking my head, I stared straight ahead as I worked through this new reality—assuming I wasn't dreaming right now. So, I was to just marry him? Connor. The prince who loathed me. The more I thought about it, the angrier I became.

I wasn't allowed to marry the prince I loved—not that I had much love for him at the moment—but I would be forced to marry the prince who hated me.

Hated you enough to save your life. Twice.

My thoughts needed to shut up.

Who did this prince think he was, making such decisions for me?

Clenching my teeth, I scowled at him, dropped my hands into my lap, and shrugged.

"So that's it then. I'm just to marry you? With no say in the matter?"

A shadow of irritation passed over his features, but then his lips appeared to be fighting a smirk. He rose to his feet, shoved his hands into his pockets, and walked slowly toward the bed.

Towering over me, he flashed me an innocent smile before mimicking my earlier shrug. "Oh, you can have a say in the matter." His features melted into a wounded expression that I was certain couldn't be genuine. "I'd like to think that marrying me holds some appeal over the alternative."

"Which is?"

"Death?" He posed it as a question, as if I had truly forgotten the punishment he'd saved me from.

"Right," I muttered. I chewed on the inside of my lip while I contemplated this predicament. Finally I peered up at him again. "I still don't understand *why.*"

Groaning, Connor looked away. His chest rose as he took a breath, but he didn't turn back to me when he answered quietly, "I couldn't let you die."

"Why? Do you have some sort of savior complex?"

I was being unfair. I should be grateful he'd saved me, but I couldn't shake this anger over having my life—and now my death—controlled by everyone else but me.

He dropped his head and rubbed his fingers over his forehead as he answered with a single word. "Perhaps."

For a long moment, neither of us moved or spoke. I couldn't even tell if he was breathing.

Was I really going to have to marry him?

Was I really going to be *queen*?

Connor turned and sat on the edge of the bed, facing me. He remained impassive, enigmatic even, when he finally spoke again.

"If you're worried about marrying me, don't be. We won't actually get married. This is just a temporary solution."

I eyed him nervously. "So you're just going to kill me then?"

He gave a single breath of a laugh and shook his head. "I didn't save you just to kill you later. I'll think of something when the time comes."

"And when will that be?" I asked with some apprehension, though I was starting to breathe a little easier knowing I wasn't truly being forced into a lifelong commitment.

"Just until after Brennan and Calla are married in the spring."

I flinched as if he'd actually pricked my heart with his answer.

"Of course," I whispered. Tears began to gather along my eyelids, and I swiped at them angrily. I didn't want to cry over Brennan. Not ever again. Not after he had abandoned me in that room.

"I really am sorry," Connor said. "If I could have found another way, I would have chosen it."

At that, I laughed, though it came out hollow and humorless. "This must be dreadful for you. I can't imagine that getting engaged to one of your staff was high on your list of dreams. Temporary or not."

"Wasn't on my list at all, in fact," he said, half-smiling.

"So what now?"

"For now, get some more rest. You still have a couple of hours until dawn. Your attendant will be in later to get you bathed and dressed."

He rose and shoved a hand into his pocket. My eyes widened when he pulled out a small box, opened it, and set it on the table beside the lamp. Inside was a simple, delicate ring of interwoven golden vines with blue sapphires nestled among them.

"This is for you," he said. "A token of our betrothal. Put it on when you're ready. We'll discuss it more over breakfast."

He'd already made it to the door before I managed to ask, "Where do I meet you?"

Looking back over his shoulder, he replied in an almost sad voice, "I'll come for you."

CHAPTER THIRTY-FIVE

Connor

I closed her door behind me and slumped back against it, closing my eyes.

What was I thinking? What was I doing?

It's only temporary.

That reminder didn't stop my pulse from racing though.

Lieke had taken the news better than I'd anticipated—not even a single yell—though for a moment there she'd had me worried. The woman had honestly seemed ready to choose death over pretending to be my betrothed. That shouldn't have stung, but I didn't know many males whose egos would survive such rejection unscathed.

Pushing away from her door, I strode across the hallway and stepped into my own rooms. I kicked off my boots and started to unbuckle my belt, desperate for at least a few hours of sleep before I had to tackle the first real day of this charade. First, though, I'd need to get rid of my brother.

"Brennan," I said. "Let's get this over with. It's been a long fucking day, and I'm tired."

Silence greeted me, and for a moment I wondered if I'd been wrong when I caught his scent in here.

I angled an ear up and listened.

There it was. A heartbeat. Faint, but clear enough.

Walking around the corner into my bedroom, I found him lounging on my bed with his arms crossed behind his head and his legs stretched out in front of him. I waited for his typical greeting, but he said nothing.

"Brother," I said with a dip of my chin as I moved toward the wardrobe and opened it. Hanging up my jacket, I spoke around the door. "What's so urgent you couldn't tell me in the morning?"

He swung his legs off the bed and sat up, but he didn't look at me.

"She hates me, doesn't she?"

Well, that wasn't what I'd expected him to say. Clicking the wardrobe door shut, I pulled my shirt up over my head and tossed it into the clothes bin in the corner.

"I don't know." I shrugged and crossed my arms, leaning back against the wall. "She didn't mention you actually."

"I fucked up," he muttered.

"Well, you certainly didn't help her any. Or your friendship. But it's better this way."

Brennan shot me a look of jealous suspicion. "Did you plan this?"

I couldn't stop my eyes from rolling. I exhaled loudly. "Yes, brother. I hoped Lieke would leave your rooms, kill a fae, and then get sentenced to death all so I could con her into being my wife."

The moron seemed to ponder the ridiculous statement as if it might actually be true. What had Lieke ever seen in my brother?

"So you weren't actually engaged," he said, and I bit back a laugh. Apparently my worry that the secret betrothal would be too far-fetched for anyone to believe had been unwarranted.

Muttering, "No," I walked into the washroom, determined not to let Brennan's idiocy delay my sleep any longer. He didn't say anything as I washed my face and cleaned my teeth. He was still sitting on the edge of my bed when I stepped back into the room.

"So are you bunking with me tonight?" I asked. "Because I'm going to bed."

He stood slowly but didn't move out of my way. Then he took a step closer to me and jabbed a finger into my chest. Was he seriously about to threaten me?

"If you hurt her…" he growled, and this time I did laugh at him.

"You mean more than you already have tonight? I'll try not to." Pushing his arm out of the way, I stepped past him and pulled the blankets back. When he didn't say anything more and didn't show any signs of leaving, I groaned. "Go away, brother. I'm tired. You can threaten me again some other time."

I climbed into bed as soon as he started walking away and was asleep before I heard the door shut behind him.

✳

The morning came too quickly, but at least I'd had a dreamless sleep. I woke up feeling more rested than I'd expected to. Still, I would have rather stayed in bed for the entire day than face the damned mess I'd created for myself yesterday, but avoiding problems only made them worse.

Forcing myself to leave the comfort of my bed, I quickly dressed—grabbing a fresh shirt and pants from the wardrobe—and made sure I looked somewhat princely before I had to fetch my fiancée. I mentally groaned. The word felt wrong, misplaced. But it was my reality now, whether I liked it or not.

Pulling the door open, I found Matthias standing there, his hand poised to knock.

"Oh good, you're up," he said with an obnoxious grin. Last night I'd managed to steer clear of him and his inevitable ridicule, but there was no avoiding him now as he pushed past me and settled himself into one of the chairs beside the hearth.

"Come on in," I said dryly, giving Lieke's door a quick glance before closing my own. I didn't bother to sit. Matthias simply kept grinning.

"Did you come here just to smile at me? Or did you have something to say?"

He answered with a slow shake of his head, that irksome smile still planted on his face.

"Seriously. I have places to be," I said.

"Right, right. Of course. Your bride awaits," he said, waggling his eyebrows.

I cringed.

"I mean," Matthias continued, relaxing deeper into the chair, "I am glad you finally listened to me about needing to find yourself a female, but I didn't think you'd choose that one. And I didn't expect you to hide it from me."

At that, I deflated. I could try to lie to him, but what was the point? He couldn't possibly believe the engagement was real. It was obviously a ruse. Slowly I walked over and dropped into the chair opposite him.

"Makes two of us," I said wearily, letting my head fall against the high back of the chair.

Matthias's brow lowered. "So it's not true."

I straightened in my seat, leaning forward to peer at him incredulously. "You thought it was?"

He shrugged. "You were rather convincing."

"And Lieke's protests before she blacked out didn't seem suspicious?" I laughed at the absurdity of all of it.

Nodding, Matthias's grin turned upside down. "I admit, that did seem odd, but then, she's a human. They're odd creatures. I thought perhaps she was just surprised to have you announce it so suddenly and publicly."

"I can't believe you actually—"

Matthias cleared his throat. "I'm glad to know it's fake though. Kind of hurt my feelings to think you'd keep something this big from me."

"Kind of hurts *my* feelings that you think I would," I said. "But no. I didn't plan it. I panicked."

"Why not just let her…" He seemed to answer his own question, because he started nodding, a silent "*Oh*" on his lips. "You couldn't let her die, could you?"

"Makes no sense, I know." I dropped my head into my hands and ran my fingers through my hair.

Matthias laughed. "Makes perfect sense actually. She's really got you all tied up in knots, hasn't she?"

"She's definitely got me frustrated and irritated, if that's what you mean."

"So irritated you opted to get engaged to her," he said, barely containing his laughter.

I pressed my fingers into my temples to try to relieve the headache that was quickly forming. All I wanted was to go back to bed, to feign illness and hide, emerging only when Brennan was safely married to Calla and we could give up this ridiculous ruse.

As if he could read my thoughts, Matthias took on a sympathetic air as he said, "There's no hiding from this now, Your Highness."

He only called me that when he needed to remind me of who I was and what I needed to do. It was why I'd insisted he be my second during the war. He'd been my friend for ages before that, but he also knew me well enough to recognize those moments when I needed a general more than a friend.

Matthias continued. "On the plus side, though, this is quite the opportunity."

Nodding, I dropped my hands and looked at him. "I know. A human queen would be—"

"No, no. Not that," he said, his expression pinching in confusion. "You never talked to her, did you? About what she did the whole time she was hiding out with her family? Maybe this is your chance to get that information from her. See what she knows. This could be our best opportunity to locate the rebels and put an end to their attacks."

"I know," I groaned, lifting my head to rest my chin in my hand. "But what if she doesn't cooperate? I don't even know if I can get her to go along with this engagement story."

"Then you make her."

"Because I've done a bang-up job of getting her in line before this."

I lifted a brow at him, hoping some of that strategic genius of his might kick in and help me.

"Ah, but that was before her life was threatened, right?"

A pathetic laugh fell out of my mouth as I remembered how she'd reacted last night. "Honestly? I don't know if that's reason enough for her."

"You could always try wooing her. I mean, she fell in love with one Durand already. Who's to say she can't fall for you too? Maybe it's time to be more like your brother."

"You mean the jackass who cared so much about her he was going to let her get dragged off to the gallows?"

"Well, maybe not *that* side of your brother, but you know what I mean." Exhaling loudly, he rose from his seat and tossed his head toward the door. "Now, I believe you have a woman to seduce. Come find me later though. We have a lot to discuss."

He followed me out into the hallway and nearly burst out laughing when I stopped at the room across from mine and raised my hand to knock. I could have had her moved into any number of guest rooms in the palace, but I'd chosen the one closest to mine for good reason. Not that Matthias would listen if I tried to explain it.

Stars, he was nearly as insufferable as the woman.

I glared at him, and he lifted his hands in surrender, backing away. Once he was around the corner and I was sure he was truly gone, I knocked on the door, hoping Lieke would be willing to play along as I needed her to.

CHAPTER THIRTY-SIX

Lieke

The curtains rustled loudly as they were thrown open, and sunlight blazed in, disturbing my fitful, uneasy rest. Pulling a pillow over my face, I rolled away from the window. What little sleep I'd managed to get had been haunted by images from the night before, forcing me to relive the king's harshness, Brennan's blatant dismissal of me, and Connor's decision to force me into this preposterous falsehood.

How could anyone believe it was true? Him? Me? They had to be stupider than I thought.

"Miss," someone said softly. It was a gentle, feminine voice I didn't recognize. Slowly I turned over and peeked out from under the pillow. A woman leaned down and peered at me with a kind smile. "His Highness is expecting you soon, and I'm to get you ready."

Of course. We all had to do his bidding, didn't we?

Leave it alone, Lieke.

Stay out of it.

Remain in your room.

Have breakfast with me.

Pretend to be my bride.

Groaning, I threw the pillow off me and sat up to find the girl was actually a fae, her pointed ears peeking out from waves of dark brown hair that complemented her olive complexion perfectly. I must have looked as awful as I felt, because she seemed to be trying hard not to giggle at me. At least Connor hadn't assigned Lola or her sister to attend to me. That would have added to my already unbearable humiliation.

"I'm Gretchen," she said, dipping her chin before flitting across the room to a small wardrobe I hadn't noticed last night—Mother's wardrobe. "I used to tend to the queen, you know. But since she passed, I've been assigned to look after any guests who visit the palace."

She busied herself with pulling my mother's old clothes out of the wardrobe, examining the items one by one, only to put them back with a wrinkle of her nose. I was about to defend the garments when she finally stopped and whispered, "Aha!" and whipped around with a simple blue dress in hand. "This one. This one for sure," she said.

Gretchen ushered me out of bed, and I sluggishly obliged. She pointed me to a large folding screen in the corner beside the fireplace.

"There's a fresh bath prepared for you just behind there. Do you need help?"

I shook my head but couldn't find any words. As I plodded across the room, I glanced around, realizing it was much larger than I'd thought last night. Passing the wardrobe and chest of drawers, I noticed a door leading to a parlor that seemed similar to Brennan's front room. Had they really put me in the royal wing? Or was this just another guest room?

I stepped behind the screen where a claw-footed porcelain tub had been set up. We didn't have anything so fancy in the staff privy. Just a metal basin that we had to fill with water heated in the kitchen.

Gretchen called from the bedroom, "Is the temperature all right, miss? Sometimes it is hard to get just right."

I dipped a hand into the steaming water. "It's perfect. Thank you."

As I undressed and slipped into the bath, I released a long sigh and listened to Gretchen's pleasant prattling.

"I heard you suffered quite a nasty fall last night. Some of the staff thought it must have been embarrassing for you to faint in front of all those guests, but if the prince had just announced to the world that he was engaged to me, I'd probably collapse from shock too."

I cringed at the thought of what everyone must have thought of me. How embarrassing indeed. She continued to chatter as I worked the rich vanilla-and-rose-scented soap over my skin and hair, but I couldn't be bothered to listen to any of her words. My thoughts instead drifted to the wild, unexpected events of last night. I still couldn't quite fathom how any of this was real.

Before I knew it, Gretchen was handing me a fresh towel from behind the screen.

"He'll be here any moment, Miss Berg," she said.

Taking it, I thanked her and stepped out of the bath. I peered down at the water and asked, "How do you drain it?"

A giggle tickled the air. "Oh, don't worry about that. I'll take care of it. You just get dressed."

Wrapping the towel tightly around me, I did as directed, nodding to her as I passed by. As I walked across the room, I heard wood scraping and turned to find her sliding the screen closed. When she snapped her fingers and the tub vanished, water and all, I nearly ran into the foot of the bed.

"What?!?" I breathed.

Gretchen peered over her shoulder and shrugged as if this was as normal as baking bread or picking flowers.

"Get dressed," she said, pointing at the blue garment lying on the freshly made bed. "I'll be back later today, but if you need anything before then, just let me know."

She was out of the room before I could ask how I should contact her. For all I knew, she could hear me from anywhere in the palace. That thought made me freeze, and I suddenly remembered all the childish, improper, and untoward things I'd uttered within these walls. I certainly hoped that wasn't part of her fae abilities.

*

Whether it was fae magic or just a lucky coincidence, I didn't know, but the blue dress Gretchen had selected fit me nearly perfectly. It was a little big in the bust, but not so much that I would be risking an embarrassing wardrobe mishap. Having a breast spill out in front of Connor might prove to be more humiliating than anything else I'd endured up to this point.

The ring stared at me from the small table by the bed. Did I dare leave it there and risk his wrath?

He did say to put it on when I'm ready.

That could be never though.

Gingerly I picked up the box and turned it this way and that, watching how the sapphires caught the sunlight. It truly was beautiful. I slipped it from its resting spot and set the box back down on the table. What was the likelihood it would even fit?

If it didn't fit, I could at least use that as an excuse not to wear it.

Until he gets it resized, that is.

But when I slipped it onto my finger, it settled into place as if it had been made for me. Absurd. It was obviously an extra piece from the royal treasury that just happened to be my size.

Flexing my fingers, I tried to ignore the new accessory as I walked into the front room to study my new living area. A small dining table with four matching chairs, upholstered in a lovely rose-gold velvet, sat off to the left. On the opposite side of the room, a chaise and a small sofa were placed in front of a fireplace, framed by bookcases that were sadly empty. Not that I felt much like reading. It would have been nice to have something to peruse while I waited though.

No sooner had I lowered myself onto the chaise than a knock at the door pushed me back onto my feet. Smoothing the knee-length skirt of my dress down, I rushed for the door and stopped. My heart thumped wildly, and I tried to draw in a breath to settle it, but it refused.

It's just Connor.

Yes, my fiancé. I gritted my teeth. I could do this. If it meant living, I could do this. It was only temporary, as he'd said.

Another knock startled me, and I shook my head at his impatience. Pulling the door open, I donned a scowl, or tried to. Connor wore a simple dark gray, button-down shirt tucked into perfectly tailored black trousers. I'd never seen him dressed so casually, and the crooked grin plastered on his face sent my heart fluttering against my will.

"Can I come in?" he asked, flicking his eyes to the room behind me.

I tried to get my bearings by pulling in another breath, but all it did was bring a fresh wave of his cologne toward me, that same stars-be-damned sexy smell that he'd left on my clothes that day in the—

"Thank you," he said as he stepped past me.

I whirled on him, irritation pulling my brow tight. "I don't remember inviting you in," I said, placing my hands on my hips.

He eyed me over his shoulder and shrugged. "The look on your face just now seemed invitation enough."

CHAPTER THIRTY-SEVEN

Connor

Lieke slammed the door closed, and a smile tried to weasel its way onto my lips as I turned away from her. I fought it back though. Why did she have to look so cute when she was irritated?

She darted around me and pressed a hand to my chest, as if that could physically stop me from moving further into her room. Still, I humored her and stopped, stepping back and struggling to ignore the unwelcome warming in my core. Watching her blue eyes lock onto mine in challenge made that nearly impossible.

She glared up at me. "You cannot just—"

I raised my brow but said nothing. Surely she realized who I was, whose house we were standing in, and what I had just done for her. She didn't back down though, and the fire in her eyes continued to blaze.

"I cannot just what?" I finally asked when she still hadn't finished her sentence. She blinked a few times, as if my question had broken her out of some reverie. "Where did you get lost just then, Lieke?"

At that, she set her jaw, and her eye twitched slightly. "What? No stupid nickname anymore?"

"I didn't think it was befitting of our new relationship." I shrugged. "But if you really want one…"

Pursing her lips, she studied me for a moment and then huffed out a breath. "Only if you can do better than *blondie*. It was a bit basic; I'd expect better from *Your Highness*."

She used my title with far less reverence than Matthias did. Casually I sauntered away from her and settled myself into the armchair in her sitting room. Lieke remained standing stiffly, though she'd turned to follow me with her eyes.

I let my gaze rove over her as if I were contemplating a new nickname for her, but I was actually attempting to determine what steps we needed to take to sell this farce.

"Shall I spin for you?" she asked in a mocking tone.

"If you'd like," I said.

"Oh, well, at least I have a say in something." She lowered herself into a curtsy before rotating slowly in place.

Stars, this woman.

I released a sigh and forced my face to relax.

Apathy would be better than bitterness if I was to convince her to play her part. Getting her to feign affection for me seemed nearly impossible at the moment, but we could at least work on her appearance while I figured out how to win her over—even if only artificially. The dress didn't quite fit her, but it would suffice on such short notice. I made a mental note to send the tailor to her after breakfast.

Indignantly, she crossed her arms in front of her, and for the first time since I'd entered, I noticed my mother's ring on her hand. It seemed to fit her perfectly, and I wasn't entirely sure how I felt about that.

"I thought you were taking me to breakfast," she said.

"Not exactly." Before she could protest, I stood and gestured to the dining table in her room. "You're not quite ready to be presented—"

"Presented," she repeated, her nose wrinkling in distaste. "Like a prize cow?"

"Something like that. Though I do appreciate you wearing the ring."

Surprisingly, she ignored that comment—as if she didn't want to even acknowledge the jewelry at all—and asked, "So I'm to be confined in here then?"

I stepped toward her, invading her space. Her sweet scent—combined now with the aroma of vanilla and roses—teased my senses, and I struggled not to pull away from it. If I was to pull this off, I'd need to at the very least be able to stand close to her.

Woo her. Matthias's words smacked me upside the head.

She didn't need to fake any attraction to sell our engagement, but it certainly would make it easier. Maybe I could just ask her to pretend to like me, but given her propensity for stubborn defiance, winning her attraction for real might prove easier.

Stars, this was humiliating.

Awkwardly I dropped my gaze to her lips before finding her eyes again. At least we didn't have an audience. Yet. Matthias would no doubt be guffawing like an idiot if he were here now witnessing my piss-poor acting.

Lieke stiffened slightly but lifted her breasts higher so I was forced to notice them. I swallowed hard, willing my body not to react. Clearing my throat, I leaned forward slightly and whispered, "Are these rooms not adequate for my bride?"

Her glare sharpened. "They're fine."

"Good," I said, straightening.

"For now," she mumbled and seated herself at the table, crossing one leg daintily over the other and smoothing her dress over her lap. "So where is this—"

A knock at the door echoed through the room.

"My bride is so impatient," I teased.

"Only when I'm being held hostage." She shot me a haughty look much like the one she'd given me in the guest room last week, and my nerves pulled tight, igniting the anger I had hoped would stay dormant at least for the morning. I was trying—trying so hard—to remain civil and kind, and yes, to coax some hint of affection out of her, but she was apparently intent on irking me.

Another knock came at the door, and Lieke opened her mouth, presumably to invite the visitor in. I dropped my hands to the table and leaned in close, so close that her racing heartbeat thundered in my ears.

"Lieke, you are no hostage here." Her mouth opened, but I snatched up her jaw in my hand, startling her and cutting off any potential protest. My anger grumbled low in my chest, begging to be unleashed, to show her how life as a hostage would actually be, but I couldn't let it take over. Not now.

Still, she needed to understand. I was not her enemy.

But my rage pushed my voice into a growl. "You are free to go. I won't stop you. But without me, the gallows are all that await you."

Her blue eyes hardened, and for a moment I worried she might truly hate me so much she would choose death. She remained silent, though, even as she yanked her head out of my grasp.

As I walked to the door, I took a steadying breath, trying to calm my temper. I opened the door to find one of the staff waiting in the hallway, holding a large, covered tray. She dipped her chin to me, and I ushered her inside. Lieke seemed to flinch as the female carried in the food, but I brushed it off as I turned to leave.

"Are you not staying?" Lieke asked me, sounding almost nervous, but I didn't care. Not when she insisted on being so ungrateful.

"I'll be back later," I called over my shoulder and shut the door behind me.

*

Matthias eyed me curiously as I dropped into the chair in front of his desk. "You're here earlier than I expected," he said.

"Don't ask," I grumbled. "What did you want to talk about?"

He studied me for a bit before his expression twisted with concern. "Sure you don't need to talk about her?"

I scowled but said nothing.

Laughing quietly, he shook his head. "Fine. Unfortunately, though, what I *need* to discuss involves her."

"Of course it does," I said flatly, then raised my brow in a silent invitation to proceed.

Matthias leaned forward and slowly unwrapped a cloth-covered bundle on his desk I hadn't noticed until now. Inside lay two identical knives, simple in their design yet beautiful, with delicate carvings in the wooden handles.

"Are these hers?" I asked.

Matthias nodded once, but when I reached out to touch one of the weapons, he reached across to stop me. "Don't touch them. Unless you have a death wish." He cocked his head. "She hasn't irritated you to that point yet, I hope."

Ignoring his comment, I asked, "They're that lethal?"

He nodded again. "Guards claim they heard the fight and came running. They rounded the corner just as Griffin fell backwards. He was dead before they made it to his body."

I gawked at my friend and then down at the knives. "What are they made of?"

Matthias lifted his hands, palms toward the ceiling. "Steel and wood. That's it."

"Magic? Are they enchanted somehow? What do the healers think?"

Clearing his throat, he clasped his hands and rested them on the desk. "A poison of some sort. But not the kind that can merely be wiped off the blades. They believe it's embedded into the steel."

"Poison? Do we think it's connected to the rebel attacks?" Another nod. I swallowed hard. "And do we think Lieke is one of them?"

"The evidence is rather damning, don't you think?" he asked. While logically, he was right, something in my gut told me she couldn't be involved with them. "We'd be fools not to at least consider the possibility. We don't really know who she was with for those three years. While she might not be a rebel herself, she could very well be the best chance we have of finding them. The healers are still looking for the poison's origin. Once we have that, we'll have a better idea of who is truly behind the killings."

Biting the inside of my cheek, I tried to organize my thoughts. We now had some answers, but there were still so many questions remaining. If anyone found out Lieke had even the slightest connection to the attacks, it would prove disastrous.

"Who knows about this?" I asked finally.

"Just us and the healers, and you know how tight-lipped they are."

"Good," I said. "Let's keep it that way. Have them continue working on identifying it, and in the meantime, I'll see what I can glean from her."

CHAPTER THIRTY-EIGHT

Lieke

I clasped my hands in my lap to try to stop their trembling, or at least hide them from Lola, who eyed me contemptuously from the side as she set the breakfast tray on the table. Why did it have to be her? Why couldn't it be Marin or even Mrs. Bishop herself?

But they had no reason to know Lola was the last fae I wanted delivering my meals, especially when I was here by myself. I'd have to ask Connor to arrange for someone else to bring my meals in the future, but after the way he'd stormed out, I wasn't sure he would care, let alone listen to my request.

"Trouble in paradise?" Lola asked in an overly sweet voice.

I couldn't answer. I couldn't even look at her.

She lifted the lid off the tray, revealing poached eggs, fried pork belly, fresh bread with butter, a handful of ripe strawberries, and a lidded mug of what I hoped was coffee.

Lola placed the lid on one of the other chairs and then stood there, staring at me.

This was ridiculous. I was betrothed to her prince. I was to be Queen of Emeryn—at least as far as she knew. Why was I kowtowing to a servant?

I forced my chin up and reluctantly made eye contact with her, hoping I was painting an adequately dismissive expression on my face so she wouldn't be able to detect my discomfort.

Averting her eyes, she started to survey the room as she pulled a chain out from beneath her collar and began rolling the blue stone pendant between her thumb and fingers. Mother's necklace. I jolted forward, and her eyes flicked to mine, stopping me from completely lunging for her. Sneering, she gave me a once-over and tilted her head.

"I don't know how you did it, Lieke. And I don't really care. But I'd rather die than have you as my queen."

The words struck home, stinging me, reminding me of my lesser status—my worthlessness. I didn't belong here in this room, and yet...I *was* here. The prince had saved me, had announced to the country that we were to wed, and as angry as I was at being forced down a path I didn't want to take, the fact remained: I was his fiancée, whether Lola accepted it or not.

Pulling in a breath, I reached for the mug and removed its lid. The sharp aroma of coffee hit my nose as I lifted it to my lips. I closed my eyes and took a small sip, hiding my wince when it singed the tip of my tongue. Watching the fae coldly, I lowered the mug to my lap. "If you'd rather die, Lola, that can be arranged."

*

I spent the rest of the morning pacing my rooms and staring out the windows. Then the palace tailor came in and measured me in more ways than I thought possible. He was an older fae, nice enough, and he was thankfully no fan of idle chitchat, so he went about his work in comfortable silence.

I had just lain back on the chaise and closed my eyes for a nap when the door to my room opened without warning. With a jolt, I sat upright.

Connor strode in, and although he appeared unperturbed, with his hands buried in his pockets as usual, the muscle pulsing in his jaw betrayed his irritability. He didn't say anything as he nudged the door closed and came to stand in front of me.

When he remained silent, looming over me with a steady, blank stare, I lifted my hands off my lap and asked, "Can I help you with something?"

He pressed his lips together into a tight line and closed his eyes, pinching the bridge of his nose. Still not looking at me, he said, "Care to tell me why you threatened one of the staff?"

Letting out a long sigh, I lowered myself back against the cushion and shut my eyes lazily. "I merely offered to fulfill her request."

I tensed, waiting for a reprimand that didn't come. Instead he let out a low, tired laugh. Cracking my eyes open, I peeked out at him and was shocked to find him lowering himself into the chair opposite me, shaking his head slowly.

"What's so funny?" I asked, not entirely sure I wanted to know. No doubt he'd find some way to deride me.

"Laughing seemed better than yelling," he said. I couldn't argue with him there, though his chuckling was decidedly off-putting. He rubbed the back of his neck. "All laughter aside, though, I can't have my future wife threatening the staff."

Wife. The word grated on me more than I expected.

Be nice be nice be nice.

I ground my teeth together behind my smile.

"Speaking of the staff, dearest husband-to-be," I said, drawing out the words as I twirled a strand of my hair around my finger. "Can I request someone else deliver meals and messages from now on?"

"Why? Because you might murder this one the next time she comes in?"

"Maybe," I muttered under my breath. He cleared his throat. I glared at him and asked, "What? She said she'd rather be dead than have me as her queen. I'm more than happy to oblige her."

His expression darkened as he studied me, and I shifted in my seat uneasily under his scrutiny. What was he looking for?

"What happened between you two?" he asked, his tone becoming almost gentle, as if he were truly concerned.

Explaining to Connor how I'd traded my mother's favorite necklace so I could see Brennan—only to be rejected by him—was not something I wanted to do today. Or ever. So I shrugged. "Just have them send someone else, please?"

He contemplated my request for longer than seemed necessary before finally conceding. "Fine. Is there anything else I can do for my bride?"

I scowled. I'd been planning to ask for a deck of cards or some books or anything to help me pass the time in this fancy prison of mine, but then he'd gone and called me *that*.

"Yes. Find another nickname. That one annoys me."

At that, he rose from his seat and closed the distance between us in two easy strides. I eyed him suspiciously as he knelt beside the chaise and took my hand in his. My breath hitched when he lifted it to his lips and kissed it tenderly.

Stars, why did he have to do that? And why did my body have to like it so much?

He lowered my hand to reveal a too-handsome smirk on that irritatingly attractive face of his. And I nearly melted when he said, "But then I'd have to find another way to make you squirm."

CHAPTER THIRTY-NINE

Connor

As ridiculous as Lieke's request seemed, I couldn't ignore the nagging feeling that something had happened between her and that female—before the whole death threat debacle. Regardless, there was no harm in making the request.

I could send a page down to the kitchens, but it had been too long since I'd visited our old cook, and I wasn't sure I could trust anyone else to deliver this message.

Several staff eyed me curiously as I ventured down the back stairs. Maybe this was a mistake. My coming down here—even if this was my palace—would fuel the rumor mill even more, but no, this was something I had to do personally.

I pushed open the kitchen door and instantly smiled at the familiar smells. This had always been one of my favorite places to come when I was younger, before the war, before my father had accepted the throne, before everything had fallen apart. I had sat on that very stool, with Brennan beside me, listening to Mrs. Bishop tell all manner of stories. I missed those times dearly, but even if war hadn't broken out, my getting older would have interfered with those visits all the same.

Mrs. Bishop stood at the worktable in the center, jotting down notes in some old journal of hers. Two fae had their backs to me as they washed pots and pans in the large sink. They glanced over their shoulders and gawked at me for a moment before whirling back around to continue their work. The old fae peered up at me from her writing and beamed.

"Boy, it's been too long since you've been down to see me. Come give me a hug!" She reached her arms out wide as she came around the table and moved toward me.

"How could I not?" I pulled her close, fighting the flood of memories that rushed at me. I'd forgotten how nice—how essential—it was to feel loved and appreciated. I made a mental note to come visit her as often as my schedule allowed. But I needed to make this quick, so I lowered my voice and whispered, "I need to talk."

She gave me a final squeeze before releasing me and clapping her hands at the two other fae in the room. "All right, girls, out. I'll fetch you when we're done chatting."

With quick nods, they rushed out of the room, and as soon as they were gone, I turned back to the cook. But when I opened my mouth, she lifted a finger to stop me, stomping past me toward the door. Yanking it open, she stuck her head out into the hallway.

"Get away from this door! To your rooms, now!" She remained hanging halfway out the door for a few more moments before finally coming back in, rolling her eyes and shaking her head. "So predictable, I swear. Now, as sad as I am that you didn't come all the way down here just to see my pretty face, if it's about my sweet girl, I'm glad to help however I can."

Not responding, I began to pace the kitchen, casting my eyes down to the floor as if I would find the words I needed among the worn stones. But where should I begin?

"What happened?" Mrs. Bishop asked in a motherly tone.

I turned on my heel to face her and threw my hands into the air. "I wish I knew, honestly."

"I heard about the *threat* to Lola," she said, twisting her lips around the last word.

"Where did that come from anyway?" I asked. "Did Lieke and Lola not get along?"

"Lola barely gets along with anyone who isn't her sister. But I noticed her wearing a new chain around her neck. It looked familiar, but I didn't think to inquire about it until that little rumor hit my ears this morning. Unfortunately I haven't had the chance to confront her yet."

"This is over a necklace?"

Mrs. Bishop's face fell, her eyes filling with a sadness I'd never seen in her. "If it's what I think it is, that's Lieke's mother's necklace. One that *your* mother gave to her."

My mind churned as I attempted to process this. Lieke's parents had been on our staff for many years, but I'd never heard about any friendship between our mothers. Not that it mattered much now.

"Why would Lola have it?"

The cook's shoulders lifted with a heavy sigh. "I don't know. But I can tell you it must have been important if Lieke parted with it willingly."

My brows pinched together. "What if it wasn't willingly?"

She shook her head. "Doesn't really matter. Either way, it explains the animosity."

"Well, I can't have her threatening staff—or anyone—regardless of the reason for it. Can we have someone else see to her meals from now on?"

Mrs. Bishop gave me a thoughtful look as she nodded. "I can, but may I ask how long you're going to keep her cooped up in that room?"

"Just until Julius can get the new dresses made for her. He works fast, so I'd say no more than another day. Maybe two."

Pursing her lips, she studied me for a moment and then offered me a sad smile. "I'm not going to lie to you, Connor. I'm not thrilled about this situation you've put her in, but I'm thankful you found a way to save her. Be gentle with her though. She's more fragile than she lets on. Whether this ends in your marriage or you somehow find a way out of it that doesn't send her to the gallows, you had better not toy with her heart. You hear me?"

I swallowed hard. How could I possibly try to win her heart, as Matthias had suggested, when I felt no affection toward her? That was the epitome of toying, wasn't it?

"Understood?" Mrs. Bishop leaned in close, her stern glare burning into me.

I nodded quickly. "Understood. But how do I get her to work with me on this? She never listens. She seems determined to undermine me any chance she gets."

The cook's brow wrinkled, and then she burst into laughter, throwing her head back before grabbing my shoulder and flashing me another smile. "My boy, you should have thought about that before you roped her into this mess."

I wanted to argue, to explain how *this mess* wouldn't even be happening if Lieke had simply obeyed the damn rules in the first place! But there was no arguing with Mrs. Bishop.

"Fair enough," I said, sighing. "But do you have any useful suggestions? Or are you just going to mock me?"

"Still all business, aren't you?" She smiled kindly and then walked toward the end of the worktable, where a tray of lunch was waiting to be delivered. "Start with taking her some food, and maybe get her something to do. She'll be nothing but a thorn in your ass if she's hungry, bored, or tired."

"So basically like all females?" I said, winking, and she threw a towel at my head.

✳

I had just arrived at Lieke's door, heavy tray in hand, when a page came skidding around the corner. His brows shot up at the sight of me, and he came running. Mentally I considered all the reasons he might be coming at me with such fervor, and none of them were good. Were they ever?

"Yes?" I asked him, doing my best to stay patient.

"His Majesty, sir. He wants to see you."

My stomach fell to my feet, my heart taking its place in my gut. While he and I had spoken briefly about my engagement to Lieke last night, I'd insisted we talk more about it later. Later was apparently now. I glanced at the door and then back at the page.

Shoving the tray into his arms, I tossed my head toward Lieke's room.

"Thank you," I said. "I'll head over there now. You take my fiancée her lunch." With wide eyes, the boy regarded me nervously. He had no trouble taking orders from the king, but having to deliver a meal to a human woman scared him? As laughable as that was, I needed him to do this.

"Yes, Your Highness," he stuttered as I walked around him.

"Oh," I said, turning to glance at him over my shoulder, "let her know I will stop by this evening to see how she's faring."

He gave me a string of small nods and gulped. Poor kid. I hoped Lieke would go easy on him. He might not recover if she didn't.

✳

"Come in," my father's voice boomed from within his study, and I stepped inside as confidently as I could. He was seated behind his desk, focused on the papers in front of him. Without looking up, he ordered me to sit down.

I did. Silently. Folding my hands in my lap, I waited for him to be ready. I'd learned the hard way years ago not to speak first. Sometimes that meant sitting here in silence for an hour. One time he had made me wait nearly three. My stomach grumbled, reminding me I hadn't eaten all day. Thankfully it only took him seventeen minutes to drop the papers onto the desk and address me.

"What were you thinking?" he asked calmly, though a storm brewed in his eyes, waiting to be unleashed on me if I answered insufficiently. If I lied to him, tried to play this off as a true engagement and not a whim, he'd lose his shit. I needed him on board with this, though, if I was going to keep her out of the executioner's hands.

"It was the best move I could think of," I admitted, holding his stare.

He barked out a laugh. "Best move. Best move?! I expect this type of harebrained nonsense from your brother, not my military commander!"

I opened my mouth to speak, but he shut me down with a glare.

"Stop. Just tell me this isn't real and I haven't spawned two idiot sons."

Roughing a hand over my mouth and chin, I searched for the best way to explain this. It had all made sense last night.

"No," I finally said, "it's not real. Mother—"

Shit. I realized my mistake too late, and my father slammed his fists down hard on his desk.

"Don't you dare bring her into this! I know she always insisted on protecting the humans. I know I promised her I would. I don't need you to remind me."

I pulled in a slow breath and exhaled fully before I tried again.

"With relations between humans and fae deteriorating as rapidly as they are, I understand why you sentenced her as you did. But executing her would have been a missed opportunity to fix this once and for all."

His sharp eyes narrowed on me, and he nodded for me to continue.

"The humans want what? Their homes back, their place in our society restored. But the fae resent them, blame them for the war. It will be difficult, I know, to convince the fae to accept this, but a human queen could be our best chance at ending the rebels' attacks. If the attacks cease, the fae—"

"Are slow to forgive, Connor," the king said, his tone softening ever so slightly.

"I know. That's why we start winning them over now. With her."

He shifted his gaze to the side as he pondered my proposal.

Finally he sat back in his chair.

"Are you sure it wouldn't just be easier to have her help us find the rebels? Surely those she stayed with—the ones who gave her those knives—have some ties to whoever is responsible for this violence.

Assuming she isn't a rebel spy herself."

"My second agrees with you. So, yes, I am planning to learn what I can from her about why they gave her the knives and what she knows about them. But she won't take kindly to being interrogated, especially if she feels it will put her family in danger. I would like to try this more peaceful method first, if you'll allow it."

The king paused, his brow lowering as he pondered my proposal. Finally, he dropped his head to the side and said, "It might work. If she's willing, of course. The blasted woman's foolish heart had to fall in love with our Brennan, and given their brazenness in sneaking about the palace together before, I don't have much confidence that she can be reined in—even by you."

I shook my head slowly. "I'm fairly certain Brennan effectively ended their ill-fated romance when he refused to help her last night. So at least that's one obstacle I don't have to worry about. I either need her to care enough to convincingly fake this engagement with me, or…"

"Or what?"

"Or find a way so she doesn't have to pretend at all."

For a moment his brow twisted in confusion, and then realization dawned on him.

"You can't be serious, Connor."

"I can, and I am."

"You really think you can get her to fall in love with you?"

I heaved a sigh, pushing aside all my doubt. "I'll do my best."

"And if she does? Are you prepared to marry her for real?" he asked, and I almost thought I caught a hint of fatherly concern in his eyes.

Would I marry her? Would I see this through to the end if necessary?

I thought back to that talk with Matthias years ago, the one in which he had urged me to find a queen and had mocked me for waiting for my mate. Was I prepared to give up on ever finding my mate in order to save my kingdom?

As painful as it was, the answer was clear.

"I am."

CHAPTER FORTY

Lieke

Gretchen stood in front of my wardrobe, her lips pursed in annoyed concentration as she flicked through garment after ill-fitting garment. She groaned quietly and tossed a look at where I sat cross-legged atop my bed.

"Every time I start to wonder why the prince insists you stay in your room, I remember these," she said and proceeded to hold up two velvet dresses with frilly lace collars adorning the high necklines. Scrunching up her nose, she returned them to the wardrobe. "They're better suited for the waste bin than our future queen."

"I'll have you know, Gretchen, those were the height of fashion when my mother was younger," I said, completely failing to show genuine offense at how she had insulted Mother's clothes. The dresses truly were hideous, and I myself had often teased my mother for keeping them.

"Oh, I remember," Gretchen said, resuming her search. "Those were dark times here in Emeryn."

"What does it matter what I wear anyway?" I asked grumpily. "It's not like there's anyone to see me except you."

She cast a sidelong look my way and smirked. "Are you saying you don't want to look nice for me?"

I shrugged. "Why bother when I'm already spoken for? And by the prince, no less."

"Yes, that does put a damper on a future for us," she said, giggling.

Gretchen finally selected a simple sage-green dress with fluttering gossamer sleeves. "I guess this one will do for today."

I uncrossed my legs and moved to stand, sighing. "Ah, yes, for my rousing day of sitting around, staring at the wall."

"Oh, come now, Miss Lieke," she said, smiling kindly as she handed me the dress. "You can always stare at the ceiling instead."

"Lucky me," I muttered as I slipped the dress over my head and smoothed down the skirt.

Gretchen ignored my scowling and went about making up my bed. It had taken two days of confinement—and one good slap on the back of my hand—for me to learn not to interfere with her duties, though I still found it difficult to watch someone else perform such basic tasks for me. I wandered into the living area and lay down on the couch to take her suggestion and stare at the ceiling.

A few minutes later, she leaned her face into my line of sight. "If there's nothing else you need, I'll be back later this evening to prepare your bath."

I mumbled my gratitude and offered her as genuine a smile as I could.

Hours went by. Or perhaps they were mere minutes. It was difficult to track the passage of time with so little to occupy my mind. When my backside finally fell asleep, I sprang up from the sofa and growled.

I needed to get out of here. Out of this room. Out of my own head.

I stalked toward the door and grabbed the handle but stopped. What would Connor do if he came by and found me gone? Or what if I ran into him in the hallway or on the stairs? His temper wasn't something

I particularly wanted to deal with today.

So what?

What could he do? Cancel our engagement and have his former fiancée hanged? Unlikely.

But possible all the same.

Still, this was the prince who had saved my life not once but twice. I wagered he wasn't about to let me hang simply for stepping outside my room. He'd be angry, of course, but when was he not?

Sucking in a breath, I pulled the door open enough so I could check the hallway to the right.

No one. Empty.

Opening it slightly more, I held my breath as I poked my head out to peer down the other side.

Again no one.

So far so good.

I stepped out of my room for the first time in days and clicked the door shut quietly behind me. At first, I tiptoed toward the main stairway, as if I were an escaped prisoner. But I wasn't a hostage. Connor had said as much himself. For all anyone on the staff knew, I wasn't an insignificant human who was currently being used in a political game; I was their future queen.

So why was I slinking around like a common thief?

Angling my chin high, I straightened and proceeded to walk through the palace like the ruler I was never actually going to be. Down the main stairway I continued, smiling kindly and nodding regally to the staff I passed—ignoring how they seemed to sneer. Did they all feel as Lola did? Did I really not have any friends here? Or were they merely jealous I'd snagged the prince?

Whatever the reason, they were clearly unhappy with my new station.

On the ground floor, I meandered through the hallways, admiring the paintings and tapestries that graced the walls, running my fingers over the soft petals of the fresh flowers placed on tables throughout. As nice as the blooms were, though, and as gorgeous as the artwork was, I longed to be out in the sunshine among the leaves and grass and vines and blossoms in the garden.

I had just turned the corner when I saw him. Connor. Prowling toward me with a vicious gleam in his eye. Of course he would have sensed me coming before seeing me.

Cursed fae abilities.

CHAPTER FORTY-ONE

Connor

I should have locked her fucking door, but I'd stupidly wanted to prove to her that she wasn't a prisoner in her own room. Even more foolishly, I'd actually expected her to listen and stay put.

Her heartbeat appropriately sped up when she saw me, so I at least elicited some fear in her, but the serene expression on her irritatingly beautiful face proved it wasn't nearly enough.

"There you are, dearest," she crooned. I clenched my jaw tighter, trying to get control of my temper. "Would you like to join me in the—"

I didn't allow her to finish her invitation. Wordlessly, I reached out, wrapped my hand tightly around her wrist, and spun her around, never slowing my stride as I pulled her with me back toward her room.

"What in the stars do you think you're doing?" I demanded quietly. Although no one was nearby at the moment, I didn't want to risk making a damned scene. She stumbled beside me as I dragged her along. The slipping of her feet started to remind me of the night she'd killed Griffin. I eased my pace so she could keep up, but I regretted it as soon as she answered.

"Taking a walk, obviously."

I growled.

Why did she have to be so stars-damned stubborn?

Without warning, I stopped in the middle of the hallway, maintaining my hold on her arm. I wouldn't put it past her to try and run away from me if given the chance.

Lowering my face to hers, I scanned her deep blue eyes for any hint that she cared one bit about the risks I'd taken to keep her alive. Of course, all I found was the same bitter pride I'd seen there time and time again.

"I told you to stay," I said, coating each word with anger.

Lieke tilted her head slightly and licked her lips. A wave of heat rushed through me. My annoyance rumbled in the back of my throat. She smirked. "Last I checked, Wolfie, I'm not a dog. You are."

As she said the last two words, she laid the palm of her free hand on my chest. My body warmed under her touch, sparking an entirely unwanted desire. Without thinking, I snatched up her wrist and forced her to stumble backwards until her back hit the wall.

A memory flashed in my mind—a dark room, my hand at her throat—but I swept it aside as I pinned her arms against the stone by her head. Turning my hips, I angled my body so she couldn't strike me with her knee. Then I pressed my body as close to her as I dared.

Her scent threatened to overpower me, but my anger was too amped up. I bared my teeth and snarled at her. Her eyes flashed down to my lips and lingered there for longer than I was comfortable with.

"Look at me!" I growled. When she obeyed, another rush of lust swept over me, and I cursed silently to myself. "So you can listen."

She pulled her head away from the wall and brushed her cheek against mine until her lips hovered over my ear. My eyes drifted closed against my will as her breath teased me. "Oh, I can be a good girl."

Fuck!

I slammed her wrists against the wall again, as if that could possibly help me regain control of this situation. Lazily she rested her head on the wall and stared at me with a haughty, bored expression.

"You will stay in your room. You will do as you're told. Or I swear to the stars, I will drag you to the gallows myself. Do you understand?"

She turned away from me.

"Do you understand me?" I growled the question again.

Flicking her eyes to me, she cleared her throat and angled her head slightly. It took me too long to realize she wasn't about to answer me; she was informing me we weren't alone.

A curse echoed in my head as I picked up on the extra heartbeat in the hallway.

Here we were, supposedly a betrothed couple madly in love, and I was angrily shoving her against a wall and yelling at her. I couldn't risk someone running off to spread word that our relationship was more toxic than loving.

Thinking fast, I pressed close to her, struggling to ignore how her breasts heaved against my chest with her next breath. I mimicked her earlier move, inching my lips closer to her ear, and whispered as quietly as possible, "Play along."

Releasing her wrists, I gently interlaced our fingers and lowered our clasped hands to our sides. When my lips tickled her skin below her ear, she shuddered against me, and I prayed to the damned stars that she wouldn't give me grief for how my body instantly responded to her. As I kissed my way down her neck to her shoulder, I desperately tried not to let myself enjoy the way she smelled and tasted and whimpered softly in my ear.

This wasn't real.

She wasn't mine.

I didn't want her anyway.

Slowly she pushed me away, whispering, "They left."

I straightened and risked a glance down the hallway before pulling away fully and dropping her hands as if they were hot irons.

"Get back to your room," I said firmly.

"Yes, Your Highness," she said sweetly, but she didn't move to leave. Instead her eyes drifted lower, trailing down my body. She pursed her lips and gestured toward my waist with her hand.

No. Lower.

"You might want to take a moment before you go anywhere though," she said, smiling. Before I could say anything more, she was lifting onto her toes, planting a kiss on my cheek, and strolling away.

CHAPTER FORTY-TWO

Lieke

Connor didn't come back after our awkward encounter. Whether it was because he was embarrassed or angry, it mattered little. I was fine with it either way, though his absence left me with hours of silence to pick apart each word and touch we'd shared.

Thankfully, the tailor, Julius, had shown up to distract me from my swirling thoughts, delivering an entire wardrobe for me—a variety of simple cotton dresses and elegant gowns of satin and lace. There were also several sets of casual pants and shirts and even some new night-gowns and undergarments, including a few intimate items that seemed altogether unnecessary. Although I supposed, with the staff believing our pending nuptials were real, it made sense that they would have supplied the more embarrassingly delicate pieces. I promptly shoved those to the back of the chest of drawers.

I wouldn't need them ever, and especially not today. Thankfully, Connor had agreed that my formal *presentation* could wait until dinner tonight.

Today, I was getting to run.

Not alone, of course. He had given me a babysitter. His second. Matthias.

The male's voice drifted in from the front room. "You almost ready, my lady?"

I peeked my head around the doorway, keeping my still undressed body out of sight, and found him sitting at the table, picking at the fruit left over from my breakfast. "Nearly. And can you not call me that?"

As I retreated, I swore I heard him laugh. "He said you were sensitive about nicknames."

"I'm not sensitive," I called as I slipped a short-sleeved, dark blue shirt over my brown leggings. Once I had my new running boots laced up—a much nicer pair than the ones I'd been gifted by Raven's parents—I strode into the front room, plaiting my hair down my back as I faced him.

He rose slowly, an almost mischievous smile gracing his lips. "My lady isn't really a nickname, by the way. It's more a title of sorts."

"Title or not, it feels too formal," I said.

His eyes lit up with humor. "You *are* my future queen. Formality seems appropriate, no?"

"Do you go around calling Connor by his title then?"

"Only when he needs reminding of it," he said, still grinning.

"Well, Matthias, I don't need any reminding of who I am and what role our dear prince has forced me into, so you can just use my name. Please?"

At that, his smile faded a bit, and he pursed his lips as he sized me up. I wanted to squirm under his scrutiny, but I forced myself to remain still. Finally, he blinked several times, as if breaking some sort of spell.

"Okay then, Lieke. Shall we?" He gestured toward the door, and I couldn't contain my excitement at finally getting some fresh air.

We didn't speak again until we stepped out of the front door and into the midmorning sunshine. I drew in a deep breath, savoring every scent the air carried—the freshly cut grass of the grounds, the pine trees that framed the stables, and the flowers that still bloomed in the expansive beds beside the entryway stairs. I stretched out my back, my arms, and my legs, eager to get the blood pumping.

"Are you sure running is what you want to do?"

"Why? Is it not appropriate for the future queen?"

He shook his head. "It's nothing like that. Just wondered if you'd be able to keep up." Bounding down the steps, he took off, glancing over his shoulder at me just before he entered the trees.

I rolled my eyes. Of course I couldn't keep up with him, but if he wanted to get in trouble for leaving me behind, that was his problem.

I ran after him, setting a comfortable pace for myself, not wanting to overexert my muscles or risk injury by pushing it too hard too soon. Once inside the trees, I couldn't spot Matthias anywhere ahead of me. Why had he agreed to come if he was just going to leave me behind? Shaking my head in annoyance, I tried to focus on the rhythm of my boots against the dirt and my breathing.

The forest smelled intoxicating. I'd missed this. The fresh air. The earthy scent. The solitude.

I didn't find Matthias again until I had looped back toward the palace and arrived at what looked like a barn. Matthias was leaning against the building, covering a yawn as I approached. "I thought you had been trained," he said through his smirk.

Unruffled by the mild affront, I laughed quietly. "And I thought you were supposed to stay with me."

Jutting his chin, he lowered his voice and said, "Who says I didn't?"

My expression tightened with confusion. "I do," I said. "I never saw you."

He shook his head slowly, clicking his tongue in judgment. "If you're to be our queen, we'll have to work on your environmental awareness. Never know who might be watching you, my—"

I glowered at him, daring him to say the next word. He raised his hands in surrender. "Lieke."

"So you were watching me?" I asked, trying to retrace my run and determine if I'd noticed any hint of his presence.

"The whole time," he said, nodding. "You're quite a sight when you're running."

I froze. "What does that mean?"

"Nothing. I'm used to training soldiers. They run with a purpose; you run like…well, like you're free."

I had to pull my lower lip between my teeth to keep it from trembling. I wasn't free. Connor claimed I had a choice here, but I didn't really. It was either do what he said or die. What kind of choice was that?

Matthias tossed his head toward a door to his right. "Come on, Lieke. Let's practice."

He was already heading inside the building before I could say anything. Part of me wanted to decline and head back to my rooms, but the other part was too curious not to follow him.

It was no barn but a training ring. Along one wall hung all manner of weapons. Most I recognized—swords, spears, axes. A few others were lined with terrifying spikes. I was perfectly fine never becoming acquainted with those. Matthias walked over to a long table and lifted two wooden swords. After tossing me one, he moved to the middle of the ring.

I caught it, just barely, and twisted my wrist around to get a feel for its weight and balance.

"Let's see how well they trained you in the ring, Lieke," he said and waved me forward with his free hand.

I stalked gingerly forward. "I stand no chance against you though."

He shrugged again as we circled each other. "You've killed a fae before, so you must be somewhat capable."

I froze as the memories rushed back—Griffin's breath in my ear, his hand on my throat, his weight atop me as I panicked—and I closed my eyes, forcing myself to breathe through it. I refused to let this haunt me. I refused to be weak.

When I finally opened my eyes, Matthias was watching me apprehensively. He started to apologize, but I stopped him with a shake of my head.

"I'm fine," I lied, wishing I could believe the words myself. Before he could say more, I lunged for him, pushing off my back foot and swinging my sword down toward his legs. He bounded out of my reach quickly and smiled.

"Good," he muttered. He didn't wait for me to attack again but came at me with a downward cut of his own that I couldn't parry in time. The flat of his blade smacked against my shoulder, and I winced.

But I didn't hesitate to strike back.

On light feet I rushed at him, swinging up. He blocked me easily, but I was already twisting my blade around to strike him from the opposite direction. Smiling, he deflected every attack I attempted, turning around and around the ring as I pursued him.

After a few minutes, I still hadn't managed to hit him, and my muscles were already becoming fatigued.

I held up a finger and bent at the waist, trying to catch my breath.

"You're doing well, Lieke," he said, and I couldn't quite tell if he was being genuine or not.

I spit into the dirt and turned to look up at him, remaining doubled over. "You have an odd definition of *well*."

He shrugged before walking over to me and offering his outstretched hand. "Here, let's get you some—"

Shifting my weight to my left foot, I crouched lower and swept my right leg at him, sending him falling onto his backside into the dirt. I stood over him as he laughed.

"Get me some what?" I asked, holding my hand out to help him up. He took it, but instead of rising, he pulled me down on top of him, rolling me over onto my back. Then he was standing again, his wooden sword tucked under my chin, before I could grasp what had happened.

Clapping echoed through the building, and I pulled my gaze away from Matthias to find Connor walking toward us. My treacherous mind conjured up memories of his lips trailing over my skin and his hands wrapped around my wrists. I managed to blink the thoughts away but couldn't rid my damned body of the warm tingling his arrival caused.

"Mind if I cut in, friend?" he asked, looking far more handsome than anyone had a right to. Even a prince.

Matthias flashed me a wink before tossing his practice sword to my betrothed. He helped me up and pulled me in close, whispering in my ear, "Knock him on his ass."

I nodded, though I was sure Connor had heard him even from twenty paces away.

He was dressed in a white linen shirt and black pants, and I tried not to let my eyes drift away from his face as he circled the ring. I pivoted as he moved, keeping my sword trained on him. Unlike Matthias, he didn't wait for me to strike first.

I barely blocked his first blow, but despite that, he gave me no time to think or recover, immediately bringing his sword around to strike again. When his sword tapped me on my back, I groaned in frustration. He simply smiled, his golden eyes dancing as he watched me. We continued for quite some time, striking, lunging, and blocking. And just as it had been with Matthias, I never did manage to hit him.

Still, as frustrating as it was to be failing, I couldn't deny I was having fun.

Sweat beaded along my forehead, and I swiped it away with the back of my hand before it could fall into my eyes.

"Does my girl need a break?" Connor asked, smirking.

I struggled to steady my breathing but managed to respond, "No, does my Wolfie?"

Matthias's single laugh hit my ears, and I smiled.

"Not until one of us is on our back," he said, and my core lit up at the prospect. I clenched my teeth, frustrated with my body's reaction. I was supposed to be mad at him—annoyed, not aroused.

Connor lunged, and I spun out of the way, swinging my sword at his back as I moved. But he moved faster, stepping just out of my reach. Spinning my sword around, I brought it over my head and down, expecting him to easily block my strike. But I wasn't prepared for him to push me backwards once our swords met. My feet slipped out from under me, and I was falling.

Before I hit the ground, his arm was around my waist, holding me up and sending a flash of pinpricks up my spine.

His face was so close to mine that his breath warmed my cheek. His eyes held me captive.

"So much for getting me on my back," I said.

He answered by planting a kiss on the tip of my nose. Then, sliding his lips to my ear, he whispered, "Oh, I'll get you on your back, but I won't have an audience when I do."

I swallowed hard, my body heating with unwanted passion once more. Even if I'd had a good retort, I didn't trust my voice, so I said nothing. He set me back down on my feet and slid his arm from around me.

"Done for today?" he asked, as if he hadn't just ignited every stars-damned inch of me.

Nodding, I handed him my sword. "See you at lunch?" I asked, trying to sound as casual as I could.

"Of course, my bride," he said, flashing me the most endearing smile I'd ever seen on his lips.

CHAPTER FORTY-THREE

Conner

As soon as Lieke left the training center, I dropped my chin to my chest. It had only been five days, and I was already worn down, more by my guilt than anything else. Every time I spoke to her or smiled at her or did anything remotely affectionate, Mrs. Bishop's voice rang in my head.

Don't toy with her heart.

Yet here I was, doing just that with every touch and look.

I tried to reason with myself, insisting I wasn't going to hurt her. But that didn't change the fact that I was manipulating her for my own selfish reasons. By doing this, I was no better than my brother. In fact, I might be worse.

"Well, that was interesting," Matthias said, interrupting my self-loathing.

Lifting my head, I avoided his eyes and moved to put the practice swords away. "Oh?" I asked, though I already had some notion of what he was about to say.

"Does this mean you've finally let go of that mate nonsense?"

That wasn't what I had expected him to say. I turned slowly. "What?"

He shrugged and rubbed a hand over his jaw as he approached me. As he leaned an elbow against the table, the corners of his mouth turned down like they always did when he was pondering something. "I mean, I know you're just *pretending*"—he made a quoting gesture with his fingers as he said the word—"but that seemed rather real from where I was standing."

I rolled my eyes and strode toward the door, tossing my response over my shoulder. "It's just acting."

He ran to catch up with me. "You're not that good of an actor, Connor."

What was he implying? That I was interested in her? Nonsense. She was attractive, of course, but there was more to a person than looks alone. Appearance was only a minor factor in the grand scheme of things.

Just before I reached the door, I rounded on him. "What are you saying exactly?"

He leaned forward, and his expression held more concern than humor now, which put me on edge.

"I'm saying, Connor, that you're going to fall for her yourself if you're not careful."

I shook my head. "That's laughable. She drives me mad."

Nodding, he widened his eyes. "Madly in love is more like it."

"You're out of your mind," I said, turning to leave, but he grabbed my arm and pulled me back.

"Just—"

"Just what, Matthias? What do you want me to do? I'm trying my best to do what's right for everyone!"

"For everyone except you and Lieke, you mean."

Pulling in a sharp breath, I asked, "What do you want from me?"

"I don't want to fight. I just want you to be open to having something good, even if it comes from somewhere unexpected."

"You mean her?"

"Yes, I mean her, you idiot."

"What happened to *Your Highness?*"

He ignored my question and continued to push the matter. "I know you, and I see what's happening to you, whether you want to believe me or not. I'm just hoping that when you do finally fall in love with that girl, you won't deny it because you're holding on to some fairy-tale mate bullshit. She could be good for you, if you let her."

"I don't have time for this," I muttered, and thankfully this time when I turned away, he let me go.

＊

Matthias's words wouldn't leave me alone for the rest of the damn day. They left me distracted and unable to focus on the reports the healers had sent for me to review. All I managed to conclude was that they'd made some startling discoveries from Lieke's knives but needed more time to chase down their leads.

Tonight would be Lieke's first dinner with my family, and even without my friend's idiotic assertions, I was on edge about how this would go. She hadn't seen Brennan or the king since the night of the banquet, and if I was being honest, I wasn't sure she was ready.

I bathed and dressed early, putting on the new suit our tailor had made for me after he'd completed Lieke's new wardrobe. I'd tried to protest, but he'd refused to take it back. Apparently Mrs. Bishop had insisted I needed it. It wasn't lost on me that the shirt was the exact color of Lieke's eyes, the color of the night sky right before the stars came out.

In frustration, I growled. It was irritating how familiar I was with her. She invaded my thoughts far more than I wanted. But given how much time I had to spend with her, it was only logical that this would happen.

Falling onto the edge of my bed, I dropped my head in my hands, squeezing hard.

Damn Matthias.

How could he possibly think there was anything real between us? It had only been five days, and my flirting was so obviously forced that I was sure she could see my true intentions behind every lingering touch and whispered tease. But I couldn't stop now.

Maybe you don't have to trick her though.

I could be honest with her, request her cooperation, if only I could trust her to not sabotage this whole plan, or at the very least not undermine me at every turn. While there had been moments she'd seemed genuinely flustered this week, all of my efforts to woo her had done little. Her anger remained palpable. If I claimed not to be irked by her continued glares and snide remarks, I'd be lying. Every time I thought I was gaining some ground with her, she did something to assure me I wasn't. She would quickly trade her smile for a scowl, hissing out insults about anything from my choice of shirt to my apparent need to protect everyone.

I hated that part of myself.

Some days I wished I could be more like Brennan and let others care for themselves.

But I wasn't my brother. I never would be.

Shit. This dinner was going to be a disaster.

Unless I prepared her—assuming she would listen to me.

I huffed a laugh. There had to be a first time for everything, right?

Pushing to my feet, I crossed my living room and stepped out into the hallway.

Lieke answered her door as soon as I knocked, as if she'd been waiting for me to arrive.

Or planning to leave on her own. Again.

"Hi," I said, smiling as I let my gaze linger on her lips for a second longer than was necessary. Her eyes darted down the length of my body, and her face flushed an adorable pink color. She didn't return my smile, though, as she stepped aside to let me in.

"You're here early," she said flatly, leading the way to the sitting area.

Although she was wearing an outfit similar to the one she'd trained in this morning, she had obviously changed into fresh clothes since then, as these showed no signs of dirt and sweat from the training ring. Her hair, still slightly damp from her recent bath, cascaded down her back in dark golden waves.

"I thought you might be nervous about tonight," I said as I lowered myself into my usual seat, nodding to the chaise. She didn't take the hint. Either that or she was refusing to do as I suggested. Instead she stood in front of me, avoiding my eyes as she wrung her hands together at her waist.

"I'm not nervous," she said, scowling.

"Are you sure?" I raised a brow at her, and her eyes swung up to mine, narrowing with annoyance.

"Of course I'm sure."

"Then why do you—"

"What was that back there?" she blurted out, her jaw pulsing as she clenched her teeth, waiting for me to explain.

"What? Back where?" I asked, playing innocent.

She squirmed, throwing her hand out to the side. "Out in the training room—"

I pointed in the opposite direction. "It's over there," I whispered. I had to bite back my smile when she pressed her lips together. I half-expected her to stomp her foot.

"You kissed me," she explained.

"Technically, I kissed your nose."

"Why?" She didn't stomp, but she stepped toward me, her glare demanding I give her a straight answer.

My smirk disappeared, and I leaned forward, staring up into her churning blue eyes. "Because you are my bride, Lieke. I was playing the role because Matthias was watching."

But she was shaking her head and gnawing on her bottom lip before I was done answering.

"No."

"What do you mean *no*?"

"Maybe that's the reason for the kiss, but not for your words. Matthias couldn't have heard those."

Angling my head to the side, I relaxed back in the chair. "I don't know. He is a fae. We have pretty good hearing."

"And the little things you do in here when we're alone?"

"I don't know what you're talking about," I lied, brushing an invisible piece of lint off my sleeve. She was quickly draining what little patience I had, and if she kept this up—

"Stop lying to me, Connor."

I was on my feet in an instant, forcing her to step back half a pace. Despite that, she held her ground. I tried to ignore how her breasts pressed against my chest. Instead I chose to focus on the vitriol in her eyes. This woman hated me. How could I have ever thought I would be able to change that with a few sweet gestures and teasing comments? Why had I bothered to come here early? Why did I care about her discomfort?

"Fine," I growled. "You want the truth? I need everyone to believe we are engaged, that this is real for both of us. And I don't trust you not to fuck it up like you do everything else."

At this, she gritted her teeth, searching my eyes. "So you're just playing the part for both of us and hoping I'll...what? Become so smitten with you I don't have to pretend? Is that it?"

"Maybe," I said before I could think better of it.

She inched closer to me and lowered her voice to an angry whisper. "As if I could ever fall for you."

"You think I like this? You're a political pawn, Lieke. Nothing more." Part of me recoiled, as if protesting the words that had just come out of my mouth.

"And how do I know this isn't some sick fantasy you're playing out? How do I know you weren't just jealous because I loved Brennan and not you?"

I threw my head back and laughed. "Yes, because all these years I've been pining for a human who was stupid enough to think she stood any chance with my brother."

"Get out," Lieke spat, throwing her hand toward the door.

"No."

She pushed against my chest, but I didn't budge. As an exasperated huff rose from her throat, she punched me with both her fists, and I let her. But when she moved to do it again, I grabbed both of her wrists and held them tight, ignoring the sense of déjà vu.

"Stop," I growled, but of course she didn't listen. She continued to struggle against my grip.

"Let me go!" she screamed, trying to pull away from me as angry tears began to well up in her eyes. I held firm, even when she drove her boot into my shins. "Damn you, Connor. Let me go!"

"No," I said, forcing my voice to calm, hating how I couldn't just let her go and walk away.

Matthias was wrong. I wasn't falling for this woman. But I couldn't send her to die, and if she could help me stop the rebels and protect the fae, I'd use her however I needed to.

CHAPTER FORTY-FOUR

Lieke

I hated crying in front of Connor, and having him holding my arms captive as the tears streamed down my face was even worse. There was no fighting him though. He would always be stronger and faster than me. He would always have the upper hand.

Yet I still had some leverage here. He needed me. Even if he wouldn't admit it aloud, there was something keeping him from changing his mind and having my sentence reinstated.

Brennan didn't want me.

Connor didn't like me.

I was nothing to this family except a pawn. While I hated the idea of being used, it was decidedly more appealing than dying. Maybe—if I could convince Connor he could trust me—I could at least have some agency. I could help. I could be more than a mere thorn in their royal sides.

Earning his trust, especially after I'd screamed at him and hit him, wouldn't be easy though. Nor would it be fun or attractive.

Clearing my throat, I peered up at him from beneath my tear-soaked lashes.

"Are you done?" he asked quietly, almost gently.

I dipped my chin a bit and whispered an apology. Suspicion clouded his features, but after I took a couple of calming breaths, he finally loosened his grip enough that I could take a step back. Sweat pooled around my forearms where his fingers remained.

"I'm not going to hit you again," I said, shifting my gaze to my wrists, silently begging him to let me go.

"I hope not," he said, and a moment later he released me. "Can we sit and talk?"

Silently I obliged, perching myself on the edge of the chaise and resting my forearms along my legs as I leaned forward. I forced myself to look at him when he sat opposite me.

"Look, Lieke, I'm sorry," he started, and my eyes widened in surprise. I waited for him to follow up with some justification for his actions, but he only sat there looking at me with what seemed like genuine regret.

"Me too," I muttered.

A small smile tugged at his mouth. "You already apologized, Sapphire."

"Sapphire?" I asked, rolling the word around in my mind.

Connor's smile turned upside down. "New nickname. Like the color of your eyes."

It was decidedly better than *blondie* and definitely less irksome than *bride*.

"I might actually like that one," I said and nearly laughed when he pulled back in surprise.

"You're agreeing with me on something?"

"I'm just as shocked as you are."

He leaned back and roughed a hand over his chin. "I would like to work together, if you're willing."

I glanced up at the ceiling, pretending to ponder the idea. Sighing, I let my shoulders drop dramatically. "That does sound better than the gallows."

"It would require you to hide your hatred for me when we're around others though."

At this, I frowned slightly. He thought I hated him?

"I don't hate you, Wolfie," I said, adding a smile.

"Are you sure?"

"Pretty sure," I said, shrugging. "Do you drive me nuts? Absolutely. Do I want to smack you? Regularly. But that's not hatred."

He smirked but seemed to be searching for any sign that I was lying to him. "Okay, so you don't hate me. And I don't hate you. That's a good start. But that's a far cry from being so in love we got engaged in secret and only announced it when we were forced to."

"Do I need to kiss you on the nose?" I asked, wrinkling my own nose as if the thought disgusted me.

"Only if you want to, I guess." He dropped his gaze to his lap and remained quiet for a while before finally focusing on me again. "Maybe we need to set some rules. I would rather not have either of us feel forced to do something we don't want to."

What in the world was he saying? What did he think I was going to do?

My confusion must have shown plainly on my face, because he laughed and said, "No need to look so nervous, Sapphire."

"That's not my nervous face, Wolfie. I'm confused. What sort of rules are you thinking of?"

"Well, we will be expected to stand close, hold hands, and—"

"Look longingly into each other's eyes?" I asked.

"I suppose."

"I can handle that. What else?"

"You got angry over a kiss on the nose. But—"

"It wasn't the kiss that bothered me. It was the questionable intentions behind it."

He nodded. "Fair enough. But kisses could get complicated."

I shot him a lopsided grin. "You might be doing it wrong if you think it's complicated."

This earned me a laugh that almost sounded sincere. "I mean, it could quickly complicate things between us if one of us gets carried away."

"Oh, are you worried you're going to fall in love with me, Your Highness?"

That question sobered him up quickly, and something I didn't recognize flashed in his eyes.

I fumbled with my words, trying to backpedal as quickly as I could. "Never mind. So you want to set a boundary on kisses then."

He nodded but said nothing. The shadow still hadn't cleared from his expression.

We were quickly running out of time before dinner, and I still needed to change into my dress, so I lifted one hand in the air and began raising a finger for each thing I listed. "Kisses on the cheek, forehead, and hand are fair game for me. But"—I lifted my other hand and spoke as I raised more fingers—"neck, shoulder, collarbone, and anywhere lower…"

"Understood," he said, chuckling nervously. "And lips?"

Instinctively my eyes lowered to his parted lips. His tongue darted out to wet them, and my mind went rogue, imagining what they would taste like. I cleared my throat, which had gone suddenly dry.

"I don't think that would be a good idea."

When I looked up at him again, he was smirking at me. My neck and cheeks began to warm in anticipation of whatever teasing remark he was about to make, but he only said, "Agreed. Now, we should probably talk about what to expect at this dinner."

Grimacing, I stood. "Would you be able to talk while I dress? I'd hate to make us late to my first dinner."

His eyes darkened a touch. "So no kissing on the lips, but you'll allow me to watch you dress? Seems rather odd."

I rolled my eyes as I turned away and headed into the other room. Waving a hand over my shoulder, I beckoned for him to follow. "I can hear you just fine from behind the screen."

Once I was safely concealed in the corner, I began to strip off my pants and shirt, folding them neatly and setting them onto the small table next to me.

"So? Are you going to talk, Wolfie? Or did you get distracted by the thought of me naked behind this flimsy partition?" When he didn't respond, I dared to peek around the screen.

Connor leaned casually against the door frame, his arms folded in front of him. The troubled look in his eyes returned.

"I thought you needed to get dressed," he said, not turning to face me, and I quickly retreated behind the screen. "You should know that my father and brother both know the truth."

I froze, holding the maroon dress barely up over my hips. "Oh?"

"Brennan accused me of planning this all along, which was absurd."

"And the king?" I asked nervously.

"He insisted it had to be a ruse, couldn't fathom that it could be real."

"Ouch," I whispered, slipping my arms into the delicate sleeves.

"I wouldn't take it personally, Sapphire," he said quietly. "But I did have to convince him this plan had merit."

Reaching around my back, I started fastening the buttons that ran up from my waist. I winced as I attempted to stretch my arms to secure the last of them. Stars, I couldn't go to dinner with my dress half-buttoned, and we didn't have time to call for Gretchen to help.

"Connor?"

"Yes, Sapphire?"

Sheepishly, I stepped out. My face heated at the way his eyes roved over me. Turning, I pulled my hair over my shoulder to reveal the final buttons I needed help with.

"Could you...?"

I cursed my racing heart as he slowly walked toward me. This was nothing. It wasn't like I was asking him to help me bathe. I wasn't even indecent; every part of me was covered. It was just a few measly buttons. Yet that didn't stop my breath from catching when his fingers whispered across my back.

Stars, pull yourself together, Lieke. Before he gets the wrong idea.

CHAPTER FORTY-FIVE

Connor

They were just buttons. It was just her back.

But with the way my whole body heated as I neared her, she might as well have been standing here in nothing but her shift asking me to help her undress. It didn't help at all that she trembled under my touch, as if I were ripping the buttons off instead of fastening them. Of course my mind had to conjure up that image, and for a moment I lost myself in the idea…until I saw them.

Scars.

So many scars.

They lined her back at various angles, lengths, and stages of healing.

Gently, I brushed my fingers over them, my anger growing as I did.

"Who did this to you?" I asked, quickly losing the grip on my control.

She bristled, the muscles in her back tensing as she muttered, "It doesn't matter."

It didn't matter? How could she think this didn't matter?

Slowly, I turned her around to face me and growled, "It matters to me. Was it your family? Did they do this?"

Her eyes met mine. "I don't need to tell you," she said firmly.

I pressed my lips together, my chest tightening with fury, but I couldn't afford to lose my temper again. Pulling in a long, slow breath, I counted back from ten in my head. In the calmest voice I could manage, I said, "Lieke, if they did this to you, their own kin, what could they do to someone else? To an enemy? To the fae?"

Her dark eyes flashed. "Are you accusing my family of something?"

Shaking my head, I raised my brow. "No, but what am I to think? You were in hiding for years and then return with poisoned knives and all these scars. Why did they send you back?"

"Because this is my home, Connor! They sent me back home!"

Her voice trembled slightly, and I caught a hint of sadness mixed with her anger, but I couldn't let it go. I had failed to have this conversation with her too many times, so I had to at least try. "And the knives?"

"For my own protection!" she shouted at me. "And apparently, it was warranted."

"That's all?" I asked. Pushing her like this was a risk, especially right before this important dinner.

She rolled her eyes at me. "You got me, Wolfie. I was obviously sent here to assassinate the family who has provided for me and protected me my whole life—including your brother, who I loved."

My teeth slammed together. "This isn't a joke."

Jabbing a finger into my sternum, she glowered. "Then don't accuse me of such laughable nonsense."

I spun away from her and stalked back to the front room, chiding myself for how poorly I'd handled that. Falling into the chair, I dropped my face into my hands and rubbed at my temples.

Between Matthias's insistence that I was falling for this woman and her clear animosity toward me, it was growing harder to focus. I needed to calm down.

Lieke cleared her throat, and I peered up to find her standing in the doorway, perfectly mimicking the way I had stood there just moments before. "I'm sorry for snapping at you," she said, pursing her lips. She sounded almost genuine.

I nodded and roughed my hand over my chin as I looked back down to the floor. "You know there are going to be questions about the scars, Sapphire," I said quietly.

For a moment, she merely hummed, but finally she said, "The unfortunate consequences of having a fiancé who insists I know how to protect myself."

"That could work," I said, though I still had my doubts.

"Are you going to be okay, Wolfie?" she asked, almost sounding like she cared.

"Of course," I lied.

Her laugh, light and airy, filled the room and poked holes in my resolve. "You'll have to learn to lie better than that if we're going to fool a whole kingdom."

"Fine," I said with a huff. "I'm nervous. Brennan is unpredictable, as you well know. I haven't seen him since that night, and I don't know how he's going to react seeing us together."

"Why does he even care?" Lieke's earlier mirth had vanished, having been replaced with bitter pain. "He abandoned me, left me to…"

Her face fell, and she nervously tucked a strand of hair behind her ear. I rose to my feet instinctively.

"He's an idiot," I said, taking a few cautious steps forward. Carefully she ran her hand beneath her eyes. Some small part of me hoped these would be the last tears she ever shed for my brother. Dropping her arms, she stepped away from the wall but still didn't look up at me. She gripped her dress in both hands, squeezing it tightly as if it were some lifeline that would get her through tonight.

"Do I look all right?" she asked, nearly whispering.

As I stepped toward her slowly, I searched for the proper response. This confident woman who had confronted her crown prince and screamed at her rulers in front of an entire room of fae in order to save her life, now stood before me looking deathly afraid to have a simple meal with those same royals.

Against my better judgment, I lifted my hand to her chin and, with the edge of my finger, tipped her face up toward mine. "You look perfect, Sapphire."

Her lips—soft and inviting—slowly curved up into a lopsided smile. "Careful there, Wolfie, can't have you making this complicated."

Ignoring the way my gut twisted uncomfortably—made worse by Matthias's warning, which echoed in my head for the millionth time—I tapped her nose playfully. "It'll only get complicated if you try to kiss me."

✳

When we entered the dining room, my jaw tensed as tightly as Lieke's grip on my arm.

They weren't supposed to be here.

They should have left this morning.

At the table, seated beside my brother and across from the king, were Princess Calla and her parents.

"Ah, Connor," my father said, lifting his glass toward us. "Right on time!"

"Appears we're a little late," I said as casually as I could, shooting my father a questioning glance.

"Our guests' bad luck with the weather is our good fortune," he explained. "They were unable to travel back to Arenysen today, so we get to enjoy their company for another day."

Smiling cordially at the Arenysen royals, I guided Lieke around the table to the other side of the room. She took my hand as she settled into her chair, letting go when I slid into the seat beside her. An awkward silence settled over the room. Lieke remained tense, staring at the place setting in front of her. I wanted to reach under the table and give her hand a reassuring squeeze, but Brennan was watching carefully, glaring at me as if I had stolen his favorite toy and then lied about it. So instead, I pressed my knee against hers, and when her eyes finally slid to mine, I smiled.

Princess Calla was the first to break the silence, leaning forward as she spoke in her kind, sweet voice. "I'm Calla. You're Lieke, right?"

Lieke slowly lifted her eyes and smiled. "I am, Your Highness. It's a pleasure to meet you. Congratulations on the engagement, by the way."

"Speaking of engagements," King Vael said, lifting his glass to his lips and taking a long sip. "I believe congratulations are warranted all around! Connor, why didn't you mention your lovely bride-to-be before?"

At this, Lieke turned to look up at me with a doting smile and slid her hand into mine. Ignoring the sparks that flew from her unexpected touch, I lifted our clasped hands to my lips and planted a gentle kiss before skirting my eyes to meet the king's.

"As you are likely aware, Your Majesty, tensions are high between the fae and the humans. Not everyone is as forgiving and welcoming as your family, I'm afraid. Unfortunately, circumstances out of our control required I announce it in a less than desirable manner."

King Vael laughed heartily. "*Less than desirable.* That's certainly one way to put it." He shifted his attention to my father. "I'm surprised you handled it as well as you did, Durand! If it had been me in your position that night, I would not have been nearly as calm."

Brennan scoffed loudly, and everyone turned to him, except my father, who instead focused his attention on me.

"*Calm* isn't the term I'd use to describe my reaction that night," he said, and quiet laughter rang out among our guests. "But after talking to my son and seeing how strongly he feels, I couldn't deny him—and Lieke—my blessing."

The queen placed her hand on her chest, shaking her head as if remembering some fond memory from her childhood and not from earlier this week. "The way you stood up for her, Connor. It warmed my heart to see."

I nodded my thanks, even as Lieke's hand stiffened within mine.

Thankfully, the servers brought in the first course—a salad of wilted greens with roasted squash—before anyone could say more about my daring rescue. The conversation turned to the details of Brennan and Calla's wedding. The Vaels wanted to hold it next spring when the apple trees would be in bloom.

Seven months.

Could Lieke and I keep this charade up for that long? Would she agree to it?

What choice did she have? What choice did either of us have?

I watched her spear a piece of squash with her fork, place it gingerly on her tongue, and chew slowly. She didn't look up from her plate, remaining quiet and seeming to have no desire to engage in the discussion. Not that I could blame her.

"And have you set a date?" Calla asked, waving her empty fork from Lieke to me.

I set my fork down, then glanced at Lieke, who was still focused on her food. Under the table, I tapped her foot with mine, caught her eye, and nodded to the princess across from us as discreetly as possible.

Clearly flustered, Lieke apologized. "The food is so delicious I must have gotten lost in it."

"This is true," King Vael agreed. "Your chef truly has a magic touch."

Calla ignored her father's interjection. "I was just asking if you two had set a wedding date yet."

I couldn't help but notice how sweet and genial this female was—certainly better than anyone Brennan had been with over the years, and perhaps better than he deserved.

"Oh, no, we haven't yet," Lieke said. She patted my arm lightly. "Wolfie here didn't want to detract from your celebration."

Brennan's head jolted up. He'd been quietly stewing most of the night, though no one else seemed to have noticed. Now he chose to speak up. "He's Wolfie now?"

Rolling my eyes, I opened my mouth to answer him, but Lieke beat me to it.

"Has been for a while actually," she said, laying her fork down on her now empty plate.

"I don't believe this," he grumbled, pushing away from the table and stomping out of the room.

Our guests stared after him in silent shock.

Clearing my throat, I looked from Lieke to Calla and smiled sympathetically. "You'll have to excuse my brother," I said. "He's still a little hurt that I...that we"—I grasped Lieke's hand in mine—"kept this from him for as long as we did."

Lieke nodded along as I spoke, adding in, "I'm sure he'll be fine. He's always been rather passionate, hasn't he?"

"Indeed," my father said, donning a smile that barely masked his ire.

"Should I go after him?" Calla searched each face around the table, but it was my father who finally offered her a shake of his head.

"No, Your Highness, he just needs some time to think. I'm sure he will come back soon."

But Brennan never returned.

CHAPTER FORTY-SIX

Lieke

By the time dinner was over, I couldn't wait to slip into a hot bath and ease away the tension I'd carried all evening. Connor escorted me back to my room in a pleasant silence, loosely holding my hand in his until we turned down our hallway. At my door, I offered him a quick goodnight before turning my back on him to open it, but Connor's hand landed on my arm. As he pulled me around to face him, I kept my eyes lowered.

"I'm tired, Connor," I said, not wanting to acknowledge how my stomach fluttered again at his touch.

His hand fell away, and he shoved it into his pocket. "I just wanted to say thank you. You did well."

My throat pinched closed, making a verbal response impossible, so I nodded. He let me turn from him this time, and as I stepped inside, he whispered, "Goodnight, Sapphire."

Once I closed the door behind me, I pressed my back against it, leaning my head back and letting my eyes fall closed. Seven months. I'd have to pretend I loved Connor for the next seven months. Could I do this? While I had full confidence I could convincingly act the part, I was more nervous that I would one day reach the point where I didn't need to fake it, just as he had originally planned.

This was temporary.

This wasn't real.

This was only a game.

I couldn't afford to lose my heart again, not after what had happened with the last prince I'd foolishly fallen for.

I needed to stop thinking about this and do something else.

Pushing away from the door, I focused on getting ready for bed.

To my pleasant surprise, I discovered that all the lanterns had already been lit, and a bath had been prepared behind the screen where I had dressed earlier. But my delight lasted only a few moments. I stopped and frowned, silently cursing. I couldn't get out of this dress by myself.

"Gretchen?" Please let the girl still be here.

Only silence answered me. There was no way I was going across the hallway and asking Connor to unfasten my buttons. I'd need to call for Gretchen. My bath would have to wait until she could arrive.

I reached for the cord on the wall to ring for her, but before I could pull it, a voice startled me.

"I can help," Brennan said. I whirled around to find him seated on the edge of my bed.

My initial shock gave way to anger. Who did he think he was, entering my room without permission? I was about to admonish him when he stood and walked toward me. In the low light, I could barely make out his expression, but as he got closer, I smelled wine on his breath and noticed the slight sway in his gait.

"You're drunk," I said, scowling and raising a hand in front of me to hold him at bay.

That was a mistake, though, because he grabbed my hand and placed it on his chest, holding it against him as he leaned in.

"Of course I am," he slurred. Then his lips curled into a sneer. "After having to watch my brother pawing you all night."

Yanking my hand away from him, I stepped backwards. "All night?" I scoffed. "Did you forget you left like a big baby before the main course? And since when is holding someone's hand the equivalent of pawing? You act like he was undressing me at the dinner table."

Brennan threw his arms out to the sides. "He might as well have been with how he looked at you."

This was ridiculous. It had to be the wine talking.

Wait. Was he seriously jealous? What right did he have to be jealous?

I stomped toward him and rammed my finger into his sternum as hard as I could, ignoring how it sent a jolt of pain through my joints.

"Why do you even care, Bren? You couldn't be bothered to care when I was about to be killed, but now? Now you think you have some sort of claim on me?" My voice was quickly growing louder than was prudent, but prudence be damned.

He tried to grab my hand again, but in his drunken state his movements were sluggish, making it easy for me to evade him. He dropped his arms to his sides, and his eyes softened with what might have been sadness or regret, but I'd been wrong about his emotions before. I wasn't going to assume anything now.

"I couldn't stand up to my father. You have to believe me."

"Funny, because your brother had no trouble with it."

"I thought you loved me," he said quietly. He was probably trying to manipulate me, but the gloom in his voice gave me pause.

"I did," I whispered. "I do. I don't know anymore. I loved you for so *so* long, and for years you acted like I had died alongside your mother."

"I've already apologized for—"

I raised my hand to silence him. "That pales in comparison to what you did that night. It was inexcusable. Who just stands there and lets their friend *die*?"

He flinched at the word *friend* and dropped his head. He was silent for a long time, staring at the floor between us. My feet ached. My body whined with fatigue. I needed rest. I needed him out of my room. When he still hadn't said anything, I turned around and reached for the pull cord again. But this time, I stopped myself.

Everyone on staff was a horrible gossip. As much as I liked Gretchen, the likelihood that she would be able to keep Brennan's presence here a secret was near zero, and that could put this entire engagement charade at risk.

"You need to leave," I said gently, but he didn't budge.

"And if I don't?" He glanced up from under his brow.

I gritted my teeth and got in his face. "Stars help me, Brennan, I will throw you out of here."

This earned me a laugh.

Lifting a hand, he tapped the tip of my nose like his brother had done earlier and smiled. "You're not strong enough to throw me anywhere."

I swatted at his hand and huffed out an angry breath. "If I can kill someone, I think I can force you to leave my room."

Slowly he backed away from me, smirking like a drunken buffoon. "Fine, I'm going. But before I do…"

He didn't finish his sentence and didn't move, just stared at me.

Becoming impatient, I sharpened my glare. "What is it?"

Instantly he was there, standing right in front of me, so close his chest brushed against mine when he inhaled. Before I could scoot back, his arms were around my waist, pulling me to him. Arching my back, I tried to lean away and put as much distance between us as possible. His eyes searched mine, desperate and hungry.

"I was stupid, Lieke," he whispered. "I can't lose you."

"You never had me, Brennan. Now let me go," I said as calmly as possible. His arms tightened around my ribs, making my next breath difficult.

"Kiss me?" he pleaded.

"You're engaged, Brennan. I won't."

He scoffed. "So are you. But we're both puppets, Lieke. We don't have to do what they say. We can be together."

My anger bubbled up in my chest, becoming harder to constrain the more he talked. Through clenched teeth, I spat out, "You lost your chance with me when you refused to fight for me."

"I'm fighting for you now!" he shouted, then slammed his lips against mine, his hand snaking up to the back of my head so I couldn't get away.

My protests were muffled by his lips and tongue as he attempted to consume me. Desperate, I slammed my fist into his ear, and he released me, reaching up to the side of his head as he cried out in pain.

"Get out! Get the fuck out, Brennan," I said, wiping away the feel of his mouth from mine. "And don't come back. I mean—"

The door to my room flew open. Connor, shirtless and wild-eyed, rushed in and punched Brennan in the face. Brennan staggered backwards, but Connor was already grabbing him by his collar and dragging him toward the door. Brennan's feet slipped several times as he tried to explain to Connor what was going on, but I didn't hear any of his words through my own anger thrumming in my ears.

"Connor!" I yelled, but the damn fae didn't stop. He threw Brennan through the doorway, sending him across the hall and into his own room. Brennan fell hard to the floor and—was the idiot laughing? Connor didn't even glance in my direction as he reached for my door to pull it closed behind him, but I slammed my hand into it, forcing him to turn around and acknowledge me.

"Did he hurt you?" Connor seethed, his gaze trailing over my face and neck before finding my eyes again. But I couldn't keep myself from staring at his bare chest and the intricate tattoo that covered half of it, reaching from his heart up over his shoulder like armor. It looked as if a chunk of his breast plate and pauldron had melded with his body, sinking into his skin.

Blinking, I met his eyes, but I didn't bother answering his ridiculous question. "I had it under control, Connor," I hissed through my teeth.

He looked at me for another breath before silently turning away and stomping back to his room.

CHAPTER FORTY-SEVEN

Connor

I kicked my door shut and stalked across the room to where Brennan had curled up on my sofa.

"What in the stars-damned fuck were you thinking?" I asked, barely keeping my anger contained.

I'd just finished bathing when I'd heard Lieke's voice, raised and upset. At first I'd thought that servant, Lola, had decided to confront her, but then she'd shouted Brennan's name.

Brennan twisted around to face me, his eyes lit up with humor.

"It's not funny," I said.

As if to prove me wrong, he laughed. "It kind of is though. Now she's mad at you, brother."

Shit, she was. I'd gone to help and done exactly the opposite.

But I would deal with that later.

"I can handle her," I said, immediately wishing I hadn't when my brother waggled his brows at me. I shook my head and said, "You're an idiot, you know that?"

His shoulder shifted against the cushions as if he were trying to shrug. "I am. I know." He was silent for a few moments before he finally glanced up at me. There was no humor in his expression now. "She doesn't love me anymore."

Seriously, how could he think she would? Before I could ask him that though, he was speaking again.

"I knew she wouldn't, but I had to at least try. I needed to know for sure."

"And you thought the best way to do that was to sneak into her rooms and…what? What did you do, Brennan?"

My body tensed as I waited for his answer, worried over what Lieke had just endured from him.

He waved his hand in the air, shaking his head. "It was just a kiss."

A kiss. It could have been worse, but still, the thought of him forcing his lips onto hers was maddening. He deserved to be pummeled again, but when I looked down at him, his eyes had fallen closed, and his breathing was gradually slowing.

Leaving him there to sleep off the alcohol and poor decisions, I returned to Lieke's door and knocked softly, half-hoping she'd also be asleep.

But I was not so lucky. Almost immediately she yanked the door open. She was still wearing the maroon dress from this evening…and still displaying the scowl she'd graced me with earlier. Her eyes flashed down to my chest, and I cursed silently when I realized I hadn't put on my shirt before storming across the hallway.

"Can I come in?" I asked, running my hand over the nape of my neck.

She cocked a hip out to the side and dropped her hand onto it. Her dark eyes burned like a cold fire, so sharp I could nearly feel them piercing me.

"So you can be an asshole again? No thank you," she said.

Fine. If she wanted to have this conversation in the hallway, I would oblige her.

"I'm sorry about my brother," I said, immediately realizing those were the wrong words.

Her brows shot up, and her jaw tightened.

"About your brother," she said quietly. "And what about you?"

"I'm sorry about me too. I shouldn't have acted so rashly."

"You should have let me handle it, Connor. I appreciate all you've done for me, but I need you to trust me. You *have* to trust me."

I swallowed hard, genuinely impressed by this woman's resolve and confidence. She might have a penchant for bad choices, but her nerve, her guts? These made her more attractive than any fancy dress could. My eyes wandered down to the low neckline of her dress and then snapped back when I realized I'd been staring. She was still glaring at me, though not as intensely as before.

"Do you need help with…" I gestured to her dress.

She shook her head slowly and offered me a smile that didn't reach her eyes. "No thank you. Gretchen should be here soon."

I nodded quickly before spinning on my heel, but I didn't want to return to my room just yet.

⁕

I banged on the door three more times before it finally opened. Matthias, bleary-eyed and visibly annoyed, took one look at me and ushered me inside.

"Trouble in paradise?" he asked around a yawn. "Need a drink?"

"I guess, and yes, I do need one, but I'd better not," I said as I stepped into the apartment. While he normally split his time equally between living here above the palace's training center and staying at the barracks with the army, he had remained here for the last couple weeks to oversee security during the Vaels' visit.

Against the far wall of his living room, underneath the large window that offered a clear view of the back of the palace, was a small table that held several bottles of varying sizes and shapes. Matthias grabbed two glasses and, shaking his head at me, proceeded to pour a generous portion of brandy into each. After handing a glass to me, he took a long draught from his before saying, "Yes, you'd better. Take it and sit down."

I didn't bother arguing with him, not when I'd just woken him up in the middle of the night. Taking a sip, I let the liquor slowly singe my throat on its way down, and then I settled into the chair closest to his small fireplace, which was currently dark and cold. Matthias didn't sit but stood next to the chair opposite me, leaning against its high back.

"Talk," he commanded, giving me a hard, albeit surprisingly sympathetic, look.

"I punched him, and now she's mad at me," I said into my glass before I took another drink.

Matthias swirled the amber liquid in his glass. "I hope you mean Brennan." I confirmed it with a roll of my eyes. Who else would I have meant? "And the human is mad at you? Or the princess?"

"Who do you think?" I asked, instantly regretting my sour tone. He didn't deserve for me to take my frustration out on him.

His mouth curved downward. "It's hard to think at this hour."

I let out a single, empty-sounding laugh. "Some commander you are."

"Last I checked, I wasn't in battle, Your Highness. I was in my bed."

Mumbling an apology, I threw back the last bit of brandy.

"Another?" he asked, and I held the glass up to him without a word. As he poured me another drink, he continued his questioning. "What did he do to deserve it? How mad is she? Like stab-a-prince mad or silent-treatment mad?"

I took the drink from him and stared at it for a long time before I answered. "After he stormed out of dinner, he must have drowned himself in wine and sneaked into her rooms."

"And? Is that it?"

"He kissed her," I muttered dejectedly, and Matthias laughed lightly, finally settling into his chair.

"Jealousy isn't a good look on you, friend."

I glared at him. "I'm not jealous."

He grinned and twisted his brow in that expression he always pulled out when he thought I was full of shit. "Spoken like a true jealous male."

"Don't make me throw this glass at you."

He scoffed. "So why is she mad? Because you hit him?"

"Because I didn't trust her."

Matthias's face pinched with confusion. "Trust her to do what? Does she know you're jealous too?"

"I'm not jealous," I started, but there was little point in arguing over that. "I guess my savior complex got me in trouble."

"Ah, that. Makes sense."

"But what was I supposed to do? Ignore her screams?"

"Apparently, yes," he said, pursing his lips behind his glass and generally doing a piss-poor job of hiding his laughter.

I groaned and flung my hands into the air. "I need to fix this. And I need to keep him the hell away from her." At that, Matthias's brow quirked up, and I pointed my glass at him. "And not because I'm jealous. But if he pulls that little stunt again, he could put this whole alliance with Arenysen in jeopardy. Again."

My friend shrugged. "So take her away."

Distance could be good, but where?

Matthias leaned over, propping his arms on his knees. "I wasn't planning to brief you until the morning, but since you so rudely assaulted my door and woke me up, we might as well discuss it now."

"What's happened? More attacks?"

"Not quite."

Widening my eyes, I indicated for him to continue.

"The fae are growing restless, and that stunt of yours with Lieke didn't help matters, unfortunately."

"Shit, I was hoping for the opposite."

"Yeah, well, maybe in time it can work in your favor, but at the moment, it's backfiring badly. We have Griffin's family riling up those in Linley, convincing them that the crown cares more about protecting the humans than the fae. If we don't do something soon, they may try to hunt down the rebels themselves."

"So we go on another tour?" I asked, already dreading the lumpy beds and stale ale and endless days of traveling from town to town. Add to that the innate danger of taking Lieke out among the fae, and the idea had no appeal.

But Matthias didn't seem to agree. He nodded slowly, his grin widening.

"Would you be joining us this time?" I asked.

He grimaced. "Why? Do you two need a chaperone?" My eyes fell to the floor, and he laughed. "What happened? Do I even want to know?"

I jerked my face up. "You're as bad a gossip as the staff, you know that?"

"Yes, but you love me more. So…?"

"Nothing really. It's just awkward having to touch her"—his eyes lit up—"*hands*, asshole. Her hands. Pretending to be smitten isn't hard, but…"

Matthias hummed thoughtfully, running his fingers over his chin. "So you take separate horses, stay in separate rooms—"

"Is that wise though? The separate rooms, that is. If the fae try to do anything—"

"Then sleep on the floor."

I scrunched my nose. The floor would be worse than the straw mattresses.

Matthias's expression became mischievous. "You can always shift before you sleep or learn to deal with the uncomfortable floor. But to answer your original question, yes, I would plan to join you as usual. Well, maybe not as usual. I'd like to bring some of the guards too."

At this, I nodded, warming up to the plan.

But in the back of my mind, I wondered if anything I did would be enough to keep Lieke from finding trouble.

CHAPTER FORTY-EIGHT

Lieke

Even if I hadn't been angry with Brennan, and even if I hadn't been wanting to get as much distance from him as possible, I still would have been excited for the journey around Emeryn. When I had traveled with Raven's family, we'd steered clear of the main roads and villages, so this would be my first time visiting any of the towns. The first stop was less than a day away from the palace, to the south—a village named Linley.

"Does Matthias always travel with you?" My question broke the long and uncomfortable silence that had settled between us since our departure a few hours ago. My horse, Honey, seemed as eager as I was to be out and about. We traveled beside Connor and his mare, Rosie. Matthias and two guards rode ahead of us and four others followed behind. Despite our easy pace, Connor didn't bother to look at me when he answered.

"Usually," he said, the single word clipped short, as if talking to me was some ghastly chore.

I wasn't going to let his bad attitude ruin mine though. Half-smiling, I nodded toward the general. "Is he your bodyguard or something?"

A short, breathy laugh came from Matthias, though he didn't look back at us at all. The two men beside him appeared to be laughing quietly, their shoulders bouncing slightly.

"No" was all Connor said.

"What's wrong with you today?" I asked, not bothering to hide my annoyance. He slid his gaze to mine for a moment before returning his attention to the trees around us.

"Nothing," he muttered. I was about to call him out on his bullshit when he amended his answer. "Couldn't possibly be that I'm riding through a dangerous forest with a woman most of my subjects want to see dead, heading for a village where…"

His jaw tightened, and I waited for him to finish. But he didn't. Instead, he went back to riding silently and acting as if I wasn't with him. Well, if Connor wasn't willing to tell me, I'd ask someone else.

"Matthias?" I called.

"Yes, Lieke?" The prince's friend turned his chin over his shoulder.

"What is in the village we're heading to?"

Connor sighed loudly, but Matthias ignored him. "It's—"

"Don't," Connor growled, and Matthias shrugged, turning forward again.

Pulling my reins back, I eased Honey to a stop. Connor let Rosie walk a few paces ahead of me before turning her head around and pulling up beside me. He glared at me, but I got the sense he wasn't truly frustrated with me. Or maybe I was only hoping that was the case.

Taking a deep breath, I calmed myself and said—as kindly as I could manage—"I told you to trust me, Connor."

"And I do, but you will not force me to speak on your terms or schedule. Have some stars-damned patience, Lieke. I have my reasons for not telling you everything."

"And what are those?" I pushed back, my frustration mounting.

He inched Rosie forward until our legs brushed against each other, then leaned toward me. His golden-brown eyes blazed in the late-morning sun for a brief moment before he seemed to realize we were not alone. Darting a quick glance toward the guards who waited nearby, he slowly lifted his hand to my cheek and brushed his thumb over my skin. Without thinking, I nestled into his touch, but he pulled away quickly.

"Maybe..." he whispered, "maybe I wanted to allow you to enjoy this first leg of our journey without being burdened by fear and worry."

My stomach hollowed, but I set my jaw, determined not to let the implications of what he was saying affect me. "I know the fae hate me and my kind, Wolfie. I know the risk I'm taking. Whatever it is, I can handle it."

His eyes narrowed slightly before he raised a brow and straightened in his saddle. "Fine, Sapphire. Linley is where Griffin was from. You remember him, yes?"

The blood in my veins chilled as my mind swirled with memories of Griffin's cruel voice and how he had attacked me in that hallway. If he was from Linley, then...

I met Connor's unsympathetic gaze.

"Good. You do remember."

"His family?" I whispered.

"They're not too fond of you, as you can imagine."

I turned to study the forest around us, as if his family might be waiting in these trees to ambush me, then asked, "So why are we—"

Wheeling Rosie around once more, Connor pulled away from me as he answered. "Because they pose the greatest risk. Not just to you, but to all humans—and by extension, the kingdom itself. We need to win them over before they can spread their discontent."

With that, he grabbed my hand, giving me a reassuring squeeze as he interlaced our fingers together. He tossed his chin toward the road ahead.

"Come on, Sapphire. Your future subjects are waiting."

CHAPTER FORTY-NINE

Connor

We arrived in Linley just before suppertime. The sun bathed the village in a warm amber glow, making it seem more inviting than I knew it would be. The streets were empty, which was to be expected at this time of day, as families would be gathering in their homes for a meal.

Lieke had been quiet for the remainder of our ride here. As we exited the trees and stepped onto the wide dirt path that served as the village's main street, her anxiety appeared to worsen. Pulling her bottom lip between her teeth, she scanned the buildings on either side of the road, and her knuckles whitened as she gripped the reins harder.

"Relax, Sapphire," I whispered. Her eyes flicked to mine, and I tried to offer her a reassuring smile, but the worry remained written on her face. Reaching over, I covered her hand with mine, rubbing my thumb over her skin in soothing strokes. Instead of pointing out that this was the fear I had hoped to spare her from, I said softly, "We aren't meeting with anyone tonight."

She didn't appear relieved, though, and her expression tightened.

Matthias slowed his horse to allow us to catch up to him. Turning to me, he gave Lieke a cursory glance. "I'll secure rooms at the inn while you get the horses situated?"

I nodded, forgetting—until it was too late—to remind him to get Lieke a room of her own.

Together, Lieke and I rode around to the stables at the rear of the inn. I dismounted first and handed my reins to the stable hand. Lifting a hand to Lieke, I offered to help her off her horse. Her hand trembled in mine, but I didn't comment on it. While she climbed down, I steadied her, and the eyes of the two guards and the stable hand burned into me, as if they were scrutinizing every move we made.

Pulling Lieke close, I cupped her jaw in my hands and lifted her face gently until she looked at me. Fear still swirled in her dark eyes.

"It will be okay," I whispered, but her face remained pale, her features strained.

With a sigh, I instinctively placed a soft kiss to her forehead, wishing I could take away her worries.

I froze.

That felt too real, too genuine.

Fuck. If I wasn't careful, I'd end up proving Matthias right and falling for her. I retreated, reminding myself this was all for show—every touch, every kiss, every longing glance—they were nothing but staged gestures needed to sell the lie.

I caught her eye once more. "Let's get you to your room so you can rest."

She didn't say anything—didn't even nod. I slid my hand down her arm and weaved our fingers together. Just inside the door, I nearly ran straight into Matthias, who took one look at our entwined hands and smiled. When he handed me a single room key, I opened my mouth to protest, but he was already explaining.

"I'm afraid they're nearly full. Only had the one room available, but I did manage to request supper be delivered to you shortly." He shrugged, the same stupid grin still plastered on his face.

I threw my thumb over my shoulder. "The stables were basically empty though."

"Not everyone owns a horse, Your Highness. I'm only telling you what I was told."

Lieke pulled the key from my hand and looked from Matthias to me. "It's okay, Wolfie. We can share the room. I'm more worried about Matthias and the men."

Matthias gloated. "See? You *can* share the room. And no need to fret about us, Lieke. We'll be just fine. We are used to improvising."

With that, he skirted around us, leaving us to head upstairs.

I turned to lead Lieke up to the room—our room—and each step I took seemed to push my stomach further up into my throat. If I found out Matthias had lied and orchestrated this nonsense, I'd lock him in the fucking dungeon for a week.

As we passed by each door, I listened for sounds of life behind them before remembering everyone was probably eating at the tavern next door.

Opening the door to our room, I held it wide and stepped out of the way so Lieke could enter. I surveyed the space. It wasn't one of the worst rooms I'd stayed in. Small and sparsely furnished, it was drab yet somehow had a quaint, cozy charm to it. The walls, undecorated as they were, could use a fresh coat of paint. The fireplace across from the door looked as if it hadn't been cleaned out since the inn was constructed. Still, fresh wood lay waiting inside it, ready to help combat the night's chill. A small chest of drawers with a lantern perched atop it acted as a bedside table, and a simple washbasin sat in one corner. The single bed, larger than most inns boasted, was covered with an old quilt and a lumpy pillow, but at least there was a spare blanket draped over the footboard.

In silence, we settled in.

Kicking off her riding boots, Lieke lay back on the bed and propped her hands behind her head. She closed her eyes, and although she looked almost peaceful, her elevated pulse and shallow breathing betrayed her nervousness. I moved to light a fire, but when heavy footsteps sounded on the stairs, I instead darted for the door, opening it before the innkeeper could knock.

The female who greeted me was older and might have reminded me of our own Mrs. Bishop, had she not been scowling. Even when our cook was cross, she didn't look this mean and sour.

"Your supper," she said curtly, thrusting two bowls into my hands and turning before I could even utter my thanks.

The aroma of braised meat and vegetables filled the room, rousing Lieke and coaxing her to sit up. Though I was certain she'd been awake, I still asked, "Sleep well?"

She only shrugged. Pulling her legs up onto the bed, she crossed them like a child and took the bowl when offered. But she didn't eat. Instead she merely stared at the thick stew.

"You should eat, Sapphire," I said, lifting a heaping spoonful to my mouth. It might have looked unappetizing, but it tasted divine. The food was perhaps the one redeeming quality of this village and the only thing I looked forward to when visiting—that and the ale at the tavern.

Once we had finished eating and piled our dishes beside the lantern, I grabbed one of the pillows and the extra blanket and dropped them onto the floor in front of the fireplace.

"What are you doing?" Lieke asked from her perch on the bed.

I didn't look at her as I answered, "Going to bed—"

"Technically it looks like you're going to *floor*."

Smirking to myself, I nodded. "I suppose so. But we should get some sleep. We'll be meeting the villagers at the tavern in the morning."

"And you're going to be able to sleep there?" she asked.

"As Matthias said, we're used to improvising."

"But you're the prince."

I swiveled my chin around to face her. "Yes, but I'm also the general of the armies. Not the kind of general who carts around feather mattresses and luxurious bedding with me into battle."

"Are you saying this"—she gestured to the room around us—"is like going to battle?"

Her question gave me pause, and it took me a moment to decide how to answer. "In a way, I suppose it is. Convincing everyone that a human queen is good for them will be a harder fight than I'd originally thought."

"What?" she asked, a stoic expression on her face. "You mean the fae who want all humans gone aren't keen on having a human on the throne? How odd indeed."

"Stop mocking me," I said flatly, kicking off my boots before sitting down on the floor.

"Then stop being stupid," she said around a smile. "Why did you think this would ever work?"

I ran my hand over my face and sighed. "Foolishly hopeful, I guess."

"But how? The fae hate—"

"Not without cause," I blurted out and immediately regretted it.

Her features twisted with curiosity. "Because of the attacks?"

"Among other things," I said. "Their anger dates back to well before the attacks began."

"Since when?"

My mind flooded with images of blood and death and screaming, memories from the war—a war started by the humans. I squeezed my eyes closed, trying to blot it all out, but still I whispered, "Since the war."

"Was it that bad?" she asked, and I turned to look at her. She couldn't be serious, yet her eyes stared back at me with innocent concern.

"It was war, Sapphire. War is always *that* bad."

"My father fought for your family, you know." Averting her eyes from me, she focused on wringing her hands in her lap. "I was just a baby when he died, and by the time I was old enough to understand where he had gone, I could never ask my mother about it."

Leaning back on my hands, I studied her as she spoke. What was it like to not know war? To grow up in the aftermath but never to be haunted by the memories of the bloodshed?

"Could I ask you about it?" she asked meekly. The images flickered to life again in my head, and I winced so obviously that she immediately muttered, "Never mind."

"Maybe another time," I said, hoping she wouldn't push the matter and ask why.

When she dropped her legs over the side of the bed and slid off, my stomach tightened. But she didn't approach me. Rather, she moved around the bed to where her pack sat on the floor. I relaxed as she retrieved a simple nightgown from the bag.

She gave me a sideways glance and a small smile. "Do you mind if I change for bed?"

"Of course not," I said.

She cleared her throat, widening her eyes. "Were you just planning to watch me?"

My cheeks warmed at my mistake. Without a word, I lay down and rolled onto my side to face the fire. Staring into the flames, I tried to concentrate on the popping and crackling of the wood instead of the rustling of fabric being pulled across her skin. I managed to not peek over my shoulder and didn't turn away from the fire even when the bed creaked under her weight and the blankets whispered over her as she pulled them up.

As uncomfortable as this floor was, sleeping here would be worth it to avoid any complications between us. This was going to be difficult enough without blurring any lines. I could handle a few nights of discomfort.

"Are you sure you don't want to sleep up here?" Lieke's question floated through the space. "There's plenty of room, and I promise not to bite."

I scoffed silently to myself. Biting was the least of my worries with her.

"Go to sleep, Sapphire."

CHAPTER FIFTY

Lieke

After the long day of riding, sleep came easily. Unfortunately, sleep brought dreams, and being here in this village summoned the worst kind.

No sooner had I closed my eyes than I was back in the forest outside the palace, scrambling backwards away from Griffin as he snarled at me. With his massive hand, he gripped my throat and squeezed. I tried to scream, but he cut off the sound with his ever-tightening fingers. The world darkened, and I collapsed to the ground. When I opened my eyes again, I was back in the dim palace hallway. My knife was in my hand as soon as the fae spoke.

"Remember me?"

My feet slipped from under me, and I fell hard onto my backside. He kicked against my shoulder, sending me toppling backwards until my head slammed into the stone floor. I opened my mouth, but no sound came out—everything was drowned out by his growled taunts, my pounding heartbeat, and my labored breathing. My knife clattered to the floor, and he barked out a laugh as he knelt over me, pinning me in place. Tears pricked my eyes, but still I had no voice, no strength with which to scream or speak.

Bucking against him, I struggled to reach the knife, but it was no use. Every time my fingers grazed the handle, it would slip further out of reach. I was going to die here. This time, I wouldn't be as lucky. This time, there would be no prince to save me and no way for me to save myself.

The fae leaned over me, his hot breath warming my face. He laughed as his eyes searched mine with the same viciousness he'd shown that night. Once more I tried to find the knife, to kill him as I had before, but I froze as his words hit my ear.

"You might have killed me, Goldie, but my family will avenge me. Maybe not here, and maybe not today, but sooner or later, I'll get my revenge, and I won't make it fast." He trailed a finger down the side of my face as if he were my lover instead of a monster. "You won't die quickly like I did. You'll suffer as you deserve when your body is torn apart, inch by wretched inch."

His hand fell to my throat, and when his fingernails pierced my skin, he ripped a scream from my lungs.

"Lieke," he said firmly. I continued to scream, flailing against him, trying to get him off me, but he was too strong.

"Sapphire." Even though he whispered the name, it slipped through my frantic shouts and stilled my limbs. "Sapphire, wake up."

That wasn't Griffin.

This voice was gentle, kind, and worried.

Sliding my eyes open, I found a pair of golden-brown eyes staring back at me.

"You," I whispered.

"Me," Connor said, his lips twitching as if he were suppressing a smile.

Sitting up, I looked around the room, half-expecting to see that I was actually in the palace hallway. But we were still in the Linley Inn. The early morning light peered in through the single window, illuminating everything with an ethereal glow.

Connor lifted a hand and brushed his fingers across my forehead to coax my hair back behind my ear. "Are you okay?"

I nodded slowly, refusing to look at him. He was sitting on the bed—altogether too close to me—with his leg resting against mine. When his fingers swept over my collarbone, every one of my nerves sparked, and my skin prickled. He didn't want to make things complicated, yet he was willing to do things like that?

"I thought you were going to sleep on the floor," I said, nodding to the blankets in front of the fireplace that he had obviously slept in.

"I did," he said, his brows knitting together.

I scrunched my nose at him—yes, that was safer than a smile—and asked, "Then why are you in my bed?"

He flinched and lifted both hands in a questioning gesture. "I'm not *in* your bed."

Shrugging a shoulder, I pulled my lips tight. "If you say so."

"You were having a bad dream—"

"Was I? Quite the convenient excuse for you, Wolfie," I said, narrowing my eyes. "If you wanted to be so close to me, you could have just asked. No need to—"

Connor blew out a breath as he pushed to his feet and stomped over to the fireplace. In silence, he folded up the blankets and returned them and the pillow to the bed.

"You're incorrigible," he griped. "Get dressed and meet me downstairs. Quickly. I'd like to get to the tavern before the townsfolk do."

My insides writhed like worms after a heavy rain, and bile rose into my throat. I covered my mouth with the back of my hand. Connor shot me a puzzled look, but I simply nodded.

From the doorway, he repeated, "Quickly" and left me to fret in solitude.

※

Matthias met us outside the tavern door with a smile that seemed altogether too happy considering what we were here to do. But then he wasn't the one the fae's family wanted to see strung up and killed. Connor, on the other hand, seemed appropriately somber, though I hoped it was due to his serious nature and not because he had a sense of foreboding. Under other circumstances, I'd likely find the contrast between the two males rather amusing, but not today.

"Well?" Connor shot his friend a pointed glare.

Matthias didn't seem at all perturbed by the scrutiny and dove into his report. "Just the tavern owner, his wife, and their server are inside. He says the usual morning crowd should arrive within the hour, though he couldn't say how many of them will actually show up. They all know we're here. Word spread quickly last night, as we expected."

Connor roughed a hand over his stubbled chin. "Let's hope they come then. I'd hate for this stop to be a wasted opportunity."

"And if there's trouble?" Matthias asked.

Dipping his chin, Connor answered, "That's why you're here."

Matthias's grin widened, as if he was hoping for trouble to arrive just so he could have some fun.

Inside, the tavern was similar to the one I'd visited in Engel, though the owner looked nothing like Mr. Marstens. For one, he was much shorter, had far less hair, and wore a bitter frown that only deepened when his eyes landed on me.

Connor ushered me to a chair at a large table in a corner, settling into the seat beside me while Matthias charmed the young female server. Positioned around the room—leaning against columns, sitting at tables, and standing next to the bar—were Matthias's guards. They waited and watched, their eyes trained on both the entrance and the door to the kitchen.

I leaned toward Connor and whispered, "I'd feel better if I had a weapon of my own." His muscles tensed, and I clarified, "Not my knives. Just anything I could use to defend myself."

"You have two generals and six guards here. You'll be fine."

"You sound rather confident for someone who looks so nervous."

"It's called being alert, not nervous."

"Whatever you say, Wolfie," I mumbled, slumping further down in my chair. Connor grabbed my elbow and hauled me back upright. I started to protest—to remind him we had an audience—but he was in my face in an instant.

Before he could say anything, Matthias cleared his throat, and Connor's gaze skirted over to him. Pursing his lips, Connor closed his eyes and pulled in a slow breath, as if frustrated by the reminder that we were supposedly in love. When he opened them again, his gaze was gentler, calmer.

"Queens don't slouch or cower," he said in a patient yet firm tone. "Own the room, Sapphire. It's yours to rule." His eyes burned into mine, as though he could convince me any of this was true with a simple look.

He was trying to help, of course, but something in me still bristled at his statement. But with the guards present, I couldn't sneer at him like I wanted to. Dropping my hand to his shoulder, I brought my lips close to his ear.

Why did he have to smell so damned good?

Focus, Lieke!

Licking my lips, I whispered to him, "It's not mine. It will never be mine. This thing between us is—"

"New, I know," he said, shifting so that our noses nearly touched. My muscles tightened. He couldn't kiss me. Not here. He'd forbidden it. But instead, he slid his lips up to my ear. I tensed as his breath tickled my skin.

"Careful here. They can hear better than you think."

I nodded stiffly once. Then his hands were on either side of my neck, and he had his forehead pressed to mine. Something about the gesture calmed my breathing and settled my nerves. At the same time, it sent my heart racing away from me, as if it wanted to run to him of its own accord, against my will.

And I couldn't allow that.

✳

We sat in the tavern for most of the morning without a single patron walking through the door. While this was decidedly beneficial for my safety, it did little good to help us win over anyone when they refused to even see us.

"How long do we wait?" I asked, pacing the small area behind our table and trying to coax the feeling into my backside and legs again.

Connor rubbed a hand behind his neck and pulled his legs down from the table, where he'd been resting them for the better part of the last hour. Before he could answer, though, the door to the tavern swung open and three fae males stepped inside. Their resemblance to Griffin was unmistakable, but even without the similarities, the murderous glares they pinned on me would have given them away as his family. The males stepped aside, revealing a smaller female who looked nothing like them.

Her red hair was cropped short, accenting her delicately pointed ears and bright green eyes—green eyes filled with malice. The long-sleeved black dress she wore covered most of her petite body, from her neck to her feet, and swished softly as she strode purposefully toward us.

More fae filed in behind her, filling up the tavern until I could no longer see the guards Matthias had stationed. As if the sheer number of them wasn't intimidating enough, none of them sat. They all remained standing, watching us.

No—watching *me*.

Connor reached behind him and took hold of my hand. Guiding me forward, he nodded to the chair beside him—a silent command to take my seat. Why would he choose to remain seated at a time like this? Shouldn't we be standing our ground or preparing to fight back if necessary? But I didn't raise any of these questions. I could ask him later—assuming I survived this. Right now, I needed to trust him.

"Renata," Connor said with a warmer tone than seemed warranted given everyone's icy stares. He gestured toward the chair opposite us. "Please, sit."

For a tense moment, she merely stood there, her eyes boring into me like fiery daggers. Every muscle in my body tightened as I waited for her to say or do something.

Slowly, Renata dropped a hand to the back of the chair and pulled it out. She lowered herself gracefully into it, and my eyes widened slightly when all the gathered fae mirrored her actions, slipping into chairs around the tables or onto stools lining the bar. Griffin's family took seats beside Renata. The continued silence kept me on edge, and I waited anxiously for them to spring whatever trap was being set for us.

Renata finally pulled her attention away from me and turned to Connor. "I wish you were visiting us under better circumstances."

"So do I," he replied.

As if their exchange had been a cue of some kind, the silence broke, the crowd launching into murmured conversations. Over the next few minutes, they kept the tavern keeper and his servers busy with their orders. Our table remained quiet, though, as did Matthias and his guards, who maintained their posts around the room.

Folding her hands on the table, Renata leaned forward slightly and asked, "Can I assume you aren't just here to pay your respects? I'd hate to think our noble prince had stooped so low as to celebrate my husband's demise by parading his killer around and demanding we bow to her."

This was Griffin's wife? I shifted in my seat uncomfortably, somehow managing to resist the urge to sink lower. I was to be queen—at least as far as these fae were concerned—and a queen wouldn't shrink away even when facing those who hated her, so I forced myself to straighten and mimic Connor's regal posture.

Connor lowered his brows slightly. "I am not demanding anything that isn't already expected of you as an Emerynian. The crown—and whoever wears it—will be respected."

Renata's eyes twitched. "She doesn't wear it yet."

As I worked hard to keep my breathing and heart rate under control, I watched them carefully, and I couldn't help but be impressed by Connor's ability to remain calm while this wretch challenged him, but then I'd seen his excellent control plenty of times. I'd also witnessed how quickly that poise could shift into rage when he was pushed too far.

Would this fae be so stupid as to goad him?

Grief made even the smartest of people act irrationally.

Connor maintained his placating tone as he responded, "No, she doesn't. But she will, whether you—or anyone else—approve or not."

One of the males next to her cleared his throat. "Then why bring her? You don't want our approval. You don't need it. So why bother?"

Connor glanced at me and half-smiled before facing the fae who had spoken. "Because I hope for peace, Enzo. An end to the attacks. A return to the harmony we once enjoyed. Having a human as your queen will appease the rebels, convince them of our desire to restore their place in our society, and stop their violence against the fae."

He spoke with such conviction that I regretted teasing him last night. But would anyone here share his vision? Would anyone believe it could be done?

Renata's lips shifted into a sad smile, and she glanced at me as she said, "You put a lot of trust in the humans, Prince." Then she slid her gaze back to Connor, shrugging. "And what happens if that trust proves ill-placed? What happens if the rebels don't accept her? What if they keep coming for us? Are you prepared to protect the fae? Or do you only offer your protection to the mortals?"

A fresh quiet blanketed the room as all conversation stopped. Every fae turned to look at Connor expectantly. My heart thumped faster under the intense scrutiny, but his people were no longer regarding him with anger. Yes, some animosity lingered, but on the edge of it lay the familiar sheen of exhausted grief and fear.

For the first time since I'd learned of the killings, I realized the fae were truly scared. And of humans, at that. What were the rebels doing to elicit such terror in these immortals?

In answer, an image of Griffin's final shocked expression flashed in my mind.

I, a weak and mortal human, had killed a fae. How?

Anna's words rushed back to me. *"These blades are special. They will protect you from the fae, but you must only use them as a last resort."*

Were the rebels using something similar? Did they have access to the same material my knives were made of? Was my family involved? My head swirled with the questions, but before I could make any sense of them, Connor was moving next to me.

Standing slowly, he slid his hands into his pockets and surveyed those gathered, already looking so much like the king he would one day be. He commanded the room without a word, and my heart fluttered involuntarily, filling with a strange sense of pride at the thought that I would someday rule beside such a strong, noble male—despite the fact that I never actually would marry him, of course.

"The crown rules over all of Emeryn," Connor said, his rich tenor reaching every corner of the crowded tavern. "Fae. Human. And any other race that resides here. Our duty is to all of you. I know you're hurting. I know you're scared. But no matter what happens, I will put the good of this country first every time. Whether the rebels accept my bride or not, that will never change. We will find them. We will stop this. We will restore peace. But that peace will only be possible if you are willing to accept it."

CHAPTER FIFTY-ONE

Connor

Silence answered my speech, filling the room with a tension that bit into my bones and twisted my stomach ever tighter. Slowly and wordlessly, the fae turned to look at one another. Even Renata was gazing intently at each of Griffin's brothers. They exchanged slight nods, which spread through the room like a wildfire.

Something nudged my leg, and I glanced down to find Lieke had bumped me with her knee. Her face was alight with cautious hope. I offered her a tight-lipped smile and turned back as Griffin's wife and brothers rose from their seats.

Renata nodded sharply. "Despite all that we've lost, we want peace as well. But this"—she waved a hand from me to Lieke and back—"is beyond difficult." Her jaw tightened. Her eyes darkened. "She killed him, and I know; I've heard the excuses. My Griffin was no saint of a male, and maybe she did do it in self-defense, but…" Renata's gaze dropped to the table between us.

I cleared my throat and addressed each of Griffin's brothers in turn as I said, "It's difficult and painful, I know. But hatred and revenge cannot dull that ache. Only peace can. Please, at least consider what I've said."

Renata slowly lifted her chin and studied Lieke for a long, tense moment before finally focusing on me once more. "We will consider it, Your Highness. But that's the most I can promise you now."

It might not have been a declaration of trust, but it was more than I had expected from them.

"Thank you," I said, nodding once. Before I could think to say more, Renata spun on her heel and exited the pub with the brothers close behind. As I stared after her, Matthias appeared beside me, leaning close.

"Do we believe her?" he asked.

Chewing on the inside of my lip, I pondered his question for a moment. I wanted to trust her, but was that merely my foolish hope blinding me from recognizing a disastrous truth?

"I don't know," I said finally, then lowered my voice. "Seemed too easy, didn't it?"

Matthias shrugged a shoulder. "Maybe. Or maybe you're just that good."

✳

We stayed at the Linley tavern for the remainder of the day, leaving just after supper. Although the rest of the crowd stayed longer than Renata had, they refused to speak to me or meet Lieke. With the next village being over a day's ride away, it made little sense for us to leave yet, so we opted to stay for another night.

When we returned to the room, Lieke remained quiet for an abnormally long time. I almost would have preferred the teasing. This quiet Lieke put me on edge and made me worry about her more than I wanted to. But when I asked her if she was okay, she avoided the question and inquired about the last thing I had expected her to.

"How does the mate thing work anyway? Is there really only one mate for everyone?" She curled her legs up onto the bed as she had the night before.

"Why do you want to know?" I asked, stoking the fire.

She shrugged. "Just curious. Mrs. Bishop mentioned it once but never had time to explain it. I mean, how do you know when you've found them?"

As I watched the flames grow, I searched for the words my father had used to explain it to me. "According to my father, your mate—only one—was chosen for you when the stars were hung in the sky. But you don't know who they are until the bond is physically formed."

Lieke's lips twisted comically. "Physically? So you have to sleep with them before you find out?"

Laughing, I sat down on my makeshift bed on the floor. "Maybe for some, I suppose. Though I've never met any who didn't at least kiss before doing that."

Her face flushed my favorite shade of pink.

Stop that. You're supposed to try and avoid *that type of thinking!*

"So a kiss then?" she asked, her eyes flitting to the ceiling as she pondered this information, but she was soon staring at me again, this time with humor filling her dark blue eyes. I got the distinct impression that I wasn't going to like what she asked next.

"Is that why you said lips were too complicated? Are you worried we could be mates?"

I dropped my head, rubbing my fingers along my forehead to shield my warming cheeks, hoping I appeared more exasperated than embarrassed. I received enough grief from Matthias for believing in mates; I didn't need to have her ridiculing me too.

"No," I said, taking a deep breath. "That's not why it's complicated. You don't need to be mates for kisses to cause problems. Just look at you and Brennan."

Immediately I regretted mentioning my brother. I was supposed to be keeping them apart. Physically and mentally. Thankfully she ignored the comment.

"How do you know you've found your mate then? Is there some clap of thunder or burst of energy or something?"

At that, I laughed again, shaking my head. "When the bond forms, it's different for everyone, from what I can gather. My father described it as being struck by lightning."

"Lovely," Lieke whispered as she wrinkled her nose.

"My mother, however, said it was like having her eyes truly opened for the first time in her life, as if the world had been nothing but a dull gray before him."

This time Lieke reacted with a swoony sigh. "That's rather poetic. My mother used to talk about Father as if he were the center of her world, and"—she choked up a bit and looked down to her lap—"I suppose he must have been, since there always seemed to be something missing in her life after he died."

How was I to respond to that? I could ask about her mother, but that path seemed too personal to tread down. Before I could find any words, though, she was speaking again.

"So I'm guessing you haven't found your mate then?"

I choked in surprise, but I should probably have expected this question to come up. Now I did wish I had inquired about her family instead.

"No," I said quickly.

Jutting her chin slightly, she eyed me with curiosity. "Are you looking for her?"

"Not at the moment, no." I smirked but was sure she could tell how fake it was.

"Well, I didn't mean right now," she said, rolling her eyes. "Obviously you're not searching for her while you're engaged to me."

"That would certainly complicate things. Someday maybe I'll find her. Matthias doesn't believe in mates though. Tells me I'm a fool to. I'm one of the few who still do actually. It's become a bit of a sore subject for the fae."

"Why is that?"

Drawing in a deep breath, I leaned back onto my hands. "The war was fought over a mated pair. My uncle, Cian Durand, discovered his mate, Ellae, was a human from Wrenwick. Ellae was unfortunately betrothed to Leif, that kingdom's prince. When she ran away to Emeryn, the humans insisted she'd been stolen, abducted, brainwashed, who knows.

Their prince declared war to get her back. Many died. Fae and human alike. The fae blamed the humans, as you know, but they also faulted the mating bond itself for all the bloodshed and eventually ceased to believe in it at all. They insisted, instead, on choosing their companions themselves rather than waiting for some problematic cosmic connection."

"But your parents were mates? Is that why you believe in it?" Lieke asked.

I nodded once, picturing them in my head—in particular the way my father was before Mother had passed. "I suppose so. I've seen the good that comes from it, the love, the dedication, the commitment..."

She remained quiet for a while, staring down at her lap. Did she think I was a fool for my beliefs? Why did I care if she did?

Clearing my throat, I finally said, "We should get some sleep. We have a long ride to Fairden in the morning."

Lieke dropped her feet to the floor and stood, heading for the door. When I gave her a pointed look, she chuckled once. "Just going to the privy, Wolfie. Calm down."

"Be careful," I said.

Opening the door, she threw me an eyeroll over her shoulder. "I'll try not to fall in."

Before I could respond, she was gone, pulling the door shut behind her. The crackling and popping of the fire beckoned my attention, and I once again let my gaze soften as I watched the flames lap hungrily at the logs I'd added earlier.

I thought back to her question—*Are you looking for her?*—but it was drowned out by the memory of my father's voice when he'd asked, *Are you prepared to marry her for real?*

Once more, I lowered my head into my hands, this time from weariness and frustration. I was no longer trying to earn her affections, of course. Yet the sweet moments with Lieke were beginning to fray my confidence that I could keep this ruse up without losing my heart to her against my will.

What if I fell for her just as Matthias had predicted? My mind then twisted my father's question into a new one, one I didn't have an answer to yet.

Am I prepared to let her go when this is over?

Outside our room, a set of boots clomped hastily on the stairs, and I whirled toward the door. Lieke should have been back by now. My throat tightened with dread as I stood.

When I stepped outside, though, I found the hallway empty. I sprinted down it, catching Lieke's scent as I neared the top of the stairs. Why had she been here?

Bounding down, I cursed as I recognized another scent mixed in with hers.

Renata.

The main room of the inn was empty, and I couldn't tell which way they had gone. As much as I hated shifting, I didn't think twice before pulling at the magic in my blood and taking on my hound form. Their mixed scents hit me, and I took off running, out the back door and into the alley that ran along behind it. Swinging my head to the right, I scanned the stables but sensed nothing except the horses. They hadn't gone there.

I turned left and took off, pushing my feet to go faster.

When Renata's rough voice hit my ears, I skidded on the cobble-stones and took a sharp turn down a side street. A growl rumbled in my chest.

Lieke, held by two of Griffin's brothers, was pinned against a brick wall. Renata pressed a knife to her throat as she hissed in her face, but I didn't hear what she said. I didn't care. She would receive no mercy from me.

Lieke's sapphire eyes shifted in my direction, but I was focused sole-ly on her captors.

Renata swung the knife around toward me, thrusting it high, ap-parently expecting me to leap at her. Instead, I crouched low, clamping my jaws on her calf. She screamed as she lost her footing, and with one violent shake of my head, I threw her body into the wall across the alley.

The two males dropped Lieke and lunged for me, but I was faster. Leaping onto one of them, I sank my teeth into his neck, ignoring the disgusting taste of his blood as I ripped and tore at his throat. The other male got his arms around me and tried to pull me off his brother, but it only aided me in tearing away a large chunk of flesh. I spit it onto the ground and watched with satisfaction as the fae collapsed against the wall, his hands frantically trying to staunch the blood pouring from his wound.

Lieke's scream rent the air.

Still fighting to get free of the other fae's hold on me, I searched for Lieke, assuming Renata must have come to and was attempting to finish her off. Instead, though, I found Lieke—my bride, my mortal, my Sapphire—rushing toward us with Renata's knife in hand. Then she disappeared from view. I couldn't see what she did, but it must have been effective, because the fae roared in pain, releasing me before his back arched and he fell to the ground.

CHAPTER FIFTY-TWO

Lieke

Blood trickled down the knife and onto my shaking hand. I couldn't move or think as I watched the fae fall to the ground. I'd buried the blade in his lower back, thrusting it up under his ribs as I'd been taught to. Something moved in my periphery, but I couldn't pull my eyes away from the pool of blood now spreading across the stone street. A hand grabbed my arm and wheeled me around until I found myself staring into Connor's golden-brown eyes.

"Are you okay, Sapphire?" he asked, his breathing as ragged as my own. "Are you hurt?"

Blinking quickly, I nodded. "I'm fine. I'm sorry."

He cupped my neck in his hands, his thumbs stroking my jaw as he narrowed his eyes. "Why are you apologizing?"

I swallowed hard, ignoring the way my skin warmed under his touch and how my pulse settled in his presence. "I should have been more careful."

He laughed quietly and brought his lips down to my forehead, kissing me softly before saying, "You're only human, Sapphire. And three fae surprising you on your way to the privy—"

"Is embarrassing," I said, my face heating. How many times was this prince going to have to save my pathetically mortal life?

Connor laughed again as he pulled his hands away from me, and I noticed the blood coating his stubbled chin.

I gestured to my own jaw. "You missed some."

Quickly he swiped a hand across his face, grimacing at the blood that now stained his fingers. He brushed them against his pants to clean them off and then looked down at the three fae that lay unconscious on the street.

"Are they dead?" I asked.

Before he could answer, though, Matthias and several of the guards came running around the corner. At the sight of us, they came to a sudden stop, and Matthias burst into laughter.

"I guess you don't need my help after all, Your Highness," he said as he walked slowly toward us, eyeing the bodies briefly as he stepped over a pair of legs.

Connor shrugged casually, as if this was any other day. Perhaps it was actually. Connor was the commander of the king's military, after all. "Actually, we could use your help," he said, nudging Matthias's arm and gesturing to the fallen males. "These two will need a burial."

At that last word, I gasped. They were fae though. Immortals. Realization dawned on me as I remembered our earlier conversation. The war. Fae had died in battle, so they weren't truly immortal. Yes, they could heal—how many times had I witnessed Mrs. Bishop's cuts and burns heal rapidly?—but they could still be killed.

Connor's voice snagged my attention, and I found him pointing to Renata's unconscious form. "And that one needs to be taken back to the palace for trial."

Matthias gave him a sharp nod. "This isn't going to bode well for your image with the townsfolk, Your Highness."

Connor rubbed a hand along the back of his neck. "No kidding. We'll need to delay our arrival in Fairden so I can meet with the village lord and do my best to smooth things over."

As Matthias turned to dole out assignments to the guards, I caught Connor's attention.

"What will you say?" I asked, cringing internally at the stupidity of my question.

"The truth, I suppose," he said with less confidence than I'd hoped for. "We should get back to the room and get some sleep."

"Well then, after you, Your Highness," I said.

But Connor offered me his arm, dropping his head to the side. "Why don't we walk together from now on."

CHAPTER FIFTY-THREE

Connor

fter the attack in Linley, I refused to take any chances, so I instructed Matthias to again reserve a single room for Lieke and me in Fairden. He teased me briefly, as expected, but her safety was worth enduring his juvenile remarks. We departed early in the morning and rode hard without stopping. When we arrived, I expected Lieke to collapse from exhaustion. Instead, she lay on the bed, staring at the ceiling. I didn't comment on her shallow breathing or trilling pulse. To be honest, I didn't know what to say or how to help—or if I even could help.

As I had done before, I moved to gather a pillow and some extra blankets from the bed, but I stopped when she shifted her head toward me.

"Connor?"

"Yes, Sapphire?" I replied, trying to guess what she might request this time.

"Would you stay with me?" Her question came out barely above a whisper, and her lashes began to glisten with the first hint of tears. My heart thumped unevenly, and I was glad she couldn't hear it as I could hers. I swallowed hard, wrestling between my innate need to help her and the desperate desire to keep things professional between us.

"I don't know if that's a good idea," I said gently. She sucked her bottom lip in between her teeth and nodded quickly as she resumed staring at the ceiling above her. I dropped the blankets and pillow back onto the bed and came around to sit beside her outstretched legs. Reaching for her would most definitely cross the line, so I threaded my fingers together and leaned forward, resting my forearms on my legs.

"What is it, Lieke?" She shot me a puzzled frown as if I had just sprouted a third eye, and I had to admit it was a rather ridiculous question. The attack last night wasn't the first time she'd ever been in danger, but I'd never seen her struggle this much. "This isn't like you."

"We haven't always shared a room, Wolfie," she said, closing her eyes.

For some reason, guilt pricked my heart, as if I had failed her somehow by not being there for her. I gritted my teeth, frustrated with this stars-damned sense of duty I'd inherited. I wasn't her keeper! I wasn't her savior!

Aren't you though? My thoughts taunted me, and a low growl rumbled in my throat.

Her eyes flew open, finding mine.

"Sorry, Sapphire. What helped in the past? Aside from having a prince sleep beside you?" I intended the last question as a joke, realizing only too late how awkward it sounded.

She didn't seem to notice, though, and shrugged. "Time, I suppose. Eventually it becomes easier to close my eyes, but the nightmares never truly stop."

We didn't exactly have time on our side here, with five more villages to visit over the next week. My eyes shifted to the space beside her on the bed, but I couldn't do it. Here I was, commander of armies, a seasoned warrior, and the crown prince of Emeryn, and I was too nervous to sleep next to a human for a few nights.

"Would it help if you shifted?" Lieke asked. I cringed, and her brows knitted together. "Do you dislike shifting? Or are you truly that averse to being so close to me?"

Both.

But I couldn't say that aloud, so I offered her a half-truth instead. "It's not the most comfortable to be in that form, so I don't do it often."

Her lips curled into a small, obviously forced smile. "Yet you've done it to save me. More than once."

I waited for her to ask the obvious question—*why?* But she never did. I explained regardless. "Actually, the first time I did, I was needing to find Brennan quickly, and my senses are enhanced when I shift."

She lifted her chin slowly. "Ah, I see. So, it isn't always for me."

"To be fair, you've only been around for a small part of my life, and I did shift now and then before we met."

Lieke looked back to the ceiling and remained quiet for a long time, but I had no idea what to say or do. If we were to have any chance at success on this tour, I needed her rested and alert. But I also needed to maintain certain boundaries.

Which was worse? Sleeping beside her as myself or as my hound?

I hated this, but I couldn't sit here all night debating it either.

Heaving a rough sigh, I stood up and padded my way to the other side of the bed. Then I glanced over my shoulder, checking to make sure she wasn't watching. I hated doing this with an audience. Not that it was embarrassing at all, but the process was uncomfortable enough as it was. Having someone's eyes on me only made it worse.

Closing my eyes, I located the thread of magic in my mind and snagged it, then stretched out my shoulders and tossed my head as I shifted into my hound form. When I turned back to Lieke, I found her staring at me with her mouth hanging slack. Rolling my eyes, I dropped my head to the side.

She didn't say anything as I jumped up. Staying at the foot of the bed, I lowered onto my belly and curled up to go to sleep. Through slitted eyes, I watched her lie back down and turn onto her side to face me.

"Good night, Wolfie," she whispered.

***

Every stop on our trip proved less eventful than our first, thankfully, but also just as futile. Few—if any—of the villagers were willing to speak to us. A handful of young fae in Shoerda had enough curiosity to venture close, but their parents ushered them away before they could do much more than gawk and giggle at Lieke's rounded ears.

With each failed attempt to connect with the locals, my hope dwindled more and more. Lieke had been right to mock me for thinking a human queen could fix the rift between our kinds, but thankfully she didn't seize the opportunity to remind me of my foolishness. Instead she seemed to go out of her way to encourage me, reassuring me with a warm look or a kind word, telling me that maybe the next town would be more open-minded. Somehow she never let the fae's disapproval get to her—or, if she did, she never let it show. She always seemed to be able to smile through the dismissals and rejections.

Until we were alone.

Each night, back in our room, she grew quiet and anxious. The smile she'd worn all day would fade, and her eyes would glaze over. There were no more questions about mates or family or anything. When it was time to turn in and go to sleep, she would lie there staring at the ceiling as the stress and fear returned, pushing her heart to beat faster. And each night, I curled up beside her on the bed in my hound form, refusing to drift off to sleep until she had calmed down and fallen asleep herself.

It wasn't my favorite arrangement, but my hound form at least offered me the additional benefit of heightened senses. If anyone wanted to hurt her again, I could stop them before they got close. Even though there had been no more violence, it would be foolish for me to assume she was safe.

"Has Matthias ever seen you shift?" Lieke asked one morning as we were getting ready to head to yet another tavern.

I ran a hand through my hair and checked the mirror to ensure I appeared somewhat presentable, laughing quietly. "Of course, but he doesn't gawk at me like you do."

She scoffed. "It's just so weird!"

In mock chagrin, I let my face fall into a disdainful expression. "Thanks. I appreciate that. Does that mean you're ready to sleep alone again?"

Lieke stilled, dropping her gaze to the floor, and I was starting to feel bad for asking the question when she peered up at me from beneath her lashes and smirked. "Are you sure *you* are, Wolfie?"

"Of course I am," I said flatly and made my way to the door. Yanking it open, I gestured out into the hallway. "Ready to go?"

CHAPTER FIFTY-FOUR

Lieke

We only had one stop left before returning to the palace, and it was one I was particularly excited about, because I would get to visit with an old friend. While it hadn't been that long since Mr. Marstens had escorted me away from Raven's camp, I was eager to see at least one friendly face.

For the last several hours, we had been traveling in silence, and that grated on me. I opened my mouth to ask Connor a question—something that would annoy him—but Matthias's scout came galloping back toward us, his face ghostly pale. He turned to ride beside Matthias, who lifted a hand, instructing us to slow while he received the whispered report. I shifted in the saddle to glean any hint from Connor as to what was going on, but he kept his gaze locked on his second. His jaw pulsed. This couldn't be anything good. We continued forward, though, and I began to relax a bit. If it were anything serious, surely Matthias would have had us stop.

Matthias turned his chin over his shoulder and mouthed something

I couldn't hear. At first I thought he must be talking to the guard beside him, but then I noticed his eyes lock onto Connor's.

Connor stiffened.

"What is—" I started to ask, but he lifted a finger. I snapped my mouth shut.

He guided his horse closer to mine until our legs touched, and I silently cursed at the way the simple contact sent my skin tingling.

"It's not good," he whispered. The rigid set of his shoulders and the dour expression on his face made my stomach churn uncomfortably.

"What if it's—"

Shaking his head, he said, "You're not in danger."

How could he possibly know that for sure?

Before I could ask that, though, he was already clarifying.

"They're gone."

Who was gone? What was happening? If no one was ahead of us, why did he seem so nervous?

A gust of wind hit us, causing the trees on either side of the road to sway dramatically. A sharp, metallic scent enveloped me as the wind swirled around us, and I froze.

Blood. And a lot of it, if I could smell it so easily.

Matthias wheeled his horse around. To my surprise, he didn't lower his voice to keep me from hearing what he said to Connor next.

"It's worse this time, Your Highness." His tone was more somber than I'd ever heard it, and he'd used Connor's title. I got the distinct impression that *not good* and *worse* were understatements for what awaited us up ahead.

"We're sure they're gone?" Connor asked.

Matthias nodded slightly. "As sure as we can be. Scout estimates it happened sometime yesterday."

Roughing a hand along his jaw, Connor asked, "Can we avoid it? I don't want her to see this. She can't see this."

Though part of me appreciated his concern, a larger part of me wanted to punch him. So I did—squarely in the shoulder—as I told him, "I'm right here, Connor. You don't need to talk about me as if I'm not."

He swiveled his head around, his eyes blazing with indignation. While I'd known he would react, I wasn't prepared when he grabbed the front of my shirt, fisting the fabric and pulling me to him, nearly yanking me out of my saddle. Resting his cheek against mine, his breath curled around my ear as he growled, "Knock it off and stop acting like a baby."

I lifted my hands to pry his fingers off me, but he pushed me away before I could. Awkwardly, I righted myself, straightening the front of my shirt. Heat rushed up my neck and over my cheeks. Connor had clearly forgotten all pretense of our engagement, so after looking from him to Matthias—whose face was unusually stern and humorless—I sneered at the prince.

"Then stop treating me like one!" I ground out, hating the embarrassment that tainted my anger.

Pressing his lips into a thin line, Connor studied me quietly for a long, tense moment. Finally, his face relaxed into an apathetic expression. He angled his head a bit, never taking his eyes from mine, as he said, "Fine, this is your decision, Sapphire."

"Thank you," I muttered, but uneasiness still blossomed in my belly. Squaring my shoulders, I steeled my features and turned to Matthias. "What is it exactly?"

He raised a palm to me, retreating slightly. "I'm not getting in the middle of whatever this is."

Connor continued to stare at me even as he issued the command to Matthias. "Tell her."

A pained sigh fell from the general, and he mumbled something I couldn't make out before lifting his eyes to mine. "In short, my lady,"—I bristled at his use of the title, but he ignored me—"it was a massacre. And a bloody one, at that."

My throat tightened, but I didn't flinch. "How bad?"

Matthias's eyes flicked to Connor briefly, but the prince was still watching me with irritation in his golden eyes. Clearing his throat, Matthias shifted nervously in his seat. "They were butchered, Lieke. Limbs severed. Entrails strewn. Eyes gouged. Heads—"

Bile rushed to my throat, and I lurched, squeezing my eyes closed, but that simply provided me with a dark canvas on which to paint the gory images in my mind. When I opened them again, Connor's brows were raised in an *I told you so* manner.

"Would you like to see?" he asked flatly. "Or would you allow me to spare you the inevitable nightmares?"

My stubborn side begged me to lift my chin and trot Honey down the road without a word, to show this prince I wasn't afraid, to prove I was just as capable as any one of his guards or soldiers. But I wasn't a soldier. Yes, I had some training, and I had sustained some wounds, but I'd never been exposed to anything this extreme. The worst I'd ever witnessed was a broken leg.

"There's no shame in avoiding this," Connor said gently.

I hardened my glare. "Would you still suggest this if I was one of your royal guards?"

"You aren't."

"But if I was—"

"Yes, I would. If one of my guards or my soldiers—or any Emerynian for that matter—could be spared from having this carnage burned into their memories, I would do that for them. This isn't because you're a human or a woman. This isn't because I don't think you can handle it. It's because I don't want you to *have* to handle it."

I could only stare at him blankly as I pondered that.

This was the Connor I had come to admire—the one who cared for others with his entire heart and soul, who served and protected them. Despite all of that, though, he had not trusted me enough to speak plainly.

It shouldn't matter.

We weren't a real couple. This wasn't a real betrothal. But if I was going to be in this relationship—fake or not—I needed this from him. I needed to be trusted to make my own decisions, or at least have a say in the decisions.

Reaching for him, I laid my hand on his and gulped. I hoped he would listen. The irritation in his eyes had vanished, replaced by concern.

"I understand, but I need you to understand something too. I am your partner in this, and I need to be treated as such. Talk to me, not around me. Help me to understand and trust me to trust you."

"There isn't always time to explain," he said, setting his jaw.

I nodded. "But there was time here."

His eyes narrowed but then softened slightly. "Did it occur to you that I might have been about to? Before you hit me?"

Shit. Stars-damned impatience.

"You still could have, instead of yanking me off my horse and growling at me," I said, noting how the guards and Matthias were inching their horses away from us.

Connor leaned back and turned his face toward the early evening sky as he shook his head. Slowly he brought his attention back to me. "I don't know if you know this, Sapphire, but bad tempers run in my family."

I pressed a hand to my chest and pulled back in feigned shock. "You? Temper? No. I don't believe it."

This earned me a soft laugh that ended too quickly.

"Forgive me?" Connor asked.

I bowed my head and asked him for the same in return. In response, he took my hand and gave my fingers a squeeze before waving Matthias back over to us. Then he looked to me expectantly. It took a quick toss of his head in Matthias's direction for me to realize what he meant for me to do.

"I would like to avoid the scene if possible. Is there a way around it?" I asked, and Matthias nodded.

"There's an old hunting trail about fifty meters back. It meets up with the road between Engle and home," he explained, pointing behind us.

I glanced at Connor and asked, "Would it be a problem to backtrack to Engle?"

Rubbing his hand over his chin and along his scruffy jaw, he shared a look with Matthias before finally answering me. "We won't be going to Engle." My brows shot up, but I held my tongue, giving him the opportunity to explain. "With the rebels active in this area, and with the drastic escalation in their cruelty, we need to return home."

"So we just give up?"

Before I'd even finished asking my question, he was shaking his head. "Of course not. We just delay the rest of our visits for a while. We need to learn what we can from the scene and then regroup before we decide how to proceed."

"But how do we learn from it if we're bypassing it?"

Connor looked around at the guards who stood watch around us. Meeting my eyes once more, he explained, "You and I are going to take the hunting trail."

"Alone?" I asked with unintentional nervousness.

He laughed quietly. I waited for some inappropriate comment, but instead he said, "No, we'll be taking Evan and Willem with us. Matthias will take the others to investigate and report back to the palace once they've laid the fallen to rest."

Matthias tossed his head to command the other four guards to continue down the road, but he didn't turn to follow them right away. Guiding his horse close to Connor's, he clapped a hand on his back and whispered something to him before riding away.

CHAPTER FIFTY-FIVE

Connor

Surprisingly, Lieke never asked what Matthias had said to me before we parted ways. A few times on our ride, she gave me a sideways glance, but I pretended not to notice, focusing on searching the trees on either side of the old trail we now traveled along.

Even if she had asked, I would have lied.

"I told you she was good for you, Connor," Matthias had said. It had been nearly impossible to keep myself from scoffing at him, but doing that would have surely piqued Lieke's curiosity to an uncontrollable level.

We proceeded in relative silence. To my knowledge, this path hadn't been used since before the War of Hearts. It had since become overgrown, but the trees had been cut back so severely they'd never fully recovered, affording us just enough room to ride beside each other. On a map, this would appear to be a shortcut back to the palace, but its twisting and winding route through the trees would, in fact, force us to travel slowly.

As we rode deeper into the forest, my earlier annoyance with

Matthias shifted into a prickly unease. The air—darkened prematurely by the thick forest canopy—chilled me, yet somehow it remained stifling. The trees, which bowed their branches over the path, seemed to close in on us. Soon it seemed as if the forest might swallow us up, and we were eventually forced to ride single file.

I motioned for Lieke to go in front of me so I could more easily watch for any danger. Her heartbeat sped up. Not much sunlight was visible overhead, but I estimated we had another few hours, at least, before darkness fell. We wouldn't make it back to the palace before then and would be forced to make camp.

Lieke turned her head over her shoulder, whispering, "What if the rebels didn't leave? Will Matthias be okay?"

I stifled a laugh. "Should I be jealous that my fiancée is worried about my second and not me?"

But she didn't seem amused as she faced forward again, saying, "Last I checked, he doesn't shift into a hound with fangs and claws."

"He'll be fine, Sapphire." Even as I offered her the reassurance, though, I sent a plea up to the stars to keep him safe. As confident as I was in Matthias's training, it did seem as though the rebels were always one step ahead of us in this gruesome dance, and we were merely stumbling along.

After another hour of traveling at a frustratingly slow pace, the trees thinned enough that we had room to let the horses graze. Hopefully soon we would find a spot for us to stretch out somewhat to sleep.

"Here," I said quietly, and Evan, who was leading the way, halted and dismounted.

Lieke searched the trees on either side of us. "What is it? Why are we stopping?"

Giving Rosie an appreciative pat on the neck, I stepped down, slipping the reins over her head and walking her off the path. "Resting," I answered, not looking up.

"For how long?" Lieke asked from her perch atop her mare.

I smirked up at her. "Scared?"

Her shoulders drooped as she huffed out a sigh. "Yes, actually. I am!

We're in the middle of this creepy forest. We left our friend with a bunch of decapitated bodies, and we don't even know for sure that the killers aren't lying in wait for us. So yes, scared seems appropriate, thank you."

I cocked my head as I considered her, busying my hands with loosening Rosie's girth strap. We would leave the horses saddled in case of trouble, but I could at least allow them to rest more comfortably overnight.

"Just for the night, Sapphire," I said, pulling my pack down from behind my saddle. "We have another full day's ride to get back to the palace, and I can't have you falling off your horse when you succumb to exhaustion."

"I'm not tired," she said, lifting her chin and promptly reaching up to cover a yawn. I let it slide and didn't comment. As fun as it was to perturb her, flirting with her would only lead to feelings I couldn't entertain.

I shrugged and moved to help Evan and Willem clear some stones and sticks to make room for our bedrolls. Lieke still hadn't dismounted when I snatched her pack off her horse. I laid hers beside mine, and when I caught the hitch in her breath, my muscles tensed.

"I knew you weren't ready to sleep alone," she quipped.

Glancing over my shoulder, I watched her step down onto the grass and lead her horse over to where Rosie stood grazing contentedly. "Oh, this isn't for my benefit, Sapphire. I can't have my woman falling ill from sleeping in the cold and damp now, can I?"

Her head jerked up, and I could almost see her mind churning. Understanding dawned on her face, and her lips lifted into a coy smile. "So will I be getting a fur blanket...or a fae one?"

Stars, this woman.

Her sultry tone sent a wave of heat through me, which settled uncomfortably low. I swung my head back around. If I couldn't get my body to fucking behave, she'd have to sleep beside one of the guards instead. That sparked a different type of heat—and I pulled my hands into fists at the thought of another male lying beside her.

Fuck. What is happening to me? She's not really mine. I have no claim to her.

I growled as I shook my head, trying to force the unwanted emotions away, but this earned me a giggle from Lieke, who must have thought I was reacting to her question.

"You're cute when you're angry," she said from closer than I'd expected.

I didn't turn to face her. "All you can see is my back."

"But it's cute when it tenses like that." The smile evident in her tone only irritated me more.

Forcing myself to ignore the growing tension between us, I fished around in my bag for some of the provisions we'd packed in case we found ourselves camping beside the road like this. I pushed to my feet, then spun around and thrust an apple, a chunk of hard bread, and some dried meat at her.

"It's not much, but it will get us by until morning."

She took the food without complaint. "And what will we have then?"

"More of the same," I said, surprised when she didn't balk at it but offered a quiet thanks.

Later, having eaten our meager meal in an uneasy silence, we settled onto our makeshift beds. I stared up at the trees that loomed overheard, pretending not to notice her watching me as she lay on her side.

"Sure you don't want to shift, Wolfie?" she whispered, a hint of teasing in her voice.

Turning onto my side to face her, I propped my head up on my elbow and lowered my lips down to her ear. "What would the guards think?"

Kissing her cheek, I retreated, thankful for the gleam of understanding in her eyes.

But then it changed into one of clear concern, and she asked, "Are you sure you're okay with this?"

I frowned at her briefly before planting another kiss on her forehead. "Go to sleep, Sapphire," I said, rolling onto my back once more and closing my eyes.

CHAPTER FIFTY-SIX

Lieke

s I lay there on my blankets, I stared up into the forest's blackness. It was so dark I couldn't even see the leaves and branches that blocked the moon from view. To my right, Connor rested with his back to me, his breathing slow and even. At least one of us could sleep. I had scooted as close to him as I dared in an effort to keep warm, but it only helped with half of my body. Even though I was under my blanket, my left side shivered.

Just roll over. You're sleeping like this for warmth, aren't you? So use him!

I had been arguing with myself for the better part of the last hour—or however long had passed since we'd settled in for the night. It was difficult to assess time, with nothing but the forest surrounding us. Slowly I turned my head toward him. Maybe he wouldn't notice if I curled up against him.

You shouldn't care if he does. This was his idea, remember?

My body trembled from the cold, as if it was pleading with me to get over my discomfort. Part of me wished he'd chosen to shift into his hound form. For all my teasing about getting a fae blanket for the night, I'd been nervous to lie next to him like this. Every little comment, every damned smile of his—stars, even every growl and scowl and roll of his eyes—made my heart flutter.

Fuck it.

I pushed myself to roll onto my right side. Curling into him with my hands tucked to my chest, I nestled my face close and breathed in the scent of cedar and spice. I shivered against him—not from the cold this time, but from my stupid, fickle heart. Why did I always have to want someone I couldn't have?

Just sleep, Lieke, I told myself. Before I could force myself to relax, though, Connor was moving, and I froze.

Slowly he rolled himself over until he was facing me. His eyes remained closed as his hand slid to my waist and down my hip where it stilled, sending a wave of heat over my skin. My heart pounded in my ears as I tried to figure out what to do.

"You should sleep," he whispered, though he appeared to still be asleep himself.

I didn't say anything, didn't move, didn't even let myself take full breaths as my mind conjured up images of things I wanted to do with him—things I shouldn't want to do. Heat pooled in my core, and against my better judgment, I inched even closer to him.

Connor didn't retreat but asked quietly, "What are you doing?"

I answered him by slowly unfolding my hands—still clasped between us—and pressing one lightly to his chest. His heartbeat quickened under my touch. When he still didn't pull away, I risked nuzzling my forehead against his jaw, as if I were merely trying to get comfortable, ready to complain about being cold if he protested.

Instead his fingers began lazily stroking my hip, igniting more flames within me. What was I thinking? What could I possibly hope to have happen here, tonight, with his guards so close?

But I didn't stop him.

"Connor?" I whispered, half-hoping he wouldn't answer, not sure I could actually ask the question that had been plaguing me for days.

"Yes, Sapphire?" he said, continuing his light caresses.

I swallowed hard. It was just a question. Mrs. Bishop always said there were no stupid questions. But then I doubted she'd ever found herself in a predicament such as mine.

"What is it?" he asked, angling his chin down so that his breath tickled my forehead.

"Do you—" I started, but panic closed my throat, cutting off my words. This was absurd. It was only a question, and he didn't have to answer it. Pulling in a deep, warm breath—letting the comforting scent of his cologne relax me—I tried again. "Do you ever wish this was real? That we were really…?"

I couldn't finish the thought, my embarrassment getting the better of me. Slowly he let his hand fall to the small of my back, and my breath hitched when he pulled me to him. An ache pulsed between my legs, but I desperately tried to ignore it.

Connor inhaled slowly and whispered against my hair, "Sometimes."

"What would you do?"

"If this was real?" he asked. I nodded, and his fingers found their way back to my hip, where they curled into the fabric of my skirt. "I'd ask why you're wearing so much right now." His whisper was rough with desire, and fire danced beneath my skin.

I couldn't help but roll my hip against him slowly, as if pleading with him to do whatever he wanted with me, not caring where we were or who we were with. But it was wrong. We weren't together. We weren't in love. Except my heart seemed to be cracking under the weight of that truth, just as it had every time I'd remembered that I could never be with Brennan.

I was over Brennan. I had been cured of my childhood infatuation. But how would I get over the cure, especially when he held me so tenderly and touched me like he might feel more than mere obligation toward me?

Reluctantly, I freed my hand from between us and rested it atop Connor's. As tears threatened to surface, I closed my eyes and retreated slightly, whispering, "We shouldn't complicate this, Wolfie."

CHAPTER FIFTY-SEVEN

Connor

I froze beside Lieke, not knowing whether to roll away from her or argue that it was too late to avoid complications.

Stars, what the fuck was I doing?

Lieke was right. I'd been the one to insist on maintaining boundaries, and I'd nearly barreled through them tonight. Had I misunderstood her question? Her movements? Was I simply hearing what I wanted to hear from her?

Clearing my throat, I started to pull my hand away, but she curled her fingers around mine and shook her head. My head spun. What did this woman want from me? What did *I* want?

"Don't leave," Lieke whispered into my chest, and my heart splintered as I realized she didn't want me, but she needed me all the same.

"You were right though," I said. "I shouldn't have—"

"It's okay," she muttered, removing her hand from mine and tucking it between us. Her voice was barely audible when she asked, "Can you just hold me?"

Drawing in a calming breath, I dropped my lips to her forehead and kissed her gently before saying, "Of course I can. Can't have you freezing to death. Mrs. Bishop would have my head if I let that happen."

Light laughter was her only response as she nestled her face into my chest, taking care to keep space between our hips. Slowly, I dropped my hand to her back and nudged her to me. She turned her head, but before she could protest or mock me, I sighed. "You can't ride your horse with frozen legs. Let me keep you warm. Unless you can't control yourself, Sapphire."

"I can if you can," she murmured.

Those words cycled around in my mind for hours after she'd drifted off in my arms.

Could I control myself with her? Did I want to?

What I wanted didn't matter though.

I had to.

✳

We packed up our camp in silence and set off again. The trail soon became wide enough that we were able to ride beside each other.

"Can I ask you something?" she said, peering inquisitively at me.

My mind whisked me back to her question last night, and I hoped she wasn't about to broach the topic of what had nearly happened—what was *happening*—between us. I only hummed in response, urging her to continue. When I didn't respond, she returned her attention to the path ahead, staring at Evan's back.

"When someone finds their mate, are they forced to be together? I mean, do they have any say in the matter?"

I flinched slightly. This might not have been the question I was dreading, but it made me uneasy all the same. What was she really wanting to know? What difference did the answer make? Was she hoping to find her own mate someday?

Pushing past my discomfort, I asked, "Why the obsession with mates?"

She merely shrugged, answering casually, "Why not? It's fascinating."

"No," I said, and I cringed at the obvious sadness in my tone. "They don't have to choose each other, but..."

Images of my parents interrupted my thoughts, and I remained silent for a long while as I recalled all the happy moments they had shared—and how her death had shattered my father's heart and spirit.

"But what?" Lieke asked, and I blinked away the memories.

"Once the bond is set, it's nearly impossible to resist. To be away from one's mate is said to be anguish. I believe it's why my father is so angry, like the rage protects him from the agony of losing my mother."

I could faintly hear Lieke's heartbeat falter and her breath catch. Tears lined her eyes, but they never spilled over. Sniffing quietly, she regained her composure and asked, "What if they loved someone else first?"

Shooting her a curious look, I responded with my own question. "If they're in love, why are they kissing someone else?"

She grimaced. "I don't know. Sometimes kisses are unsolicited."

While she was obviously—hopefully—referring to Brennan's little stunt in her room, I couldn't help but wonder if the comment was targeted at me as well. Before I could say anything though, she was asking another question.

"Have you ever met anyone who denied it?"

"Anyone who ignored the bond? No. Not personally anyway," I said. "Generally, we don't go around giving out kisses to just anyone. Well, most of us anyway." My eyes skirted to hers as I said that last part. She looked away quickly, visibly uncomfortable, so I continued, "If it has happened, I would expect it wasn't a fae who walked away."

"Oh, right. You said the war started when a bond formed between a fae and a human?"

"Yes," I said quietly. "Fae-human pairings weren't uncommon, hence our demi-fae population. But many assumed it was a fae thing only, because the bond hits them harder."

"What do you mean harder?"

I laughed. "Feeling pushy today, are we?" She didn't respond, except

341

to stare at me until I started talking again. "Fae senses are stronger than those of humans, and that's not limited to just our hearing. All our feelings are amplified, for better or worse. Grief, anger, betrayal, love—the bond—all affect us to a greater degree."

"That sounds terrible," she muttered.

"Feeling nothing would be worse," I said.

She shrugged again. "I don't know. I would happily live without the pain."

I was shaking my head before she finished speaking. "Even our pain helps us grow, Sapphire."

She seemed to lose herself in thought for a while before shooting me another curious glance.

"Speaking of pain… Your tattoo…"

I breathed out a quiet laugh as a smirk tugged at my lips. "What about it?"

"What is it exactly?" she asked.

Glancing at her sideways, I angled a brow. "You mean, you didn't get a good look at it while gawking at me in your doorway?"

She squinted at me. "Oh, you mean when you were being a shirtless jackass?"

She wasn't wrong, so I nodded. "Yes, when I did that."

"No, I was too angry at you to really study it. So are you going to answer my question or not?"

"My Sapphire is so impatient," I said, chuckling lightly. "It's designed to look like my armor."

"I got that much, Wolfie," she said. "What are the words above it? Along your collar?"

I stiffened yet somehow managed to keep my voice steady. "It's something my mother always said to us: *Live to serve until the stars fall.*"

At that, she pressed her lips together, regret pulling her features tight as silence fell heavily between us.

CHAPTER
FIFTY-EIGHT

Lieke

Up ahead, Evan said over his shoulder, "Approaching the road, Your Highness."

"Almost home," Connor said quietly, and I allowed myself a relieved exhale.

"How much farther once we're on the road?" I asked, dreaming of a hot bath and Mrs. Bishop's lamb stew.

Connor looked up to where the branches offered us occasional peeks of the sun and said, "It's late morning now? I'd say, a little over half the day left."

A smile crept across my lips, but then I remembered Matthias and our other guards. "Think we'll meet up with Matthias?"

Connor shrugged. "Doubtful. My guess is it will take them a while to study the attack and lay the dead to rest. He'll probably arrive home after we do."

At the edge of the road, Evan dismounted so he could peer around the trees, turning one way and then the other. When he returned to his horse, he nodded quickly to Connor, who signaled for him to proceed. As I urged Honey from the soft grass of the hunting path and onto the hard-packed dirt of the road, my stomach clenched with unease.

It was likely nothing—just my imagination running amok after thinking about Matthias and the scene we had bypassed. I looked over at Connor, who offered me a thin smile. Taking a deep breath, I closed my eyes, willing myself to relax.

I opened my eyes in time to see Evan slap his neck as if a bee had stung him. When he pulled his hand away, he held what looked like a small needle. Slowly he turned back to us, his questioning eyes suddenly widening into shocked horror. I'd seen that look before—the terrified gaze of someone who knew they were dying—on Griffin's face right after I'd cut him.

"No!" I screamed, reaching forward as I kicked Honey to get me closer to him, even though I knew it was too late. Evan's eyes rolled back, and his head lolled to one side. His body fell to the ground with a dull thud just as an arrow flew from the trees, piercing his horse's chest.

Connor and Willem rushed to my side, swords drawn, circling around in search of the attackers, but I knew it was no use. Whoever was out there was using the same poison that had been on my knives, a poison that killed fae and killed them quickly.

"We can't stay here, Connor," I said. "We need to run!"

To my surprise, he nodded.

But he didn't move.

He leaped from his horse, calling Willem over. My heart pounded against my sternum like a war drum counting down the moments until the rebels' next attack as I watched Connor lift the dead fae up to the other guard.

"Get him home," Connor commanded, already remounting Rosie.

Willem took off, kicking his mount to move faster, and we followed close behind.

The air was ripped from my chest, though, when I watched an arrow punch through Willem's head just as another struck his horse in the neck. Their bodies crumpled before us, and I opened my mouth to scream, but no sound came out.

Rosie and Honey started to back up instinctively, but Connor corrected his horse, screaming at me, "Go! Keep going!" Honey and I raced off, her hooves thundering against the ground as loudly as the blood pumping in my ears.

Harder and harder, I pushed her onward, desperate to get away before the rebels could get us too.

My heart leaped into my throat.

Something was wrong.

Connor wasn't beside me.

Glancing over my shoulder, I still didn't see him anywhere near me. *No no no no.*

When I wheeled Honey around, I saw him. So far behind me. On the ground.

No no no no. This can't be happening.

Leaning over Honey's neck, I begged her to go faster. She skidded to a stop when we reached him, and I slid down from the saddle. Rosie had fallen, an arrow in her belly. Her breathing was uneven as she struggled on the ground. Connor lay beside her, eyes closed, one leg trapped underneath her. I rushed to him, reaching out my shaking fingers to his neck to find a pulse.

It was faint, but it was there. He wasn't dead. Why wasn't he dead?

I searched for any sign of the same dart that had killed Evan but found nothing. Connor's neck was fine. No puncture wounds. No cuts.

Quickly I hovered my hands over his body, hunting for what had hit him.

There, in his back! I pulled his shoulder toward me to see a slender needle drooping toward the ground, barely hanging onto the fibers of his shirt. Had it not gotten enough poison into him? Is that why he was still alive?

I pulled it out and quickly stored it in the pouch at my waist.

"Let's get you moved, Wolfie," I whispered, shuffling my way around his head and slipping my hands under his arms. I pulled with all my might, but I couldn't move him. As desperation mounted, a tortured scream tore from me. I needed Rosie to move. She was fading quickly, and if I couldn't get her to move now, I'd have no hope of getting her dead weight off him. Crawling across the dirt, ignoring how the sharp rocks dug into my knees and shins, I reached Rosie's face.

I was about to coax her to move when a pair of boots came into view. My tears welled up as I laid eyes on our attacker and the bow in her hand. I knew this face—those deep brown eyes and crooked nose. I'd seen her before, though we had never spoken to each other. She was a member of Raven's group, one of the hunting party. What was she doing here?

"Why? Why do this?" I shouted, my voice choked by tears.

She showed no remorse as she narrowed her heartless gaze on me. "Because they're fae."

"But they are good!" I screamed, leaping to my feet and rushing toward her. Although the woman was slightly shorter than me, she looked at me scornfully as if I were a young child in need of discipline.

"You are a fool," she hissed. "I told them you couldn't be trusted, that your love for them would make you weak, but they insisted."

"Who is *they*?" I demanded, but I knew. They'd given me those daggers. They'd encouraged me to pursue Brennan despite his engagement. Had they orchestrated this whole thing?

I was nothing but a pawn. Again. Always and forever someone else's tool to be wielded.

I was about to say this when a woman spoke behind me.

"You've done well, Lieke."

I whipped around and locked eyes with Anna, who stood a few paces away beside her husband. Neither wore the warm smiles or friendly expressions I was accustomed to seeing on their faces. Today, these two weren't the loving parents of my best friend.

They were rebels.

Murderers.

"But not well enough," Owen added, frowning.

My mind flooded with questions, but that didn't matter right now. There was one thing I cared about at this moment, and I shoved all other thoughts aside so I could focus on it.

"Tell me how to heal him," I demanded.

Anna's eyes glided down to the ground where Connor still lay, breathing shallowly. "But this isn't the prince you love."

"Why should that matter?" I challenged. "He's still good and noble and deserves to live. He's trying to make things better for all of us!"

Owen barked out a laugh. "Is that what he has you believing?"

"I've seen his goodness with my own eyes. Now HEAL HIM!" I screamed as tears spilled over and trailed down my face. I didn't bother to swipe them away.

Anna walked slowly toward me, studying me as she approached. When she was within arm's reach, my hands fisted by my sides, and I had to fight with all my strength to refrain from punching her in the face. She pulled one side of her mouth up into a snide grin. "He's not going to die, Lieke. Not yet anyway."

"What? What do you mean? I saw the needle in his back."

"Those were my idea," Owen called from behind his wife, as if I should congratulate him for his murderous ingenuity.

Anna ignored him. "The one that hit him was treated with a different poison. It merely knocks them unconscious for a spell. The guard, though, got one coated in—"

"The same poison as my knives," I offered, glaring at her husband and then at her.

She nodded. "We need you to finish your mission, Lieke."

I flinched away from her slightly. "I have no mission here, and I'm not going to help you!"

"Ah, but you do. And you will. Because if you don't—if you don't stop this alliance with Arenysen—we will kill your precious prince."

"No, you can't kill Brennan."

Anna shrugged casually. "Brennan. Connor. Who knows which one we will go for?"

"But why would you kill Connor? He's not the one marrying Calla."

Clicking her tongue, she shook her head at me and smiled at my apparent ineptitude. "But if he dies, who is left to take the Emeryn throne?

347

Brennan. And if Brennan takes our throne, he is not free to marry into the Arenysen royal family. So no, he may not be marrying Calla, but his death will serve us just as well."

I opened my mouth to respond, but I had no words. How could I save both of them? How could I stop the wedding?

As if she could hear my thoughts, Anna said, "You'll think of something, Lieke." She began to back away. "But don't try to betray us. You aren't our only eyes and ears—and hands—in that palace. We'll know if you try anything stupid, like telling him about any of this." She pointed at Connor before reaching behind her back and pulling out a knife. Flipping it, she caught it by the blade and offered it to me. I simply stared at her. Her eyes remained cold and distant. "He'll wake up in a couple of hours, but you'll probably want to take care of his horse soon."

"I can't move him," I said pathetically. "I can't move the horse off of him."

Anna snapped her fingers in the air, signaling her husband to help pull Connor's body out from under his horse, dropping him roughly in the dirt. She said nothing more as she turned on her heel and disappeared back into the trees with Owen and the other woman close behind.

CHAPTER FIFTY-NINE

Connor

The last thing I remembered was watching Lieke race away, and then Rosie's legs buckled underneath me. Something stung my back as we crashed down to the ground. Blackness engulfed me. Sleep pulled me away from this world and into one of sweet nothingness, a place where there were no rebels, no brothers, no servants, nothing.

Just darkness, comfortable and blissful.

Voices echoed somewhere off in the distance, but I couldn't be bothered to care. Here I could rest, finally. No one needed me here. In the far reaches of my mind, something poked and prodded, urging me to remember what I'd been doing when I'd fallen. But I shoved it away.

Until the pain hit, and I groaned.

Rocks dug into my spine as I shifted my weight, and my eyes snapped open. Bright sunlight pierced my skull, forcing me to close them immediately.

"Connor?" a voice called, sweet and light and scared.

"I'm here," I said. Or at least I thought I said it. I must not have, though, because the voice called my name again.

"It's me, Lieke."

I knew that name, but as I hovered here in the peaceful fog of my mind, I couldn't quite remember how.

"Please wake up," she pleaded.

But I was awake. Wasn't I?

Something squeezed my shoulder, and I turned my head toward the pressure, forcing my eyes open again. A pair of eyes sank into my line of sight—eyes of a sparkling deep blue that reminded me of a star-studded twilight.

"Lieke?"

"Are you okay?" she asked, and I wanted to smile but couldn't. I was okay, wasn't I? I mean, I had been a moment ago. But the pain shot through my leg again, a brutal reminder that I was, in fact, not okay.

"My leg hurts," I whispered, reaching a hand toward it.

"You broke it when you fell," she said.

Her voice cracked, and she sniffed back a tear. I was going to heal quickly, so why was she crying?

"What happened? Where are we?" I said, though I didn't know why I'd asked that last question, because it was fairly obvious from the trees lining the edges of my vision that we were still on the road and not yet back home.

"The rebels," Lieke said quietly. I pushed myself up onto one elbow, and she rushed to grab my shoulders, helping me to sit up. I leaned back on my hands and looked around. We sat in the middle of the road. One horse lay dead back down the road behind me. Another was stretched out beside us, blood pooling around its head. Two bodies—Evan and Willem—lay motionless nearby.

Dead because of me. Not just these guards. So many fae had been killed on these roads. They had all died because of my failure to stop the rebels. Panic snaked around my heart with icy tendrils, tightening its grip as it filled me with guilt and despair.

I lifted a hand off the ground to press my fingers to my forehead and nearly toppled over, but Lieke caught and steadied me.

"I should have been more careful," I mumbled. "I should have—"

"No, there's nothing you could have done differently. Not against their poisoned weapons."

"Are you hurt?" I asked, though I knew they probably wouldn't have attacked another human. Had she talked to them? I didn't wait for an answer to my first question. "What happened after I fell?"

"I'm fine, relatively speaking," she said, dropping her gaze to the ground between us. "I came back when I realized you weren't with me. Found you on the ground, trapped under Rosie's body. The dart they shot you with—the needle?—it must not have been the same kind they got Evan with, because it killed him instantly. You, it obviously didn't."

"You didn't see them?"

She shook her head slowly, her eyes still cast down.

"And the needle?"

"I have it in my pouch to take back to your healers. Thought they might be able to compare it to whatever was on my knives. But, Connor…" She grabbed my hand as her blue eyes, full of sadness, found mine again. "Rosie… I had to…"

Rosie. She'd collapsed beneath me. Right before I'd blacked out. Where was she? I pivoted my head around until I found her lying nearby. Tears gathered as I leaned back to look at the sky. It had no right to be so brilliantly blue when my girl was gone.

"I'm so sorry, Connor. I tried to end her suffering quickly," Lieke said, pulling my attention back to her. Her bottom lip quivered as she watched me, but my vision quickly glazed over. This wasn't the first horse I'd lost, but she had been the best one, and now I couldn't even bury her. Not by myself. The embers of my anger sparked to life, spreading through me as I stared at Rosie, growing hotter when I caught sight of the other fallen bodies around us. The rebels needed to be stopped. Giving them a human queen wasn't enough, and I'd been a fool to think it would be. We needed to find them, to end them.

But how?

"We need to get home, Connor."

She wanted me to go home now? To just leave my fallen guards?

"I can't," I muttered.

"Is it your leg?" she asked, gingerly reaching for me.

"No, it's not!" I snapped, and she froze in place. Pressing my teeth together as hard as I could, I waited for Lieke to yell at me in return. But she didn't.

Leaning back, she sat on the ground and pulled her legs up to her chest. She rested her chin on her knees and watched me as she chewed on her lower lip. We sat there staring at each other in silence, which was fine by me. I didn't want to talk. I didn't want to yell. I didn't want to do anything but process everything.

And she let me.

The entire world seemed to be pressing against my chest, threatening to crush me. I couldn't escape this reality. My people were being slaughtered by rebels I couldn't find. My country was falling apart around me while I did what? Paraded this woman around? All in hopes of convincing everyone that she could help us, of wanting to prove to myself that I hadn't completely fucked up by saving her life.

Time and time again, I'd saved her. Had I been wrong?

"I can't do this," I whispered.

Lieke tilted her head slightly as her brow creased with concern. "Do what?"

My shoulders fell with my weary exhale. "I can't save anyone. Except you, apparently."

Her lips twitched as though she were fighting a smile. "You can. You have. But you can't save everyone, Wolfie."

My sternum caved inward. My throat tightened. She was right, of course, but that didn't make it any easier to accept. I was their prince, soon to be their king, and I couldn't keep them safe. What good was a ruler who couldn't even protect his people?

"You're carrying too much," she said carefully.

I scoffed. "Because I have to."

"Do you though?"

Pushing myself forward, I leaned toward her. "Who else is there, Sapphire? My brother?" I threw a harsh laugh in her face. "My father?

You?"

"You're not alone, Connor. This may be your burden to bear, but you don't have to shoulder any of it alone. You have Matthias. You have me. Let me help you."

"What if I fail?"

"Then you keep going, I suppose. You make another decision. You take another step." She reached a hand over to my chest, hovering her fingers lightly over the words inked into my skin. "Until the stars fall, Connor, you keep going, because it's what you do. It's who you are."

Dropping my chin, I closed my eyes. "I'm so tired."

Though she didn't respond, I could hear her shifting against the ground, could feel her warmth growing closer. Her hand, soft and gentle, cupped my jaw as she slowly lifted my face to look at her.

"Let's get you home. You can rest and regroup as you planned to." Her eyes pleaded with me to listen to her, but I couldn't leave.

"What about them?" I asked, nodding toward the horses and guards.

"Matthias will come through here on his way back. We could leave him a note, or we could send someone from the palace to come care for them."

Closing my eyes, I considered her suggestions. I knew she was right; we couldn't do anything ourselves, and we couldn't just sit here, waiting for Matthias. Slowly, I nodded, agreeing to trust her.

CHAPTER SIXTY

Lieke

While Connor scrawled out a message for Matthias—letting him know we were okay and had survived this attack, I prepared Honey for our departure, retrieving Connor's pack from behind his saddle and strapping it onto my saddle alongside mine. Behind me, he groaned in pain, and I spun around to find him pushing himself to stand.

"Is your leg healed?" I asked.

"Healed enough," he said, shrugging as he limped toward me. I stepped back a bit, careful not to stand too close to him. It was ridiculous, of course, since we had been even closer last night and were about to be again for the next several hours.

"Ready?" I asked, failing to keep my voice steady.

Connor didn't say anything—didn't even look at me—as he offered me his hand. I swallowed hard as I accepted his help climbing onto Honey's back, shivering as the contact sent a cold ripple up my arm. Scooting as far forward as I could in the saddle, I waited as he lifted himself up behind me. When his body settled against mine, my breath caught, and my face heated with embarrassment. Then my skin ignited, and tiny icy flames danced along my shoulders as he trailed a hand across my neck to sweep my hair over my shoulder. Snaking one arm around me, he took the reins and whispered in my ear, "I'm ready, Sapphire."

My whole body tensed as he pressed his legs against Honey's middle and clicked his tongue quietly. She settled into a gentle trot. Connor's injured leg tightened against mine, and he hissed softly through his teeth.

"We can go slower if you need to," I said.

Connor adjusted his position slightly, and I froze, as if any added movement on my part might send us toppling over. He pressed his chest into my back with a deep inhale, and then his breath warmed the top of my ear as he spoke.

"I'm fine, but you'll be hurting if you don't relax." There was a hint of laughter in his voice. "You didn't seem to have any problem cuddling up to me last night."

I pulled my bottom lip between my teeth.

Well, at least one of us can joke about what happened.

Or didn't happen.

With a long, exaggerated sigh, I melted back into him and let my head rest against his jaw, ignoring how the rough stubble snagged my hair and scratched the side of my face. I smirked when he tensed. But then his body reacted to our closeness, and he hardened behind me, bringing the unacceptable warmth back into my core, my chest, and my cheeks.

I needed to focus elsewhere, so I teased him instead, saying, "Seems like you're the one who needs to relax now, Wolfie."

I expected him to stop the horse and maybe shove me out of the saddle or at least make me ride behind him, but he did nothing of the sort. Instead he released a ragged breath and wrapped his free arm protectively around my midsection, holding me close.

We didn't say anything for the remainder of the ride, even when we stopped to stretch and rest before sundown. In silence, we ate standing up, trying to relieve the stiffness in our legs a bit. Every now and then I'd glance at him and catch his eyes darting away from me as soon as our gazes met.

When we were almost finished eating, he handed me the last piece of bread, brushing his thumb over my fingers when I accepted it, and a fresh wave of desire washed over me.

Why did he have to do that?

If he was trying to keep things uncomplicated between us, he was failing.

We climbed up into the saddle and eased back into the now too-familiar position. Not long after we started back down the road, my heart tightened in fear as I contemplated what the rebels had said to me earlier. I'd been forcing myself to not think about it since Connor woke up, but now my exhausted mind was too weak to keep it at bay any longer. I was to break up Brennan's engagement, to disrupt the alliance. Perhaps I could talk to Connor. Sure, Anna said they had spies in the palace, but we weren't back there yet. We were on the road, with no witnesses.

Connor shifted his arm around me and sighed contentedly into my hair. Panic sparked in my chest. If I told him and they found out—if somehow they learned I'd warned him—they'd kill him. Or Brennan. I might be angry with Brennan, but I didn't want him dead. If anything happened to either of them, especially because of me, I would never forgive myself.

You'll think of something.

Anna's assertion repeated in my head.

Yes, I would think of something, except there was one problem.

I was falling for him.

I didn't know when or how it had happened, but the thought of being without Connor now created an unbearable ache in my chest. Unfortunately, no matter what—whether he died because I told him or he hated me because I sabotaged the alliance—he would leave me.

He wasn't mine though, not really. I had no claim to him. This had never been real. It had always been a ploy, a way to save me from the gallows. Nothing more.

Tears surfaced, and I squeezed my eyes closed, capturing them in my lashes and holding them hostage before they could fall freely. I choked back the sobs and bit my lip, desperate to keep him from noticing.

He had so much on his shoulders already. He didn't need my problems too.

Even if my problem was him.

Matching my breathing to his, I worked to settle my mind and my heart. With the rhythm of his pulse in my ear and the steady rise and fall of his chest against me, I drifted off to sleep in his arms.

＊

"Sapphire."

The word floated softly into my ear, and my eyes fluttered open. Darkness surrounded us, and the smell of dust and hay and horses enveloped me.

"Wake up. We're home," Connor whispered gently. All I could do was hum in response.

A shiver crept down my back when he pulled away from me, swinging his leg back over the saddle and stepping down to the ground. My hands gripped Honey's mane as if she were galloping at full speed instead of standing still inside the palace stables. Connor reached his hands up to me, his golden eyes searching mine with a tender eagerness. Turning, I leaned toward him, letting his hands trail slowly up my ribs as I pulled my leg up and over my horse's back. His hands settled below my arms, and I rested mine on his shoulders, never pulling my gaze from his as he lowered me down to the ground.

"Connor," I whispered, not sure what I planned to say.

He stepped closer, dropping his hands to my waist and pulling me gently to him. My stomach tightened in anticipation. I licked my chapped lips, and his focus drifted down to them and lingered there for what felt like forever. I should say something—remind him again of the rules, tell him we couldn't do this.

But I didn't want to.

And when he caressed my neck, all remaining hesitation melted into a desire that refused to be ignored.

All I wanted was him. His hands. His lips. His eyes. His heart. I wanted all of him, and the realization scared me.

Trailing my trembling hands up his neck, I lost my fingers in his hair, my thumb brushing over his ear. He lowered his face to mine, and his breath lingered teasingly over my lips. His scent wrapped around me like a warm embrace, as if welcoming me home to his arms.

"This is really going to complicate things," I murmured, my voice cracking nervously.

Connor's eyes sparked. "Then tell me to stop," he said.

I couldn't. I didn't want him to change his mind and realize how stupid this was, so I shifted forward slightly in invitation, and he took it. His lips claimed mine with a hunger and a passion I'd never known. All doubt, all fear, all worry vanished, and I gave myself over to him, parting my lips for him, offering my heart to him. He tasted of bliss and security, of desire and belonging, of peace and…

He was leaving.

Pulling out of my arms. Backing away from me. Staring at me with trembling fear.

He lifted a hand to his lips as if to wipe away any trace of me. Then he spun around and left me in the stables to wonder what I'd done wrong.

CHAPTER SIXTY-ONE

Connor

My mate.

I'd found her, and I'd run from her.

Slamming my door closed, I dropped my forehead against the cold wood. A growl roared from my throat as I punched my fist into the door. What the fuck was I going to do? This should be a good thing. I should be happy. Lieke was my mate. She was the one I'd been waiting for—hoping for, even.

But it wasn't supposed to be *her*.

It couldn't be her.

Yet it was.

When our lips had met and she'd melted into the kiss, a jolt of energy had seared my nerves, my skin, my heart. Everything I'd known about the world and myself, about love and life, had been ripped from my mind and replaced with something new. It was like the world had shifted around me, and I could now clearly see my purpose.

My purpose was her and always had been.

It had always been her.

I knew her though. She hated having decisions made for her. She feared not being in control over her own life. I'd already taken that freedom from her once; I couldn't do it to her again.

She could deny the bond.

My chest caved from the pain of that thought. To have her reject it, to live my whole life with a mate who didn't want me? How could I ever take another queen after that?

You will if you must. You live to serve. What's one more sacrifice for your country?

I couldn't tell her. I couldn't put pressure on her to choose me out of some sense of obligation. Even if it meant forfeiting my own heart, I wouldn't do it. If she recognized our bond herself, that would be different, though it was unlikely. Humans didn't feel things like we did.

So that was it.

I'd made my choice. I would reject the bond. I'd live with this pain forever.

For her.

✳

I'd barely lived with the pain for a few hours when someone began pounding on my door. Again.

I ignored whoever it was—as I had the previous two visitors—rolling over on my bed and placing the pillow atop my head. Just a few more minutes and they'd give up and leave. The knocking continued, loud and insistent. This one was apparently more tenacious than the others. When it finally stopped, I tossed the pillow aside and sat up. My stomach growled, angry at me for ignoring its need for sustenance, but I brushed off its protests as easily as I had the knocking.

I didn't want food. I didn't want visitors. I just wanted to wallow in my misery. At least for a few days. My duties as prince wouldn't allow me much longer than that. Stars, they didn't allow for even that long, but I needed time and space and—

"Connor Durand, you had better open this door right this instant," a familiar voice bellowed from behind the door. Mrs. Bishop. I stilled, as if that could keep her from hearing my erratic heartbeat. When I still hadn't moved after a minute, she resumed pounding on the door, and I remembered just how stubborn my old governess could be. Once, she had stood in the hallway staring at Brennan and me for nearly an entire day until one of us confessed to swiping a pie from the kitchen. When the sun had begun to set and my legs had started to shake with exhaustion, I finally spoke up. Of course she had sensed the lie the moment I opened my mouth, and she had withheld desserts from us both for an entire month.

No, there was no waiting out this old female. She would knock on my door until I answered, no matter how much work she had to abandon to wait me out.

With a heavy exhale, I stood and made my way to the door slowly, but I didn't open it. The knocking ceased, and I braced myself for her to yell at me again.

Instead, she said gently, "I know you're hurting, boy. And I know you think you can shoulder all of this on your own, but sooner or later, you need to stop carrying everything yourself." My eyes closed as I mulled over her words, but still I said nothing. She sighed, her disappointment and sadness evident even through the door. After a moment, she cleared her throat quietly. "Take some time, and then talk to her. I'm leaving some supper out here for you. You need to eat. Just remember, I'm here for you. You know where to find me if you need anything."

The tray clinked against the stone floor, and then her footsteps moved down the hallway.

As usual, Mrs. Bishop was right. I needed to talk to Lieke.

If only I knew how.

✳

That night, I drifted off to sleep easily enough—thanks to the faerie wine I had hidden in my desk drawer. Unfortunately, while alcohol might help bring sleep, it did shit for escaping life's problems. Although I'd successfully avoided Lieke all day by hiding in here, there was no evading her in my dreams. Every night since I'd saved her from the gallows, I had relived our encounters in my sleep—saving her, scolding her, challenging her, teasing her. Even in my dreams, though, I had never dared kiss her. It was as if my subconscious had been protecting me from discovering the truth.

Tonight, we were back in the room we'd shared in Linley. I'd dreamed this before, and everything appeared to be the same, with Lieke sitting on the bed, her legs tucked in front of her as I lounged on the floor and leaned back on my hands. Despite the familiar scene, something was notably different. Instead of an awkward silence filling the room, a tension now stretched between us, like a string being pulled taut, drawing us together.

It was the bond, of course. It had to be.

Lieke also looked different somehow, or perhaps there had merely been a shift in how I viewed her. Was this part of the bond as well? Her appearance was the same—her blonde hair falling in waves around her shoulders, her dark blue eyes shining as she stared back at me, her mouth still twisting into a scowl as if I had just done something to irritate her.

All familiar, but now I was seeing it through the eyes of her mate.

Stars, this was complicated. How was I to tell this woman that she was bound to me but not to worry about it because she didn't have to accept it? Even though I'd then be destined to spend my entire existence alone or in a loveless union, knowing my mate was elsewhere?

"Why?" Lieke's firm tone snapped me out of my thoughts.

"Why what?" I asked, my brain hunting for any clues about what she was referring to. It could be any number of things, honestly. Why had I saved her? Why had I kissed her?

Tossing her feet to the floor, Lieke rested her forearms on her knees and leaned forward. Her scowl deepened. "Why are you avoiding me?"

Apparently, my subconscious had decided to give me as much grief as Mrs. Bishop. There truly was no escape, was there?

When I still hadn't answered after several breaths, Lieke raised a brow and scrunched her nose. "Well? Let's hear it, Wolfie. What…" She paused, and her eyes softened with vulnerability as she lowered her gaze to her hands. "What did I do wrong?"

"Nothing," I answered, perhaps a little too quickly, because I had no other words ready. Slowly she lifted her face, revealing fresh tears, and my heart cracked open. The pain in my chest instantly pushed me to my feet and sent me across the room to her. Falling to my knees at her feet, I covered her hands with mine, stroking her legs with my thumbs. Silently she pleaded with me to give her an answer. But I couldn't, not even here in my head.

This isn't her, I reminded myself. *You can talk to her. What better time is there to practice what to say?*

My stomach writhed, and I uttered the first thing that came to mind. "I'm scared."

It wasn't what I *needed* to tell her, but at least it was true.

Lieke's brow creased with concern. "Scared of what? Me?" She laughed nervously.

I shrugged and offered her a tight smile. "Well, yes. Actually."

Slowly, she slid her hands out from under mine and began to wring them in front of her chest, averting her eyes again. "You don't think I had something to do with the attack, do you? Because I didn't. I didn't know they were going to… I didn't know."

Her voice broke into soft sobs that throbbed in my chest as if they were my own.

"No, it's not that," I said, joining her on the bed and wrapping my arm around her shoulder. I winced as she nestled against my collarbone. As much as I wanted this—wanted her—this wasn't real. This was just a dream.

Then let yourself enjoy it, my mind urged.

No, that was wrong, selfish. Wasn't it? To enjoy her company here as I slept while avoiding her otherwise? That wasn't fair to her.

Yet when her hand settled on my chest and her fingers curled around my shirt as if I were the one thing she needed, I couldn't deny the heat that pooled within me. Reaching around, I ran my fingers along her neck and under her chin, coaxing her to look up at me, but her eyes fell squarely on my lips. Without thinking, I allowed my tongue to sneak out to wet them.

My breath ceased as she lifted her face, letting her lips whisper over mine.

I shouldn't do this.

Mates or not, I shouldn't be allowing this, not when she didn't know, not when I hadn't figured out how to tell her.

Her exhale warmed my skin, and I closed my eyes as I drank in all of her.

"I shouldn't." This time I whispered the words aloud, but I didn't pull away.

Lieke's lips grazed mine. "Then tell me to stop," she whispered back, and my resolve melted away.

Dream or not, I needed her like the stars needed the heavens.

Sliding my hand along her jaw and tangling my fingers in her hair, I pulled her to me, molding her lips to mine, urging her to open so I could savor her—her lips, her tongue, her breath—as I hadn't been able to in the stables. I explored her slowly, cherishing the way she moved with me. Tears laced her kiss, healing and breaking me all at once as I consumed her. My soul sighed with more contentment than it had experienced in years—or ever.

Her fingers worked to undo the buttons of my shirt, and my thoughts resumed warring inside my head, arguing over whether to stop her out of propriety or take this wherever she would allow. I was still fighting with myself when she swung her leg up and over mine to straddle me.

Fuck. The curse echoed in my head as her center pressed against me.

I can't do this!

Yes, you can!

My mind continued to rage until finally I forced myself to focus on her alone. She threw my shirt open and shoved me back onto the bed, creating an unbearable chasm between us. My protest froze in my throat at the sight of her studying my inked chest. Her fingers traced the edges of the armor and glided over the words along my collarbone.

"Until the stars fall," she murmured, sliding her eyes to mine, capturing me in those dark blues and pulling at the last thread of my resistance.

Then I had her down on the bed, rolling her onto her back so that I hovered above her, drinking in the cocktail of emotions swirling in her eyes. Sadness. Fear. Doubt. I wanted to save her from each of them, even if only here and now in this moment I alone would remember.

Gently I pushed a lock of her blonde hair away from her face and placed a kiss on her forehead before losing myself in her again. Lifting her hand to my chest, I pressed her palm against the family crest that covered my heart.

"Until the stars fall, Sapphire, I serve you. My bride. My love. My mate."

CHAPTER SiXTY-TWO

Lieke

Throwing the pillow off my head, I stared up at the ceiling, which was dimly lit by the soft moonlight pouring in through my open drapes. Although I was alone in my room, heat crept into my cheeks as I thought about the vivid images from my dream. It had seemed so real, as if we had truly been back at the inn, but it couldn't have been anything except a dream. Not with how he'd looked at me.

And what he'd said.

My mate.

Don't be ridiculous. Dream Connor simply said what you wanted to hear.

But was that, in fact, what I wanted to hear?

Reaching up, I clutched my hand to my chest, right over my heart. It thumped wildly, and I wished I could ignore the thought of his body against me. Dreaming of him and holding onto these fake memories would not help me in the long run. Even so, why had the dream ended before anything actually happened between us? Why had I woken up before he'd really touched me?

Grumbling, I rolled over and roared into my pillow.

Pull yourself together, Lieke. It will all be okay. It will all work out as it's meant to.

But why had he run from me in the stables? Why had he ignored me when I stopped by his room yesterday? It was absurd to think he was legitimately scared of me. How my brain had come up with that gem of an answer was beyond me.

Well, he couldn't ignore me forever. After all, we still had a betrothal to fake—and for several months, at that. If he refused to be around me or speak to me, this would all fall apart, and then where would I be?

The gallows appeared in my mind's eye, and my hand flew to my neck protectively.

He wouldn't let that happen.

But with how he was acting now, I wasn't so sure that was still the case.

*

Embarrassed and humiliated by Connor's dismissal, I refused to take my meals in the dining room with the Durands, and Gretchen was dutifully delivering my food to my room. But Mrs. Bishop had sent a message with my lunch today, insisting I come join her for supper this evening. As much as I hated risking a possible run-in with Connor—or anyone else, honestly—Mrs. Bishop was not one to be ignored.

So as soon as the sun began to sink below the treetops, I tentatively opened my door and stared straight across the hallway to his room. Had he come out at all since we'd returned? Or was he in there devising a way to spend the next six months without having to see his fiancée?

Without thinking, I tiptoed over and lifted my hand to knock. Faint footsteps inside his room gave me pause, and a new wave of fear crashed into me. It wasn't like the fear of being sent to the executioner I'd experienced before. This was new, different. If I knocked again—if I tried to speak to him—and he refused me, the rejection would be unbearable.

Mrs. Bishop laid her fork across her now empty plate, which she pushed to the center of the small table in her room. She studied me quietly as I took the last bite of roast lamb.

"Have you seen him lately?" she asked, and the bluntness of her question had my hand freezing in midair, my fork hovering over my plate.

I blinked my initial surprise away and settled back in the stiff dining chair. "I assume you mean Connor?" She nodded, concern written plainly across her face. "No, I haven't."

She released a long, tired-sounding exhale and rolled her eyes to the ceiling before mumbling something I couldn't hear. When she looked back at me, though, she smiled gently. "How are you faring, Sunshine?"

The question was simple enough, and yet I had no idea how to answer it. The dream had made a mess of my heart—and other parts of me. On top of that, there was the daunting and terrifying task of having to find a way to do the rebels' bidding before my failure got one of the princes killed. Neither could be mentioned to her though, and I stumbled over one thought after another.

"That good, huh?" Mrs. Bishop asked with an empty laugh. "Well, that's understandable, I suppose. Given what you both endured on your journey."

I straightened slightly, bolstered by the hope that Mrs. Bishop might have some insight regarding Connor's odd behavior. "Has he spoken to you about it?"

She shook her head and lowered her gaze to where her hands rested, clasped together, on the table. "No, but he will when he's ready." Peering up at me from under her lashes, she then asked, "Why don't you talk to me though, Sunshine? What happened out there?"

I said the first thing that came to mind. "We were attacked by—"

"Not about the attack," she clarified. "Between you two."

Heat flooded my cheeks, and I half-expected the old fae to laugh at me for being so obviously embarrassed, but she simply looked at me expectantly.

"Honestly? I'm not sure," I said, searching her eyes to make sure she could sense the truth in my voice. "I thought we had finally turned a corner, that maybe I was no longer just a thorn in his side, but…"

Mrs. Bishop's expression turned thoughtful, tightening with concern. "But what?"

I shrugged. "I don't know. I don't know what to think. I keep racking my brain, trying to figure out what I did wrong, why one minute he looked at me as if he—" I huffed out my frustration, unable to say the words aloud. "Only to have him run away as fast as he could? What am I to think?"

Mrs. Bishop lifted a hand to her lips. Shaking her head slowly, she watched me as I finished my rambling. I averted my gaze, as much to avoid the pity in her eyes as to hide my inevitable tears. I didn't want to cry over this when I wasn't even sure what *this* was. Hadn't I shed enough tears over the Durands already?

"You asked me about mates once," she finally said. My throat tightened. "I found mine. Long ago. But I was much like you in my youth. Stubborn. Independent. I didn't want to be tied down, so I rejected the bond and walked away from Hugh."

"Hugh? Hugh Marstens? In Engle?" Mrs. Bishop nodded silently. "But you had a daughter," I said.

"I eventually married, later on—Nicholas Bishop—and we had a child, but there is one consequence of denying your mate that I hadn't expected. I could never open my heart to another. I was never able to love another, and neither was Hugh. I wanted to love my husband; I did. I cared about him, of course, but it was never—"

"But if you loved Hugh, why leave? How could you ignore it?" I asked, trying to wrap my head around this.

"It wasn't easy, Sunshine. But if you want something else strongly enough, it's not impossible to walk away from that bond. I wanted my independence so badly, I walked away from the only love I was destined to have."

"If you could go back, would you choose differently?" I asked.

Sadness clouded Mrs. Bishop's eyes. "I've asked myself that same

UNTIL THE STARS FALL

question so many times, and my answer changes day to day. It doesn't matter though. The point is, Sunshine, we only get this one life, and some decisions cannot be fixed. We have to live with the choices we make, accept the consequences, and remember there are some mistakes not even a fae prince can save us from."

"Why are you telling me all of this?"

A rueful smile graced her lips. "Because I want you to think long and hard before you make a decision you'll regret."

CHAPTER SIXTY-THREE

Lieke

As I fell into bed that night, my whole body tensed in anticipation of seeing Connor again, which seemed rather absurd since I was only seeing him in my dreams. Still, spending time with my imaginary version of him there held more appeal than sitting around, waiting for him to come out of his room.

My eyes fell closed, and when I opened them again, I frowned. I was alone in a dark room that wasn't mine. For a brief moment, I panicked, wondering if I had accidentally walked in my sleep to some unoccupied guest room, but then I caught the familiar scent of spice and wood.

Looking down, I noted I was wearing my old servant's uniform instead of the nightshirt I'd put on before bed. I let out a relieved sigh, thankful I hadn't meandered around unknowingly, but disappointment pricked my chest when I realized I was here alone.

This wasn't just any random room; it was where I'd foolishly confronted Connor after Brennan and I had been caught together. I spun around to find the spot beside the door where he had pinned me against the wall in his anger, and my core tightened in response.

"Fond memories in this room?" Connor's voice struck my ear from where he stood close behind me, but his tone seemed more nervous than playful.

Slowly I turned to face him, and my shoulder brushed against his bare chest, sending a prickling wave of anticipation over my skin.

"What happened to your shirt, Wolfie?" I teased, hoping he wouldn't catch the slight waver to my voice.

His lips parted slightly as his eyes flashed to my mouth, and I instinctively tucked my bottom lip between my teeth. When he answered, the edginess I'd detected earlier had been replaced with the confident tone I'd come to expect from him. But this time, it was desire—not anger—that made his voice rough.

"Just starting where we left off."

Reluctantly I pulled my eyes away and glanced around the dark room. "I seem to remember we left off with me on my back," I said, turning to read the words etched across his skin.

Without warning, Connor hoisted me up in his arms, his hands supporting my backside. I wrapped my legs around his waist. Taking his face in my hands, I cupped his jaw and searched his golden eyes. What I hoped to see, I didn't know. Maybe I wanted some sign that this wasn't just my imagination run amok. Maybe I hoped I'd wake up and he'd really be lying beside me.

Stars be damned. Just enjoy this, Lieke!

I'd be awake soon enough, thrown back into my role of being temporarily engaged to a male who couldn't even look at me. The Connor holding me here, though, was doing far more than that.

He claimed me, consumed me, threatened to undo me with nothing but his gaze.

"Wolfie?" I whispered, and part of me screamed in protest at my hesitancy.

Connor's eyes roved over my face hungrily. "Yes, Sapphire?"

My mind blanked, and all words escaped me when his lips pulled back in a smirk.

Never mind.

I thrust my lips against his. Sliding my hands past his pointed ears, I kneaded my fingers through his hair as I ran my tongue along the seam of his still smirking lips, begging him to recreate the sensual dance of tongues we'd shared the night before. A moan thrummed in his throat, and I whimpered as his hands pulled me tighter against him. Then we were across the room. My back slammed hard against the stone wall.

Connor's lips refused to release me. Pinning me to the wall, he pressed his hips against mine and eased his hands up to my waist and over my ribs. He continued kissing me slowly, leading me deeper into a blissful world where there were no alliances or rebels, no rules or pretenses. A world where we could be wrapped in each other, needing nothing more than moments like this.

But then his lips slipped away from mine, and fear flooded my heart. Holding my breath, I closed my eyes, not wanting to witness his inevitable regret and retreat again.

"Open your eyes, Sapphire," he whispered, his breath warming my jaw as I obeyed. He pulled his face back just enough to catch my gaze, his golden-brown eyes shining with loyalty and devotion and promise and…a question. "I'm yours," he said, "if you'll have me."

All I could manage was a nod before he was kissing me again, the first in a string of tender kisses that trailed along my jaw and down my neck. I dropped my head back against the wall as his soft lips caressed me and his tongue swept across my skin. Then his kisses became hungry. Dropping one hand back down to my thigh, he clasped the other onto my neck. Firmly, he held me captive to his ravenous lips, which continued to taste and explore inch after inch—down my neck, across my shoulder, along my collarbone. A whimper escaped my lips when his kisses turned to nibbles, his teeth nipping their way back up to my neck. I gasped as his teeth sank into the tender flesh above my collarbone, plunging me into a drunken ecstasy I never wanted to end.

My heart pounded in my ears, loud and urgent, when his lips found mine again. I needed him, needed more. Frantically, I dropped my hands. My fingers fumbled for his belt, and without pausing his kisses, he adjusted me in his arms to grant me access to what I craved. A low note of need rumbled in my chest as I gripped him, guiding him out of his trousers.

"Are you sure?" Connor whispered against my mouth. I laughed darkly, and he pulled away slightly.

"If I wasn't, would I be doing this?" I asked as I slowly and greedily stroked him with my hand.

He groaned, his eyes darkening, and his fingers slipped beneath my undergarment to find me more than ready for him. With a wicked grin, he slid the thin fabric out of the way and inched his hips closer to me, teasing me for several tortuous breaths. When I pulled his lips back to mine, cradling his jaw in my palms, his hands lifted my hips and he pressed himself inside me so slowly I almost growled in my impatience. My eyes fell closed, and another moan of pleasure hummed in my throat. Each inch of himself he offered dragged me deeper into an epic bliss edged with pain and fear.

I rolled my body against his, shuddering with each thrust as he met my every move. When his lips found my breasts—his tongue and teeth and lips devouring each pebbled peak with slow, deliberate attention— my head fell back against the stones, and I looked up toward the stars. He lifted his face to mine and slipped his fingers deep into my hair, forcing me to stare into his eyes—eyes brimming with a warmth and desire that overtook my heart.

"You're mine, Sapphire," he said, his breathing ragged as we moved together. "And I'm yours. From here and now to forever and beyond, we are one."

"Forever and beyond," I breathed, nodding my agreement as tears clouded my vision.

Then his mouth was back on my throat, claiming me, consuming me as his hips pushed faster. Thrusting harder and deeper, pulling moan after blessed moan from my soul, he guided us together—as one—to that precipice among the stars—glimmering, dancing, falling around us. And then I was careening toward a blissful end I'd never imagined, made even more perfect because Connor was with me, for every breath, every heartbeat. We collapsed against one another, sighing. Our foreheads pressed together as our names graced each other's lips, whispered with utterly satisfied breaths.

But as I looked into his eyes now, I realized the horrible truth.

I might never have this—never have him—outside of my dreams.

And this wasn't enough.

✳

After I awakened, I was restless and agitated, aching for something I couldn't have. I couldn't sit still in my room any longer. I needed to get out of here, get some fresh air into my lungs, get myself moving. The palace was still quiet as I made my way to the front door. When I stepped out into the chill morning air, I was greeted by the sound of approaching horses. My throat tightened when Matthias and the guards rode into view. The fae commander caught sight of me and turned his mare, dismounting before she'd come to a full stop.

"Is he okay?" Matthias asked, concern deepening the creases in his brow as he searched my face.

I swallowed hard, my mouth suddenly going dry. "I don't know," I finally managed to say.

Matthias's eyes widened slightly. "What do you mean you don't know?"

Images from last night's dreams flashed into focus, and my throat tightened as the now-too-familiar feeling of rejection overwhelmed me. I took a slow breath and forced my voice to remain steady as I responded, "I haven't seen him since we got back."

"And when was that?"

"Two days ago. He just sits in his room—as far as I know. I've knocked on his door, but he doesn't answer."

Matthias's lips tightened into a thin line as he handed me the reins. "Take her to the stables for me? I'll talk to him."

I nodded silently, and he slipped past me quickly.

CHAPTER SIXTY-FOUR

Connor

I slouched lower in my armchair as I stared at the fire, replaying last night's dream in my head for the millionth time. It had felt so real. *She* had felt real. I could almost taste her blood on my tongue and feel her hands around my—

The door to my room flew open, startling me when it banged into the wall. Matthias entered, threw the door closed behind him, and stormed toward me. His mouth was set in a firm line. His eyes blazed with fury.

"What in the fuck are you doing?" he asked, standing directly in front of me, resting his hand on the pommel of his sword.

I met his glare for a moment before shifting my gaze back to the flames. "Guessing you saw Lieke?"

"Yeah, I saw her. What did you do to her?"

My eyes slid closed, and I pulled in a slow breath. He wasn't going to understand. Stars, I understood it—somewhat—and still couldn't figure out what to do. It had been two days since I'd kissed her, and ever since then, I'd been hiding in here like a coward. She'd tried to visit, but every time she knocked, I pretended to be out.

"It's complicated," I said, huffing out a pathetic laugh at my choice of words given the rules she and I had set up to prevent this problem.

Well, not exactly *this* problem. This was the last thing I had expected to happen.

Matthias let out a loud sigh as he lowered himself into the other armchair. "She was out front when we arrived, Connor. Said she was worried about you."

I laughed quietly, though none of this was funny in the slightest. I had already known she was worried. Somehow I could sense it. It was tugging at my nerves, as though her worry was now mine—along with her feelings of rejection and abandonment.

I dropped my head into my hands.

What was I going to do?

Matthias cleared his throat, but I didn't look up. "You've been home for two days, and she hasn't seen you since then? What happened?"

"I kissed her," I mumbled.

My friend breathed out an *okay* and then asked, "And that warrants you becoming a creepy recluse...why?"

Raising my head slightly, I rested my chin on my clasped hands. "She's my mate."

Matthias's eyes widened slowly and then narrowed, his brow tightening as he regarded me carefully, like he thought I would joke about this. "You're serious?"

My face fell, dejected. "No. I'm lying."

"You're serious," he repeated; this time it was not a question.

I nodded, pressing my lips together.

"Wait," he said, sitting back in his chair and crossing an ankle over his knee. "Why is this a bad thing? You need a queen. You're already engaged. And boom, your betrothed is your—"

"I can't tell her," I blurted out.

"Um, yes you can. You just told me. Pretty sure she understands words."

"I'm not saying she's stupid, Matthias. It would crush her." I pushed to my feet and stormed into the other room. I needed a drink. Matthias watched me carefully from his seat as I poured myself a generous portion of brandy.

"You're right," he conceded, shrugging. "It would certainly devastate the woman to know the male she's fallen for is destined to be with her."

My hand paused on the bottle I'd just set back down on the table. Sure, I'd noticed love in her eyes before, but only in these dreams I kept having. "How do you know she— Did she tell you?"

Matthias rolled his eyes dramatically. "No, she didn't tell me. She didn't need to. It's painfully obvious that she loves you. I told you that back in the training room, didn't I?"

As I considered a response, I returned to my seat, swirling my drink around in my hand. "No, you predicted I'd fall for her. You didn't say anything about her loving me back."

"Close enough," he said, a thoughtful frown appearing on his face. "Still, I'm not wrong."

"I can't take the choice away from her again. I already did it once with the engagement stunt."

He looked like he wanted to smack me, and he might have if I'd been closer. "How are you taking anything away from her? Even if she didn't already love you, being your mate doesn't require her to choose you, does it? And if she doesn't, you can always go back to suffering as you are now."

"But she knows enough about the bonds to know we only have one mate. What if she feels pressured to accept it?"

Matthias threw his hands up and stood. "Then you live happily ever after!"

"There's no happily ever anything if she doesn't love me."

"Fine. Don't tell her. Go on avoiding her," Matthias said.

He stalked away.

"I'll tell her," I muttered as my friend opened the door to leave. "I just don't know how to do it yet."

"Well, don't take too long. She won't wait around forever for you. Even true love fades when it's neglected."

CHAPTER SIXTY-FIVE

Lieke

I walked slowly out of the trees toward the palace, my hands resting behind my head as I greedily pulled in air. Sweat covered the back of my neck, pooling under my plaited hair, and my clothes stuck to me uncomfortably. Still, this was less suffocating than being in my room waiting for Connor to stop being stupid.

"Good run?" someone asked from behind me, and I spun around to find Brennan leaning against a tree, his arms folded casually in front of him. I smiled at him, surprised to find I was happy to see him—not like a lovesick woman pining over her first love, but more like a sister toward her sibling.

"Are you following me now?" I asked.

"Maybe," he said, shrugging. His easy smile faded slightly as he pushed away from the tree and strode toward me. "Can I walk you back?"

I nodded, and we walked in silence for a bit before he cleared his throat quietly.

"I wanted to apologize," he said. He laughed half-heartedly before adding, "Again."

"Oh?" was all I could manage. Lightly he touched my elbow and brought me to a stop, turning me to look at him.

"I shouldn't have kissed you." He dropped his hand from my arm and lifted it to the back of his neck. "Or gotten drunk. Or entered your room."

Unsure how to respond, I just stood there, staring at him blankly.

"You know that first time we kissed, in my mother's room?" he asked. I nodded. "I actually hoped you'd end up being my mate. I thought maybe if you were, my father would let me off the hook."

"Really? You mean that was like some kind of test?" I asked, and he merely shrugged in response. "And what about the second one? Was that a test too?"

Shaking his head, he gave me a sad smile. "That one was just me being stupid. Like when I didn't stand up to my father for you." He paused, his smile shifting mischievously. "Though, I think everything worked out as it was supposed to in the end."

As thankful as I was for his apologies, I couldn't keep from rolling my eyes. "Oh, yes. I was destined to find myself in a fake relationship with a male who can't even bear to see me after—"

Clamping my mouth shut, I stopped myself before I accidentally confessed what had happened in the stables. Brennan's eyes narrowed in suspicion for a brief moment, but then he blinked a few times and shrugged. He pivoted back toward the palace, offering me his arm as we resumed walking.

"Is it fair to assume you're no longer waiting for me then?" he asked. "I won't have to worry about you trying to sabotage my wedding?"

I laughed nervously, thankful he couldn't detect lies like Mrs. Bishop. I peered sideways at him to find him trying to hide a smile. "Only if you ask me to, though I get the impression that something's changed. Is it possible you're actually happy?"

"In fact, I am," he admitted, glancing at the ground as a boyish smile pulled at his lips. "The king and queen returned to Arenysen after you and Connor left, but Calla remained here for several days. She is…

well, she's incredible. She's really something else. Smart and witty. Kind and sweet. Gentle but with a bold fierceness too. Basically she's everything I don't deserve."

My heart warmed as I listened to him, and I noted the genuine contentment in his voice. "Nonsense. You deserve to be happy. I'm happy for you. Truly," I said. Inside, though, my gut wrenched itself into uneasy knots over the task the rebels had given me. The idea of breaking up their engagement had been bad enough when I'd thought he wasn't happy about it. How could I do that to him now that I knew he was?

Brennan hummed softly. "What happened to the woman who swore to wait for me until my vows were uttered?"

Laying my head on his shoulder, I drew in a slow, deep breath and sighed. "I think you already know."

CHAPTER SIXTY-SIX

Connor

With a growl, I punched the wall beside my window and turned away from the sight of my mate clinging to my brother as they walked toward the palace. My mind ran wild with scenarios for why they were coming out of the forest together. None of them were desirable.

Closing my eyes, I dove into my own consciousness, seeking out Lieke's emotions within myself. How this worked, I didn't know, but the entire run from the stables after I'd kissed her—after the bond had formed—it was like she was running alongside me. Her confusion, her rejection, her pain—they'd accompanied me all the way back to the palace. It was like all she felt had seeped into my own veins and singed my nerves.

It had overwhelmed me then, but now—as I watched her hold onto Brennan's arm, lean her head against his shoulder, and smile at him—I longed to know what she was feeling. Did she still love him? Did she still want to come between him and Calla?

All I found inside myself, though, was my own anger and bitter jealousy.

Desperate for a distraction, I picked up the message Matthias had sent earlier. The healers had discovered something.

✳

"It's blood?" I asked Quinton, our lead healer. His white hair bobbed in the air as he nodded. Pushing his spectacles further up on the bridge of his nose, he reached for a paper on his desk and handed it to me.

"And not like any blood any of us have ever seen, Your Highness," he said, his voice as smooth as old leather.

"Can you tell how it works?" Matthias asked, peering over my shoulder at the report in my hands.

"Not yet," Quinton said. "But we're working on that, while trying not to kill ourselves in the process."

"What about the needle or dart or whatever it was that struck me?" I asked. "Lieke said it must have been something different."

"Indeed. It's most fascinating actually. It has many of the same markers, which has us believing it's from the same individual—or at least within the same family."

My brows shot up. "Family? You mean it's not from an animal?"

Quinton shook his head casually. "Not an animal. A human actually. More or less anyway."

"What do you mean, *more or less*?" Matthias asked, stepping up beside me.

"Well, just that it's human. But it's also not," Quinton said, as if it should have been obvious. "Something's altered it, shifted it into a venom of sorts, which they've used to create poisons of varying degrees of potency. How they did it, we don't know, but we can venture to guess why."

"For the rebellion," Matthias and I said in unison.

"Is it related to the poison that killed my mother?" I asked quietly.

Quinton shrugged, and his face fell. "We still don't know, and we might never know. Without examining the weapon or knowing the delivery method used in her case, we can't truly compare them."

"Do we know where it's coming from though?" Matthias asked.

Quinton lifted a finger in the air. "Ah, yes, that we can tell you. We found faint traces of pollen from a plant that does not grow on our land. It's native to the island of Dolobare."

"Dolobare?" Matthias and I asked in unison.

Matthias then asked, "Do you think the night stalkers have some hand in this?"

The healer's brows rose over his weary eyes. "It appears that way, but nothing is certain. How this poison is getting here is anyone's guess, but if it is from their island, it would have to be going through one of the ports in Arenysen."

Matthias leaned close to me and whispered, "It's a good thing your brother's marrying their princess."

＊

Lieke didn't visit me in my dreams that night. Instead I chased invisible rebels across my kingdom and beyond. But no matter what I did, I couldn't catch them, couldn't stop them. Scene after bloody scene assaulted my mind. And all the while, the victims—the families, the guards, the lone travelers—haunted me as I searched for the humans responsible. I woke with my muscles tight and my head pounding.

A voice echoed from far-off, and my heart sank when I realized it wasn't Lieke's.

"Your Highness, it's time for breakfast."

I opened my eyes to find my page staring down at me apologetically. Rubbing my hand over my face, I groaned. "Set it on the table as usual."

"Afraid I can't, sir. His Majesty insists you join the family this morning in the dining room."

CHAPTER
SIXTY-SEVEN

Lieke

I only afforded Connor's door a cursory glance before slipping into my own room. On the dining table, a folded piece of paper had been left—a note from Matthias. He had talked to Connor, and Connor was "fine." That should have relieved me, but it only made his behavior in the stables—and over the past few days—more painful.

If he was *fine*, it meant I'd done something wrong.

Except I hadn't.

Setting the note back down, I walked to the bedroom and sat on the edge of my bed. I had replayed the kiss—stars, I'd replayed the entire trip—in my head so many times, and still I couldn't find any logical explanation for his reaction.

He had held me! He had kissed me!

I never should have let him. I never should have ignored our rules.

Had I simply imagined his growing feelings for me?

Had I simply seen what I wanted to see?

He initiated that kiss though, I reminded myself yet again. Why would he have done that if he didn't feel anything for me?

Maybe he was testing you like Brennan did.

My head snapped up from where I'd dropped it into my hands.

A test.

Was that what the kiss had been?

A test to see if I was his mate?

The words from my dream echoed in my mind.

My bride. My love. My mate.

Scoffing at the absurdity of it all, I rolled my eyes, but I couldn't completely shake the niggling in the back of my head that this was it; he'd been testing me.

And I'd obviously failed.

I searched my memories for the moment when his lips had hit mine, and I could almost feel them caressing mine, could almost taste him on my tongue. Had there been some kind of magic spark? Some lightning bolt like his father had described? Connor had said humans didn't notice the bond like fae did. Was it possible I just couldn't feel it like he could?

And if it was the case that I really was his—I couldn't even think the word again—why had he run? Why had he been avoiding me? Why would he refuse to talk to me?

※

That night, I didn't find Connor in my dreams. I was back in the forest on the old hunting trail at the small clearing where we had camped. The horses grazed while the guards—Evan and Willem—huddled together near a tree. Tears pricked my eyes at seeing Connor's men and horse alive and well.

I called for Connor, but he wasn't here.

Grabbing Honey's reins, I climbed into the saddle and took off down the trail in search of him. He had to be here somewhere. I blinked and found myself back on the main road. When I spun Honey around in a circle, my grief slammed into me. Evan, Willem, and their horses lay dead on the road in pools of blood.

"Connor!" I called out again, but my voice sounded muffled and distant, like I was screaming through water.

Honey continued turning, and the forest spun around me, making me dizzy. Then I saw him, and I pulled Honey to a stop. I couldn't move. There in the middle of the road, Rosie was on the ground, suffering as her blood seeped into the dirt. Connor lay beneath her, trapped. Not moving. Not breathing.

No, no, no!

This wasn't how it had happened.

Sliding out of my saddle, I hit the ground and ran to him. My fingers fumbled around for a pulse but found none. My vision blurred with tears, and sobs violently wracked my body.

"We warned you," a voice said, slicing through the air. I didn't need to turn to know it was Anna. "We told you what would happen if you failed."

"No!" I screamed, jolting up. I found myself back in my dark and empty bedroom. My heart thundered as I wiped the tears away from my cheeks and looked around the room. I was alone. He wasn't coming this time.

CHAPTER SIXTY-EIGHT

Lieke

The door to my room opened, and someone walked quietly through the living area before appearing in the bedroom.

"Good morning!" Gretchen said, her voice as cheerful as the sunshine pouring in through the curtains. She headed for the wardrobe and yanked the doors open, flipping through my clothes. "We are running a little late this morning, so I'm afraid there's no time for me to draw up a bath for you." After pulling out a light blue dress, she closed the doors and hung the garment on the dressing screen in the corner.

Stepping out of bed, I stretched my arms overhead and padded my way across the room.

Her nose wrinkled briefly, but she offered me another smile, though it was a bit tighter this time. "Perhaps the royal family wouldn't mind waiting a bit longer." Then she waved her hand in the air, and the steaming bath appeared. No matter how many times I'd seen her do this, I never got used to it.

Placing my hands on my hips, I angled my head at my maid.

"Gretchen, are you trying to tell me something? Should I be offended?"

The poor girl pulled one corner of her mouth down as she cringed apologetically. "Well, it's just that ever since you came back, you've kind of…smelled?"

The comment might have mortified me if I hadn't been certain Gretchen was imagining it. Lifting my shoulder, I sniffed my skin. I couldn't detect anything different or unusual. I lifted the front of my nightshirt to my nose and took a deep breath, but all I caught was a faint hint of Connor's damned cologne. It seemed ridiculous to argue with the girl and let a perfectly good bath go to waste, so I shrugged and stepped behind the screen to undress.

I had just lowered myself into the water when someone knocked at the door. Gretchen ran to answer it. Pulling my hair away from my face, I twisted it up and leaned back against the tub to hold it in place while I listened for any hint as to who had stopped by. Hope made my heart thump faster. Maybe Connor had finally gotten over whatever had kept him away. Maybe he was finally ready to talk to me. But I couldn't make out any voices, let alone any words.

A few moments later, Gretchen stuck her head around the door-frame. "Lieke, the prince is here to escort you to breakfast. He's waiting in the living room."

My heart leaped into my throat, and I tried to contain my smile. "Can you tell Connor I'll be out in a moment?"

Sheepishly, Gretchen lowered her eyes to the floor and opened her mouth to respond, but another voice called out from the other room first: "Not that prince."

Brennan.

I wanted to sink down under the water and hide, but since I didn't particularly feel like drowning, I cleared my throat and said, "Sorry, Bren! I'll hurry."

Swearing under my breath, I hurriedly scrubbed the soap over my skin and lathered it into my hair. Gretchen held a towel out for me, and I shared an embarrassed look with her as I dried off and she helped me dress.

When I stepped into the living room, Brennan was already standing with his arm held out, waiting for me to take it. I slipped my hand under his elbow, and he leaned close and whispered, "Don't worry, I won't tell my brother that you confused me for him."

Rolling my eyes, I sighed. "Not sure he'd even care at this point."

"Well, we're about to find out," Brennan said, pulling open my door and leading me into the hallway. "The king's forcing him to dine with us this morning. And since Connor isn't me, we all know he'll dutifully comply."

I stumbled like I had tripped on a loose tile—as if the palace would ever have such a thing—earning me a laugh from my friend. "Don't worry. I'll be right there with you the whole time."

"I can handle your brother," I said.

"Oh, I know you can. But it seemed like the right thing to say regardless."

During the entire walk to the dining room, my stomach flipped and flopped uncontrollably, like a fish trying to find its way back to the water. Pressing my hand to my chest, I tried to soothe my racing heartbeat. But when Brennan guided me into the room and I caught sight of Connor occupying his usual seat, all of my efforts failed. His eyes lifted to mine and held me hostage.

Heat flooded my face.

The last time I'd seen him was in that dream when we'd—

"Breathe," Brennan whispered into my ear, and I blinked away the memories. He pulled out the chair beside his, and I sat, never looking away from my betrothed. His expression was blank, as if he were bored, except—there!—faintly, the muscle in his jaw pulsed. Was he that upset about having to see me? Was he jealous about me sitting beside his brother? Had he expected me to hide in my rooms for days until he was ready to fetch me?

The questions swirled around in my head even as I smiled at the king and said, "Good morning, Your Majesty. I apologize for being late."

The king waved a hand. "No need for that, Lieke. After what you endured on your journey, it's understandable if it's harder to face the world some mornings."

I nodded appreciatively, trying to avoid Connor's scrutiny. A server I didn't recognize set our meals before us, and Brennan eagerly dug in, heaping eggs and potatoes onto his fork. "So, brother," he said, lifting the loaded utensil toward Connor, "you're alive!"

Sneaking a glance at Connor from under my lashes, I noted how his eyes flicked to me before returning to Brennan. "I am," he said dryly, then returned to eating his breakfast.

"Well, we missed you," Brennan said. He elbowed me in the arm and flashed me a mischievous smile. "Didn't we, Lieke?"

Heat returned to my cheeks, and I tucked my bottom lip between my teeth. Keeping my eyes on my food, I nodded, asking Connor, "Where have you been anyway?"

Connor pierced a potato. "Around."

When our eyes met again, I could have sworn there was an angry sadness swirling in them, but why would he be mad at me? What was his problem? At least before I'd known where I stood with him. I was a thorn in his side, a problem to be overcome. Now? Now I didn't know what I was. Stars above. I wanted to throw my fork down and demand that he tell me, but this wasn't the place or time. But would he ever agree to speak to me again? Would I ever have the chance to ask him?

The king's fork clattered loudly onto his empty plate, drawing everyone's attention, and he leaned his forearms onto the table as a server whisked away his dishes. He shot a pointed glare in Brennan's direction. "Leave him alone, Brennan," he said, sounding more like a father than I'd ever heard before. "Connor has simply been busy working to assess the rebels' last attacks."

He was lying.

I didn't need to have Mrs. Bishop's sixth sense to know he was covering for his son, but why? My head swirled with even more questions, but I had no hope of finding any answers.

"Apologies, brother," Brennan said. "Hopefully you'll have some free time soon, or I'm going to have to keep entertaining your fiancée while you're otherwise occupied."

Damn it all, I was blushing again, and I could sense Connor's anger swelling even without looking at him.

"I'm free this afternoon actually," Connor said, his tone bitter and hopeful at the same time. "If you're available?"

I swallowed hard as dread settled heavily in my gut. I'd been hoping for a chance to talk to him, but now I wasn't sure I wanted to hear what he had to say.

"Of course, Wolfie," I said around a tight smile.

CHAPTER SIXTY-NINE

Connor

My feet slipped on the dirt floor of the training ring, and I barely lifted my practice sword up in time to block Matthias's strike.

"Sloppy, Your Highness," he said, his voice serious and unyielding.

"I can't do this," I said, pushing him back and retreating a few paces. "And no, I'm not talking about the sparring."

"Glad you clarified that, but either way, yes, you can. And you will." He spun his sword around to attack from the opposite side. I parried easily but couldn't strike back quickly enough before he was coming at me again. "Just talk to her."

"I can't even look at her," I insisted, lunging at him and wincing when my sword clashed against his.

"Then keep your eyes closed," he said flatly, catching me off guard just long enough to bring his weapon down hard on my forearm.

I groaned from both the pain of the hit and this blasted situation I found myself in. "I know I need to talk to her. It's why I invited her here, but I don't know how to even be in the same room with her."

Slumping against the wall of the training building, I slid down until I was sitting in the dirt. Matthias tossed his sparring sword onto a nearby table before joining me on the ground.

"I thought this was what you wanted," he said. "To find your mate, I mean."

I threw my head back against the wall, appreciating the sting as it hit hard. "Honestly? I hoped I never would."

Matthias stiffened. "What?"

"Losing my mother was hell for me, and I was just her son. Her death is slowly killing my father, and the thought of enduring such pain myself…"

"So what? The bond is there now, whether you like it or not, right?"

Dipping my chin slightly, I said, "Yes—"

"Pain is part of life," Matthias said. "You can't hide from it or escape it."

"I can delay it though."

"At what cost?"

I let out a hollow laugh. "It should be easier, shouldn't it? She's my mate—our souls are destined to be together—yet I can't even talk to her."

"To be fair, though, how many mates met because one was in love with the other one's brother?"

He had a point, but that didn't make any of this easier.

"Look, Connor," Matthias said, pausing to take a long inhale. "She'll be here any minute. You can do this. You've saved this girl so many times. The least she can do is hear you out, and if she can't handle this bond, if she can't accept it and she walks away, at least you can go on knowing you tried. Trust her to make her own decision, whether it's the decision you want or not."

"You're right," I said, lifting my head and giving him a sideways glance.

"Of course I'm right," he said around a smile. "That's why you keep me around."

"That and because you're the only one willing to call me out on my bullshit."

"Yes, that too." He rose to his feet and offered me a hand. "You can do this. I'm heading out to check in with the soldiers, but find me tomorrow? Unless, of course, it goes really well and you're too busy."

CHAPTER SEVENTY

Lieke

I was a mess the entire walk to the training ring. My pulse was going so fast by the time I arrived that I half expected Connor to hear it and greet me at the door. He didn't though, so I took the opportunity to pause outside and gather my thoughts.

As my emotions wreaked havoc on me—covering my chest with nervous tingles, filling my stomach with excited flutters, prickling my skin with a cold fear—I took deep breaths, filling my lungs with the pine-soaked air. Acknowledging each of my emotions, I reminded myself that they weren't the enemy. They were simply a part of life. They only ruled over me if I let them.

I had nearly calmed down when something new slammed into me, pressing against my heart with such intensity that I pressed a hand to my sternum as if I could quench it.

Guilt.

My nightmare flashed into focus, Anna's words spinning around in my head. *"We warned you. We told you what would happen."*

I had lied to Connor after the attack. I'd done it to him to save him and Brennan, sure, but I had lied all the same. And here I was about to demand that he be honest with me.

It's different.

But was it? I was trying to protect him. How did I know he wasn't keeping his distance to do the same for me?

Swallowing hard, I forced my feet to carry me through the door. As I entered, Connor rose from where he'd been sitting against the wall, brushed the dirt off his dark pants, and shoved his hands into his pockets. His eyes caught mine briefly before darting away to look elsewhere.

"You came," he said softly, seeming to drop the words at his feet rather than saying them to me.

I stepped forward cautiously, as though he might retreat if I moved too quickly. "I've missed you," I said meekly, immediately questioning whether that was the wrong thing to say. A faint smile tugged at his lips, but he didn't respond, causing fear to spark within me once more.

He still didn't look at me, didn't move.

This was far from the confident royal I'd come to know. This wasn't the same fae who had come to my rescue too many times to count. What had changed? What had happened to cause this shift in him?

But a different question spilled out of me. "What did I do wrong?"

The muscle in his jaw pulsed as it did when he was angry. His gaze burned into me, but not with anger or frustration. With regret.

"Nothing," he finally said, swallowing hard.

Another step brought me close enough I could almost reach out and touch him if I dared.

I didn't.

"Then why?" He started to shake his head slowly as I moved even closer. His scent engulfed me, but I ignored the desire that warmed my core. When I was less than an arm's length away, I stopped, wringing my hands in front of me. "Why did you do it if you were just going to regret it?"

His lips pursed in concentration, and his eyes tightened slightly. I could almost see the thoughts churning in his mind as he worked to find the right words, debated how to answer me.

"You think I regret it?" he asked quietly, pinching his brow tightly.

"Why else would you run away? And then refuse to see me?" My voice wavered, my frustration and pain colliding into one confusing mass of emotions in my throat. "Was it some kind of test to see if I was your mate?"

Connor flinched, and his nostrils flared, but he remained quiet.

Dropping my hands to my sides, I straightened with feigned confidence. "That's it, isn't it? A fucking test. Just like Brennan."

With a growl, he spun away from me. "It wasn't a stars-damned test."

He wasn't going to avoid me this time. I wouldn't allow it. I deserved some answers. Grabbing his arm, I tried to pull him around to face me, but he held firm, keeping his back to me. When I stepped in front of him, his hand snatched up my other wrist and pulled me to him so our chests were pressed together. His breath, ragged and uneven, shifted my hair against my forehead.

He released me immediately but didn't fully pull away. "I'm scared," he admitted softly.

I froze, my breath catching as my mind raced to remember where I'd heard him say that before. An image of the Linley Inn came into focus.

My dream.

"Scared of what? Me?" I laughed nervously as I repeated the same words I'd said in the dream. His eyes widened expectantly, like he was waiting for me to say something more.

"What, Connor?" I asked, lifting my shoulders. "What do you want from me? Do you want me to leave you alone?"

He shook his head. "No, I don't want—"

"Then what?" My gut churned with my growing frustration. "Trust me enough to talk to me!"

Connor's expression darkened, and his voice came out low and rough as he said, "Trust goes both ways, Sapphire. I'm not the only one hiding something, am I?"

The guilt that had assaulted me earlier flooded back in, but I couldn't tell him what I was hiding, not when the sight of him lying dead in the road haunted me whenever I closed my eyes. Shaking my head, I tried to fight the tears that sprang to the surface.

"That's different," I stammered.

"How?" he growled. I blinked rapidly, racking my brain for some excuse. When I came up with nothing, he huffed. "That's what I thought."

He started to turn and retreat again, and fear erupted in my chest, driving my tears to spill over and stream down my cheeks. "Connor, please. Just trust me when I say I can't—"

Rounding on me, he pinned me with a wounded glare. "Can't what? Just say it, Lieke. You love Brennan. I can see how you look at him. And it doesn't matter that…"

He paused to take a shaky breath, and I held mine as I waited for him to complete his thought.

But he never did.

Instead, he simply muttered, "None of it matters."

I wanted to close the distance between us, to take his face in my hands and tell him exactly how I felt. How my world was empty when he wasn't around. How my life lost all meaning without him beside me. How I couldn't bear another minute apart.

But I couldn't.

Telling him any of that would guarantee his death. Or his brother's.

We couldn't fight the rebels. We couldn't stop them. And I couldn't be with him.

I had no choice but to do as they demanded, and Connor had just handed me a way to do that.

"Brennan can't marry Calla," I choked out, trying to reassure myself this was for the best. This was what had to be done.

"So I'm right. You still want him?" Connor whispered, watching me.

I nodded once, unable to utter the lie aloud.

He cleared his throat, shrugging his shoulders as if to avoid someone's unwanted touch. "He's never been there for you, and you'd still choose him."

"I—"

"He just *stood* there as you were sentenced to death!" he said, sending each barbed word straight at my heart. His chin dropped in defeat as he muttered, "Fine."

For a long moment I stood there, unable to speak, biting my lip to keep it from quivering.

Finally, he broke the silence. "You should know—" he started. But then he pressed his lips together into a tight line and closed his eyes, shaking his head, as if reconsidering what he had been about to say.

"What?" I asked.

When he opened his eyes, he stared at the floor and nodded toward the door, muttering, "You should go."

I hesitated, fighting the urge to run to him and tell him it was all a lie, that I only wanted *him*, but Anna's warning echoed in my head again, reminding me why I couldn't.

So without a word, I turned to leave, certain he could hear my heart shattering as I walked away.

CHAPTER SEVENTY-ONE

Connor

It was better this way—better she didn't know our hearts were bound by the stars.

Especially when she still wanted to give hers to Brennan.

The prick.

But if that asshole would make her happy, then I could shoulder the pain and loneliness of our bond alone.

Yes, this was better.

Better felt like shit.

I couldn't sit here in the dirt all night, but I couldn't go back to the damned palace yet either. I glanced at the ceiling, to where Matthias's apartment was situated on the second floor. With the recent influx of new soldiers, his visits would keep him out late, affording me enough time to hide out there until I could stomach going back.

Reaching into my pocket, I pulled out the spare key to his rooms. He'd given it to me for emergencies, and this felt like a stars-damned emergency to me.

Once inside, I grabbed a bottle from the table under the window, not caring what it was. Ignoring the clean, empty glasses, I unstopped it and tipped it up to my lips. It burned my throat and settled in my stomach like liquid fire, mixing with all my pain and jealousy and worry over Lieke. After several long draughts, though, it began to numb everything.

Just as I'd hoped it would.

My stomach grumbled loudly in the quiet room, reminding me I had missed supper. Perhaps Mrs. Bishop wouldn't mind me popping into the kitchen like I used to when I was younger, when my nights were spent having fun in taverns rather than trying to keep our kingdom from collapsing. Taking the bottle with me, I stumbled out of his apartment and shut the door behind me—at least, I was pretty sure I shut it.

When had our property gotten so big?

I didn't remember it ever taking this long to get home before.

When I finally arrived at the palace, it was quiet, and I slowed my steps so as not to make too much noise as I made my way downstairs. My father wouldn't take kindly to my making a scene. Again. I chuckled at how ridiculous I must have looked that night, standing there in front of all our guests, trying to think of a reason not to kill Lieke.

Looking around, I wondered how I'd ended up at the kitchen so quickly, but it was no matter. I was here, and I could smell our cook's delicious food even from the hallway. I leaned my shoulder against the wall and tapped the lip of the bottle against the kitchen door, closing my eyes as I waited. The door swung open faster than I'd expected, but when I opened my eyes, my mouth fell into a frown.

"You're not my cook," I said, pointing the bottle at the female who seemed altogether unimpressed that her crown prince was standing before her.

"Neither are you," she said around her scowl.

Recognition dawned on me, and my brows shot up I leaned my head closer to her. "I know you. You're Laura."

"Lola," she corrected with no amusement on her face.

"Right, that's what I said."

Laura or Lola—or whatever her name was—angled her head to one side, studying me more than I should have allowed. Before I could order her to stop, she smiled sweetly, though I got the distinct impression there was nothing sweet about this female. "I knew it was only a matter of time before she drove you to drink."

A string of laughter bubbled up from my chest as I lifted my hand, still holding the bottle, and placed a finger to my lips. "Don't tell anyone, Laura, but my bride doesn't like you very much."

The female's smile faded, her eyes icing over. She sneered. "The feeling is mutual."

I dropped my gaze to the dark blue stone lying against her chest.

"That's not yours," I said, glancing briefly up to her eyes.

She clutched the stone in her hand. "It is now. She gave it to me."

I narrowed my eyes. "Why?"

Mischief played upon her mouth before she said, "In exchange for getting to take your brother his dinner."

Of course. It was always about Brennan.

Peeling myself off the wall, I set my jaw as I stared at her. "You know what? I don't think I like you very much either." Before she could react, I grabbed her wrist with my free hand, squeezing hard until her fingers released their grip on Lieke's necklace. Tossing her arm to the side—a tad miffed that it didn't smack into the door—I snatched up the necklace and tore it from her neck. Forgetting about my hunger and my quest for food, I stepped back, turned slowly around, and headed upstairs.

CHAPTER SEVENTY-TWO

Lieke

I was still crying when I returned to my room. Thankfully, I hadn't met anyone along the way, and Gretchen wasn't here to ask the reason for my sobs. Falling into bed, I buried my face in my pillow, letting my tears flow freely and silently and for as long as they needed to.

I must have fallen asleep at some point, because the room was dark when I sat up to the sound of knocking at my door. My heart took off running ahead of me as I walked slowly to answer it. At first I assumed it was probably just Mrs. Bishop, here to insist I eat something, but somehow—even before I opened the door and found him standing there with his head hanging low toward his chest—I knew it was Connor.

Dressed casually in his black trousers and grey button-up shirt, he looked much like he had the first time I'd opened the door to him. Except this time his hair was mussed—one stray piece hanging haphazardly into his eyes—and his shirt, while tucked in, hung loose. The top three buttons were undone, revealing enough of his chest and tattoo that I nearly forgot how to breathe.

"Connor?" I said sheepishly, not intending it to come out a question.

He lifted his chin just enough to bring his eyes up to meet mine, and a smile crept lazily across his lips. "Sapphire," he breathed out.

Under any other circumstances, I probably would have giggled, but with how we'd left things this afternoon, I was more worried than amused. "You're drunk," I said.

He lifted a nearly empty bottle toward me as if offering to share, but he said nothing. Gingerly I took the bottle from him and invited him in. When he stepped forward, though, he stumbled, catching himself on the doorframe. He shifted slowly, running his hand up the wood to grip the molding overhead. His movements were so smooth, they almost appeared intentional. Almost.

Leaning against the doorframe, he angled his head and gave me the most flirtatious smile I'd ever seen on his face—outside of my dreams anyway. "I am indeed…drunk."

I held the bottle up and eyed its label before sloshing around the last bits of the amber liquid in the bottom. "What is this anyway?"

"The good stuff," he purred before laughing softly. "Matthias is going to kill me for swiping it."

Slowly, I stepped toward him, reaching out as I whispered, "You should come in before someone sees you like this."

He grabbed my hand but didn't step inside. Pulling me close, he guided my hand to his waist before releasing it. His hand was at my throat before I could take another breath, his thumb stroking the underside of my jaw while his fingers crept into my hair. He angled my face up so I had to look into his eyes. Our breaths mingled between us, tickling my nose, and my core heated, reminding me of my recent dreams. I swallowed hard under his palm, unsure of what to do.

"Sapphire," he whispered over my lips, and it took every ounce of willpower not to sink into him. His hand tightened slightly at my throat before he moved to bury his fingers deep in my hair. He pulled me to him and kissed the end of my nose as he had during training weeks ago. Slowly and tenderly, he brushed his cheek against mine until his lips tickled my ear.

"I think I need to sit down," Connor muttered.

When he released me, I pushed aside my disappointment and led him inside to the sofa, where he promptly lay down with his legs stretched out. Kneeling beside him on the floor, I pushed the hair off his forehead. He hummed contentedly.

"Before I forget…" he started. Reaching a hand into his pocket, he pulled out a chain. His fist hovered in front of my face as he let the dark blue pendant fall and dangle from the chain. "I brought this for you."

After looking from him to the pendant and back a few times, I snatched the necklace from his hand and clutched it to my chest. I'd never thought I would hold it again, and he'd gotten it for me. "How did you—"

He waved a hand dismissively, his eyes falling closed. "Had a lovely chat with your friend, Laura."

"You mean Lola?"

His eyelids fluttered open. "That's what I said."

"Thank you," I gushed, smiling despite all the reasons I shouldn't.

"It's nothing," he said, and a shadow of sadness passed over his eyes.

"This isn't nothing," I said.

His jaw pulsed beneath clenched teeth, his expression hardening. His eyes fell closed again as his lips softened. "Don't worry though. It's the last time."

"What do you mean?" I asked quietly, not sure I wanted to hear the answer.

"The last time I save you—or your jewelry," he said matter-of-factly. Sighing deeply, he continued. "It's over. You and me, the whole thing. We no longer have to pretend. I'll get Brennan out of the engagement for you."

"What about the king? The princess?"

He said nothing but lazily waved a hand in the air before letting it fall onto his chest.

Silently, I watched as his breaths lengthened and his body relaxed. His hair fell across his forehead again, and this time when I nudged it out of the way, I let my fingertips graze the side of his face. He seemed so at peace—more relaxed than I'd ever seen him before—as if he were finally free of all his heavy burdens.

CHAPTER SEVENTY-THREE

Connor

When I woke up from my dreamless, booze-induced slumber, I found myself staring into two very irritated blue eyes.

"You're an asshole, you know that?" Matthias said.

"Good morning to you too." I winced as my voice bounced around inside my aching head.

My friend scoffed loudly. "What were you thinking exactly?"

I squinted at him, trying to get my brain to focus, but it refused. "What did I do this time?" I asked.

A bottle drifted into my line of sight, making my friend appear wavy and distorted. I laughed and then groaned as the next wave of pain hit.

"Oh, that."

"Yes, that. And then I had to come drag you off of Lieke's sofa? What were you even doing there? And while drunk?"

At that, I sat up, looking around. I was in my own room, lying on my own sofa. Leaning forward, I rested my elbows on my lap and squeezed my head between my hands. No amount of pressure helped ease the throbbing headache though.

"I didn't tell her, if that's what you're wondering," I said, fairly certain I hadn't confessed anything in my sleep.

"I know that much." Matthias's voice had softened, albeit only slightly. The sofa shifted as he sat down beside me. "If you had, you'd be sleeping in her bed instead of on your couch."

"How did you know where I was?"

"Lieke heard me pounding on your door last night."

I knew I should probably apologize for breaking into his apartment—though to be fair, I'd used my key—and stealing his booze. I had no excuse for that.

Instead I said, "She's still in love with Brennan." Each word grated on my nerves and poked fresh holes in my heart.

"I told you—"

I lifted my head, ignoring the resulting bolt of pain, and glared at him. "You didn't see them together."

"You don't know—"

"She told me." My shoulders slumped under my defeat. "She loves him."

Matthias's eyes narrowed. "And what about last night? You can sense her emotions through the bond, right?"

"I don't know. The drink clouded everything, maybe," I said, running a hand through my hair. "I love her, and I can't have her."

"But you didn't tell her she's your mate."

"I couldn't. Not after she asked me to call off Brennan's engagement," I said.

"So what are you going to do now?" Matthias asked, his expression tightening with concern.

"I need to talk to my father."

CHAPTER SEVENTY-FOUR

Lieke

atthias, thankfully, had taken one look at the drunken prince on my sofa and promptly hauled him away without a word, sparing me the pain of explaining. What would he think when Connor told him? Would he think less of me? Would he hate me for hurting his friend?

Why did I care?

All that mattered now was stopping the rebels' assassination.

The attack on the road had proven their impatience. I needed to inform them immediately that I'd stopped the wedding—and the alliance—or that I'd at least secured the crown prince's promise that it wouldn't occur. I couldn't risk them taking action before it was officially finalized. I could only hope Connor's promise would be enough to keep them from making good on their threats.

Reaching under my pillow, I retrieved the knife Anna had given me after the attack—the one I'd had to use to ease Rosie's suffering. I slid the weapon into my pack, cinched it closed, and hauled it over my shoulder as I rushed for the door. The sun was barely beginning to rise, so I couldn't linger if I was going to make it out of the palace unseen. I stepped out into the empty hallway as quietly as possible. My heart raced at the sight of Connor's door. Part of me yearned to rush into his room and see him one last time before I left, but what more was there to say? Goodbye? I'd already hurt him enough.

It had taken so much strength to deny him twice already; I wasn't sure I could do it again.

Tiptoeing past his room, I held my breath until I reached the main stairs. As I'd hoped, the palace was still slumbering, so I slipped out the front entrance without issue, running across the courtyard to where Honey was stabled.

Pain pricked my chest as the familiar scents of hay and dirt and horses hit me, yanking my mind back to the last time I'd been in here.

With him.

Tears surfaced, and I swiped them away. I didn't have time to cry. I needed to find Anna and let her know it was done. Honey tossed me a seemingly sad glance as I saddled her and tied my pack into place.

"Don't look at me like that," I whispered. "It had to be done."

Someday he'll understand.

And if not, at least he'd be alive.

＊

Given the rebels' nomadic habits, they'd likely already moved on from their last camp, so I couldn't waste time heading there. Thankfully, I knew someone who could direct me straight to them. Pulling the hood of my cloak over my head, I rode into Engle shortly before suppertime. Although it would do little to hide my humanity from the fae locals, it at least brought me some sense of security.

Outside the tavern, the stable hand warily approached me to take Honey's reins, darting away as soon as I'd handed them over. Inside, the tavern was virtually empty, unlike the last time I'd been here. A lone individual sat at the far end of the bar, hunched over the tankard he cradled in his hands. I strode toward the bar, debating whether to call for Mr. Marstens or simply wait for him to appear. The door to the kitchen swung open as I settled onto a stool.

Mr. Marstens jerked to a stop as soon as he saw me, and for a split second I worried he might be working with Anna as more than her courier. Would he hurt me if commanded to? My mouth went dry as I pondered the question, but when a wide grin spread across his face, I relaxed.

"Didn't expect to see you here!" he exclaimed, pulling a tankard down from where it hung overhead. "Drink?"

I didn't really have time for one, but I had ridden nonstop from the palace, so I nodded. "Thanks."

After placing the ale in front of me, Mr. Marstens straightened and cocked a brow. "Now, what brings you here? I assume it's not just to gaze upon my handsome face."

I returned his smile. "That would be reason enough, of course, but no. I need directions."

"Ah," he said thoughtfully and roughed a hand over his mouth and chin before reaching into his pocket. "I was actually waiting for a courier to come fetch this to take to the palace."

My pulse quickened as I took the envelope from him. It was obviously from the rebels, but it could contain any number of messages. They weren't likely to send me notice they were about to follow through with their threat, but would they issue me another warning?

Before opening it, I caught Mr. Marstens's attention. "Do you know where I can find them?" I asked in a low voice.

His friendly expression turned remorseful, and he shook his head. "All I know is they moved on. Didn't tell me where this time, though to be honest, they don't always."

I huffed out a sharp sigh and glanced back down at the envelope—my last hope of finding them.

Mr. Marstens rapped a knuckle lightly on the bar in front of me. "I'll leave you to it. If you need anything, I'll be right over here."

Nodding, I slid my finger under the flap and broke the wax seal, pulling a single folded page out. I recognized Raven's handwriting immediately.

Lieke,

I don't know what to do. My parents have done something awful, and I don't know who to turn to. I can't stay with them, but I don't know where else to turn.

Please.

My mind rushed through the memories of my time with them. Had she truly not known her parents were part of the rebellion?

They had sent her out of the tent when they'd given me the knives. That didn't prove anything though.

At the bottom of the note, she'd scrawled a location: *The old farm outside of Engle.*

I knew this farm. We'd often used it as a marker on our runs. I'd be a fool not to suspect a trap, but if my friend truly was in trouble, I couldn't ignore this. Lifting my eyes to the bartender, I debated asking him to accompany me, but if he was also in the dark about their activities, I didn't want to be responsible for dragging him into it and potentially getting him hurt. Or worse.

My stomach roiled as I recalled the gruesome sight of the fae guards on the road, pierced with arrows, their blood soaking into the dirt. Connor's words sprang to mind: *Lieke, if they did this to you, their own kin, what could they do to someone else? To an enemy? To the fae?*

I knew what Anna and the rebels did to their enemies. I bore the scars from what they forced Raven to do to those she trained. If Raven had learned the truth and fled—if she had betrayed them—what might they do to her?

I needed to get Raven back to the palace where we could keep her safe.

CHAPTER SEVENTY-FIVE

Connor

A hot bath and some fresh clothes didn't completely cure my hangover woes, but they helped enough for me to make the trek to my father's office. As soon as I knocked, he called me in, and to my surprise, he set down the papers he'd been reviewing and waved me over to sit down.

"What is it, Connor?" The king had an odd look in his eye, as if he knew something I didn't, but I mentally waved it aside and straightened in my chair.

"I want to give up the throne."

He shifted forward slowly, eyeing me as if he hadn't heard me. "Why? How?"

"Give it to Brennan," I said. He actually choked, but I held up a hand before he could respond. "Let him marry Lieke. I'll take his place and marry Calla."

My father sat back in his chair, steepling his fingers in front of his mouth as he considered me. "The princess chose Brennan though. We don't know that she'd accept you as a suitable replacement. And even if that weren't the case, why? Why would you do this?"

"It's what Lieke wants," I said.

"Are you sure about that?" he asked.

"She loves him. She's always loved him. Nothing's changed."

He raised a brow. "Yes, it has. Everything's changed since you returned."

I shrugged. "It was a difficult trip."

His gaze softened. "I know she's your mate, Connor. I could hear it in your heartbeats. Perfectly in sync."

"It doesn't matter," I said, looking down at the floor.

"Have you lost your stars-damned mind?" He was leaning forward again, his eyes blazing with intensity. It seemed like he honestly thought I had gone mad. Maybe I had. "Of course it fucking matters!"

"Why? If she doesn't love me, why does it matter?" I challenged.

My father pressed his lips together and studied me for a long moment. I was about to press him for an answer to my proposal when he released a heavy sigh and settled back in his chair. "How have your dreams been lately?"

I stilled, confused. "What?"

"After you returned—after the kiss and the bond—was Lieke in your dreams?"

I shrugged slowly, trying to ignore how my face warmed at the memories. "Yes, but—"

"Can I assume by the shade you're turning that these weren't *bad* dreams?"

My stomach knotted. "So? They're just dreams."

"Mates *share* dreams, Connor. But only if they're both thinking of each other. Not fleeting thoughts either. If she was there, she was thinking of you as much as you were of her."

My heart sank into my stomach, and all my blood seemed to rush from my head. I was going to be sick.

The dreams had been real.

Every sensual, blissful moment. Every touch. Every kiss.

It had been real?

That didn't prove anything. We did all sorts of things in dreams that we didn't mean, acted on impulses we wouldn't otherwise, and even though I had meant every single word I'd uttered to her, that didn't mean she had meant hers.

"It doesn't matter," I repeated, shaking my head. "I spoke with her. She chose Brennan." My throat tightened around those last words, as if the reality of them might actually strangle me. I needed to trust her. She'd told me what she wanted. Shared dreams or not, bond or not, I would honor her wishes, no matter the cost.

"Does she know?" my father asked slowly, deliberately.

My heart pitched itself into my throat, cutting off my voice so I could only mouth the word "*No.*" I lifted my eyes to the ceiling and tried to blink back the threatening tears.

"She deserves—"

"Why?" I asked sharply, flashing my attention back to him. "So I can trick her—guilt her—into being with me instead? I want her to choose me because she loves me, not because of some stars-damned bond. And yes, I know, she could decide to deny the bond, but it's better this way."

"Better for whom, Connor?" he asked, but I had no answer to offer. He sighed deeply and continued. "Look, I know the pain of losing a mate, of having the other half of your heart stolen, of drowning in unbearable loneliness. But it was worth it for the joy I shared with your mother—a joy you could have with Lieke, if you give her the chance."

A chance.

She'd already rejected me once, and though I'd survived battle after battle and attack after attack, facing that pain again…

I sucked in a deep breath and forced myself to remember how Lieke had stood in that training ring, staring at me as I asked her about Brennan. I recalled the emotions that had swarmed me in that moment as if they were my own: love, guilt, regret, fear…hope.

I lifted my eyes to my father's once more. "So your answer is no then?"

He frowned, genuine sadness written across his face. "I will allow Brennan to back out of the engagement if he wants to, but *only* if Lieke agrees to this after you've told her the truth. She deserves to know."

***

I couldn't talk to Lieke yet, not without ensuring Brennan was going to step up and be there for her. As soon as I knocked on his door, my stomach sank at the realization she could very well be here with him.

The door opened, and Brennan—standing alone—looked me up and down. "Hello, brother. What happened to you?" I waved away his question and stepped past him into his room. "Come on in," he said, already closing the door behind me.

"We need to talk, Brennan." I pivoted on my heel in the middle of his living room and shoved my hands in my pockets.

"Oh no," he said, his mouth pulling down into an exaggerated frown. "Don't say it. You're breaking up with me. It's you, not me. Is that it?"

In silence I stared at him until he finally shrugged. I pushed the words out before I could change my mind. "I'm letting you off the hook. You don't have to marry Calla."

Brennan lowered his brows and regarded me skeptically for a moment, then scratched casually at his chin. "Is that so? And what about the alliance?"

"We'll secure it another way," I said, trying to get my pounding heartbeat under control before he could comment on it.

"And how's that? Are *you* going to marry the princess?" He smirked, but it soon melted away into a solemn expression when I didn't answer. "You can't be serious, Connor. What about Lieke?"

Hearing her name on his lips grated on my nerves, but somehow I managed to utter, "She's all yours."

Stars, it hurt to say. Like piercing my throat with a hot iron. My breath shuddered, and I tried to cover it up with a feigned cough. Brennan studied me carefully. I wanted to shake him, tell him to just accept this and be good to her.

"What makes you think she wants me?" he asked finally, crossing his arms and tilting his chin up.

"She's always wanted you, Brennan. Still does. I spoke with her yesterday, and she chose you." Each word sliced at my heart, like I was physically cutting away pieces of it and dropping them at my ungrateful brother's feet.

"And you're okay with this?"

"Of course I am," I lied. "It was my idea. Why wouldn't I be?" I shrugged, but the gesture was stiff, forced.

"Oh, I don't know, brother. Maybe because she's your mate." His eyes widened in challenge, and I stepped back as if he'd shoved me.

It was one thing to have our father recognize the bond, but Brennan?

"Come on," he said. "I knew as soon as you both came home. She smells just like you—definitely one of the weirder signs of the bond, I swear. Honestly, it was getting harder and harder to sit so close to her."

"It doesn't matter. She loves you, not me."

Brennan scoffed loudly. "You think she still loves me?" I nodded, cringing at having to admit it. "Do you remember when we were younger, and Mother would go on and on about how she hoped we'd find our mates, just as she and father had found each other? Remember what she said about it?"

I tried to recall, but my mind was a chaotic mess.

Brennan continued. "After the bond, any feelings you hold for someone else are overshadowed. Lieke might still care for me, but she doesn't love me anymore. Not like she used to. She's not *all mine*. She's yours, and you are hers, so stop being a fucking martyr, and let yourself have this!"

My chin dropped to my chest, and I stared at my feet as I bit the inside of my lip. Lifting my hand to my neck, I tried to rub away the tension. Could I really do this?

I didn't look up as I asked the one question that wouldn't stop haunting me.

"What if she doesn't want this?"

Brennan slapped a hand on my shoulder. "And what if she does?"

"I hate forcing this on her," I confessed, suddenly feeling like the younger brother here.

"You aren't, Connor. It's not your fault. If anything, you can blame the stars. Now, get your ass out of my room and go find her."

CHAPTER SEVENTY-SIX

Lieke

As Honey and I turned onto the road that led to the old farm, I slowed her to a walk. At the edge of the trees, I stopped, keeping us in the shadows. The barn and the house, surrounded by grass that hadn't been cut in ages, appeared just as empty as they always had been, but then, Raven would know better than to leave any sign she was here.

This could be a trap, I repeated to myself for the thousandth time. Trap or not, I wasn't going to leave my friend to whatever fate she faced here.

Slowly, I dismounted. Retrieving my knife from my belt, I patted Honey's neck and whispered, "Stay here, girl, but be ready to leave in a hurry if needed." She gave her head a gentle shake, as if to say she understood, which was preposterous.

On nearly silent feet, I stalked my way through the waist-high grass, taking cover behind an old plow and then a rotten bale of hay. I decided to start my search with the barn, as it was closest to me. Peeking around the hay bale, I watched the building for a moment but couldn't see anyone. I cursed myself for not waiting until at least dusk, when the shadows would be long and provide more cover. Midday was the worst time to be sneaking about—or attempting to.

Crouching low, I tried to plan my route while keeping an eye on the barn for any sign of movement or activity. I was just about to sit down and resign myself to waiting for dark when a female voice whispered loudly, "Lieke?"

I couldn't see anyone though.

She said my name again, a little louder this time. "In the barn! Come around back."

I sneaked a glance at the barn one more time and couldn't help but smile in relief. Raven was peering out of the window. She lifted her fingers over the sill to wave me over. Immediately, I shifted forward, but then I stopped, hesitating as the hairs on my neck prickled in warning. My gut tightened.

What if it's a trap? What if Raven is—

No, I wouldn't consider that possibility. Not Raven.

You're a fool not to.

Uneasily, I contemplated what to do, until Raven hissed at me, "Get in here, Lieke!"

Taking a final look around me, I inhaled sharply, held my breath, and ran for the back of the barn.

I'd barely rounded the corner when arms encircled me, holding me tight.

"I missed you, Lieke," Raven whispered tearfully. "But what are you doing here?"

Gently I pushed her back and eyed her intently. "You sent for me," I said. "The note?"

Confusion spread through her dark brown eyes, but it was quickly replaced by worry. "I didn't send any note."

With shaky hands, I dug the note out of my pocket and shoved it at her. My pulse raced, beating so loudly in my ears that it nearly drowned out my own voice. "It's your handwriting."

Raven shook her head as she read the note, whispering, "I mean, it looks like my writing, but I swear I didn't write this."

"What happened?" I asked, gripping her arm as I started to panic. "Why are you here?"

"Our camp was compromised. We got warning just in time to pack up and disperse before the royal guard arrived. My mother instructed me to come here and wait for further instructions. You're the last person I expected to show up, but—"

"I shouldn't have," I muttered, warily searching our surroundings. Running wasn't an option, at least not until dark, and we were too exposed standing out here. We needed to get inside the barn. I nudged her backwards and guided her inside.

Pacing the dirt floor, I tried to gather my thoughts.

For all the rebels knew, I hadn't stopped the alliance, and now they needed to kill one of the princes.

Dread pooled in my gut.

I wasn't the target.

I was the bait.

What would they do when no fae prince showed up to save me?

CHAPTER
SEVENTY-SEVEN

Connor

Stars, I hoped Lieke was in her room.

My boots skidded on the stone floor as I rounded the corner into our hallway, and when her door opened, my heart jolted.

But it wasn't Lieke stepping out. It was Mrs. Bishop.

The cook immediately caught sight of me, her eyes wide and full of worry. On quick feet we rushed toward each other, and she grabbed both of my arms, gripping me tightly.

"Did you tell her?" Mrs. Bishop asked, and I didn't bother to ask for clarification. It seemed everyone but Lieke knew of our bond.

"I was on my way to just now. Is she in?" My eyes darted over her shoulder, but the door was closed. The old fae shook her head, her lips quivering, and my gut twisted. "Where did she go?"

I didn't care how frantic I sounded. I only cared about finding my mate.

"I—I don't know," Mrs. Bishop stammered. "Marin came and fetched me early this morning when she found her room empty. I thought she was overreacting, but some of Lieke's clothes are gone, and her pack's missing."

Yanking my arms from her grasp, I started toward Lieke's room, asking over my shoulder, "Where's Gretchen? Did she see anything?"

Mrs. Bishop caught up to me and pulled me around to face her.

"No, Gretchen fell ill last night. That's why Marin was there instead. But I have a bad feeling about this. It doesn't make any sense for her to just leave. Did something happen between you two?"

Guilt flooded my chest, and I dropped my chin to hide my shame. "We fought," I said.

"About?"

I shrugged like a child being cornered into confessing some misdeed.

"Brennan?" Mrs. Bishop asked, and I reluctantly peered up at her. "Yes, I know she loved your brother. We all knew. It's partly why I sent her away like I—"

The fae stopped mid-sentence, and her eyes glazed over as if focusing on something hovering in the air.

"What is it?" I demanded.

She blinked several times. "Her family. It's the only other place she'd go."

"Where are they?"

"They move. Always moving. Never staying in the same place twice."

Slamming my teeth together, I growled. "How would she find them?"

"A demi-fae in Engle, Mr. Marstens. He was friends with Lieke's parents. No doubt that's who she'd see."

I was already running past her before she finished speaking.

✳

There was only one official way off the royal property, and it led in the completely wrong direction from Engle. Thankfully, my uncle had thought to construct three other gates. They were known only to a select few outside of the royal family. The gate I needed was set in the northwest wall.

As soon as I entered the trees, I shifted into my wolfhound form, running as fast as I could. I marveled at how the shift no longer irritated me as it used to.

It didn't take me long to reach the wall, and I slowed down to hunt for my exit. This gate was nothing more than a narrow fissure in the thick stone, hidden beneath heavy curtains of ivy and moss, making it extremely difficult to find. As I paced along the wall, I tested several spots, sticking my snout behind the ivy here and there.

Shit, I should have marked the damn gate, but it had been years—decades, even—since I'd bothered to use any of the secret entrances. I muttered another curse, which came out as a canine whimper.

Someone laughed behind me, and I spun around, snarling.

Matthias's eyes lit up with humor. "Anyone ever tell you you're cute when you're mad?" he asked, leaning over and patting his knee, calling me over like any ordinary hound.

Shifting back into my fae form, I crossed my arms and glared at him. "I don't come when called."

I realized too late my unfortunate choice of words, and Matthias was instantly smirking. "I honestly don't want to know what gets you to come."

"Why are you here?" I asked impatiently.

"Ouch." He flinched in mock offense but recovered quickly. "Saw you head into the trees and shift like it was no big deal. Never seen you do that without a lot of fretting first, so I figured there must be a good reason and maybe you needed help."

Pushing out a sigh, I pivoted back to the wall behind me. "Well, since you're here, you might as well be useful."

He marched past me, slapping me on the shoulder as he did. He walked along the wall, but his eyes watched the ground. "Why are you looking for the gate anyway? Decided to run away from Lieke rather than just hide from her?"

He must have found something among the grass and leaves and

roots, because he abruptly turned and pulled back the ivy to reveal the opening I'd been hunting for.

"Running after her actually," I said, joining him. I moved to step through the gate, but he grabbed my arm, pulling me back.

"Wait, did she actually refuse the bond?" he asked, all humor now gone.

"No, she's gone."

"Gone? Why? Where?"

"I don't know, maybe to see her family. I just—I need to find her," I said, gritting my teeth anxiously. "You coming?"

Matthias's brow twisted. "Of course. Though it's really too bad you don't shift into something more useful, like a horse."

"Like I'd let you ride me if I did."

He pushed me through the gate, laughing. "If only you could be so lucky, you mean."

CHAPTER
SEVENTY-EIGHT

Lieke

I adjusted my grip on my knife as the barn door opened and daylight washed over us. Anna stepped inside, followed closely by Owen. Clicking her tongue to the beat of her steps, the woman stopped a little more than an arm's length away from me and never once even glanced at her daughter, who stood beside me.

"Of all the things that could have derailed this mission, I never thought it would be this," she said.

I lifted my chin. "An abandoned farm? Why would you?"

Anna's expression hardened, and her hand struck fast, slapping me on my cheek and sending my head reeling to the side. Raven shouted something at her mother as I reached a hand up to my face. I clamped my eyes shut but said nothing, straightening to face Anna again.

Sneering, the older woman scrutinized me, and her lips curled into an unnerving smile. "I see you've brought my knife back to me. Hand it over." She offered me her open palm, but I didn't bother to acknowledge it.

I leaned forward slightly. "When I return it, it'll be in your neck."

I braced myself for her to strike me again, but she simply stood there.

Raven gripped my elbow, pulling me around to face her. "What are you doing, Lieke?"

Instead of responding, I twisted my head around to face Anna. "Why don't you tell your daughter what you did to all those fae on the road? How you butchered them for no reason."

Raven slowly released me and turned her attention to her parents. "What is she talking about?"

Anna looked at Raven plainly. "We've killed many fae, some more brutally than others. But it's only fair, given how many of our kind they slaughtered as they drove us from our homes after the war."

"I thought…" Raven started, shaking her head. "All the training—all the pain I had to inflict on Lieke and the others—it wasn't merely for defense."

Anna shared a bored look with her husband. "Maybe she's not as dumb as we thought."

Raven didn't seem at all bothered by the insult, but my blood heated at Anna's callousness. "That's your daughter!"

"Unfortunately, yes, she is," Owen said wearily.

"Still, she's proven useful enough, has she not?" Anna said, angling her head to study my friend.

Lunging, I swung the knife toward Anna's side, hoping to lodge it below her ribs, but the older woman had faster reflexes than I'd anticipated. She caught my wrist and squeezed hard as she pulled it up and back in an awkward angle that dragged a groan of pain from my lungs. I dropped the knife into her free hand.

Raven screamed in protest as her mother buried the blade in my belly. I released a ragged gasp. My friend's horror-filled eyes were the last things I saw before everything went black.

CHAPTER
SEVENTY-NINE

Connor

Even without horses, Matthias and I reached the outskirts of Engle sooner than we would have if we'd ridden out of the main gate. As we approached town, a familiar scent pulled my attention down an old road that was overgrown with weeds, and I stopped mid-stride.

"What is it?" Matthias asked, nearly running into me.

"Lieke," I muttered, and without a second thought, I veered off the main road.

"So she went"—he paused, scanning our surroundings—"to an abandoned farm? Not the tavern like Mrs. B thought?" Matthias dutifully followed after me. "Why—"

"She's been here." My voice was strained under a growing sense of foreboding. "She wouldn't have come here first, not if she was seeking directions in town."

"Fair," Matthias mumbled, dropping his hand to the hilt of his sword. "So do you have a plan at least? Or are we winging this mission?"

"Claws out? Teeth ready?"

"That will surely win her over if she's just sitting down to tea with her cousin," Matthias said, smirking.

"Let's hope that's what she's doing."

＊

Tall cedar trees lined the driveway all the way from the main road to the farm, where they circled the property. An old house stood to our left in a field of tall grass, while a dilapidated barn sat in the center. Matthias and I stopped at the edge of the property, remaining in the protective shade of the trees as we observed the clearing.

"I don't hear anything, do you?" Matthias asked quietly.

I shook my head. Lieke's scent lingered, but knowing she was meeting her family twisted my gut. These were the same people who had repeatedly stabbed her in the name of *training*, and I couldn't determine whether I was more concerned for her safety or worried that she'd come here to betray me.

"You go get a look around," Matthias suggested. "It will be quicker with your super hound senses than having both of us tromping around in our boots."

Seeing no issue with his reasoning, I backed up a few paces and shifted forms before bounding off along the tree line. On my padded paws, I crept my way around the property, searching for any sign of who was here. I'd nearly made it to the other side, where the barn lay closer to the trees, when I heard them.

Voices.

I couldn't discern the words, but I clearly heard at least three individuals: two female, one male. And none of them sounded like Lieke.

My heart pounded against my sternum as panic threatened to take root.

She was here. I knew she was.

I raced back to Matthias, shifting before I reached him.

"Three in the barn."

"Human?" he asked, and I paused, my mind turning over what I'd observed.

There had been no scent other than Lieke's. Not fae. Not human. I should have sensed them. Why hadn't I?

"Should we go around the front? If we come around that way, we should be concealed from the windows," Matthias said.

"Unless they have other rebels lying in wait somewhere," I noted.

"Well, let's hope that's not the case then," he said, stretching his neck in circles like he did before battles and sparring matches. "Claws out?"

I rolled my eyes at him before shifting again, and we stepped out of the trees together.

CHAPTER EIGHTY

Lieke

I opened my eyes to find Anna gripping my shoulder hard, preventing me from backing away from her and the blade she still held lodged in my gut. My eyelids fluttered, but I fought to keep them open despite my blurred vision.

"What are you doing, Mother?" Raven demanded again, but Anna's gaze was locked firmly on me.

"You'll see soon enough," the woman said in an almost cheery tone. She lifted a hand to cup my cheek. I tried to retreat from her touch, but my muscles refused to obey. The edges of my world were quickly darkening. She patted my face gently and crooned, "It was almost too easy, Lieke."

"What is she talking about?" This time Raven seemed to be addressing me, though I couldn't be completely sure.

"He's not coming. You're wasting your time," I said. Something warm and sticky pooled in my mouth, and I spit it out into the dirt just as Anna let out a patronizing sound of regret.

"Don't be so pessimistic," she said sweetly, but then her fingers tightened in my hair. She yanked my face close to hers. "A fae can't deny the stars. He will be here."

She was talking nonsense now, or perhaps the blood loss was affecting my senses.

"It doesn't matter anyway. I ended it."

"You did what now?" Anna asked, genuine confusion in her tone.

I spat more blood onto the ground. "The alliance. It's ended. Just like you demanded."

Snarling, she jammed the knife deeper into my stomach, pulling another pained groan from me. "You stupid girl," she said. "The alliance doesn't matter now. Not after—"

"What?" I rasped out, opening my eyes wide as I tried to focus on the woman and what she was saying. "But you said—"

"That was before you let him kiss you," Anna said in disgust.

How did she know about the kiss? Had a spy of hers seen us in the stables? And why did a single kiss matter to her?

"I don't understand," I muttered, wincing and hissing with pain as Anna slowly pulled the knife free. Raven rushed toward me with her hands outstretched, but Anna whirled on her daughter.

"Tend to her and the next thing this blade cuts is your hand."

Shakily, my fingers found their way to the gash, slipping in the blood that was pouring from it. I staggered back a step, and Anna followed. When I doubled over, she slid the tip of the blade under my chin and forced me to lift my face to look at her.

Her dark eyes blazed with hatred and a hint of confusion. "Why do you think he won't come?"

I closed my eyes—from both the pain of my injury and the agony of remembering the look on Connor's face when I'd chosen Brennan.

"Because," I said, "he told me. He's done saving me. It's over."

The words pierced my heart. I blinked, trying to maintain my balance, to stay awake. But sleep sounded rather nice right now.

My head spun. The barn began to sway. Anna cackled as I fell to the ground, and my world went black.

CHAPTER EIGHTY-ONE

Connor

atthias and I rushed through the tall grass, pausing behind a large hay bale. My blood chilled in my veins as a sinister laugh rent the air. Matthias glanced back at me and nodded toward the barn.

He had only taken one step forward when the quiet groan of a bow being drawn reached my ears. An arrow slammed into Matthias's shoulder, throwing him backwards with such force, the archer had to be close. A terrified whine escaped me as my friend doubled over. Falling to his knees, he met my gaze.

"Go!" he said, and I didn't wait for him to collapse before I was darting forward.

I skidded around the corner of the barn and didn't slow even when I saw a woman standing there casually, holding a bow down at her side, as if inviting me to take my revenge. Growling, I sprang off my hind legs and sank my teeth into her neck. She fell to the ground under me, and I tore her apart, ripping away hunks of flesh with my teeth and shredding her body with my claws. I didn't stop until long after she'd gone still.

A pained groan came from the barn, and I snapped my head up. *Lieke.*

Leaping off my kill, I bounded for the door, but a man's voice stopped me mid-step.

"Tie her up over there, Raven."

"No," a woman protested meekly. I caught the unmistakable sound of a hand striking a face. Soft sobbing and labored breathing filled the barn as something—or someone—was dragged across the dirt floor.

Rage burned hot in my chest, rumbling low and menacing in the back of my throat.

"Let our guest in," an older woman commanded.

The door creaked open, and a young woman with black hair and tear-streaked cheeks appeared.

"I said let him in, Raven," the other woman barked, and the black-haired woman stepped back to allow me to enter.

My eyes adjusted quickly to the dim light inside, and my lips curled back over my teeth when I spotted Lieke sitting in the dirt, tied to a support beam. Her head lolled to one side, and her complexion was quickly losing color. Blood soaked through her shirt, but her heartbeat, though weakening, reached my ears, confirming she was still alive. I stalked toward my injured mate, letting my hunger for vengeance surge with each step.

A throat cleared nearby, giving me pause, and I slowly turned. The older woman and man stared at me, seeming almost impressed.

The woman raised a brow and said, "I can assume—by the fresh blood on your muzzle—that you've killed Caroline, my archer. We hedged bets, you know, about whether you'd take the bait. Unfortunately for me, I won't be able to collect my winnings, but I knew it was a risky wager."

Snarling, I prepared to lunge at the woman, but when I pushed off my back legs, I faltered, stumbling rather than jumping. I barely kept from falling onto the dirt. A sinister laugh pulled my attention back to the couple watching me.

"Works quickly, doesn't it?" the woman asked, and my heart jolted.

Had she poisoned me? I mentally assessed my body, checking for any sign that I'd been struck by a dart or needle or something. Aside from my shaky, weakening legs, I couldn't sense anything.

As if she could read my thoughts, the woman explained, "This method of delivery doesn't act quite as efficiently as our barbs and knives, but you have to admit, it's rather ingenious. Caroline spent the past two years drinking the solution daily. Of course, she started the practice with the sole purpose of healing her injuries faster. Was simply by chance we discovered that doing so infected her blood, making it toxic to the fae."

The archer had poisoned me by…poisoning herself?

The woman continued. "As adorable as you are in this form, Your Highness, you might want to shift back. I'd hate for you to die as a hound, unable to say any last words to her."

The edges of my vision were already dimming, and I slowly turned to Lieke. I hated doing anything this woman said, but she was right. I had to shift. I couldn't stay like this, couldn't die like this.

The thread of my magic had thinned, though, becoming barely more than a wisp of power. I reached for it with my mind and tugged, but it slipped out of my grasp. A whine filled my chest, and I had to fight to ignore their chuckling.

Squeezing my jaw tight, I concentrated harder. Lieke's voice filled my head, pushing me to not give up. *Until the stars fall, keep going.*

There. I snagged it again and pulled as hard as I could, begging my magic to do my bidding.

Blinding pain shot through me as the shift brought me back to my fae form. A deep, guttural groan escaped me as I forced myself to push past the aching fatigue and the throbbing fire coursing through my veins. Somehow I remained standing.

It must have surprised the humans too, because their eyes widened slightly.

"Interesting," the woman mused. "I wonder…"

The man beside her leaned close to her ear. "Do you think it's the delivery? Or the bond?"

As if in response, Lieke let out a soft, pained whimper. My heart leaped into my throat as her eyelids fluttered and opened slightly. Tripping and stumbling on legs that failed to bear my weight, I rushed over and dropped to my knees beside her, but I kept my hands back, lest I cause her any more pain by jostling her.

"Sapphire, I'm here," I whispered. "You're going to be okay." But even as I said this, my eyes drifted to her blood-drenched shirt. I needed to fix this, needed to save her, but how? As gently as I could, I pulled her shirt up to get a glimpse of the wound. When she whimpered, I tried to soothe her. "I know it hurts. I just need to—"

The gash in her side was worse than I'd expected. Blood continued to pour out of her with each slow beat of her heart. Awkwardly, I pulled my shirt off in one painful, jerky motion and pressed it tightly against her wound. Stroking the side of her face, I brushed her hair off her cheek.

"I'll fix this."

CHAPTER EIGHTY-TWO

Lieke

arkness enveloped me—not the warm, comforting darkness of a pleasant sleep, but a cold, terrifying loneliness that gripped my weakening heart in a vise. Every shallow breath brought a fresh stab of pain, and all I could focus on was the agony in my side. Voices danced along the edges of my consciousness, and I tried to pry open my eyes to see who was speaking. I attempted to call out, hoping someone would help ease the torment.

The only response I got, though, was a new searing pain. It tore through me relentlessly. Someone must have been attempting to staunch the blood flow. How many times had I done the same to a wound I'd sustained during training? But it had never been like this. Never this deep. Never this painful.

"I'll fix this." A whispered voice lured me away from the pain.

I knew that voice.

I loved that voice.

Connor.

Was he truly here, or was my weakened mind grasping for some bit of happiness before the end?

I tried to open my eyes wider, but my body refused to cooperate.

Fear tangled itself around my heart, threatening to strangle any bit of hope I had. I was going to die here, and he wasn't going to save me.

As if in answer, though, two words floated to me.

"I'm here."

I wanted to believe the voice, wanted to trust it, but fear tightened its black coils around me. Then something shifted beside me, and the voice shouted again, sharper now, angrier. "You said the solution heals?"

It took me a moment to realize he wasn't talking to me. Then someone else spoke. The voice was muddled and indiscernible but notably real, and I let myself hope.

Connor had come for me after all, despite all I'd said to him, despite all the pain I'd caused him.

He barked out a command, harsh and desperate. "Then heal her! Now!"

A different voice—feminine and familiar—repeated his plea.

Raven? Raven was fighting for me.

"Why can't we heal her?"

Two soft thuds were the only response, and I didn't have the strength to deduce what had happened.

My world started to slip away, and the darkness turned bright around me. The pressure at my side lessened, replaced by a soothing coolness that reminded me of the balm my mother had often used when I'd spent too much time in the sun. The pain eased as another beloved voice called to me—my mother.

"Smile, sweet girl. It will all be over soon."

Those should have been happy words, but instead they pricked my heart with sudden panic. Connor's brown and gold eyes flashed in my mind briefly before disappearing. I cried out, pleading and begging.

"I don't want it to be over! I want to stay. I need to stay. With him."

I repeated the words, screaming them into the nothingness that surrounded me, until the darkness flooded in once again. My pain returned, though now it was more of an ache, lingering like an annoying, tenacious gnat.

"Sapphire, can you hear me?" Connor's voice, soft and stilted, guided me through the darkness until I opened my eyes to find him staring at me.

"You," I whispered, lifting my lips into a half-smile.

"Me," he said, and although relief shone in his eyes, a wince contorted his features.

"What's wrong?" I tried to reach for him, but my wrists were bound behind the wooden post I was seated against. I struggled against the bindings. The coarse rope cut into my skin but didn't loosen at all.

Connor ignored my question, straining to ask his own. "Are you okay? Are you in pain?"

"It still hurts, but it's better," I said. I shifted to examine my wound but stopped when I realized he was shirtless. "What happened to your shirt?"

"You needed it more than I did," he said. A weak laugh tumbled from his lips. He pulled the fabric away from my midsection, and his expression darkened. Tension pulsed in his jaw as his eyes squeezed shut and a growl rumbled in his chest. "You said it would heal her!"

Anna hummed quietly from where she stood a short distance away. "I wondered if this might be the case," she said flatly.

"What is she talking about?" I asked Connor, but his arms suddenly went slack, and his body heaved as he struggled to breathe. He hung his head, resting it lightly against my shoulder. I glared at Anna and Owen. "What is wrong with him?"

"It's the poison," Owen offered casually, as if that should have been obvious.

Anna sighed and added, "But we didn't poison him. He did that to himself when he attacked Caroline."

"Who the fuck is Caroline?" I asked through gritted teeth.

"Our archer?" Anna clarified. "You met her several times, I believe." I vaguely recalled the few encounters I'd had with her.

Before I could ask them anything further, Connor lifted his head off my shoulder enough to turn slightly toward the humans. "Why isn't it healing her?"

His voice held only a fraction of its normal strength.

"The bond," Anna said. "That's my best guess anyway. When applied directly to the wound, the tonic heals surprisingly quickly…normally. But it seems like now that your mating bond has been established, she's no longer a mere human. Her body no longer reacts to the solution as a human's would. That's likely why—"

"We're mates?" I didn't realize I'd said it aloud until Connor turned to me, his tired eyes pleading with me, as if he was worried I would be angry.

Anna laughed lightly. "Oh dear. Has he not told you?"

"I'm your…mate?" I asked shakily, my heart bursting with a terrifying joy. I yearned to hold him, to take his face in my hands and tell him how elated this made me. Resting my forehead against his, I sighed as I hunted for the right words.

"I didn't know how to tell you," Connor said, his words barely loud enough for me to hear. A tear escaped and slid down my cheek, settling at the corner of my smile. He pulled back slightly, and his soul connected with mine as our eyes met. "And now it's too late."

Connor sucked in one final, shallow breath and collapsed on my lap.

CHAPTER EIGHTY-THREE

Lieke

Mates.

We were mates.

Bound and fated and destined for…not this.

It wasn't supposed to end like this.

How could it be over before it had even begun?

I wouldn't accept it. I couldn't.

We were meant to be together.

He couldn't be gone.

Lifting my tear-soaked face to Anna, I shook my head as I screamed my pleas. "Heal him! Save him! Please!"

Anna shrugged. "Even if I could, why would I? I told you this would happen!"

My eyes darted back and forth over the dirt floor in front of me. She'd already known I was his mate, even before Connor had arrived. She'd mentioned our kiss. But how? How had she known?

The spy.

But who? Who was working for them?

I stared down at Connor—my fiancé, my mate—who was quiet, unmoving. He was still breathing, but too slowly.

It didn't matter who the spy was.

It didn't matter how Anna had known.

There was no fixing what had already been done.

"What now?" I asked pathetically.

Anna stepped toward me, and my entire body tightened when she nudged Connor's foot with her own. "Nothing good, I'm afraid. We can't exactly allow you to return to the palace and inform anyone about what happened here."

"You can't be serious, Mother!" Raven's voice pierced the air from somewhere behind me. I twisted my neck but only caught a glimpse of her in my periphery as she walked slowly forward. She glanced in my direction but didn't look at me. She was focused on something over my head, beyond me. Tossing her head toward me, she turned back to her parents. "She's family. Are you really considering killing her?"

"Sometimes we must sacrifice for the better of everyone," Anna said. My stomach turned to stone.

"Do you mean I wasted three years training her—putting up with her blathering and her whining and her incessant pining for a filthy fae— all so you could just kill her? How does that serve the greater good?" The vitriol in Raven's voice was like acid in my veins, peeling open every old wound I'd suffered at her hand. Through gritted teeth, I growled quietly, mentally forming insults of my own to throw at my supposed *friend*, but from behind me came a hushed warning to remain quiet.

"Don't move, my lady."

Matthias.

Of course he'd come with Connor.

Relief shot through me, but I did as he commanded and remained still. Keeping my eyes forward and my lips pressed into a stern line, I worked to hide my wince as he began cutting the ropes digging into my wrists. When they fell away, I forced myself to ignore the desperate call of my muscles to be shaken out and stretched. Matthias pressed the etched wooden handle of a knife into my palm, and I wrapped my aching fingers around it.

"Wait," he whispered, and I signaled my understanding with my other hand.

"Life is a gamble," Anna said musingly to her daughter, her annoyance seeping into each syllable. "We had no way of knowing Lieke would prove so worthless."

Owen cleared his throat with what sounded like an oddly placed chuckle. "Not completely worthless. She brought us the crown prince, after all."

"True," Anna said, and a tense silence pulled the air taut around us. Raven shifted her weight. To anyone else, the movement would appear casual, but after three years of constant training, I knew her tells. She was anticipating an attack. And she was nervous about it. Understandably so. She had no weapon in hand, and I could see none at her back or thigh or ankle. She was unarmed, facing two ruthless humans who had slaughtered countless fae.

"Why did you try to stop us earlier, Raven?" Anna asked. "If you hate the woman so much, why defend her?"

Raven tensed, and though I couldn't see her face, I could easily picture the disdainful smirk she likely flashed her mother, as if to mock her for not realizing the obvious. "Simply protecting an asset. I didn't want all the stars-damned work I did to be tossed aside. She could still be of use to us. Alive."

Anna was quiet for a few moments before she hummed briefly and said, "I disagree. She's been compromised by her bond to the fae. Just like my sister was when their king stole her from us."

"What are you talking about?" Raven asked at the same time that Matthias's whispered curse hit my ear.

Confusion swept over me. The queen hadn't been a human. Who was Anna referring to? Who was her sister?

Anna answered her bitterly. "Ellae abandoned us to be with her mate, and it started a damned war. She never even would have met him had she not been here visiting our cousin, Alora."

"That doesn't explain why Lieke needs to die!" Raven said, lifting her hands to her sides.

Anna shouted loudly, "Because it's what she deserves! Just like all the fae!" I flinched, and Raven stepped back half a pace as if her mother had struck her. Anna's slow inhale pierced the air before she said again in a steady but firm tone, "You are either with us, Raven, or you're not."

"And if I'm not?" Raven asked, straightening so she stood a bit taller.

Anna sighed loudly. "Don't be stupid. The fae reign is coming to an end. You don't want to be on the wrong side when it does."

Raven's shoulders lifted with a long, slow breath, and then her head lowered as she whispered, "What do you need me to do?"

"You know what to do," Anna said, pulling her knife from its leather sheath. Raven lifted a hand to accept the weapon.

"I do," Raven said. Glancing over her shoulder, she shot me an apologetic look like the many she'd offered me before our training sessions. "This is going to hurt both of us."

My breath caught as I waited for her to come at me. My arms—having been stuck in this position for over an hour—would be sluggish, but I had to at least try to block her.

When Raven moved, though, she didn't attack me. Thrusting the blade in front of her, she aimed for her mother. Anna easily blocked the strike, forcing the blade into the dirt at their feet. Then, hooking her leg behind Raven's ankle, Anna knocked her daughter onto her back, crouched beside her, and grabbed her throat.

"You know what I despise more than fae?" Anna hissed. "Liars."

Raven's feet scrambled against the dirt as she fought with both hands to loosen Anna's grip, but it only seemed to make Anna squeeze tighter. When Owen knelt to pick up the knife, Matthias rushed out from behind me. Crouching low, Matthias sent his own blade flying at the man, and it struck home, burying itself to the hilt in Owen's eye.

Anna roared in vicious agony as her husband's body slumped to the ground. She glowered at the fae commander, who was now standing tall and stalking toward her. Releasing her daughter, she grabbed her knife from the ground and rose.

Raven gasped for air and rolled toward me.

"Are you okay?" she asked in a hoarse whisper. I nodded, despite the lingering pain in my side, and brought my aching arms around in front of me.

Slowly, I shifted Connor's head off my lap and brushed my fingers over his weak pulse before I laid him gently onto the floor. My muscles protested when I forced them to move, but it was the sharp sting in my wound that made me draw a hissed inhale through my teeth. Somehow I managed to get onto my hands and knees. I settled back into a crouch beside my friend to watch and wait for an opportunity to help.

Anna lunged for the fae with her knife, but Matthias leaped out of the way just in time. She sneered. "I told Caroline we should have poisoned the arrows too, but she didn't want to waste what little we had left."

"If it makes you feel better, it still hurt when she shot me," Matthias said as he knelt quickly to retrieve the knife from Owen's face, never taking his attention from his opponent.

Anna shrugged, circling the fae, and nodded toward the knife in her hand. "Enough to treat my own blades at least."

My heart plummeted.

Matthias's eyes widened briefly, but that was the only indication that he understood the gravity of the situation. He kept his distance from Anna, assessing how she moved. They circled each other until Anna's back was to me. Over her shoulder I caught Matthias's eye, and he tipped his chin up slightly.

Pushing to my feet, I slipped past Raven. She grabbed for me, whispering a warning to stop. My legs burned, my shoulders ached, and my side screamed, but I ignored it all as I forced myself forward on quiet feet. Aiming for Anna's lower back, for the painful spot that would drop her quickly, I struck.

Anna shifted at the last moment, and my blade merely grazed her side. She reached her free hand across to her injury and twisted around to face me. Growling, she plunged her knife into the existing gash in my torso.

Fire tore through me, and I screamed out in pain.

Through blurred vision I watched Matthias rush forward. He spun Anna around to face him. I didn't see what happened next, because I slammed my eyes shut. Stumbling backwards, I fell hard onto the packed dirt floor. The sickening sound of metal slicing into flesh echoed in my ears.

CHAPTER EIGHTY-FOUR

Lieke

A hand shook my shoulder. A voice called my name urgently. I opened my eyes, and slowly the old wooden beams overhead came into focus.

"Lieke, we need to go." Matthias leaned over me, worry and fear twisting his brow as he studied me. "Can you sit up?"

Instinctively, I shook my head, though I hadn't even tested my muscles at all.

"Check her wound," Raven said from somewhere nearby.

"Connor," I whispered hoarsely, craning my neck and turning toward where he lay on the ground behind me. "Is he—"

"He's alive. For now." Matthias said, reaching for my wound and carefully ripping my shirt away from the knife still lodged in my side. When he gasped sharply, I whirled my head back around to face him.

"Is it that bad?" I asked.

His brow tightened as he studied my injury. "Actually, no. It almost looks like it's healing around the blade."

Raven dropped to her knees on my other side. "That's exactly what it's doing. She may be changed by the bond, but she's still human. We'll need to remove the knife carefully and stitch her up."

Matthias nodded, but when he reached for the knife, I lifted my hand to stop him. "Let Raven do it," I said. "If there's any poison remaining, I don't want to risk it."

He tilted his head, donning an incredulous smile. "You know, I've done this sort of thing before. I'm capable of removing a knife from a wound without cutting myself."

"Even so," I muttered, "I don't want to chance it." I sighed softly when he conceded. He nodded to Raven to proceed.

I flinched as she slid the knife out.

"Just like old times, eh?" she asked, pulling out the small field kit she always carried on her belt.

Although there had been no humor in her tone or expression, I let out a breathy laugh. "Almost. It's been a while since I haven't had to stitch myself up."

"The least I can do after what my parents did," she said.

I gritted my teeth as Raven went to work, while Matthias sat to the side and observed. I focused on his face to distract myself from the sting of the needle.

"Will Connor—" I couldn't finish the question before fear lodged in my throat.

Matthias offered me a tight smile. "We need to find a healer. Unless there's some antidote to the poison?" He posed the question to Raven, who shook her head solemnly but said nothing.

"Can the palace healers—" I started to ask, but Matthias was already shaking his head. "Then who?"

"There's a mage who might help, but…" Matthias turned his gaze to Connor.

"But what? If there's even a chance they can help, we have to try," I insisted.

"Then you get to tell Connor who saved him," he said, smirking half-heartedly.

Raven tied off the end of the thread and patted my shoulder. "All good. You should be fine, but just in case…"

She stood and walked away. Matthias helped me sit up as Raven stooped down beside her father's body. She rummaged in his jacket pocket until she produced a small crystal vial that appeared to be empty. Returning to my side, she offered me a hand to help me stand, then placed the vial in my palm.

"This is the last of our tonic, as far as I know, but there's no telling what else my parents kept from me." I followed her gaze as she turned to look at her mother. Bile rose in my throat at the ghastly sight of Anna lying in a pool of blood and entrails.

"Are you okay, Raven?" I asked, cringing at how absurd the question was, given all she had lost today, but her expression was blank, as if she hadn't just witnessed the horrific deaths of her parents.

Swallowing hard, she faced me again. "Did they really massacre all of those fae?"

"Someone did," Matthias said, tossing the words over his shoulder as he rushed across the barn to Connor. He knelt at my mate's side. "Whether it was your parents or someone else, I don't know, but that scene will haunt me as much as any battle I fought in the war."

Raven lifted a hand to her lips. "How do I make this right?"

I wrapped her in a hug, careful not to pull at my fresh stitches. "It's not your job to fix their wrongs," I whispered.

"If I don't do that, then what do I do? Where do I go?" she asked, her voice trembling with oncoming tears.

I had no answer for her. Before I could ponder any options, Matthias was calling my name. Pulling away from Raven, I turned to find him holding Connor in his arms.

"We need to hurry. He's running out of time, and Minerva is a half-day's ride away."

Nodding quickly, I said, "I left Honey at the edge of the trees, but we can't all ride one horse."

Raven stepped forward. "My parents' horses should be nearby. I left my mare in the stable near the old farmhouse. I can take care of things while you save him."

I smiled unsteadily. "Come find me at the palace when this is done. We will help you."

CHAPTER EIGHTY-FIVE

Lieke

The forest had darkened with the setting sun by the time we arrived at a nondescript cottage built among the trees. The stone structure was covered in moss, and it blended in so well with its surroundings that I likely would never have noticed it had Matthias not stopped directly in front of it. Small circular windows, black and foreboding like the eyes of a demon, sat on either side of a wooden door. Chills flashed across my skin, and somewhere in the dark corners of my mind a voice whispered for me to run.

But I couldn't.

Matthias dismounted, pulling Connor into his arms from where he'd been lying across my lap like a sack of grain. I stepped out of the saddle, despite the gut-twisting desire to flee from this place and forget it existed. Staying behind Matthias, I followed him to the door. It opened before we'd come close enough to knock, and I stilled, fear holding my feet in place.

Who was this mage? And why was Matthias so apprehensive about telling Connor we had brought him here? Why did Connor not trust—

Before I could finish the thought, a lovely, song-like voice floated toward us on the still air. "Ah, Matthias Orelian, it appears dire circumstances bring you to my door. Dire indeed."

The soothing, feminine voice didn't match our surroundings, and I leaned around Matthias's arm for a glimpse of the mage. Against my will, my lips parted in shock at the frail wisp of a woman who stood in the darkened doorway in a fitted cloak the shade of dried blood. White hair, nearly translucent, sprouted sparsely from her head, leaving much of her scalp visible. Her face was gaunt and deeply creased, with paper-thin skin that wrapped around her sharp bones. It looked as if anything more than a light breeze would sweep her away like ash.

"Miss Berg," the woman said, and my eyes widened—more from hearing such a lovely voice coming from the old woman's cracked lips than the fact that she already knew my name. "It is not polite to gawk."

I blinked quickly and averted my eyes, but my mouth had gone dry, making any verbal apology impossible. The old crone didn't seem to mind though, and she beckoned us to follow her inside. Matthias did so without hesitation, and I scrambled to stay close behind him, not wanting to be left alone in these eerie woods. As we neared the dark, gaping hole of the entrance, I strained to make out anything within the pitch-black cottage. But I could see nothing.

As we stepped inside, a sharp breath escaped me.

"What in the stars?" Now the room was warm and bright, lit by a fire in a large hearth that filled the far wall to my left. Candles of varying sizes and shapes lined the sills of every window, which appeared larger here than they had from outside.

The old woman waved a hand in the air, clearing away the bundles of herbs, stacks of books, and rows of vials from the worktable as easily as Gretchen whisked away my bath. She motioned for Matthias to lay Connor on the now cleared surface.

"Thank you for seeing us, Minerva," Matthias said, bowing his head slightly.

"It has been *too* long, General," she said, her dark eyes roving over

Connor's still form.

"I suggested we see you sooner, but—"

Minerva reached out, and her hands hovered over Connor's heart. "The prince here wouldn't allow it." It wasn't a question.

"Can you save him?" I blurted out, stepping up to the table and glaring impatiently at the old mage.

She let out a long and irritating hum, closing her eyes and angling her head to the side as if listening for something.

"Interesting indeed," she murmured, and I clenched my fists at my sides to keep them still. Smacking her for not moving fast enough wouldn't be the best way to encourage her to help us.

Her eyes slowly opened, locking onto mine. "Your impatience is understandable, Lieke. The threat of losing one's mate—especially so soon after bonding—is not an easy burden to bear."

My bottom lip quivered, and I had to pull it in between my teeth to control it. Hiding anything from this mage would be impossible, but if I let the tears start now, I feared they'd never stop.

Matthias laid a gentle, reassuring hand on my arm and said to Minerva, "He's been infected by some unknown poison."

"Unknown to you, perhaps," she mused, her piercing eyes narrowing under her wrinkled brow. "It's new, yes, but the prophecy behind it is ancient. And this is not the first time I've seen it at work."

"The queen?" Matthias and I asked in unison. The mage nodded.

"If you couldn't save her then, how can you—" Matthias started to challenge her, but she lifted a frail hand to quiet him.

"I didn't save her, no, but that doesn't mean I couldn't. Unfortunately for Keeva Durand, her husband refused to pay the price all magic requires." Minerva lowered her eyes to Connor and almost appeared sad.

"What was the price?" I asked quietly.

Minerva didn't look up as she answered, "The life of one of their sons."

My eyes went wide, and I turned to Matthias, but he didn't seem as scared as I was. Had he not pieced together what the price of healing Connor would be?

Matthias gave me a warm but sad smile. "And what is the price to save him?"

The mage laughed quietly. "The price is never the same twice, so no need to fear."

"How can you say that?" I demanded. "He's dying! Of course I'm afraid!"

"Understandable as his mate," she said sympathetically, almost as if our bond itself saddened her. "His years have already been cut short by his bonding to a mortal. The world will lose a good fae much sooner now that your souls are intertwined. Your lives have been sewn together—one shortened, the other lengthened—forming a new life where there had once been two. If he dies now, you won't be far behind him, so it's understandable that you'd be afraid."

"I'm not afraid of dying," I said, trying to keep my voice steady. "But I can't lose him. The world can't lose him. Will you help or not?"

She ignored me, though, as she brushed a hair off Connor's forehead. His breathing had slowed considerably, and my heart tensed, trying to draw me inside its protective walls where loss and grief and pain couldn't hurt me.

"You know, I didn't always look like this," Minerva crooned. My impatience flared, and my hand twitched as if wanting to rise and strike her, but Matthias gently touched my arm, stopping me.

Instead, I muttered an annoyed, "Obviously."

Minerva continued, seemingly unperturbed by my childish reaction. "I wasn't born with these abilities like this prince here. I paid to inherit them. My sister and I both did—she with her voice and me with my beauty. But that wasn't the only price for our powers. We were forced to be separated, destined to live and serve others in two different realms, kept apart not by mere oceans—but by time and space itself. So trust me, Lieke, when I say I know what it is to pay heavily for what we want, just as I know the pain of loss. I do not ask this of you lightly, nor do I take pleasure in making you choose."

My breath stuck in my throat as sweat gathered in my palms.

"What is the price?" Matthias asked again before I could.

Minerva's gaze continued to rest on me, as if I had been the one to speak. "There is a stone—the Starfire—that holds the incredible power to amplify one's magic. That is my price."

I shook my head, bewildered. "But he's dying now! I can't possibly find this rock in time. There has to be something else."

"It is not far," she said. When I shrugged and looked at her expectantly, she lifted a crooked, bony finger and pointed at my chest.

My hand lifted to my sternum, as if she were casting a spell on my heart that I needed to block, but then my fingers brushed the chain hanging around my neck. Mother's pendant. I pulled it from underneath my shirt and held it out to inspect it.

"This?" I asked. When I pulled my attention away from the stone, I found the mage's eyes alight with a devious hunger. The same voice from before whispered from the far recesses of my consciousness, warning me not to give it to her, but every nerve, every bone, every fiber of my being ached. Every second I stood here deciding, Connor's breaths were weakening, his heart slowing. I couldn't let him die. Even if our hearts and souls hadn't been knit together by the bond, I would have done anything to protect him.

I lifted the chain over my head and offered it to Minerva. Her fingers trembled as they touched the stone, but she didn't take it. Her eyes burned into mine.

"Do not make this decision lightly, Lieke," she warned. "This stone in the wrong hands could have disastrous consequences for all worlds and realms and peoples."

Without hesitation, I shoved it at her, pressing her fingers around it with both of my hands. "Then guard it," I said, knowing full well that I might have just placed it into the very hands she had cautioned me about.

"Are you sure?" Matthias whispered harshly in my ear.

I gave him a sidelong look. "You said she was the only one who could help him. I can't lose anyone else, Matthias."

"But you could lose everyone—we all could—if what she says is true," he said flatly.

I shook my head, fighting to keep my tears from surfacing. "Then we will face that when the time comes—together."

Minerva shoved the necklace into the pocket of her cloak. She snapped her fingers, and an empty teardrop-shaped vial appeared in one of her hands. Placing her free hand over Connor's heart again, she pressed down on his skin right where his family's crest was inked. Her lips fluttered, but no sound came from them. As I watched her eyes slip back into her head, I reached for Matthias's arm, gripping his elbow with both of my hands.

She lifted her chin toward the ceiling, and slowly, the vial began to fill with a clear liquid tinged with blood. With each drop added to it, Connor's heartbeat strengthened and his breaths became deeper, healthier. I didn't track how long it took; my mind was too focused on watching my mate's face regain its healthy color.

I jumped, startled, when Minerva's head snapped forward again. She blinked once and held the now-full vial in front of her eyes before closing her fingers around it. When she opened her hand once more, the vial wasn't there. Where it had gone, I didn't know or care.

I looked down at Connor and leaned over him, resting my hands on his shoulder.

"Why isn't he awake?" I asked, worry soaked into every word.

Minerva said in a slow, labored voice, "The poison is gone, but pulling it from his blood takes the strength of both the mage and the subject. He is healthy, but his body is worn out. He should wake in a day or two."

"Thank you, Minerva," Matthias said. "Should I tell him the truth about his mother? It seems unfair for him to hold it against you for a decision that wasn't yours."

"I'm used to life being unfair, General. I'd rather he hate me. The truth would only come between him and his father."

CHAPTER EIGHTY-SIX

Connor

Too late.

Those were the last words I'd said to my mate before the darkness swallowed me.

Voices whispered in the distance, and I desperately tried to find them. But no matter how hard I ran, I could never make out what they were saying, never could tell who was speaking.

When they ceased, fear crept back in.

I wasn't dead. I could still feel her—my mate—woven into the fabric of my soul, ever-present and breathing and living and surviving for us both.

The poison's flame singed my nerves, licking greedily at my blood. Slowly it faded to glowing embers until it was quelled completely, as if a cool water had been washed over me, dousing the fire and cleansing me of every last ember.

Still, the darkness persisted.

I waited, because running after nothingness only brought fatigue of both my mind and spirit.

When my body was ready, it would bring me back to her.

At least, that's what I hoped.

✳

"Wolfie." Her voice pulled my heavy eyelids open. The darkness lingered at the edges of my vision as I stared up at a familiar ceiling. A fire glowed in the fireplace, warming the left side of my face. Shifting my body on the sofa, I turned toward the warmth to find a pair of sapphire eyes sparkling in the firelight.

Lieke.

"Sapphire," I breathed. Raising a hand, I traced my finger along her forehead, tucking a blonde wave behind her ear before my arm fell weakly across my stomach. "I'm dreaming, aren't I?" I asked wearily.

She nodded, a sad smile touching her lips before she said, "You should wake soon enough, but I couldn't wait that long."

"How did you know about the dreams?" I asked, quirking a brow lazily.

She lifted her shoulder in a slight shrug, and her face flushed an adorable pink. "Your father told me."

Heat spread through me as I recalled the last dream we'd shared, when we'd given all of ourselves without realizing it. I moved to sit up, but her light hand on my shoulder settled me back down.

"You got me home then."

"With the help of Matthias"—she gulped and cleared her throat quietly—"and Minerva."

Ice filled my heart. Clenching my hands tightly and scowling, I bit down on the inside of my cheek to prevent my tongue from unleashing my anger on my mate. I might have despised the mage, but I couldn't fault Lieke for doing whatever she needed to save me.

"The price? What did she demand?" I asked quietly.

Curiosity sparked in her eyes. "You knew there'd be a cost?"

"All magic comes at a price, Sapphire," I said. "I never knew what she required of my father—only that her price was more than he could pay and she refused to accept anything else."

"My mother's necklace," she said, and now it was my turn to eye her curiously. She answered my unspoken question. "Turns out it's some powerful stone or something."

A powerful stone.

In the hands of a mage.

Dread crowded my heart as I pondered what Minerva could achieve with such an object in her possession.

And Lieke had simply handed it over? Had she not thought about the consequences? But even as I contemplated that, I knew I'd have done the same thing if the situation had been reversed.

Releasing a deep sigh, I whispered, "I'm sorry. I should have told you sooner."

"Yes, you should have." She picked something off my sleeve and flicked it away as she asked, "Why didn't you?"

"Do you remember when you first woke up in this room?" She nodded once. "You nearly chose death over pretending to be my betrothed."

"To be fair, Wolfie, you weren't my favorite fae back then."

I reached for her hand and interlaced our fingers. "You are independent, stubborn—"

"Is this your idea of flattery?" she asked, and I laughed lightly.

"Those aren't bad qualities. I forced you into our engagement—"

"Not forced," she corrected. "I could have chosen death, remember?"

"Regardless, I didn't want you to feel forced to choose me. I wanted you to choose me because you wanted me and not because of some bond or some sense of obligation. I was going to tell you, but then—"

"I chose Brennan," she said quietly.

My chest caved. Even having her here with me, knowing she'd saved me, I realized that didn't mean she was choosing me.

"Why? Why did you?" I asked, although I was unsure I wanted to hear the answer.

"The rebels threatened me. They told me if I didn't stop Brennan's marriage, they were going to kill one of you."

"You could have told me—"

"No," Lieke said. "They would have found out."

Fear had forced her to lie, just as it had convinced me to hide from her. It was understandable and to be expected, I supposed, but one thing still bothered me.

My heart thumped erratically, and I pulled in a shaky breath.

She smiled. "You don't need to be nervous with me, Wolfie."

"How do you know I'm nervous?"

"Your father told me a lot about this bond of ours," she explained. Of course she would be able to sense my emotions even in these dreams.

"If there'd been no rebels, no threats—if I hadn't been stupid and had told you the truth—what would you have done?"

Lieke leaned in close, pressing her forehead against mine briefly before she planted a light kiss on the tip of my nose. Then she whispered seductively, "Wake up and I'll show you."

CHAPTER EIGHTY-SEVEN

Lieke

Connor didn't wake up though.

For two days he remained in his bedroom, and I lay beside him, only leaving when Brennan forced me to eat or Gretchen insisted I bathe. By the second afternoon after returning from Minerva's cottage, Mrs. Bishop came up herself to retrieve me. Since Connor's condition had remained unchanged—even after our shared dream last night—I agreed to accompany her.

Walking arm in arm, we made our way downstairs in silence. Once in the kitchen, she pulled the kettle from the fire and poured boiling water into two cups while nodding to me to sit at one of the stools at the worktable. She didn't sit but rested her hips against the table's edge.

"Marin left," Mrs. Bishop said, looking up at me from beneath her lashes.

"What? Why?" I asked.

"Honestly, Sunshine, I was hoping you might know." She paused to take a long, cleansing breath. "She left with no word, no goodbye. When she didn't show up for her shift the other day, I went to her room and found it empty."

"And none of the guards saw anything?"

"I've been meaning to ask Matthias, but he's had a bit too much on his mind with Connor still unconscious," she said.

Lifting my cup, I blew across the hot drink. "I can talk to him for you if you'd like. I've been meaning to check on him anyway." She nodded her thanks, and after another moment of silence, I said, "That reminds me though. I told my friend, Raven, to come to the palace so we could help keep her safe."

"There have been no human visitors—actually no visitors at all—since you left," she said.

I sighed, my shoulders hanging low as I bent over the table.

Where did you go, Raven?

What are you doing?

"I'm sure she's fine," Mrs. Bishop said in her most hopeful tone. "But if she does arrive, rest assured I have a spot for her in my kitchen."

✳

When I returned to Connor's room, I found his heartbeat had quickened and grown stronger. Sitting beside him, I pulled his hand into my lap and held it while I watched for any sign he would wake soon. For hours I sat there waiting, hoping, and fighting my growing disappointment. When the sun finally set and the room grew dark, I reluctantly released him so I could light the lanterns.

I had just lit the first one when Connor stirred. My name fell from his lips, barely audible.

"Sapphire."

I nearly tripped over my own feet as I rushed to his side. "I'm here."

He turned his face toward me, opening his eyes and finding mine at once. A tired smile crept across his lips, and before I could stop him, he was slowly lifting himself up to his elbows and then into a seated position.

"Feels good to move again." His voice was so quiet that he could have been speaking only to himself. Swinging his feet off the bed and dropping them to the floor, he reached his hands out for mine and pulled me toward him so that I stood between his legs. He regarded me, a contented look lighting up his face.

"You're not mad at me for taking you to Minerva?" I asked quietly, immediately kicking myself. Why was that the first thing I said to him?

He shook his head before raising a brow quizzically. "I am awake, aren't I? This isn't another dream?" I dipped my chin once in answer. "Then I believe you have something to show me?" He posed it as a question, as if I might not remember what I had told him in our shared consciousness.

My core heated, sending tendrils of warm desire through my veins. *Stars, this male.*

My mate.

Memories of the dreams we'd shared flashed in my mind, and my body tensed at the thrilling realization that Connor was truly here, his hands in mine, his body close to me. And he wanted me, a lowly human servant, who—for some strange reason—fate had chosen as his mate.

He was mine. I was his.

Part of me wanted to push him back onto the bed and show him the extent of my feelings for him, but another part of me remained bruised from his earlier rejection when he'd kissed me and run. That piece of my heart—though on the mend—needed reassurance that I was truly loved not because I was his mate but because I was *me*.

Looking down, I folded my hands together. Then I slipped the sapphire ring from my finger. Stepping back half a pace—lamenting even the small amount of space between us—I held my hand out with the ring resting in the center of my palm.

His eyes lowered to it but lifted back up to mine quickly, questioning me with fresh worry.

"The last time I accepted this ring, I hated you," I said. "Now, I hate the thought of not being with you."

"So naturally you must return it," he said, a hint of humor in his tone.

My lips quivered as I smiled timidly. "Next time you offer it, I promise not to faint."

His expression turned hopeful. "And you're sure you want it back?"

As I gave him a string of small nods, he plucked the ring from my hand, pinching it between his finger and thumb. Slowly he rose to his feet, wavering slightly as he fought to find his balance before leaning over to set the ring on the bedside table.

"Matthias used to mock me for believing in mates, let alone waiting to find mine. I never admitted to him, though, that my insistence on waiting was an excuse—an excuse to avoid any connection. Because connection brought love, and in the end, love only brought sorrow."

Swallowing hard, he continued.

"Losing my mother is killing my father. Gradually but surely, his heart is withering away without his mate, and the thought of the same happening to me—the thought of experiencing a pain infinitely worse than what I've already suffered with her death? It terrified me. Yet that paled in comparison to the piercing fear of watching you being dragged away to the gallows that night. As though the stars themselves had burst within my chest, and I hated it. I hated that I needed to protect you, hated how I wanted to save you, hated that I didn't understand it at all."

He paused to brush his hand along my jaw and tuck my hair behind my ear. Trailing his fingers down my arm, he clasped my hand tightly in his.

"Now I know it was the stars. They knew before I did. They pulled my heart toward you before I even knew what was happening. But I need you to know, Sapphire, that my heart was yours before our lips ever met. And even if the stars had chosen differently, I would have bound my soul to yours a hundred times over to never be parted from you again. And I know that sounds absurd, because I abandoned you. I fled when I should have stayed. But I couldn't bear for you to feel obligated to choose me. I needed to know you loved me not because you had to but because you wanted to. And I was deathly afraid you never could."

My heart soared. Blinking away my tears, I reached for him, cupping his face in my hands. Rising onto my toes, I pressed my lips to his. He tasted of unwavering devotion and fearful desire, as if he still doubted my love for him.

And then I realized. I'd never told him.

Reluctantly I pulled away just enough to search his eyes.

"I so wanted you to find your mate because"—I paused to breathe through the new batch of tears that threatened to make my words impossible—"because you deserve a love written in the heavens. I feared I couldn't give you the kind of love you're worthy of, but stars, I hoped you would have me, mate or not. Then you ran, you avoided me, and my mind taunted me in my dreams, giving me glimpses and tastes of what we could be."

"Those were some delicious glimpses," Connor interrupted, smirking.

"I thought that was all I'd ever have of you, and I tried to be content with that."

"But it was real," he reminded me. "You're mine, Sapphire."

My core heated as the blissful memories sparked a new aching desire.

"I'm yours," I said, repeating what he'd said in that blessed dream when he'd claimed me wholly for himself.

"Forever and beyond," he whispered, pulling me to him. He lifted me effortlessly, and I wrapped my legs around his waist as I pressed my lips to his, kissing him hungrily, desperately.

I needed him. All of him.

As if he could hear my thoughts, Connor whirled around and lowered me onto his bed so that he hovered over me. A wicked grin spread across his lips, and desire flared in his eyes. "I finally got you on your back."

"Shut up and kiss me," I said, but he didn't move except to raise a brow.

"Where?"

The rough need in his voice sent a flash of pinpricks over every inch of me.

"Anywhere," I whispered huskily. "Everywhere."

His devilish smile shifted as he licked his lips and bared his teeth briefly. A low growl thrummed in his throat. Then his ravenous mouth was devouring me with deep kisses and sharp nips along my jaw, behind my ear, down my neck, and across my shoulder. He coaxed my shirt out of the way. Arching my back, I sank my fingers into his hair as he consumed me inch by inch, and I giggled darkly when he ripped open my shirt to free my breasts.

His deep, heavy sigh hummed over my skin as he took one peak between his lips, his tongue teasing me in a way it hadn't in our dream. Stars, he was going to undo me before I'd even gotten him out of his clothes. My body shuddered beneath him, and I whimpered as he pressed me closer and closer to the edge. Teetering there, my toes curled as though they were trying to physically keep me from falling too soon.

My eyes rolled back, but my rough moan was cut short when he suddenly retreated. I flashed my eyes open to find him staring up at me as he kissed his way over my ribs and across my belly.

Stars, what was he doing? Where was he—

My thought fell away unfinished when he slipped his hand under the top of my skirt and undergarments and trailed his fingers along my hips before sliding my clothes down. I squeezed my eyes closed, suddenly embarrassed at being laid out and exposed for him.

"You don't need to be nervous with me, Sapphire," Connor said, repeating the exact words I'd uttered last night in our dream. My heart swelled, my pulse steadying as I relaxed underneath him. As he slid my legs apart, my breath caught again. He ran his hands up the insides of my thighs until he reached their apex. I anticipated his touch where I needed him, but his fingers retraced their path back down my legs. I opened my mouth to protest, but my words were transformed into breathy curses when his lips pressed against me and his tongue commenced a delicate dance around the very spot he'd neglected with his hands.

If I'd thought I'd been close to unraveling earlier, that was nothing compared to the sheer ecstasy he gifted me now with every slow stroke and eager flick of his tongue. Squirming against the bed, I pressed a hand over my eyes, trying to ward off the inevitable, delay it for as long as possible. I didn't want the pleasure to be mine alone. I wanted him with me as we came undone together. But his hand ran up my hip to rest below my ribs, a gentle reminder that he was in control, that he had me.

As though sensing my hesitation, he retreated, placing gentle kisses on both of my thighs, but I still hid beneath my hand. He hovered between my legs, his warm breath tickling my skin.

"Look at me," he commanded quietly but firmly. Peeking out from under my hand, I met his gaze and sucked my lip between my teeth. "Do you want me to stop?"

I shook my head and breathed out a ragged "No."

"Good," he said, his eyes darkening. "Because I told you I'd worship you, and I intend to."

He'd barely uttered the words when his mouth found me again, thrusting me toward the cliff's edge with eager precision. Rounding my back, I angled my hips up for him, and when his fingers slid past his tongue, burying themselves deep within me, I moaned his name. It was a plea for more, for him, for all he offered. Greedily, hungrily, he consumed me, like he couldn't get enough. A growl roared in his chest as he pushed himself faster, guiding me toward my utter demise. When I finally slipped over the edge, I pressed against him, wanting more, craving more, needing more, until I slammed into pure bliss with his name bursting from my lungs.

I giggled uncontrollably, my smile refusing to be contained as he lifted himself back up to me. Kissing my nose, he hummed contentedly. Timidly I pulled my hand away from my face and gazed into his eyes, which were brimming with love and reverence as if he truly was worshiping me.

"Better than any dream," I managed to say, still somewhat breathless.

He smiled knowingly. "I should hope so. I didn't get to do that in our dreams."

My eyes trailed down the length of his body, and I faked a pout. "You seem to be wearing an awful lot, Wolfie."

"So I am," he said, scrunching his brow as if trying to figure out how to remedy the situation.

I pushed his shoulder, forcing him to roll onto his back, and made quick work of catching him up to my level of undress. He showed no sign of the embarrassment I'd had when he'd laid me bare before him. I hunted for some sassy comment to make, but my mind went blank as I studied all of him.

"Is this when you *show* me something, Sapphire?" he said, studying me as he ran his fingertip back and forth along his bottom lip. The heat in my core flared, but I was suddenly painfully aware of how inexperienced I truly was. It was one thing to do this in a dream, but here, in reality, my naivete was more obvious.

But this was Connor. My mate.

I don't need to be nervous with him.

Straddling him, I leaned forward and kissed him deeply, raking my fingers up past his ears and curling them into his hair. His hands, strong but gentle, gripped my hips, lowering and guiding me onto him. He swallowed my gasp, never taking his lips from mine, as I eased myself lower, my body trembling with each slip of him further inside me. What I'd shared with him in our dream couldn't compare to the slow, sensual rhythm our bodies discovered now, as we savored each roll of hips and tongues and lips, committing all to memory.

Finally pulling my lips from his, I continued to rock against him. My heart stumbled over itself, its beats skipping as my love for him overwhelmed me. A love that wasn't unrequited, wasn't merely mutual, but was stars-bound…this was my love. A love I'd never imagined would be mine, with a male who had loved me long before he'd ever recognized it—who had saved me more often than any one person deserved. And he was mine. All mine.

And I was his.

Completely. Wholly. Eternally his.

As we moved as one, I began to understand the gravity of what we shared. Tears filled my eyes—tears of elation, not sadness. When they spilled over, Connor lifted his hands to cradle my cheeks, brushing them aside with his thumbs before pulling my face back down to his. My lips quivered even as he kissed me, and embarrassment flooded me again.

Against my lips, he whispered, "I've got you, Lieke. Always. It's us together."

My eyes closed, and I whispered back, "Forever and beyond."

And together—our two souls bound to each other, our two lives intertwined—we tumbled over that edge of pleasure, not letting go until our bodies calmed and our hearts slowed back down.

"I have something to ask you," Connor said as I cuddled against him, and I relished the lazy circles his fingers traced along my hip.

"Should we get dressed first?" I asked, giggling.

He looked down at me like I'd suggested something absolutely absurd. "What's the fun in that?"

"I don't know, Wolfie. Some things require clothing. Like having breakfast with your family in a few hours."

Sighing loudly, he shrugged. "Perhaps. But this doesn't." Before I could say anything, he was stretching his arm out to the side, reaching for something. When he turned back to me, his lips wore an elated, peaceful smile as he held up the ring—my ring.

"I never asked you properly before, and for that I apologize."

I giggled quietly, quirking a brow at him. "And this right here—naked in your bed—is what you consider proper?"

He ignored me and pulled in a long breath. "Lieke, will you accept this flawed heart of mine—my temper, my impatience, my odd timing of serious questions—and be my wife?"

Joyful tears stuck in my throat, holding my voice hostage so that all I could do was nod. Connor slipped the sapphire ring back onto my finger. Placing my hand over his heart and reaching my lips up to his, I whispered my answer.

"Until the stars fall, Connor, I live for you and you alone."

EPILOGUE

Connor

Zieke fidgeted beside me as the carriage pulled up to the front of King Vael's castle in Arenysen. I had to fight back a chuckle. With how nervous she was, one would have thought it was our wedding day and not my brother's.

"Settle, Sapphire," I whispered, squeezing her hand once.

Dropping the curtain back into place, she turned from the window and eyed me sheepishly.

"I don't know what's wrong with me today," she admitted.

I wrapped my arm around her shoulder and tucked her close to me. Planting a kiss into her hair, I sighed and hunted for the right words to put her at ease. But what could I say when I didn't know what was bothering her?

"Do I really need to wear the crown? It feels wrong when we're not married yet," she said, and I glanced down at the gold tiara in her hand. Its large sapphires, accented by diamonds, were almost as dazzling as my mate's eyes.

"It's not wrong when it's tradition," I explained. "My mother actually wore this crown when my Uncle Cian married Ellae. Granted, that was a slightly less formal affair than today's."

"Impending war does tend to put a damper on things, doesn't it?"

"A bit," I said, regretting that I'd taken the conversation down such a depressing path.

The carriage door swung open, and I leaned over to kiss Lieke's temple before inching away from her and lightly settling the tiara into her golden waves. I waited, watching as my bride took the footman's hand and stepped out into the late afternoon sunshine. Joining her, I offered my arm, and together we strode into the castle's grand foyer.

The bright, cheerful voice of Calla Vael greeted us at once, as she and my brother strode toward us. Calla immediately stole Lieke away, and Brennan elbowed me.

"Hello, brother," he said, flashing me a crooked grin.

I flicked a glance toward Calla and Lieke, who now walked ahead of us, arm in arm. "Your bride looks happy. So do you actually."

Brennan lifted a shoulder. "She may not be my mate, but I feel blessed all the same. Not sure what I did to deserve such a female—or what she did wrong to get stuck with me."

"You have more to offer than you think," I said, and he laughed.

"No need to flatter me just because it's my wedding day." He paused to look behind us toward the door. "Where's your right-hand man? I didn't expect you to travel without your bodyguard."

"He had to stay behind. We're still looking for that spy that got away."

Brennan's brow tightened with worry. "There haven't been any more attacks, have there?"

I shook my head. "Not since that little incident at the farm."

"Six months with no rebel action?"

"I know, I keep expecting some kind of response from those that scattered, but so far, it's been quiet."

"Quiet's good though," he said. "Might as well enjoy it while you can. I doubt your life will be quiet for too long after your own vows."

Calla dropped Lieke's arm and spun on her heel to face us, a playful scowl gracing her expression. "Brennan," she chided, "leave them alone."

As Brennan and I caught up to them, Lieke wrapped her arm around my waist. "What did he say?" she asked.

I leaned down and whispered close to her ear, "I think he's predicting an Emeryn heir within the year."

Lieke's face flushed a warm pink, and Brennan laughed heartily. "Still so quick to blush. Nice to know some things never change."

"You still a cheater at cards?" Lieke teased back, and before he could answer, Calla's brows shot up.

"Yes! He's the worst!"

"Hey!" Brennan protested with mock offense, wrinkling his brow.

Calla's dark eyes turned mischievous. "Well, the worst at cards anyway. He's okay at other things."

"Okay? Just okay?" Brennan said. "That's not what you said last night…or should I say screamed last night?"

Calla swatted at my brother's arm, playfully rolling her eyes before she dragged him to her, kissing him passionately as if Lieke and I weren't standing right there.

Cringing, I turned to Lieke. "I think I'm going to be sick."

Brennan broke free of the kiss long enough to say, "Careful, Calla, my brother has a habit of waltzing in uninvited." Then he lowered his voice to a loud whisper. "He likes to watch."

I growled a warning, but there was no genuine anger behind it. With the rebels ceasing their attacks for the time being, Brennan securing this alliance with Arenysen, and my mate standing by my side, there was little to rile my rage these days. Even our father had softened toward us and was showing regular glimpses of the loving parent he'd been in our youth. I credited the change in him to Lieke's presence in our family; she brought a ray of much-needed sunshine into our dreary lives.

Lieke laughed as she pulled my face down to hers and kissed me sweetly. Then she turned to look sidelong at my brother and his bride. "Who knew things would end up quite so perfectly?" she asked softly.

Reaching my hand up to her neck, I buried my fingers in her hair and trailed my thumb along her jaw, angling her chin up. As I breathed in her sweet scent that had become my whole world, I lost myself in her dark eyes and marveled at her—my love and my mate.

"The stars, Sapphire," I whispered. "The stars knew."

THE END

THE SPICE RACK

Please review this list if you would like to be aware
of the chapters with intimate content prior to reading.

2 - one brief scene

63 - one scene

87 - one longer scene

Coming Up Next

ONCE the SKIES FADE

**The law is clear: she must remarry or lose her throne.
But when she refuses to trust her heart,
she'll force her suitors to risk their lives.**

With the queen suspected of murdering her husband, one general is tasked with entering her tournament and getting close enough to learn the truth—and assassinate her if she is guilty.

But when a secret comes to light, he will find himself choosing between the friend he's served for years and the queen he cannot live without.

Once the Skies Fade is the second installment in a fantasy romance collection of interconnected stand-alones, sweeping you to a dangerous land of blackened hearts and cutthroat competition. A gender-bent Cinderella meets the Hunger Games in this enemies to lovers tale of a morally grey queen and the sarcastic warrior who could mend her wounded heart... if he doesn't stick a dagger in it first.

ACKNOWLEDGMENTS

We took a risk with this book, and yes, I say "we" because so many people had a hand in bringing it to life.

Jourdan and Merrit: You saw me through multiple panic attacks and high-stress moments this year, and I am beyond thankful to have you in my corner and by my side. You believe in me when I can't seem to and remind me regularly to celebrate my wins. I love you both so much.

To my alphas and betas, Crystal, Jess, Morgan, Marie-Lyne, Megs, Heidi, Sarah, Erika, Fedy, Vanessa, Jessica, Jourdan, Merrit, Candace, Stephanie: You put in countless hours reading multiple drafts and brainstorming endlessly with me on how best to write their story. Thank you for being there for me every step of the way.

To my street team, Megs, Merrit, Fedy, Kellie, Kayla, Talia, Sarah, Karissa, Allyn, Candace, Valerie, Nicollette, Sasha, Kitty, Maryanne, Stephanie, Kelsy, Ashley, Danielle, Ashlee, Savannah, Ciara, Elsa, Elise, Kiley, Allison, Jordan, Morgan, and Heidi: Thank you for all of your hard work hyping this book! I truly appreciate every post and story and reel.

To my author friends, especially Rachel, Jenny, Jaclyn, Vanessa, Jessica, Hillary, Nicole, Lauren, Olivia, Mary, and so many more: This job is hard, but we aren't going it alone! Thank you for keeping me going!

To the bookstagrammers and readers who let me bother them in DMs regularly: Emily, Lauren, Tina, Zura, Shannon, April, and all the Queens of Chaos.

To my publishing team: Emily, Rachel, Gerralt, and Fran. Thank you for lending your professional expertise to this project!

To the cast of New Girl for keeping me company, the folks at Keel & Co. Distilling Company for creating amazing gin, and the Laramie County Library for having one of the best quiet spots in town for writing and editing.

To my husband, Joel, and our kids: Thank you for your constant, unwavering support of this crazy dream of mine. I know things get a little stressful at times, but your patience and understanding has been beyond helpful. I love you all so much.

And finally to my Lord and Savior, Jesus Christ, for the undeserved and unbelievable gift of redemption and salvation.

Vanessa Rasanen loves a good cliffhanger, judges books by their covers, and wishes she could write faster. She lives in southeast Wyoming with her pilot husband and four kids. When she's not writing you can find her mixing up a gin & tonic, rewatching New Girl, running a small business, and wasting time on Instagram.

Connect with Vanessa:
http://www.vanessarasanen.com
http://instagram.com/vanessarasanenauthor